THE FACELESS

ALSO BY SIMON BESTWICK

Tomes of The Dead: Tide of Souls
Pictures of the Dark
Angels of the Silences

THE
FACELESS
SIMON BESTWICK

SOLARIS

First published 2012 by Solaris
an imprint of Rebellion Publishing Ltd,
Riverside House, Osney Mead,
Oxford, OX2 0ES, UK

www.solarisbooks.com

ISBN: 978 1 907992 75 9

10 9 8 7 6 5 4 3 2 1

A CIP catalogue record for this book is available from the
British Library.

Designed & typeset by Rebellion Publishing

Printed in the US

Photography by Astrid Westvang

For Dorothy Ann Smith
15th May 1915 – 6th December 2010

Only the dead have seen the end of war.
– George Santayana.

ARMISTICE DAY

'A' BLOCK

There are quiet rooms here. There is less sound to shut out now than ever, but these were built for stillness, and a certain kind of intimacy. In one such room are two leather-upholstered chairs. The leather is cracked now, the wood rotted; the air of the North is not kind to such things. Here men rocked, twitched and stammered, or fitted bodies contorted by paralysis into the least painful postures they could find as they tried to speak of unspeakable things. On the floors above, the patients' rooms are bright and airy; this was, once, a place of healing. The view from the windows, grimed and foxed though they are, shows the now-overgrown lawn; beyond that lies woodland and beyond that, rolling moors and hills. A fine view, to be sure. Even though it's cut into sections by the bars across the windows.

CHAPTER ONE

ARMISTICE DAY IN Kempforth, an old mill-town high in the Lancashire hills. Terraced houses of biscuit-coloured stone; blunt ugly high-rise flats; brutalist council offices like relics of Stalin's Russia. Tall detached Victorian houses at the edge of town; beyond them, the craggy rolling moorland, scrawled with naked trees warped sideways by an unrelenting wind.

Eleventh of November; eleven am.

The Town Hall clock struck the hour. A small crowd, silent, round the High Street Cenotaph. At the front, a row of old men, medals polished; bronze and silver gleamed dully in the rain. All wore a red poppy; wreaths of them lay round the memorial's base. The only sounds: the wind's moan, the growl of distant cars. Dead leaves; horizontal rain.

The two minutes ended. A bugle sounded the Last Post. Brief words of prayer were spoken. The plea to remember, unheeded year on year.

The crowd was gone; just another day. Work or the

dole. Living high on the hog or scraping for coins. And the wars continued, big and small.

THE LIVING ROOM of an Alma Street terrace. The reek of stale cigarette smoke, cheap air-freshener, old chip-fat. An ashtray brimming on the coffee table. Grimy, threadbare carpet. The babble of the TV, volume down low.

"God's *sake*, Martyn."

"Sorry, love." He sounded drained, like *he'd* been the one working all day. "Forgot."

"Forgot–" Eva closed and opened her eyes. "All I asked you to do was boil a few spuds and grill some bangers. Not rocket science, is it?"

"I'm *sorry*." Martyn stood head down, like a kid getting rollicked; the patch where his hair was thinning showed. "Just leave it, alright?"

"No, I won't leave it, Martyn. I always bloody leave it. I'm not, this time." The words were out before she could stop them. "What do you *do* here all day?"

"Pick Mary up from school."

"Like I did every day before I went full-time? What you want, a medal?"

He looked up, jaw clenched. "Not my fault I got laid off."

Eva breathed out through her nose.

"What?"

"Nowt."

"In't my bloody fault there's no work."

"Never said it was."

"Thinking it, though."

"Don't tell us what I think."

"Think I'm not doing enough."

"Just said, don't tell us what I think."

"I look for work."

"And I'm ruddy working." He looked down. "So come on, what *did* you do today? Wasn't the housework, wasn't the tea, so just what did you bloody *do*?"

"I'm not having this. My own house."

"And who's paying the mortgage right now? Eh?" She'd seen two friends lose their homes, unable to keep up payments. That wouldn't happen to them, not while she had breath. "I'm working my arse off, Martyn. All I'm asking for is some flipping help."

"Don't. Just don't." He spread shaking hands towards her.

"What?" She mimicked the act. "What's all this in aid of?"

He flinched back, looked away. His hands became fists, then opened. "Don't take the piss. Just leave it. Leave it." His voice had risen. He was shaking.

"Martyn, keep it down."

"Don't tell us to keep it down in me own house."

A dull, sick ache formed in her gut. She wanted to shout. Didn't. Did nothing, said nothing. Didn't trust herself. The living room door was ajar; Eva went and pushed it shut.

"What you doing?"

"I don't want Mary hearing."

He shook. A long, rattling breath escaped him. He slumped into one of the armchairs. It was like watching the air go out of something, seeing it collapse. She started towards him, stopped. He didn't answer. "Martyn…" She closed her eyes. "You've got to get help."

His eyes flicked up towards her, scared and wounded.

"What's that supposed to mean? There's nowt wrong with me."

"Love, we both know that's bollocks."

His breath went in and out through his teeth. "So... what? I'm a fucking nut-job now?"

He was shaking. She wanted to shout. Didn't. Did nothing, said nothing. Didn't trust herself. Until, finally:

"I'm gonna check on Mary. Then I'm off out."

"What?" He looked up at her again. Christ, that look in his eyes – scared, lost. Like a sheep. When did he get like that?

"My night class. Remember? It's a Monday."

"Oh." He looked down again. "Right. Forgot." But he looked relieved as well. She couldn't leave him; he wouldn't last a week on his tod. But something had to give. There was Mary to consider.

"Just get the dinner on for Mary," she said at last.

"'Bout you?"

"I'll grab something on the way."

"Eva–"

"Just get it done, Martyn, please. I'm gonna go see Mary."

"You... you could knock it on the head, just for tonight. Stay in."

"And do what?" They hadn't even shagged in four months. He couldn't. But she couldn't say that. Too cruel. "No. That's the *last* thing I need right now."

She opened the living room door.

"I love you, Eva."

Her eyes flicked to the wedding photo on the mantelpiece: Martyn grinning and straight-backed, without the belly he'd grown. That was all they'd needed. The way he'd looked at her – still did – was enough: there was pure bloody worship in his eyes. She'd never seen that before. *My big bear*. She'd married that, not this slumped thing in the armchair.

"Eva?"

Anna. She'd give Anna a bell. She was a bit funny, but she was bright. And she'd want to help her brother. Anna'd know what to do.

"Just look after Mary," she said, and pulled the living room door shut behind her. Music came from upstairs. Mary's room. At least she hadn't heard all *that*. Or maybe she'd been crouched on the landing and she'd heard the lot. No way to be sure. Eva breathed, slow and deep, checked her eyes for excess redness in the hall mirror, and climbed the stairs.

```
THE TESTAMENT OF LANCE-CORPORAL CUTHBERT WINTHROP
the initial impact didnt hurt it was like a punch
to the face it was only later that i felt it
when the air hit the nerves tried to scream but
couldnt didnt realise it was cos i had nothing
left to scream with felt like there was a chicken
bone in my mouth then realised it was part of my
jawbone couldnt smell the trench either thought
that was a blessing at the time all i could smell
was copper blood
```

NEAR-DUSK IN Kempforth Precinct; shops closing, lamps slowly coming on. The different groups shuttled past Anna: mums with prams, teenagers trying to look trendy. Farmers in flat caps, boots and anoraks. Two bearded Asian men wearing shalwar kameez under pullovers and old suit jackets.

On a corner, a bulky, headscarfed woman said "*Big Issue*, please," over and over; it might be the only English she knew. Four white lads in hoodies and jogpants pushed past; one said something. She looked away. Tension filled the air like static as they neared the Asian men, then dispersed as they passed. Anna breathed out.

No goths or moshers here; no-one different. Thugs had kicked a goth girl to death in a nearby town only a few years before. This part of Lancashire didn't welcome strangers. Ranks closed, lines were drawn; if necessary, fists were clenched. Home-grown misfits weren't liked either. But for better or worse, this was home; where she'd fled when all else fell apart. If she hid who she was, she was safe. She didn't like doing that, but she couldn't just think of herself.

She never liked being out on her own in Kempforth; she longed for her little 'study' – Dad's old loft extension – sat at the computer with a coffee close to hand, Arvo Pärt on the CD player, opening her files and reviewing her notes on Ash Fell. Well, what else would fascinate her here, but what Kempforth closed its ranks around and tried to hide?

Her mobile rang. Anna closed her eyes, sighed. Briefly she considered ignoring it. But of course that wasn't an option.

"Hello?" Static hissed; voices murmuring in the background. Must be a crossed line. "Hello?"

"… Anna?"

"Eva?"

"Yes."

"What's wrong?"

A long breath. "Martyn."

She talked; Anna listened.

"I'm really getting worried now. I know it's been a rough few months–"

"Nearly a year."

"–but the state he's in… and there's Mary to think about too."

Mary. "Yes, of course. What can I do?"

"Anna… I think he needs to see somebody. He needs help."

"Eva, we can't *force* him to see anybody, unless he's a danger to someone. I mean, do you think he is?" Was he a danger to Mary? That, most of all.

A low, deep sigh. "I don't know, Anna. Don't think so. You know he'd never hurt her."

"I know. Of course."

"But it's affecting her. Seeing him like this. Us. And… I don't know what to do. I need him back the way he was."

She sounded almost petulant, but Anna bit back any urge to tick her off. "I know." The static rose to a screech; it and the voices on the crossed line drowned Eva out. "Hello?"

"… interference."

"Yeah, I know." She didn't mention the voices. In case Eva hadn't heard them; in case they were only in Anna's head. No. That had been just two months of her life, nearly ten years ago. After the divorce. Gone now. Done.

"Just thought, maybe if you talk to him. He might listen to you. I'm at my wit's end, Anna."

"OK. Look, why don't we meet tomorrow? Lunchtime? The Creamery? We can talk about this properly over a coffee éclair."

Eva laughed. "You're talking my language now."

"Pleasure's all mine. It's the high point of my social life, these days."

"Well, that's your fault. Told you before, I'll give you a makeover. Some guys like their women tall and thin–"

"And flat as an ironing board."

"Some men do."

Yes, Eva, but it's not men I'm interested in. She didn't say that. "*Anyway.* I'll see you tomorrow, yeah?"

"OK. One o'clock at the Creamery."

"See you then."

THE TESTAMENT OF LANCE-CORPORAL CUTHBERT WINTHROP CONTINUED shrapnel wound to chin and fractured mandible whole of chin and floor of mouth destroyed tongue still present in and out of hospital for four years wife left me couldnt face it hell I couldnt face it took the kids with her my little boy crying everytime daddy came near never looked right again managed to get work

ONE DETECTIVE SERGEANT was on duty at Mafeking Road; a small wiry man in his late forties, with iron-grey hair and a thin, craggy face. He looked gentle and for the most part was; some thought him a soft touch. A few had learned the hard way he wasn't.

"Mike."

Stakowski looked up from his paperwork, tried not to sound as glad to see her as he felt. "Hello, stranger."

"*Ma'am* to you, you old buzzard." Renwick, Joan. Rank: Detective Chief Inspector. Age: twenty-nine.

"Nice to see you too. How's it been?"

He shrugged. "Same old. You?"

Hair: Glossy and brown. Skin: still tawny from summer in the Algarve. Build: lean and sleek from morning runs and gym sessions. Face: strong and wide; not quite pretty, but men looked twice. Eyes: blue-grey. Nose: aquiline. She puffed her cheeks out and released a long breath. "Busy. Knackered. Stressed."

"Owt I can help with?"

"Not really. Got to go to Manchester week after next. Baldwin trial."

"You've time to prep for it, then."

"Time to get it bloody right. Why I'm knackered. I want them throwing the key away on that bastard. What?"

"Nowt, boss. Just... be careful, you know."

"Of what?"

"Permission to speak freely?"

"Do you ever do anything else?" A fair point, but then they both went back a long way.

"That's what you love me for, ma'am. Look... I know what you're like when you've got the bit between your teeth. And that case were a rough one. I remember how it got to you."

"So do I."

"Sorry."

"The concern's appreciated, Sarge. I'm not looking forward to going through it all again, either. But I'll be OK. Even got someone to look after me now."

Stakowski nodded. "Heard there were a new feller."

"That got round fast."

"I'm a detective. Should try it sometime, ma'am, you might be good at it."

Renwick raised two fingers.

"Going alright, then, that?"

"*Yes*, it is, thank you very much. He moved in a month ago, if you really must know. Any further questions? Plans for Christmas?"

"Back to the Wirral, see your old man?"

Her smile vanished. "No. Me and Nick were more thinking a quiet Christmas for two."

"Oh."

"Oh, what?"

"Nowt, ma'am." Pause. "You had another barney with your Dad, then?"

"Sergeant."

"Sorry."

A sigh. "Yes, I did." She shrugged. "That's the way it goes."

"You should be spending Christmas with your family, ma'am."

"Yes, and with a name like Mike Stakowski you should be tearing round New York City having shootouts and chasing the girls."

"Chance'd be a fine thing. Oh, and you forgot 'not playing by the rules like those desk-jockeys at City Hall', ma'am. Otherwise, full marks."

Renwick chuckled, shook her head. "Why do I put up with you?"

"Because I'm a genius detective and all round charming devil, boss."

"Yeah, right. Anything else? Or can I get on with my work now?"

"No. I'm just glad you're doing good. Ma'am."

A silent moment; they looked at each other. "Thanks, Mike."

Stakowski shuffled papers. "Long as the bugger knows how lucky he is."

"What?"

"Nothing, boss."

"Whatever. So, anything tonight?"

"Regular crime-wave. Been a break-in at the B&Q."

"What'd they take?"

"That's the weird bit. Plaster of Paris, car batteries, paints. Shedload of other stuff worth a sight more, but they didn't touch it."

Renwick's computer groaned into life. "Christ. This thing was a horse, you'd shoot it."

"I know the feeling."

"Doesn't surprise me. What've we got?"

"Not much. CCTV was on the fritz."

"Great."

"SOCO are still working it. Might find something."

"Bunch of students off their heads on magic mushrooms. Betcha."

Stakowski grinned. "It's a jungle out there."

"Fancy a brew, Sergeant?"

"Love one, ma'am."

"Me too." Renwick opened a file, donned reading glasses. "You know where the kettle is."

"Don't strain yourself or owt, will you?"

"I'll do my best."

"Bloody slavedriver."

"Heard that."

"You're a bloody slavedriver, *ma'am*."

"That's better. Now chop-chop. CID won't run itself."

"As you wish."

Stakowski filled the kettle. Outside, the streetlamps' light thickened into luminous orange cones as mist gathered in the street below.

*   *   *

PENCILS AND CHARCOAL scratched on paper; Kev's heels clicked on the floor. Otherwise, silence, except for the moaning wind outside.

Even in a sweater, Eva was cold. God knew what it must be like for Mark, stretched out naked on the dais in the middle of the life-drawing class. She could see the goose-pimples. Still, the college paid him for it. His eyes met hers; he winked.

"*Quite* still, Mark," Kev said primly. "If you don't mind."

Mark looked up innocently. Eva felt her face burn. Beside her, Jayne bit her lips and looked down.

Kev came over, bald patch gleaming under the striplights. "Very good, Eva." He sucked his paunch in, walked on. "OK, let's take a break, people."

Mark reached for a blanket. "Aw," Jayne whispered. "Was enjoying that."

"You'll be copping another eyeful soon enough," Eva whispered back.

"Yeah, but I'm trying to keep my mind on the drawing. Alright for you. You could get a private showing any time you fancied."

"Bog off."

"You know he fancies you."

"He's twenty-one. Go after a sheep if you put a skirt on it."

"So? He's got standards. Some lads wouldn't bother with the skirt."

"Well, you've always got Kev."

"Oh, stop it."

"Come *on*. Just imagine that beard tickling you."

"*Eva.*" But Jayne was already giggling. It was catching, too; Eva could feel it bubbling up in her.

"*Honestly*. And you a married woman."

"Yeah."

"Oh. Shit. Did I say the wrong thing?"

Eva forced a new smile. "Forget it."

"'Kay. Change the subject." Jayne nodded at the window; it was white with fog. "Lovely weather we're having. *Shit!*"

"What?"

Kev bustled over. "What's wrong?"

"Someone was looking in. Bloody perve–"

Something whacked hard against the window. She turned and saw it. A hand, splayed out flat. A moment later another slammed into place alongside it, so hard the pane cracked across. Between the hands, through the mist, what might have been a face began to take shape.

Someone screamed. Eva turned and saw a figure standing in the corner; tall and thin, clad in a black, tattered cape. A soft cloth cap hung down and shadowed its face.

A dark shape hovered in the air beside it like a shadow projected onto mist. Another appeared beside it. And another.

"Oh fuck." Jayne had grabbed Eva's forearm; her fingers sank in like claws. "What the fuck? What the fuck are they?"

The shadows were moving. One moved to bar the door. What good would that do? It was a shadow. But it was thickening, growing darker, more solid. They all were. There were a dozen in all, thin black tattered shapes, like the one advancing on them. Liz had stopped screaming; instead she stood rooted, face white, lips trembling, eyes fixed, even when it stretched out an impossibly long, clawlike hand towards her.

The room wasn't cold anymore, Eva realised. It was warm; hot even. Strange she should notice that. And then the first of them was in arm's reach, and as it reached for her she saw what it had for a face.

She screamed – everyone else was, even Kev – but then the warmth became searing heat and the world was suddenly made of fire.

"OI, SARGE?" RENWICK turned in her chair. "Where's me brew?"

No reply. At the window, Stakowski was still, leaning forward.

"Mike?"

He turned and looked at her. No smile, no glint in his eye. She went over to him. He pointed. In the distance, she saw it: an orange glow, brighter than the streetlamps, flickering ever brighter through the fog.

It took her a moment to realise what it was. And as she did, behind them, her phone began to ring.

THE TESTAMENT OF LANCE-CORPORAL CUTHBERT WINTHROP
CONCLUDED kept my head down literally down so no-
one saw lasted another thirty years like that
thirty fucking years gin helped gin and whisky
but thats what finished it in the end cause of
death cirrhosis of the liver and then howling
into the dark the void howling we are all here
all howling no peace no peace even in death no
peace for us none

* * *

In the Alma Street living room the clock ticked. Almost midnight. Martyn sat staring at the TV as he had for the last hour; saw nothing.

Get up. Do summat. But couldn't. Like having flu. Couldn't so much as get up. Every little job was suddenly massive. A monkey on your back; gripping tighter, squeezing harder, never letting go.

Eva'd be in the pub now, sipping a Britvic orange juice with her girlfriends, that ponce of a tutor. And that pretty-boy model – Christ, he wasn't even *thinking* about him. Eva was everything. Even more than Mary. He knew it shouldn't be like that, but it was. And Eva still turned heads. Men still looked at her. But she wouldn't. She wouldn't cheat. Would she?

The doorbell rang. Relief; she was home, and getting out of the chair was suddenly easy. The bell rang again.

As he turned the handle he remembered: Eva had a key. Why ring the bell, then? But the door was already open, and a blue light flashing in the street outside.

THE PAINTED MASK

'B' BLOCK

Dead hair and rodent bones in lightless corners; layers of dust on wooden sills and steel surfaces. Windows dimmed with grime. Thin pale light gleams on motes in the disturbed air and settles on dusty rows of ceramic arms that hang from hooks on the wall, fingers caught seemingly in the act of closing, as if they'll form fists the moment your back is turned.

CHAPTER TWO

Monday 16th December.

IT WAS FIVE miles' drive from Roydtwistle Psychiatric to Kempforth, over dull brown moors thick with mist. Anna turned Minnie the Micra's foglights on, palms damp on the wheel; nearly ten years on, places like Roydtwistle still made her feel cold and alone.

"You're in my room," she said.

"Eh?" In the passenger seat, Martyn blinked. Jeans, sweater. Two days' stubble and an old carrier bag in his lap. A wavering smile and dark rings under eyes that flicked from place to place. Her brother. This was her brother, now.

"Mary's in the spare room. She'll want to be near you."

"I can't take your bed–"

"I've got a camp bed in the study."

"The *what*?"

"Loft conversion. Remember?"

"*Study?*" He chuckled. "Get you."

If he could joke, that was a good sign. Wasn't it? "I'll be fine. Used to it." He didn't look sure. "Honestly." She needed some privacy. Pull up the drawbridge. "I've moved all my stuff upstairs anyway."

Remember your family, lass, Dad had used to say. *Owt else comes and goes, but your family's always there.* Something else she'd have to do. The monthly trip to the Garden of Rest. Take Dad some flowers.

The hills around Kempforth came into view as she turned onto Dunwich Road North. Her gaze drifted to the furthest one, lost beneath its thick growth of pines and rowans, like a pelt of fur and bones: Ash Fell.

Eyes front, she told herself, and drove on.

HER LITTLE TERRACED house on Trafalgar Road. Slate-roofed houses of grey or yellow stone. Hers was yellow. Dad's old house. Mum and Dad's. Hers now. She filled the kettle, put it on. Coffee, milk, sugar. Checked her mobile.

"There's plenty of time yet."

"Mm? No, it's not that. Just checking to see if Carole's called."

"Carole?"

"From work? The library?"

"Oh."

"There was something I was trying to find, about Ash Fell."

"That place again."

"Anyway, she was going to let me know if she found it." Change the subject, Anna. Something less morbid. "There's some of your stuff in the bedroom. From... anyway, it's there."

30

"From Alma Street."

"Yes."

"You can say it. I'll not fall apart if you do."

"OK. Look, I'd better go pick up the princess."

"Already? School's not out yet, is it?"

"Mrs Hartigan wants to see me."

"Alright. I'll... unpack."

"She's really glad you're back." She didn't say *back home*. For Martyn, *home* was still Alma Street, radioactive with the past.

"Mrs Hartigan?"

"Mary, you silly sod."

"Aye?"

"We both are." But Mary most of all. "I got her a present from you."

"Eh?"

"Christmas. You'll need to sign the label for it."

"Right."

"You'll be OK, yeah?"

"Aye. Go on."

"OK."

"Anna." She turned at the front door. Martyn drew himself all the way upright, took a deep breath. "I'll do me best not to let you down."

"It's Mary you've got to not let down."

"I know," he said. "What Eva would've wanted."

His whole face trembled when he spoke her name.

MRS HARTIGAN LEANT back in her chair. A Newton's Cradle clicked on her desktop; a small Christmas tree wrapped in threadbare tinsel perched on the windowsill.

"So how is Mary's Dad?" she asked.

"He's only come home today." Click, click, click. The headmistress steepled her fingers. "He seems OK. But... the whole point is that it's on a trial basis. Just for Christmas. For now anyway. The doctors at Roydtwistle thought it might help. A first step."

"Sounds to me like they're treating his daughter as a guinea pig. It's been less than a month since–"

Ten days after the college fire, two days after the funeral, Mary had called her at the library, scared and weepy. Anna had come over; Martyn had been slumped in his chair, conscious, but unmoving and silent. Once Mary was out of the room, he'd calmly told Anna how he'd spent the night planning to hang himself from a ceiling beam. Anna had called their GP straightaway. Sod *keep it in the family;* better Mary saw her dad sectioned than dangling from a rafter.

Anna kept her voice level. "Mary loves her dad. And he's pretty much all she's got right now."

Click, click, cl– "She has you."

"And I love her. I've given her all the love and care I can. But she's still, effectively, lost both parents. At least she sees one of them for Christmas this way."

"Well," Mrs Hartigan sniffed and glanced away. "The decision has been made."

Bite your tongue, Anna. Don't rock the boat. Martyn's not out of the woods yet. And no-one else knows you're gay. That shouldn't stop them letting you care for Mary. Times have changed and it's not even as if you *do* anything about it. But this is Kempforth, and here old attitudes die hard.

Click, click, click.

"Where's Mr Griffiths now?"

"At mine."

"Alone?"

"He's not a suicide risk anymore."

"Let's hope not."

It won't come to that. It won't. But if it does, make sure Mary doesn't see. She comes before everything else now. She blinked. Calm down, Anna. Don't be silly. He's not at risk. With your past you ought to be more understanding.

Mrs Hartigan tapped a pencil against her teeth. Then smiled. "I'll walk you to the classroom. May as well meet Mary there."

"Thank you."

Children ran shrieking down the dim corridor, fell silent when they saw Mrs Hartigan. Watercolour paintings of Father Christmas in various guises grinned from the walls. Mary's classroom was at the far end, the door open. A few children still struggled into coats. Miss Rhodes, Mary's teacher – a sweet, rather vague woman with unruly hair, huge glasses and a liking for baggy sweaters – tidied papers at her desk.

"Hi Mary."

Mary's blue eyes flicked to Mrs Hartigan, then back to Anna. A heart-shaped face, achingly solemn for a child of ten; Eva's copper hair.

"Say hello to your aunt, Mary," said Mrs Hartigan.

"Hello, Aunty Anna."

"Hey, princess. Guess who's waiting for us back home?"

Mary's eyes went wide. "Daddy?"

"Got it in one." She took Mary's hand. "And how about fish and chips for–"

Thud. The crack of glass. Mary grabbed Anna's arm. A black shape at the window, hands splayed against the glass. Thin silver cracks fled outwards from them; a HAPPY CHRISTMAS banner peeled loose from above and fell.

Anna's heart thudded. Her last fight had been thirty years earlier, in the playground outside, and she'd lost. But she stepped in front of Mary. It wasn't courage; just simple necessity.

"Get away from the window!" Miss Rhodes shouted.

Two other figures stepped up to the window to flank the first. Miss Rhodes – vague no longer – strode towards them, metre ruler in hand. "Children, get out into the corridor. Do as you're told. *Now.*"

Anna recognised them. But from where? The man seemed very tall and very thin; a black cloak hung in tatters around him, clinging to him one moment, then flapping loose. His face – pale, immobile, like a mask. You'd remember a face like–

The newcomers spread their hands against the window. Fingers long and thin as broom twigs scraped the glass. They couldn't be real.

And Anna remembered. No, they couldn't be real – not just the fingers, but the men themselves. They couldn't be real. Couldn't. She'd seen them when she was–

More screams, further down the corridor.

"You!" Miss Rhodes advanced on the window, aiming the ruler at the central figure two-handed, like a sword. "This is school property. Go away at once."

The three stiff, smooth faces all turned to stare at her. Miss Rhodes stopped in her tracks. "I'll call the police," she said, but with less authority than before.

Anna thought Miss Rhodes would look away from them at any moment, but it was the three cloaked figures who turned away, as if they'd been called. Perhaps they had, further back in the mist Anna saw a fourth figure: tall and cloaked like them but different, somehow. The fourth turned and vanished into the mist; the others trailed almost meekly after it, and were gone.

Mary's fingers dug into Anna's arm; she covered the small hand with hers. Miss Rhodes put the ruler down and went to one child who was crying. In the corridor, Mrs Hartigan was still pressed, frozen, against the wall.

"WERE YOU FRIGHTENED?"

"No. I know how to deal with nasty men like that."

Anna had to laugh. "Oh do you now?"

"*Yeah*. Kick 'em in the goolies and run. That's what Mummy–" She stopped.

Anna almost ruffled her hair, but didn't. Mary was sunk down in her seat, looking dully out of the window. When she spoke again, her voice was quieter – older, even. "We shouldn't tell Daddy about this, should we?"

"No," Anna said. "Probably not."

"No. He'd get upset."

"Do you want some music on?"

Mary grinned, eyes bright again. "Yeah. Please."

"OK, princess. What shall we listen to?"

"Silly-bellus?"

"Sibelius it is."

She let the music fill the car, focused on that and driving Minnie the Micra safely back across town. Better that than thinking of thin, immobile faces, black cloaks blowing tatters around bodies of sticks; she'd seen them when *she'd* been in Roydtwistle. Her and no-one else. Because back then, she'd been insane.

CHAPTER THREE

SHE DROVE OUT of their way, through the town centre; Mary loved the Market Hall, a Victorian gothic beast in sulphur-coloured stone. The town centre's lampposts were Victorian too: black-painted, wrought-iron, electric bulbs installed in what had been gas-lamps. Any days of greatness Kempforth had known had been in the nineteenth century; no wonder it looked back to it. If it made Mary smile, Anna didn't care.

Mist and dusk thickened together as they drove; when they got home visibility was down to five feet. "There we go." She turned off the engine, cutting off *The Sorcerer's Apprentice*. "Come on princess, out you get."

Mary turned back to Anna at the front door, grinning.

"How about Chinese for tea tonight, princess?" She knew one that delivered. Better that than braving the mists again.

"Yeah!" Fish and chips were forgotten; Chinese food was the one thing Mary loved more. Anna smiled back at her, feeling her eyes prickle. Other people never know what they do to us, how their tiniest act can melt us somewhere deep.

Better to think of that than what she'd seen at the school. Or that others had seen the same. She unlocked the front door and pushed it wide. Silence. A faint whiff of cigarette smoke. She'd have to speak to him about that.

"Martyn?" Her hand on Mary's shoulder – hold her back, she mustn't see if–

"Daddy!" Mary shot past into the house; Anna's hand grabbed only air.

"Who's that I can hear?" Footsteps on the stairs.

"Dad-*dy*!"

Martyn embraced Mary slowly, as if she'd break. Anna hung up her coat and went into the kitchen. Martyn said something Anna couldn't quite catch. She only heard the low-pitched timbre, so very like Dad's voice: solid and rooted, like an old oak tree. Mary still thought he was. God knows what Dad would've said if he could've seen his son now. Nothing good, most like. In the living room, Mary laughed.

There was a voice message on her mobile. Anna played it back.

"Hi, Anna. It's Carole. Just wanted you to know, I found that file you were looking for. Had a root around in my lunch hour." Nervous giggle. "Anyway, it's in your desk drawer. Hope everything's OK. Byeeeeee."

Anna put the kettle on. Her hands had almost stopped shaking now.

THEY ATE IN silence, but not the kind that'd filled the car on the way back from Roydtwistle; this was easy, companionable, comfortable, broken by the occasional giggle from Mary at a wink from Martyn. For the first time, Anna had the genuine sense things might work out.

Afterwards, she took the dishes into the kitchen. Normally Mary helped her, but tonight she was snuggled up to Martyn on the sofa in the warm glow from the gas fire and the glimmer of the Christmas tree's fairy lights, both arms wrapped round one of his. Clinging fast, so as not to lose him. Let her have this time.

"I've got an idea, for the weekend," she told them. "How about we all go to Witchbrook for the day? I'll pack us a lunch. Make a day of it."

"In this weather?"

"Be alright if we wrap up warm."

Martyn nodded. "Sounds right to me. What about thee, poppet?"

"Yeah. Suppose." As long as she was with Daddy.

They was a comedy programme on the television; Martyn stretched out on the sofa and Mary curled up beside him, punctuating his rumbling chuckle with giggles and shrieks. Anna felt a strange, bitter pang watching them. Yes, he was Mary's father and she was just an aunt – it was natural Mary should love him best – but even so she ached to be the centre of Mary's world, as Mary was of hers. Jealousy: was any emotion so pathetic?

"Best get off," she said. Martyn blinked up at her. "Promised I'd go see Nan."

"OK. Give her my love. Have to go see her soon."

"Maybe Saturday." Anna fetched her coat. "Sithee later, princess."

"Bye bye, Aunty Anna."

A tight hug. The sweet clean smell of the child. Anna's eyes prickled; she kissed the soft cheek, smoothed the red hair. "Be good for Daddy now."

Small arms tightened round her. "You're coming back, aren't you?"

"'Course I am, daftie." She squeezed back. "Just going to see Nan."

Martyn saw her to the door. "Look after yourself."

"You too."

"No. I mean... out there."

"I'll stick to the backstreets." He didn't look reassured. "You OK?"

He shrugged. "Feels like I'm learning everything all over again."

"It will, for a while."

"Was it that way for you?"

"Let's not talk about that now, please."

"OK. Just... I'm scared, sis."

She squeezed his arm.

"Thought I were better than that."

"Than what? Me?"

"Stronger, then. That I'd hold up."

"It wasn't just one thing. You know that."

"Aye."

"The fire was just the last straw."

"Big bastard straw."

"I know." She pecked his cheek. "Don't worry about me. Worry about yourself. And *her*. Her most of all. The rest'll sort itself out."

The door clicked shut behind her. She stepped out onto the cold, shrouded pavement and started walking.

*   *   *

ANNA HAD KNOWN the maze of backstreets between Trafalgar Road and Stangrove Wood Residential Home all her life, but that didn't seem to help just now, in the dark and the mist. At least she could hear the murmur of televisions in front rooms as she passed the houses, see the blurred glow of lit windows. It wasn't exactly reassuring, but it felt safer than the main road, which had heavy traffic even in these conditions.

She walked at a brisk pace, tugging her coat tight around her and wishing she'd brought a scarf. Footsteps clicked behind her. Her breath caught. Foolish. Just a late-night shopper, or someone like her, with commitments, obligations. She walked faster, all the same.

Where was she now? Marshall Street. Turn left here. Then right onto Kenborough Lane. Behind her, still, the click, click, click of her follower's boots. She should have gone for the main road after all. Stupid. He wasn't following her.

A crossroads. Straight over for Stangrove Wood. To the right, traffic sounds came from the main road. She stopped to look both ways. Behind her, the footsteps stopped.

Anna looked behind her. Nothing to see; just mist and a cone of blurred orange streetlight. Click, went a bootheel on the cold damp pavement. Click, click, click. The streetlight flickered. Someone was moving deliberately round its edges, not venturing into plain view.

She turned off the backstreets towards the gathering noise of passing cars on the main road; the sound had never been so welcome. She thought she heard the footsteps following, but they were soon lost in the traffic and when she looked back, she saw nothing.

*   *   *

AT STANGROVE WOOD, Anna punched in the flat number on the keypad by the door.

"Who's that?"

"Anna."

The door buzzed open. The community lounge was empty; the Christmas tree's lights had been switched off. Anna had a spare key to Nan's first-floor flat; she let herself in. "Nan?"

"In here, love." As if she'd be anywhere else this time of day. Anna passed the framed photos in the hallway – Nan as a young woman, Dad as a boy, Mum and Dad, her and Martyn as kids, Martyn and Eva with Mary – and went on into the living room.

"Oh hullo there, darling." Nan's throaty Welsh-accented voice – she'd smoked well into her seventies – always made Anna think of a rusty squeezebox. "Are you alright?"

"I'm fine." Anna kissed her cheek – old, wrinkled, and softly furred with a light down – and caught the scent of the Imperial Leather soap Nan had always used. "D'you want a cup of tea, Nan?"

"Oh, go on, then. If you know where to find everything."

She always said that, as if she regularly swapped everything around to keep Anna on her toes. "Yes, Nan. You just stay there."

Tea for Nan, coffee for Anna with half a spoonful of sugar. Well, a girl had to have some indulgences. She pulled off her gloves and coat.

THINGS FOLLOWED THE usual pattern after that. They talked a little, put the TV on. Nan drowsed off in her chair and snored softly, arms folded, head bowed. Her hearing aids made thin piping and squeaking sounds, like far-off whale music. The TV murmured; subtitles scrolled across the bottom of the screen.

The TV murmured. Nan gave a small muffled grunt and shifted in her sleep; the hearing aids squeaked softly. Anna slipped a sheaf of print-outs from her bag; a chapter from her book. She crossing out a word, scribbled a note in the margins. Slow work; she'd precious little writing time these days. But she'd do what she could, when she could. If it helped keep her sane.

Time passed. Anna rubbed her eyes and looked up, studying the mantelpiece above the fireplace. There were Christmas cards from her, Mary, a few of the home's other residents; there was the card from Buckingham Palace, hand-delivered two years ago on Nan's hundredth birthday. A photograph of Grandpa, in his army uniform; another of him with Nan on her wedding day.

And Nan's father. Here he was in puttees and webbing belt. It was from 1918, after he'd been wounded; his face was slack, eyes staring off past the edge of the frame, seeing god knew what. There was one of him at Nan's wedding too, his daughter on his arm, all in white. Nan had married in her mid-thirties, quite late for those times, but even allowing for the twenty-five years that had passed, Anna would never have guessed it was the same man if she hadn't known. His face had creased and thickened, eyes sinking deep in their sockets as if in retreat from what they might see, and while he was trying to smile, it was a weak shadow of a thing.

Shot at the battle of Passchendaele, wounded in the

chest and arm. The arm amputated at the elbow. And yet he could tie his shoelaces unaided, fasten his tie. Not that there'd been much choice. No welfare state back then, no safety net. You provided for your family or watched them starve, that or scrape by on a means-tested pittance. The changes he must have seen; he'd fought in one world war, seen out not only its successor but a whole world, a way of life. There must have been almost nothing left, at the end, he could recognise.

Time passed. Anna glanced at the clock. Christ, the time. Had the mist thinned out? Let it clear up tomorrow; she hated driving in conditions like that.

Nan grunted again, stirred awake, blinked sleep-small eyes and fumbled for her glasses. Her hair had faded over the years from a dark grey, when Anna had been little, to near-pure white, and she'd shrunk, grown smaller and thinner. She couldn't walk without a frame. But her vitality hadn't ebbed. Despite it all, she was often taken to be in her eighties, at most. Some people were only convinced when shown the card from the Queen.

"Faffing round with that book of yours again?"

"Yes, Nan."

"Wish you'd leave it. No-one wants to hear about that horrible bloody place."

Old argument; no point repeating it now. "I'll have to go in a minute, Nan."

"What's that?" Nan blinked and squinted.

"I said, I'm going to have to go, Nan."

"Alright, love. Ooh, Anna?"

"Yeah?"

"Could you do me a favour?"

"'Course I can. What is it?"

"As long as it's no trouble."

"'Course not."

"You going to the Garden of Rest this week?"

"Can do."

"If I give you some money, could you get some flowers for your dad?"

"'Course."

Nan counted out change. "Wish I could go myself."

"It's OK."

"I'd go if I could."

"I know." Nan had always cherished her independence; precious little now remained.

"Thank you, love. You're too good to everyone, you know, Anna. I do feel bad sometimes, making you run errands for me all the time."

"Don't be silly."

"You should have a life of your own."

"Do my best."

"I know, love, but I do worry sometimes."

Anna embraced the thin body, kissed the papery cheek. "Love you, Nan."

Nan squeezed her back. "Love you too." It'd become a ritual of late; at Nan's age, you could never be completely sure she'd still be there next time.

"He was here before, you know."

Anna turned. "Sorry?"

Nan nodded towards the mantelpiece. "Before you got here. I saw him. At the window."

"Who?" On the mantelpiece the only pictures – the Queen aside – were of the dead. Nan didn't answer at first. They'd never really talked religion; as far as Anna knew Nan still had the simple, straightforward Welsh Methodist faith of her childhood. Anna didn't share it, but it had got Nan through the last century, so fair enough. But Nan had never claimed to see the dead. Assuming that was what she meant. "Who?" She felt foolish just asking. "Grandpa?"

Nan shook her head. Her eyes glistened and just for once, her age seemed to show in full. "My father," she said at last. "Outside. I saw him." Anna bit her lip. "It's alright. Don't worry about me, dear. But I did see him. Always had a bit of the second sight, you know. Runs in our family. I always thought—"

"What?"

"You might have a touch of it, too."

Anna kissed Nan's downy cheek again and let herself out. She went fast. The night was very dark all of a sudden, the mist very deep.

She didn't think about what Nan had said. Couldn't. Eva dead, Martyn damaged and healing only slowly, if at all. And most of all, Mary. The fear she couldn't protect the child; the vow that she would. And now Nan, seeing a father dead for over sixty years. Let it just be the tail-end of a dream, half-remembered on waking. Let Nan not be going mad. There was only so much Anna could shoulder. Not that she could talk about sanity. *You might have a touch of it, too.* Thanks, Nan. What would be worse: seeing things that weren't there, or things that were?

On she trudged. Home now, then bed. Too late to write anything else; she had to be up early, make sure Mary got to school. Maybe a few pages of *The Brothers Karamazov* before she slept – she was determinedly struggling through it – as long as neither Martyn nor Mary had more pressing needs. And then sleep.

This was her life now.

Your family, lass. Your family.

So on she walked, and told herself the only footsteps echoing in the mist were her own.

CHAPTER FOUR

Thursday 19th December

BRIDGE STREET, MANCHESTER. Christmas lights glittering on the lampposts; shoppers weaving like columns of ants to and from the shops up on Deansgate. The River Irwell shining like mirrorglass. And Renwick on the courthouse – *Justice Centre* – steps, sipping coffee, breathing crisp cold air, checking mobile messages and praying the jury reached a verdict today.

Two weeks' leave, starting tomorrow. Enough sleep and maybe Julie Baldwin's accusing ghost would fade. *You were supposed to keep me safe.*

First message:

"Joan? Dad. Just wondered… your plans for Christmas. I know we…" A pause, a sigh. "Be good to see you. Invite's still open. You *and* Nick. Both welcome. Got the spare room all made up. Just… even if you're not coming, let us know, eh? Alright. Lots of love."

Next message:

"Joan? Nick. Wanted to let you know: last of my stuff's moved out. Left the key on the kitchen table. That should be it now. All done." Pause. "Bye."

Last message.

"Joan? Detective Chief Superintendent Banstead. Assume you're still in court. I'm calling from home. Call me when you're done. The number's–"

She replayed the message, jotted it down. Only a select few got the Bedstead's home number. Now she was one of them. Which might be good news or bad.

"Detective Chief Inspector?" She turned. "Jury are coming back in."

She breathed out; one prayer answered, anyway.

EVER SINCE HE'D been arrested, Tom Baldwin had worn the same pious, martyred look. He'd kept it through the trial; it didn't change when they read the verdict out.

"Thomas Baldwin, you have been found guilty…"

Got you, you bastard.

Baldwin looked up at the public gallery as if he'd heard her thought.

"… of the rape and murder of your daughter, Julie Baldwin…"

He met her eyes, pursed his lips, sighed and shook his head. *Joan, Joan, why persecutest thou me?*

"… the culmination of years of abuse, practised against your own child…"

For a second Renwick wished she had a gun. She turned and walked out fast.

*   *   *

50

SHE STOPPED INTO Waterstone's to get a book for the journey. No crime fiction; good old-fashioned sword-and-sorcery. Life wasn't that simple, but it was nice to pretend.

As well as all the Christmas shoppers, she saw several large black-and-white pictures of a fortyish man with dark, silver-sprinkled hair, immaculate teeth and a phoney grin. She knew the face. Then she saw the book's title: *The Realm Of Spirit* by Allen Cowell. Christ – *him*. She'd seen his TV show; how could anyone take him seriously for even five minutes? But people did, if they were scared, bereft, battered by fate, looking for meaning. She didn't mock or judge them. It was all too easy for that to happen. She paid for her book and cleared out fast.

On the train, she called the Bedstead. The phone rang; the reception was terrible. And there was a crossed line; she could hear other voices mumbling under the static's hiss.

"Joan. How was Manchester?"

"Pleasant enough, from what I saw of it, sir."

"Did we get a result?"

"Guilty, sir. Unanimous verdict. Any luck and his Honour will throw the book at the bastard."

"Good. Good. Excellent." Banstead let out a harsh coughing fit. "Christ. Sorry. Down with this bloody flu."

The Bedstead, off sick? "It's going around, then?"

"Vicious strain of it too. Got half the force laid out up here. We're critically short-staffed. I know you're due some leave–"

Shit. "Sir?"

"There's a case. Well, two. Missing persons. One's a

two-year-old child. Got Stakowski on that one, but I want you in charge."

Shit shit shit. "Is there a problem with Mike, sir?"

"Not at all. Fine officer. You know that. But I want someone more senior in charge. Two cases, possibly connected. Plus... well, talk to Stakowski when you get back. And DS McAdams as well, he's handling the other one."

The train rattled. Static hissed. The distant voices mumbled. "OK, sir."

"Thank you. Appreciated. Good luck."

The phone went dead. Renwick speed-dialled Stakowski's number.

KEMPFORTH WAS TWENTY miles from Manchester and nearly three hundred feet higher; Renwick glimpsed boxy industrial estates and huddled grey towns clumped together in the rain from the window before mist engulfed the train. When she stepped out onto the cobbles outside the station the air was ice cold and white mist blanketed Dunwich Road. Traffic growled; pale blurred foglights swam back and forth. A car pulled up.

"How do."

"Mike." She could've hugged him. Best not.

"Been pining for me, then?"

"Oh yeah, you old buzzard. Absolutely."

Stakowski frowned. "You OK, lass?"

"I'm fine." Lie. "Long trial, that's all."

Stakowski held the car door open for her. "How was Manchester?"

"Bright lights, big city."

"And the trial?"

52

"Guilty."

"Good work."

"Thanks, Dad." She flopped back in her seat.

"Shall I book a table at the Good Luck?"

"Once you've briefed me, yeah."

"The missing kid? Roseanne Trevor. Got the interview with her mam on video. You want to see it?"

"What do you think?"

A THIN WOMAN in her early twenties: narrow face, small dark eyes. Gold hoop earrings, fake tan, bleach-blonde hair. Too much makeup, streaked down her face by tears. She scrubbed her cheek with a tissue; the skin beneath was sallow.

Stakowski froze the image. "Stacey Trevor. Twenty-one, no steady partner. The dad's called Andy Kirkland. Did a runner when he heard Stacey was pregnant."

"Real prince among men."

"Aye. Lives in Bradford now. Local fuzz picked him up."

"And?"

"Clear alibi. Plus he's shown no interest in the kiddie since she were born. Still checking, but doesn't look like he were involved." Stakowski pressed play.

"Took our Roseanne down Dunwich Park." Stacey Trevor's voice; sullen even through the grief. *All coppers are bastards*. "She'd been acting up. Pushed her on swings a bit, then she wanted to go on roundabout. So I let her." Her lips wobbled. "Could hear her laughing. All's I did... all's I did were get me *Take A Break* out for a second. Just a minute. I kept glancing up to look at her." She was crying again. "I'm not some slag. I'm not a shit mum.

Just wanted a minute to meself, just that. Could hear her laughing. Kept looking up. Then I heard summat, behind us. Bushes. Rustling. Looked round. Case it were a Spindly. There were *someone*. Fuckin' swear, mam's life. Then they were gone. But there *was* someone. Fuckin' tellin' tha." Her voice had risen. Now it faltered. "And then... took us a couple of secs to realise. Couldn't hear Roseanne." Her breath hitched, became sobs; she flapped her hands to ward the camera off. "Looked. Roundabout was still spinning, but our Roseanne were gone. Screamed for her. Ran round an' round that fuckin' park. But there were nothin'. Nothin'." She pursed her mouth, stuck out her unformed chin. "So – rang you lot and here we are." A muffled keening, then her mouth buckled, her face crumpled and the keening became a wail that raised the hairs on Renwick's arms.

"Christ, Mike."

"Soz." Stakowski switched the video off.

"Think she's on the level?"

"If she's not she should be on bloody stage."

"Skeletons in the cupboard?"

"No serious debts – well, nowt worse than anyone else on the Dunwich. No involvement in owt dodgy. No signs of drug abuse."

"Ransom?"

"She's on benefits. Council accommodation. No rich relatives. Nowt worth a kidnapper's while."

"That's what I was afraid of."

"Aye. Sorry boss. Most likely explanation's some bastard paedo."

"Or more than one. Very convenient, those bushes rustling when they did. Team effort? One distracts the mum, one grabs the kid?"

"Or some sick bastard saw an opportunity and took it. Either way, doesn't look good for the kiddie." A moment's pause. "You're thinking on the Baldwin lass." It wasn't a question.

"Baldwin didn't mean to kill his daughter. He'd been abusing her for years – went too far one night, panicked... But this looks planned. Deliberate."

"Aye."

"So what've you done so far?"

"Pulled in every known sex offender in the Kempforth, rung CID in Blackburn and Accrington about theirs. SOCO did a fingertip search of the scene. Background checks on family."

"But?"

"Nowt. Whoever took her knew what they were about. Only chance of catching them is finding summat."

Renwick breathed out. "Like a body."

"Or summat. Plenty of other things–"

"Chances are we'll never find her. Or she'll turn up in a shallow grave ten years down the line and the killer'll be long gone. Even if he's not, he'll have worked his way through a dozen other kids first–"

"We can't afford to think that way, Joan. You know that."

He didn't often call her by name. When he did, she listened. "Yeah," she said at last, "I know."

Stakowski frowned. "You shouldn't need me to tell you that, normally. Everything all right with you?"

"Oi. Sergeant. We're working here."

"Sorry, ma'am. Another coffee?"

"No. Yes."

Stakowski put the kettle on. "Best thing you can do for the kiddie is keep your head clear and do the job, boss. Cross the t's, dot the i's. Don't miss owt. Best chance we've got."

"Yes, alright."

"Sorry." Stakowski waited. The kettle boiled.

Renwick sighed. "Split up with Nick."

"Sorry."

"I'm not. Better finding out now before it got serious."

"Thought it already was."

"So did I. Not like I didn't tell him how it was gonna be."

"I remember. Late nights, broken dates, having to dash off at any minute. Nearly had tears rolling down me face by the end. Did you actually start playing the violin or was that my imagination?"

"In your case I'd say senile dementia. He said he understood."

"Probably thought he did. You can know summat and not know it."

"Very profound." Renwick raised her cup in a mock toast. "Least I won't have to spend it in Yorkshire with his whole bloody family. All ninety-six of them."

"Now you're exaggerating."

"Felt like ninety-six when I was there. All gawping like I was a circus freak."

"You were in Yorkshire. They're not used to fingers that aren't webbed." Renwick laughed. "So what are you doing for Christmas now? Seeing your Dad?"

"No."

"Just asked."

Renwick sighed. "Expect I'll be too busy anyway, with all this."

"Still not much of a Christmas."

"I just don't fancy scooting off to the Wirral to hear Dad banging on about me getting 'left on the shelf' again like I'm an alarm clock. That's *Morwenna* talking. Not my idea of fun. Downright embarrassing, in fact. Dad and his new child bride."

"She's older than you.

"Just."

"If he's happy…"

"He's my *Dad*." Renwick sighed, shook her head. "Sorry. Forget it."

Stakowski shrugged. "I wouldn't panic about the shelf thing yet. You're still young."

"Thank you, old-timer."

Stakowski smiled, tipped an imaginary hat. He thought of the duck he'd bought from Kempforth Market for his lonely Christmas dinner, the rest of it, like as not, lasting him the week. More than enough for two. He almost said something. Then didn't. There was always enough for two, and only one to eat it. Ever since Laney. "Got him owt for Christmas?"

"Didn't have time. Had a shufti round Waterstone's in Manchester, but I couldn't move for pictures of Allen Cowell."

"That *prick*."

"Whoa. Easy Mike."

"Sorry. Can't stand his sort. Bloody parasites, feeding off people's grief."

"OK."

"Sorry." There was silence between them for a spell; Stakowski broke it. "Joan…"

"What?"

"Why do you think you've got this case?"

"They're short-staffed."

"The real reason."

"Enlighten me."

"Think it's a coincidence you get this one after damn near working yourself into the grave on the Baldwin case? Right before you're due to go on leave? Banstead's not stupid. He knows this kind of case pushes all your buttons. So he gives you this. *This* one."

"There's the other one, too – Dave McAdams' case."

"But he makes sure this is the one you hear about first. Get briefed on first. Another Julie Baldwin."

"Mike…"

"Look – what state were you in when you got posted here?"

Renwick looked down. "You know better than anyone."

"Yeah. Bloody mess would be putting it kindly. Pissed every night, hungover every morning, and towing some real specimens back home with you at the end of the night."

"Do you mind?"

"Stop me if I'm wrong." No answer. "You were going great guns back in Manchester – transfer to CID, recommended for promotion to DS within a year of *that* – cos of your work on another case involving kiddie-fiddlers, as I recall–"

"Yeah."

"And then…"

"And then Mum died and I went off the rails. Thank you for reminding me."

"There's a point."

"Then make it."

"Look… lot of people had written you off back then. But look at you now."

"Thanks. I think."

"You've done bloody well. But sooner or later the

ones like you all bugger off back to big city. 'Cept you didn't. Even when you made DCI . You've already turned down one post back in Manchester. Plum job too, I believe."

"How the hell did you find out–"

"I'm a detective, boss. You should try it sometime."

"Piss off."

"Point I'm making is here you are going up, up and away, and you're not leaving Kempforth. There's only one more rank between you and Banstead."

"He thinks I'm after his job?"

"Or that the powers that be'll start thinking it's time he hung his boots up. But there's a reason the Bedstead's been Divisional Commander this long."

"Age and treachery will always defeat youth and idealism?"

"Summat like that, but I wouldn't use all those long words."

"There's a surprise." Pause. "You think he's trying to set me up."

"I know the bastard."

"So what am I supposed to do? Pull a sicky? Say I've got this flu that's going round?"

"You could."

"No I couldn't."

Stakowski smiled. "No."

"What then?"

"Watch your back."

"How about you watch it for me?"

"Did you really think I wouldn't?"

Renwick nodded, sipped her coffee. "So… what's a Spindly?"

"Eh?"

"On the interview. She said she thought it was a Spindly, in the bushes. The hell's one of them when it's at home?"

"We had a report, Monday afternoon. Between three and six individuals faffing round the playground at Primrose Hill Primary, looking in through windows, banging on the glass. Scared hell out of the kids."

"And?"

"Kids started calling them the Spindly Men. And it's caught on. Since Monday there've been reports flying about left and right."

"Any actual criminal offences?"

"Nowt we can pin down."

"So? Older kids pissing round. Students home for the Christmas break. Get up to all sorts of stupid shit, that crowd."

"Speaking from personal experience, ma'am?"

"Yes."

"I'd have said same, except for one thing."

"Don't spin it out, Mike. Come on."

"Sorry. Just remember me Mam telling me about them once. Her Dad used to tell her when she was a kid – they were a sort of bogeyman. Don't go into the woods after dark or the Spindly Men'll get you." Stakowski's father had fled to England after the war, but the farmhouse he still lived in had been home to generations of the Pidwell family, up to and including his mother.

"So they're what, a local legend?"

"Pretty old one, I think. But you'd be hard put to find anyone under the age of seventy who's heard tell of them."

"Explains why you'd know, then."

"Cheeky madam. They were supposed to live in the

woods above the town, and – well – prey on the unwary. Not much more to the story than that. No real meat on the bones. But it's pretty obscure. I only know cos me Mam told me. Whoever it is, they're even dressing the part: long, tall and thin, tatty black coats, masks."

"Masks?"

"Aye. Mam said it was cos they had no faces of their own, so they'd steal yours off you if they could."

"Ugh."

"Aye."

"So someone's acting out an old local legend. Still sounds like some sort of prank."

"Maybe, maybe not. Was thinking I might pop down the library tomorrow. See if they've any books on it."

"What good'll that do?"

"Might shed some light on why they're doing it. Maybe some sort of weird cult. And maybe see if anyone's checked those books out lately."

"Not bad thinking for an old geezer."

"You're all charm and grace, lass. Now how about a Chinese dinner?"

"Best idea you've had all night."

THE TESTAMENT OF PRIVATE WOLFIE JACOBS gather round and hearken to my tale brave boys for i can say few soldiers paid a price throughout the war as grievous as mine for as you can tell brave boys i was a smooth talker and by such dint did loosen the stays and skirts of many a fair maiden in my native london town for much to the head shakings of my greybearded father oi vey and the tears of my dear old mother hear o israel my

cock was well seasoned with the drippings of an
thousand cunts ere a boche bullet blew it off in
nineteen sixteen oh i was a right one brave boys
well valued by my platoon for twas i could always
get you a smoke a drink a knife a gun a willing
woman all so long as you were not of too choosy
a persuasion and then i was shot a bullet wound
sustained in the act of storming an enemy trench
the wound was caused by a 9mm pistol bullet
striking at the base of the penis and severing
it except for two or three connecting shreds of
musculature before tearing through the scrotum
and

THE GOOD LUCK Restaurant. A faded print of a misty
mountain range. Electric light filtered through paper
lanterns. Faux-traditional Chinese synth music piped
from speakers, fighting with the Salvation Army band's
rendition of God Rest Ye Merry Gentlemen from further
down the High Street.

Stakowski rubbed his hand together. "Hot and sour
soup to start, I reckon–"

*Sizzling Beef Szechuan with a dish of Peking ribs.
Dunno why you even bother with that menu.*

"And then Beef Szechuan, and some of them Peking
ribs. What about you, ma'am? I know how tough it is
for you lasses to mek your minds up."

Renwick raised two fingers without looking up from
the menu. "Made mine up while you were still trying
to remember where you were, Sarge. They shouldn't let
you out on your own at your age. Crab and sweetcorn
soup, steamed pork dumplings–"

"– and king prawns in black bean sauce with stir-fried noodles?"

"Amazing. You read tea-leaves as well?"

"No, but I do a great routine with balloon animals. I'm all the rage at kiddies' parties."

"Whatever."

The food came. They ate their soup in silence, started talking again as they started work on the mains.

"So what about the other misper?"

"Dave McAdams can tell you more than me, but he's off-shift till tomorrow."

"What *do* you know?"

"Asian lass. Name escapes me. Seventeen. Vanished off High Street."

"Someone snatched her off *this* High Street?"

"Yup. Broad daylight." Stakowski nodded at the mist beyond the windows. "Well, not so broad. Been like this all week. Makes it a lot easier."

"Even so. You don't snatch someone like that on the spur of the moment."

"Spare rib?"

"Just the one. Watching my figure."

"Watch it for you if you–"

"Don't even *think* about finishing that sentence."

"Ma'am." Stakowski took another rib.

"So? What happened with this girl?"

"Like I said, you should talk to Dave–"

"–and I will…"

"But… someone heard a scream, just found but the girl's handbag. Nowt taken – driving licence, bank card, money still there."

"But she'd vanished."

"Thin air. Broad daylight. No trace."

"Just like Roseanne Trevor."

"Just like."

"So there's either two sets of kidnappers–"

"–pretty long odds round here–"

"–or one group. Who on the one hand snatch a toddler, on the other a pretty well-developed teenager. There was a paedophile ring in Kempforth some years back, wasn't there?"

"Allegedly. *Long* way back. 'Bout '85, if I remember right. Before you were born."

"Piss off. But that was pretty well-organised, wasn't it?"

"Mid 80s? Before my time. But I heard something of it. Don't think they ever nailed the buggers, but I doubt any of them'd still be around either. Could always talk to the Bedstead."

"Eh?"

"Well, I think he was a DS at the time. Might have heard something."

"Leave that one well alone for now. Might as well just print a t-shirt saying *I'm Clutching At Straws*."

"Your call, boss. So, how do you want to play it?"

"I want to talk to McAdams first thing tomorrow before I make a final decision."

"But?"

"For now, a single investigation. You head up the Trevor case, McAdams stays on the missing teenager. Pool information, see what we get."

"And the Spindly Men?"

"Make your trip to the library and we'll see."

"'Kay."

"Anything else?"

"Just remember to watch your back on this one, boss. That's all."

"You're watching it for me. Remember?"

"Oh aye."

```
THE TESTAMENT OF PRIVATE WOLFIE JACOBS CONCLUDED
pulverising both testicles and the worst of it
my cullies the big bastard laugh was that we fell
back from the trench with not even that poor gain
to show for the loss of my manhood whose tattered
remnants were left to rot in germanic earth or
earth held by the german bastards anyway oh i
hated them and why should i not had i not good
cause but not as much as i hated the pity and
the horror and the disgust on the faces of the
nurses and the vads who changed my dressings and
saw and saw and saw for oh women had uncovered
my nakedness before but with very different
expressions before my tool stabbed them and
now i dreamt of stabbing with other implements
implements made of metal or wood but i did not
do so give me credit brave boys i did not but
endured the smart of pity and revulsion and a
more sickish brew than that there never was for
eleven years before at last weighting my pockets
with stones and wading the waters of old father
thames one last time in search of peace perfect
peace but finding it not brave boys finding it not
for the quality of peace is not rare but indeed
non existent it abideth nowhere nowhere at all
```

RENWICK SHUT THE door of her third-floor flat behind her just after ten pm, weary to her bones, and dropped her suitcase in the lounge.

She wanted a shower, but not because of dirt or sweat. *Baldwin*. She felt greasy at the thought of him. But too tired. An excuse not to ring Dad, anyway. Tonight at least. *Tomorrow is another day*. She made her way to the bedroom, shucking off suit jacket, blouse, unfastening her belt.

Nick had left the wardrobe doors open, showing all the gaps where his clothes had been.

Renwick kicked away shoes, trousers. Peeling her socks off felt like too much effort, so she kept them on as she pitched onto the bed. She groped for the alarm clock, held it to her bleary face and set the time. "Think I'll become a nun," she muttered, and slept.

CHAPTER FIVE

Friday 20ᵗʰ December.

THE MEETING ROOM at Mafeking Road. Scraggy ropes
of tinsel hung glittering from the ceiling. *Merry bloody
Christmas.* Renwick, Stakowski and McAdams – a
fortyish Detective Sergeant with thinning ginger hair –
facing a dozen journos: the *Kempforth Chronicle*, local
rags from neighbouring towns, even – the big time – the
Manchester Evening News and *North-West Tonight*.
Cameras flashed. Renwick breathed deep; she'd only
had ten minutes to talk to McAdams about the other
missing person.

"Tahira Khalid, aged seventeen, from the All Saints
district of Kempforth." A photograph; a soft-faced
girl with wire-rimmed glasses, shyly smiling. "Last
seen Monday afternoon, Kempforth High Street. A
scream was heard around the time she was last seen. A
handbag identified as Tahira's was found near the War
Memorial."

"Are the two cases being treated as connected, Chief Inspector?"

"Could this be an honour killing?"

"Is a paedophile ring operating in Kempforth?"

"There's no hard evidence either way at this point; we've two separate investigations that will share information. There's no indication of that. There's no evidence to support that view either."

"Then with respect, Chief Inspector, what information *do* you have?"

"We have leads we are investigating. When we've got information to share with you, we will share it. Any further questions? Thank you."

THE SQUAD ROOM, and Renwick viewed the rest of her team: four Detective Constables, all the flu outbreak and the usual pre-Christmas crime rise had left available.

"So... Tahira Khalid. What do we know?"

McAdams coughed. "She were working part-time as a shop assistant, doing a Theatre Studies A-level at Kempforth College before it burnt down." A moment's silence. Nearly all of them had seen the charred remains, mostly unidentifiable, carried from the college's ruins. At least it'd happened at night; by day it'd have been ten times worse. "Went to Primrose Hill Secondary School after work most days, where they've been holding some of the college classes. Work colleagues were fairly non-committal about her."

"Non-committal?"

"Nowt to say against her, but nowt particularly for her either. Fades into the background sort of thing. Nice enough lass, good worker, but distant, away with the fairies."

"Any boyfriends?" asked Tranter, the youngest – early twenties – of the detectives, in a smart suit a size too big. Pale grey eyes, dark frizzy hair; a receding chin and a prominent nose.

"Gonna ask her out if we find her?" smirked Janson. Renwick winced – Janson's volume always seemed to be set two notches too high. One of Renwick's few female colleagues in Kempforth CID, God help her.

"Sue," said Renwick.

"Sorry mum." Janson blinked. Her eyes were small and too close-set; what little bone structure her face had was lost in pale, doughy flab.

"Go on, Colin." Tranter was painfully earnest – downright humourless at times – but capable.

He flushed. "I was thinking exes, maybe. Rejected suitors."

"That occurred to me," McAdams said. "So I asked DC Crosbie to speak to the family."

"Shot down," Janson cat-called. Tranter went redder.

"This isn't the playground, Janson," McAdams said.

"Sarge."

"Alastair?"

About Renwick's age, but dressed ten or twenty years older, Crosbie wore grimy spectacles and an old suit jacket with dandruff on the shoulders. "She was seeing a laddie called Usman Khan, but he dumped her a fortnight after starting Uni. Nae-one since."

"What about the family itself?"

"Parents, grandmother, four brothers, two sisters – all crammed into one semi-detached house, Christ knows how. Plus an older sister, married and moved out."

"Any problems at home, that we know of?"

"None we could discover," Crosbie said. "Spoke to

DS Ashraf over at the Dunwich – he came in, helped translate. The granny didnae have great English."

"They only do when it bloody suits them."

"Something to share, Janson?"

"No mum."

"Good. Alastair…?"

"There'd been talk of marriage."

"Arranged?"

"Aye."

"And was she happy with that?"

"She wasnae bothered. That's what they all said. Whole family, even the kid sisters. All said the same. Lad she'd been seeing had upped and left her. Seems she thought an arranged marriage might be less painful – bit less chancy."

"Not bein' funny, mum, but they're not gonna just come out and say it, are they? Course they're gonna say she were up for it."

"Some girls do enter into arranged marriages of their own volition, Janson," Renwick said. Not that Janson was necessarily wrong, but how she'd crow if she were right. "Let's not jump to conclusions."

"Yeah, but–"

"Yes?"

Janson shifted her bulk in her chair. "Just saying, can't just take their word for it, can we?"

"Which is why," said McAdams, "we interviewed both neighbours and Tahira's friends." He glanced up at Janson. "Some of whom were actually white. All said the same thing. She weren't bothered. Took things as they came. Away with the fairies. Lived in a world of her own."

"Any suspicious persons reported round the time she

went missing?" asked DC Wayland, who'd arranged himself into a casual slouch most likely copied from a cop film. He was actually good at his job when he wasn't posing.

"Nothing."

"Any other questions? OK. Mike?"

Stakowski relayed much the same information he'd given her the night before. He was thorough, as always; if he'd left it out of the report, it hadn't been there to begin with. No questions afterward, not even from Tranter, and no gobbing off from Janson; toddlers didn't run away from home.

"OK, then," Renwick said. "DS Stakowski will handle the Roseanne Trevor case – DS McAdams, Tahira Khalid. Janson, you're with Dave – Tranter, Wayland, you're with Mike. We'll be running them both in tandem out of here." She hated the idea of Janson going near the Khalid case, but better there than Roseanne Trevor. And she knew she'd put her best two officers on the Trevor case. She should be trying to weight both investigations equally. Could she live with it if they found Tahira Khalid dead? She didn't know, but she *couldn't* live with finding Roseanne Trevor that way.

"What about me, boss?"

"Hadn't forgotten you, Crosbie. We're short on bodies, so we'll all be out in the field a lot – Mike, Dave and myself included. We need a point of contact here in the office. That's you."

"Nae hassle, ma'am. Fine by me."

Wayland grinned. "Trust you to get the cushy detail, you Jock git."

Crosbie flicked a ball of paper at him. "You hear that,

ma'am? Outright racial abuse, that is. Ah should make a formal complaint."

"So should I," called Wayland. "You all saw him cob that at me. That's assault, that is."

"You hurt ma tender feelings, ye bloody Sassenach."

"Alright, children, settle down." Even McAdams couldn't keep a straight face.

Stakowski chuckled. "Kids, eh? Who'd have 'em?"

"They grow up so fast," said McAdams. "It's when they become teenagers you've got to worry."

"One more thing." Renwick took a deep breath. "You've all heard, I'm guessing, about these so-called Spindly Men."

"Kids pratting around," Janson mumbled.

"Maybe, maybe not. They showed up around the same time people started vanishing. Stupid not to check. So – Crosbie, collate any reports pertaining to them. See if anything jumps out. Rest of you, report any other sightings or reports you come across to DC Crosbie. Questions?"

Janson, predictably. "With respect, mum, there's no evidence even the two cases are connected. Most likely is that the Paki girl–"

"*Janson!*"

"Al*right*, the *Asian* girl, Khalid – that her family did something to her. That or she did a bunk, slung her bag to throw us off. We should be focusing on the Trevor girl. And the Spindlies... come on, that's just–"

Someone tapped on the incident room door. "Come."

"Sorry, boss." Joyce Graham, the desk sergeant, stuck her head round the door: tubby and thirtyish with two teenage sons, but handier than she looked if pepper spray and truncheon were required. "Dave?"

McAdams rose. "Yeah?"

"Call from DS Ashraf, out on the Dunwich. He said to let you know there's been another disappearance, over at the Trinity. Macy Court. Two folk together this time." Graham hesitated. "And one dead."

"Christ," said Stakowski. "They just graduated."

Renwick flicked the last of her coffee into the bin. "You all know what to do. Dave, get the Khalid case rolling. Mike, get your team to work. Then you're with me."

CHAPTER SIX

THE DUNWICH WAS near the edge of town, like the weird kid no-one wanted to be near. A concrete bin smashed by hammers; a metal one blackened by fire. Beyond squat low-rises and flat-fronted houses in dull grey pebbledash, Renwick glimpsed far-off craggy hills veiled in mist. Hoodies with muffled faces watched them pass. At the estate's black heart stood three tower-blocks: the Trinity. Among them, Macy Court.

The lift was broken. The stairs reeked of piss; Renwick counted one fresh-laid human turd and three used syringes as they climbed. She breathed through her mouth. "Where's the crime scene again?"

"Twelfth floor."

"Christ."

"Small mercies. Could've been thirteenth."

A big man with a spade-shaped beard appeared. "Chief Inspector? DS Ashraf." His handshake was an iron clamp, gently applied. "This way."

The corridor had faded blue concrete walls smeared

with shit or blood. One striplight flickered; the others were smashed. An old man with yellowed eyes and a drinker's reddened face stood in his doorway giving a statement. An obese woman with a pallid, doughy face and greasy dark hair, vast slack breasts hanging to her navel beneath a stained top, stood screaming at another officer, spit flying from her mouth. She saw Renwick and lunged at her; the officer held her back. "Fuck you lookin' at, bitch? Eh? Eh?" In her flat, three kids aged between three and thirteen sat gazing slackly, faces lit by a TV's cold dead flicker.

There was incident tape across the hole where a steel door had been smashed down. Inside were the SOCOs in their white suits; among them, a thin, fiftyish woman with short black silver-sprinkled hair.

"Dr Wisher."

"Chief Inspector. Come in if you're coming. I haven't time to print invitations."

Renwick waited until Wisher turned away before rolling her eyes. Stakowski winked, took out a jar of Vick's menthol rub. They and Ashraf smeared a little under their noses to counteract the stink of the place. Renwick had been in flats like this before; the very air made her want to scrub her skin with wire wool. They donned the white protective bunny-suits and entered.

THE TESTAMENT OF PRIVATE TOBY GOODWIN from the suffolk fens farm labourer by trade reserved occupation could have stayed at home but i chose to fight for king and country to risk my life for greater good and this is my guerdon such is my reward i fought hoping for a better world to come but it was not to be shrapnel tore my guts

out at passchendaele resection of four feet of
large intestine other smaller resections carried
out along the colon and another in the duodenum
constant pain there was constant pain and this bag
this bastarding bag filled with my own liquescent
shite that i carried a constant rebuke to my old
high minded dreams and still i did not despair
but laid my hopes at the door of education and yet
this too came to naught as i lived to see another
war more terrible than the last and in its embers
a last flicker of hope a new world rising but this
too this too pulled down and now only the ashes
and the embers remain and in it crawl such things
as these men and women sunk lower and fouler than
dogs was it for these i fought was it for these
my entrails were torn asunder was it for these i
bled in the wind and rain the filth and shellfire
the flanders mud and such were my thoughts when
i lay gasping out my last breaths in a hospital
ward with cancer eating up what innards i had
left with the crabs pincers rending at my guts
in 1962 year of the cuban missile crisis when it
seemed certain that the world would end leaving
us all burnt offerings on the sacrificial altar
of our leaders pride as so many of us had been at
passchendaele the somme the marne loos mons and
so i died thinking nothing changes and so i think
now watching from the blackness at the world we
fought for the country we helped to save

BLOOD GLUED CLUMPS of hair to the walls, dried slowly
dark on the cheap tiled floor.

"*How* many dead?"

"One." Wisher folded her arms; her spectacles glinted. "As I told Sergeant Ashraf. Did he forget, or you?"

"Neither, Doctor Wisher. Just wanted to check."

"I *do* try to be sure of my facts before making a statement," Wisher said. "But I take your point. It does resemble the scene of a massacre."

"Where's the body?"

"Kitchen. Just follow the blood trail."

Red handprints on the kitchen door; blood on the draining board and countertop, thickening on the tiles. A man sat against the sink unit, shirt open. Two kitchen knives beside him, blades red; a third still in his hand. Matted hair hung from the red-black ruin of his head; his eyes were ragged holes.

"Christ on a bike," said Stakowski.

Renwick took a breath. Stay calm. Objective. There was one question here: whether this connected to her investigation or not. "What the hell happened here?"

"You know me better than that, Chief Inspector," Wisher said. "We're still processing the scene."

"An educated guess?"

"Alright. This is of course a provisional statement *only*. But if you look, his nose is broken, the skin on his forehead badly split – apparently from smashing his head against the walls. If he fractured his skull, it wouldn't surprise me. Look at his fingers and you'll see hair stuck to them from where he ripped it out of his scalp. And then he went to work with the knives."

"He did all this to himself? Are you serious?"

"Have you ever known me to joke, Chief Inspector?"

"Fair point," Stakowski muttered.

Renwick stepped back in. "Some kind of episode,

then? What? Drugs?"

"Possibly, or he could simply have a history of mental illness or self-harm. Formal identification and a toxicology report will help. Without that, I can only offer guesswork, and I'll thank you not to build your case on that. I have a professional reputation to maintain. Now, if you'll excuse me–"

"With pleasure," Stakowski muttered.

"I heard that."

IN THE CORRIDOR, the obese woman was still screaming at the same unfortunate copper, who had to hold her back when she lunged at Renwick again.

"Stairs?" Stakowski suggested.

At the top of the staircase, Stakowski offered Ashraf a cigarette. The two sergeants lit up. Renwick found herself wishing she smoked. "What else have we got? Manzoor?"

Ashraf released a stream of smoke. "Two missing, ma'am."

"So who's who?"

"The flat's registered to a Danielle Morton. Officially single, but neighbours say she shares the place with two men, a Pete Hardacre and a Ben Rawlinson."

"Ben Rawlinson?" Stakowski tapped ash out of the window. "Used to play pool with his dad, if it's who I'm thinking of. Pulled him in a few times. He were a decent lad once, but he had some problems upstairs. Hearing voices and that. Last I heard he'd hooked up with a lass who was as tapped as him."

"So what about Hardacre? Who's he?"

"Small-time dealer," said Ashraf. "They're both

addicts. He provides – provided – them with a supply of drugs in exchange for a place to stay. Also, according to the neighbours, there was something of a *menage a trois* going on."

"*Menage a trois?*"

"Threesome."

"I know what it means, Manzoor. Just surprised anyone round here did."

"I'm paraphrasing. The most polite version I heard was 'she's a fucking slapper doing it with the pair of them'."

Renwick laughed. Stakowski chuckled; after a moment, Ashraf smiled too.

"A dealer and junkie," she said. "Bit of luck, we can ID him off fingerprints."

"Bloke in the kitchen had grey hair," said Stakowski, "head and chest. The Ben Rawlinson I know's only twenty-odd."

"That matches the neighbours' description," said Ashraf. "Hardacre's in his forties, with long hair. Big man."

"Most likely him, then." Stakowski leant back against the wall.

"Let's get a formal ID first. You know what they say about assumptions."

"The mother of all fuckups, ma'am. I do believe it was me taught you that."

Renwick raised two fingers. "So what's the connection to Roseanne Trevor?"

"Or Tahira Khalid," said Stakowski. Renwick gave him a long look; he held her gaze.

"Or Tahira Khalid," she said at last.

Ashraf stubbed his cigarette out on the window

frame, pocketed the dimp. "Did you see the flat door?"

"Solid steel," Renwick nodded. "Standard dealer issue. Gives you enough time to flush your stash before the old dibble get in."

"'Old dibble', ma'am?"

"Shut up, Stakowski."

"The neighbours called us when they heard screaming and crashing around," Ashraf said. "That's something in itself – most people here would cut their own arms off before ringing the police. The old man next door had his eye to the spyhole all the time – he says nobody left. We had to break the door down."

"They'd have to go past his flat to reach the staircase?"

"Absolutely. There's no other way."

"In which case," Stakowski said, "where *did* they go? Out of the window?"

"It's the only other way out."

"And the windows were shut," said Renwick. "And then what? Abseil down? Climb in through a window below? They get picked up in a helicopter? What?"

"I think a helicopter would have been noticed," said Ashraf.

"With two hostages," Stakowski said, "both presumably doped up. And the big question: why kidnap these two to begin with?"

"Locked-room mystery," said Renwick. "Bloody hate them. So two people vanish into thin air and a third hacks his own face off with steak knives. Anything else? Raining frogs? Four Horsemen of the Apocalypse?"

"There was one other thing," said Ashraf. "Might not be relevant."

"What?"

"Residents report seeing the Spindly Men in the forecourt outside, before this happened."

Renwick took a deep breath, let it out again. "OK. Anything you find, copy us in on. Forward it to DC Crosbie."

"You think it's connected, then?"

"Think so. But god knows how."

"Speak frankly, ma'am?"

"Don't you always?"

"We're overstretched already. You've got seven officers – including you, me and Dave – overseeing two investigations. Now you want to make it three?"

"It's Ashraf's investigation, Mike. We're pooling information, that's all."

"Boss, they're not convinced we're going in the right direction as it stands."

"Aren't they?"

"No. Janson was gobbing off about having to do the Khalid case all by herself."

"What you'd expect."

"Aye, but that's a point too. She's easily the weakest officer on the team, and she's all Dave's got to work with in the field."

"Yeah, I just–"

"Didn't want her messing up the Trevor case?"

Renwick didn't answer.

"We're overstretched as it is. Add this case to the load, you'll make it worse."

"I can handle Janson."

"Sod Janson. It's Banstead I'm thinking of. He gets a sniff there's trouble at t'mill, he'll throw you to the wolves. You know that."

"Wanna know something, Mike?"

"Alright."

"I don't give a shit, as long as we find Roseanne Trevor alive."

"And Tahira Khalid?"

"Yes, her too."

"But Roseanne Trevor most of all."

"Yes! Alright?"

"Is it though, boss? Alright, I mean?"

"What do you want from me, Mike?"

He was silent.

"I can't handle another Julie Baldwin, Mike. Just can't."

"Boss–"

"I know. I'm supposed to be objective. I'm being as objective as I can. But there is a link. I'm sure of that."

"Well... not me you've got to convince."

"You're not happy, Mike, put in for a transfer. Or tell Banstead to pull me off the case."

"Don't talk wet." He was silent for a while. "Anyroad. Cracked the whip on Janson back at the station. Told her you knew what you were doing and to shut up and get on with the job."

Pause. "Thanks, Mike."

"Any time."

"No. Thank you."

CHAPTER SEVEN

MANCHESTER, SEVEN-THIRTY PM. The city centre was almost quiet; a lull between tides. The office workers had gone (except those who'd gone straight to the pub from work) and the late-night revellers were yet to arrive in force. The closest Vera came to liking the bastard North was times like this, when it seemed no-one was there.

Outside the Opera House, Christmas lights glowing all along Quay Street, she smoked a cigarette and yearned for home; the house on the Downs, where nobody spoke with a Lancashire burr or said *thee* or *thou*. That was home now. Not here.

In a few hours there'd be men bellowing threats at each other in the street; girls crying on steps, vomiting in gutters. Bestial: drink, fuck, fight, puke. The bastard North. The black sun.

For an instant the hand that held the cigarette looked like a bird's claw. She blinked, and it was a hand again. But she could see the skin drawn tight across the bones, the veins raised. Age always showed in the throat and hands, the wrists. God. How many years left? Morbid thoughts. It was coming back here that did it. This place. Everything she'd fled from was here; she could gladly turn her back on it, never return. But for Allen it was different. He came back, always, year on year.

"Got to do it, sis," he'd say. "Our bread and butter, this neck of the woods." And yes, the pickings up here were rich, every time. But that wasn't it, not really. He was like a moth, circling a lamp. Or a tongue probing a wound, unable to leave it alone to heal as best it might. They'd go to Manchester, to Liverpool – even, once, to Blackburn. But never to the heart of it; never to Shackleton Street and Adrian Walsh. Never to the Dunwich. Never to Kempforth. Orbiting the black sun, never flying into it. She could live with that. She thought.

There was a steel box on the wall for spent cigarettes. Vera ground out the last of her Sobranie, dropped the extinguished stub into the box and went back inside. Tiny embers danced in the air, died before they touched the ground.

TEN TO EIGHT. Backstage. Everything was ready. Vera heard the murmuring from the stalls. They loved him here. All those cow's eyes, pleading. *Tell me. About my mother, my father. My brother, my sister. My daughter, my son.* She could feel the force of their need even from here. On stage it must be like a wind, dragging you every way at once, threatening to tear you apart.

Best go check on Allen. No. Not *best go. Better go.* She'd taken the elocution lessons too, even though she didn't perform for audiences. She'd just wanted it gone from every part of her – Kempforth, the Dunwich, the bastard North. She tapped on the dressing-room door.

"Who is it?" High and choked with panic.

"Vera."

"Come in."

Inside, Allen was staring at his reflection. He wore a light blue suit jacket and trousers, a white roll-neck sweater. A difficult colour to wear, but it gave the right image. Besides, he worked out, ran every day, ate right. Vera made sure of it. A small gold cross at his throat. A thin gold bracelet on his wrist. Black hair with little traces of silvery-grey.

His forehead gleamed. She picked up a powder puff; he flinched away. "Don't fuss, woman." A trace of Lancashire in his voice too. Always was, when he was stressed. Stage fright. Christ, if only that was all it was.

"Just making sure you look right."

"I'm fine, for Christ's sake. Fussing over me like a bloody mother hen." His breathing was ragged. She took his hand; he pulled away. She took it again, stroked the back of it with her thumb.

"You'll be OK."

"Don't know how much longer I can do this," he whispered.

He said it every time, but it always sent a twinge through her. *This* was all they had, why they had the house on the Downs, the Bentley, the Land Rover, the servants – *servants*, for two Dunwich kids like them. Lose it, and what remained?

"You'll be fine," she said. And he would. His breathing had slowed and deepened. His forehead was dry now. He was calming.

They had money in bank accounts. A share portfolio.

Gold in a safe at home. It could all be lost, this way or that. Starting as low as they had, could she ever be sure of not falling back? Could they ever be high enough for that? Vera closed her eyes, squeezed his hand hard; perhaps for her there could never be enough distance. She was killing him, for money.

"I'll be right there," she said. "I've got us a table booked later. Or back to the hotel. Whichever you want."

One day, perhaps, he could stop. Maybe. Before this killed him. When she was sure they were safe. Then they could rest, enjoy the fruits of their labours. The best care for him, to help him heal. Until then, this had to carry on. Nights like this. The fear and the calming. The nightmares and the comfort. Binding him tighter to the killing wheel.

But then, it wasn't just her binding him there. So many thought him a liar and a fraud. And sometimes – even often – he was. But not always. And that, even more than her, wouldn't let him rest.

"Ready?" she asked.

"Nah." Then he grinned. "But what the hell, let's crack on anyway, eh?"

She laughed softly, and kissed the back of his hand.

IN THE LIGHTING box, she watched. A couple of the lighting techies glanced her way, then looked back at the stage below.

"Thank you – all of you – for coming here tonight. I know why you've come. Why you all come. You're looking for answers..."

She tried to relax; her part was done. She handled

publicity photos and press releases, tax returns, website updates and investments; this part was Allen's.

"First," he said, "there's no such thing as death. If you've come to one of these before you'll know that. If it's your first time, that's what you have to understand. All that happens when we 'die' is that we abandon a garment. That's all our physical bodies are. What we are – what we *truly* are – can never die, only change form. We're all sparks; sparks of divine light. That's what we truly are, and death frees us to exist wholly at that level. And that level is the world... of spirit." He smiled. "When you come down to it, it's just a change of address."

Laughter. Vera scanned the audience for potential hecklers: militant atheists or religious maniacs, come to brand Allen a fake or the Devil's spawn. And the biggest fear, of course – the one who'd come to wound with more than words.

He's a fucking angel, you bastards. If you knew what he'd suffered, how damaged he still is. You bastards. You want to send us back to that, or never have left it. You're no better than Fitton or Walsh, or the copper, or that fucking priest.

"We can't see the world of spirit," Allen said, "but we can't see infra-red or ultra-violet light. Or radio waves. Are they any less real? Of course not. They just exist on a frequency beyond our normal aural or visual range. My only talent is that I can hear – sometimes *see* – slightly higher, or lower, frequencies than most people. That's all it is. And because of that, the departed will come to me, at times such as this, because they're aware of my gift, and know their loved ones are here too, seeking knowledge and reassurance."

Vera bit her lip, pressed a knuckle to her chin.

Allen closed his eyes; his ragged breathing echoed through the theatre, amplified by the microphone on his lapel. His eyes, Vera knew from past experience, would be rolling under their lids. And then he began to speak.

AFTER THE SHOW, the round of autographs and book signings. Requests for private readings went to Vera, who explained the pay rates, checked the diary and made the appointments. It took up time; it was close to eleven when they were done, which was why she'd booked the restaurant for that time.

"Still want to eat?" she asked.

Allen grinned. "Thought you'd never ask. Bloody starving."

They ate at Savjani's in Rusholme, on the Curry Mile; it offered both discretion and an upstairs room for privacy. Vera picked over her chicken biryani while Allen shovelled down lamb madras, pilau rice, and two garlic naans.

"Gym for you tomorrow, my lad," she said.

He laughed, but the charge was already ebbing out of him. By half-twelve he was flagging, eyelids starting to sag. She called a taxi and steered him to it.

The performances often did this to him; euphoric at first, then crashing suddenly into sheer exhaustion. Performances, yes; of course none of it was real, and thank Christ for that. Tonight it had all been an act; a spectacular piece of improvisation, nothing more. Vera had seen the real thing; seen it, and what it did to him. She and only she knew it when she saw it; even Allen didn't seem to anymore. He believed his own lies. And that couldn't be healthy either. He needed to get out of this, to retire and rest. Everything pointed to that. And he would. He would. She promised he would, and soon. Just not yet. Not quite yet.

Back at the hotel, she helped him to their twin room. She helped Allen off with shoes and trousers, jacket and shirt, unclipped his watch and bracelet and put them on the bedside table. Allen's eyes were closed already, but still she took her nightdress into the bathroom to change for bed; they'd known one another all their lives, and shared a home throughout, but still, there was decorum to observe.

SUDDENLY, ALLEN'S WIDE awake. He blinks. The room is silent. That's not right. It's Friday night in Manchester; something should be filtering in from outside, however faint and distant. But he hears nothing. Not even Vera's snores. He looks: yes, she's there, in the opposite bed. Asleep and snoring, but he can't hear her, not now.

The digital clock at his bedside gives the time as zero. The red numbers on its screen don't blink; it hasn't reset after a power cut. They're frozen at zero, not moving at all.

And so he knows. He did already, of course. That thick smothering silence always means the same thing.

The boys are back in town.

A half-smile dies on his lips. It isn't funny. It's never funny. Mark and Sam and Johnny aren't funny. None of it is. None of it was.

Nothing dies. Nothing. And sometimes that's no comfort to anybody.

They're waiting, patiently, as they always do, for him to look; for him to see.

This is the price; this is the toll. The Sight's lifted him out of poverty, given him wealth and comfort. But this is the price.

Allen rolls onto his back, closes his eyes. The covers make no sound. He releases a deep breath that no-one hears. Then he sits up and opens his eyes.

They stand at the foot of the bed, red tear-marks on their pale cheeks. They cried a lot, before they died. All of them.

Sam speaks first. Sam was nine. Wiry and brown-haired, jug-eared, but with that cocky, cheeky look to him. Some of Walsh's punters had liked that. Sam had been the cunning one; he knew how to please the punters, make them happy. He'd shielded the other kids sometimes, but at others he'd let them get the worst of it, to save himself pain. They didn't judge him for that. And it hadn't saved him, anyway, in the end.

Sam's lips move. There's no sound, but Allen hears, *feels* it; the words seem to print themselves, in dully burning red, on the fuzzy darkness of the small-hours room: **You abandoned us. You left us to die.**

Allen shakes his head. He'd been a child. A child.

Johnny speaks next. Johnny was the posh lad – a little bookworm in his glasses – and the eldest after Allen, ten years old at his death. He still wears his glasses. The lenses are cracked. He was the quiet one. Tried to pretend it wasn't happening. Part of the fun for Walsh and his friends was proving to him it was.

Johnny's lips move. **So were we. And you left us to the Shrike.**

Hours seem to pass as he sits there without any answer. In the morning, in the light, he'll tell himself over and over how he lives to put what happened right, to atone for his failure, until he believes it. But no donations to the NSPCC, to Save The Children will save him from the times like this, when the years fall away and he's one of them again; four boys, naked, bound and gagged in a cold, reeking cellar while the Shrike circles round them in the darkness, whispering.

This is how they were, before. There's that much mercy, at least. He's seen them as they looked after death – hours, weeks or months later. But tonight, he knows, looking from face to bleak, solemn face, there are worse things than them to see.

Mark speaks last of all. Mark was the littlest, at eight years old. Fair hair, large blue eyes. They'd all tried to shield him, when they could. Of all of them, he'd been most like Allen himself – no defences, none of Sam's cunning or Johnny's ability to wish himself away; everything exposed, an open wound walking, but younger. A delight to the likes of Fitton. Walsh. The masked copper. Father Joe. Always popular, Mark; always in demand.

Mark's lips move. **We have something to show you**, he says, and turns his back. They all do. Facing the far wall, where the shadows have thickened and Allen sees only formless black.

As one, the boys swivel back to face him. Allen saw a picture once: ice mummies, dead Inuit whose bodies had freeze-dried in the Arctic cold. A child, face framed in a fur-lined hood, a fringe of inky hair. Lips shrunk back from the teeth. Skin the colour and texture of wood. And no eyes; just holes. Their shape remained – the eyelids hadn't decayed – but the eyes themselves were just apertures of black.

The boys' faces are like that now. Ancient, dried, eyeless. The black holes pin him, hold him. The shrunken lips move, and Allen knows what they'll say. His bowels and bladder feel ready to fail, because he knows. He's always known they'd say it one day; now it's here he's almost relieved.

It's time, Alan, says Mark. Not Allen, Alan. The name he was given; the one they all knew him by.

The reckoning, says Johnny.

The atonement, says Mark.

And then, together: **We call you home.**

The blackness spreads, drowning the filtered streetlight seeping through the hotel room curtains. The three boys sink away into it, as if into black, deep water. But out of the dark swim other shapes, closing on the bed. The blackness now covers the whole far wall, and it spreads across the carpet like a tide. Vera sleeps on, silent, as it flows up over the foot of her bed and then the covers, her feet and her legs; the other walls, the ceiling. Flanking him and hanging overhead, surrounding him.

The dark flows over Allen's feet. It's almost total; nothing can be seen in it unless it wants to. And something does. Many somethings. Some are at the foot of the bed; others approach on either side of him. He can't see them properly yet; just enough to know he doesn't want to. But in a moment, he will.

Allen tries to scream. He really tries. But there is only silence.

RATS SQUEALING; VERA woke flailing at them. Horrible things. Teeth, claws, disease-ridden – she was awake. Rats. Oh Christ she was back in Shackleton Street. No no no. Not that. Please. Everything else had been a dream. No no no. The squealing. The rats. But this wasn't Shackleton Street, this was their room at the Midland.

Not rats. Allen. She hit the light. He twisted to and fro in his bed. His arms and legs were stiff, unmoving. A spasm. His head whipped side to side, the neck tendons thin steel rods. He was trying to scream, but his jaw was clenched, so instead he made the rat-sound.

Vera threw the covers back. Her heart wasn't hammering so much now. She knew what this was. She'd done this a hundred, a thousand times. Once it'd seemed a price worth paying. Now, though – would she still be doing it at sixty, or older? She knelt by the bed.

She switched his bedside light on. Sometimes that'd wake him, but not tonight. Still screaming, or trying to. She grabbed his shoulders, flinching – he lashed out sometimes if you did that. She'd had to hide bruises on a couple of occasions. Last thing he needed, stories like that. Appearances were all.

Allen stopped thrashing; now he shuddered instead. Shaking. His skin was hot and slick with sweat.

"Allen. Allen. *Allen!*"

His eyes rolled under the lids. The clenched scream became a whimper.

"Allen. Sweetheart." She stroked his cheek, his forehead. Kissed his forehead, his cheek. A faint moan. "Allen. It's me. I'm here. It's OK."

His eyelids flickered open. Another moan, then a ragged breath. She let her own breath out, forced a smile, stroked his forehead again. "It's OK. It's OK."

A night might come when she couldn't bring him back, or when the terror stopped his heart. If it did, she wasn't sure if she'd grieve or rejoice. But tonight wasn't that night.

"Sis."

"It's OK."

He reached up for her, like a child. She held him; he shook, whimpered, cried. She stroked his hair, kissed his cheek, prayed he'd need no more than this. She sang, softly, the old song Mum had sung to them: "*Heelya ho, boys, let her go, boys, swing her head round and hold together…*"

Slowly, he calmed and relaxed. "Toilet," he said. "Need–"

"OK."

"Scared. The dark."

She turned on all the lights, opened the bathroom door for him. Allen slid out of bed. His body shone with sweat. The bathroom door shut behind him. She didn't believe, but she prayed: that she'd done enough; that he wouldn't need more.

The toilet flushed; water ran in the sink. Allen came back, naked, still shaking.

"Sis?" He whispered. "Sis, I… I…"

Her prayers had gone unheard. Still, that was nothing new. "Alright."

Ever since Shackleton Street: his raw need, her comfort. Back then, it'd been the only kind she could give. Now, it was the only kind that worked. Allen crawled back into bed; Vera peeled her nightdress off, turned back the clammy sheets, climbed in beside him and guided his hand between her legs.

THE MORNING LIGHT woke her. What time? Panic. If someone came in – even the rumour would be lethal. Damp sheets clung to her; she fought to thrash free, then found the narrow bed empty save for her.

"Al–"

He was at the window, elbows on the sill, barefoot in polo shirt and jeans. She fumbled for her nightdress. The bedside clock read 8.43 am; time for breakfast if they were quick, made themselves presentable. She'd need to take a morning-after pill later. Be safe. Forty-six years old and still no menopause. Christ. She always had three or four in her handbag, courtesy of a pharmacist friend. Always best to be both prepared and discreet. "Allen?"

"I'm sorry, sis." He looked old, suddenly; the greying hair, the face tired and slack. And he was the younger. Where had her life gone? "Cancel the show tonight."

"*What?*" Tonight was Liverpool; it was sold out.

"I need you to cancel it, Vera." His voice was quiet but very level. Determined. She wasn't used to hearing him sound that way.

"What did you see last night?" she asked. Because she knew he'd seen something. Allen might not know the real thing anymore, but she did.

"I've got to go back," he said. "Today. Right now."

"Where?" she asked. But she knew. Of course she knew.

"Kempforth," he said at last. He smiled; she saw terror and bliss entwined in it. "I've got to go back to Kempforth."

And she didn't know whether she felt more terror or relief. After all these years of circling, finally, he was flying into the black sun.

CHAPTER EIGHT

Saturday 21ˢᵗ December.

NAN'S LIVING ROOM; Anna and Martyn perched on chairs, Nan sunk in hers. Mary at Martyn's feet, huddled against his leg.

"Where you going today, then?"

"Just off to Witchbrook, Nan."

"Ah well. Bit of fresh air. Do you a lot of good, that. 'Specially you, Martyn." Martyn flinched a smile back, looked down.

"Now, Mary, come here a minute. Come on, I don't bite. Something for you." Kendal Mint Cake in dark chocolate; Mary's favourite. "What do you say?"

Mary had inched over. "Thank you, Nan."

"Give your great-gran a hug, then."

She didn't. "Mary," said Anna.

"Go on, love," Martyn said. Mary reached out thin hesitant arms. Nan pulled her close. "Bless you. You're getting a big girl." After a moment, Mary hugged her back. Nan released her. "Now, you go and have fun at Witchbrook."

"OK."

"And if you're good," said Anna, "we'll go to the Creamery after." Mary loved the place, although Anna couldn't forget arranging to meet Eva there.

Nan winked. "Spoils you, your Aunty Anna. Get fat, you will."

"No I won't!"

"Mary," said Anna.

"Don't talk to your Nan like that," said Martyn.

"Soz."

"Not soz," said Anna. "Sorry."

"Sorry."

Nan reached out to ruffle Mary's hair; the child flinched away. Anna opened her mouth, but Nan shook her head. "It's alright, love." They looked at each other for a moment, then Mary went back to Martyn and threw her arms round him, buried her face in his side. Nan studied him. "You take care as well, boy. Look after the little one."

"Aye, Nan, will do." Martyn kissed her cheek.

"Go on with you."

Mary almost ran out, Martyn lumbering after.

"I'm sorry, Nan," Anna said. "Don't know what got into her."

"I'm old, that's what. Could pop off any second."

"Nan."

"It's true. She's already lost her Mam. Nearly lost Martyn too. And I'm still here and her Mam's gone."

Anna shouldered her bag. "What about you, Nan? You OK?"

"Just the usual. Old age cometh not alone, mate." A

smile. "Know what you're on about. Have I seen any more ghosts, that's what you want to know."

Anna looked down.

"Anna, love, it's alright. I'm not going off my head."

"Never said you were." Her grip on reality wasn't so tight she could judge.

"You were thinking it, though." She didn't answer. Nan eyed her; she'd snapped at Anna before for questioning her memory. Finally she shrugged and nodded. Anna bent to kiss her cheek; Nan's thin hands rose up and met in the middle of Anna's back.

"Love you, Nan."

Nan's grip tightened. "Love you, too, Anna. And don't worry about me."

"But I do, Nan. I worry about everyone."

Nan sighed, nodded sadly. "I know."

The door clicked; Myfanwy Griffiths didn't hear it, but knew she was alone. She'd always known when she was. The Sight, her own *nain* had called it. But it wasn't just seeing, there was feeling, too.

And what did she feel now? Myfanwy studied the pictures of the dead. The dead and the lost looked back at her. Her own son among them; wrong, that was, surely, to outlive your own child. But he'd made his mark; there was still Anna, Martyn, little Mary too. The family would continue, after she was gone.

Her father's photograph: the dazed, bleak eyes fixed on some distant vanishing point. It had come and gone over the years; sometimes he was with them, sometimes somewhere else, somewhere terrible. Late at night with a drink in his hand until his eyes glazed; he might have peace after that, or wake screaming in the small hours. A terrible sound, that. By breakfast he'd have put himself back together again – how many cigarettes, lit with shaking fingers, did that take? And nobody would talk about it because you didn't, about such things.

And he went out to work, whatever kind a one-armed man could get – you didn't ask, not back then; if your father put bread on the table that was all that mattered. And age and drink ate him away. In the wedding photo, in the black suit jacket and bowler hat, he held her arm, tried to smile. The weariness: on his face, in his eyes. Myfanwy took a tissue from her sleeve, dabbed away the beginnings of tears.

ANNA WENT UP the cemetery path alone, Nan's flowers beneath her arm; neither Martyn or Mary had felt able to come. She didn't mind, some solitude was welcome.

"Hi, Dad. Nan sends her love." She replaced last month's withered bouquet, took out wet-wipes to clean the plaque. "Miss you. Wish you were still here…"

She stopped. There was no god, no afterlife. They were all gone. Dad, Mum, Grandpa – Nan's dad, too, even if she'd started seeing him at the window. Hard but true. She doubted conversing with the non-existent was a habit someone with her history should cultivate. But after a moment, she went on anyway.

"I'm worried about Nan. She's started seeing her dad, would you believe? Don't think I could face it if she…" She shrugged. "Well, I'd have to. Wouldn't I? That's my job." A sigh. "I know. Stop feeling sorry for myself. Maybe it's just her mind getting itself ready. She can't have long left, can she? She's had a good innings." That didn't help, she realised. She didn't want anyone else to go anywhere, anyone else to leave. A child's thought, she knew. This was just how it was. "Alright. Best go."

Anna dropped the dead flowers into a bin near the top of the garden. On impulse, as she passed the church, she went to the door and entered.

Cold air. She smelt must, varnished wood, polished brass. Her shoes clicked on wooden tiles. Rows of pews; tall pillars held the roof aloft. High rafters pointing skyward; a stone angel looking down, placid and unconcerned. Stained glass windows lit by winter light. Christ raising the dead: *Lazarus, come forth*. Christ casting out demons: *Call him Legion, for we are many*.

Anna found a pew. She didn't pray. She didn't believe. She didn't come here for that. She came as she'd once come to woods, rivers, hillsides, seashores: for stillness, peace, to calm herself. She couldn't go to places like that alone anymore, there wasn't the time. Everyone needed something from her – Mary, Martyn, Nan, work. Everyone claiming a piece. *This is my body; this is my blood.* But she mustn't break down. Couldn't. She closed her eyes, breathed deep, until she felt ready. When she opened her eyes, the pews were full of dark, blurred shapes.

She blinked, but they wouldn't come into focus. There were dozens of them, black and silent, in the pews and aisle. At the periphery of her sight some details – clothing, hair colour – came almost clear, only to vanish if she looked straight at them. They didn't seem aware of her; they all faced the wall to her left. A single spot on it flashed and gleamed; gold or polished brass.

There was no sound. She stood. Silent. Silent. Get away unseen. But as she rose they turned, the seated ones rising. Their faces were blackness, but in a moment she might see them. She overbalanced, fell back into the pew. She thought she cried out but heard nothing.

Leave her.

She felt rather than heard it. Her imagination, perhaps. But she looked, and the church was empty.

"Oh fucking hell." Sound had returned; her voice, her fast, panicked breath. Anna gripped the pew's edge, saw the knuckles whiten. She stood; her fingers shook when she put them to her forehead. "Not this," she heard herself whisper. "Not again." It was the strain. She'd have to see her GP. She couldn't afford to break down. Not again, not now. At least they hadn't been like the things she'd seen when she was in Roydtwistle; those black, tattered things, so similar to what'd been lurking outside Mary's school.

She had to get out of here, away from things she hadn't, couldn't have, seen. Back to Martyn. And to Mary, always Mary. But instead she was going down the aisle, to the brass that gleamed on the wall. *That* hadn't been her imagination. It was curiosity and it was something else. Defiance, perhaps. A whistle in the dark. I'm not scared. *I am the master of my fate; I am the captain of my soul.*

A brass plaque. She touched it; it was polished, smooth.

In memory of the officers and men of the 'Kempforth Pals,' killed in action, 4th July 1916.

Nan: *You might have a touch of it, too.*

Martyn. Mary. Nan. They were real, to be held on to. Anna turned and walked out fast.

THE TESTAMENT OF PRIVATE LEONARD BLOOR halfway across no mans land bullets whizzing by like wasps going past your earhole they did that in a summer meadow when i was a little boy whizz they went whizz whizz whizz buzz buzz buzz like wasps and me breaking into a run across no mans

land jinking as i did like on the make do soccer
pitch in the park back in blackburn cos i could
play and that was my plan that was my dream to
play football but it wasnt going to happen except
as we went across no mans land i thought it was
could hear all the bullets going past missing me
and i thought im special im something special
same as every kid does cos thats all i was a kid
a stupid little kid and i thought they werent
going to touch me id been spared picked chosen
but then oh then oh then the blow the blow to my
leg and it was knocked out from under me and i
was in the air for a second only a few feet up but
in the air looking down at that shitten reeking
field of mud and then i slammed down into it and
the pain hit and oh god the pain the worst pain i
had ever known german rifle bullet 7.92mm tearing
through the large muscle of the left thigh and
directly impacting the femur shattering the bone
into fragments damage to the femoral artery also
patient suffered severe blood loss and would
have perished had not one of his comrades applied
a tourniquet thus saving his life however the
amputation of the left leg immediately below the
hip was necessitated hopping along hopping along
on fucking crutches didnt eat hardly slept only
drank everything gone the one way out and nothing
left for me now nineteen years old and back to
blighty and hopping along on fucking crutches
and dont care if its swearing i will swear i want
to bloody swear ive earned the fucking right and
back in blackburn watching the lads a few years
younger than me play footy in the park

*   *   *

WITCHBROOK WAS A deep, sheltering combe carved into a hillside above the Dunwich Estate. A stream ran through it, there was a picnic area, a playground, rocks to climb, thickets to hide in. The winter wind keened but didn't reach them here.

"Faster, Daddy!"

"Don't spin her quite so fast, Martyn."

"Don't worry. Be alright."

The roundabout spun; Mary clung on, squealing happily. Martyn laughed.

Your family, lass; your family.

Anna sat at a picnic table. Below was the sprawl of terraced streets enclosing the town centre's medley of brutalist and Victorian. Enclosed was the word; small and cramped, sealed in by grey sky and dour faith. She needed more than that; without it she was withering away.

But your family, lass–

Now on the swings, Mary shrieked again as Martyn sent her flying.

Daddy was back, and Anna could never be Mummy. That had to be faced. Perhaps she could leave, finally, once Martyn was well again. No more excuses. Dad's death, Eva's, Martyn's troubles – they'd all given her reasons not to go.

But your family, lass.

Mary tore past en route to the slide. Anna smiled and waved.

Beyond the town, the green-grey moors; beyond them, Manchester and its busy gay scene. Twenty miles, that was nothing. She could be there in half an hour if need be. Stay in Kempforth and she'd wither into respectable spinsterhood. There was still time, but only if she left now.

But your family, lass–

Mary laughing, coming down the slide. *You have to go, for yourself. You have to stay, for them.*

Martyn sat beside her; the table creaked and shifted. "Dear God. Worn me out, she has."

"Happens when you get old."

"Bog off. Watch out the witches don't get you, Mary!" Mary laughed.

"There aren't any."

"Eh?"

"Witches, round here."

"Why call it Witchbrook then?"

"*Dun*wich Brook. Ran all the way down to Dunwich Road until they built the estate over it. Good place to get water for you or your horses."

"The bloody hell's Dunwich, anyroad?"

"Used to be a city on the Suffolk coast. The Dace family up here married into a shipping family down there after the Norman Conquest."

"Get you, Miss Smartypants."

"Buzz off. Then Dunwich started falling into the sea – all gone, now – and the harbour silted up. The Daces' in-laws moved to Ipswich instead, but the name stuck."

"Well, you learn summat new everyday." Martyn looked around. "Where's Mary?"

The slide was empty. The roundabout turned slowly and a swing rocked gently back and forth. Anna stood, a cold hand in her stomach, long spiny fingers coiling around her guts. The wind keened. "Mary?"

"Mary!" Martyn shouted. He blundered into the thicket, the thin black tree-trunks looked like prison bars.

Anna started across the playground. The hand in her guts clenched. Not Mary. She'd never forgive herself. Nor would Martyn – either of them, him or her. God, no, anything but this. "Mary!" Her own voice sounded shrill to her, almost hysterical. No. Mary. No.

She saw the future, what would come. The fruitless hunt; the call to the police. The lines of bobbies marching down the hill, beating bushes, dredging pools. Fishing some bedraggled, weed-tangled manikin out of the water.

Or in the gorse bushes on the moors, or the winter-withered buddleja in a vacant lot in Kempforth, they'd find torn bloody clothing and some cold white remnant. Martyn wouldn't be able to identify the body; it'd fall to her. As always. *Your family, lass.* What family, after that? Neither she nor Martyn would survive the loss. Nan would die soon after. Their family would be gone.

"Mary!" she shouted again. Focus. The moment. The future hasn't happened yet, that's why it's the future.

"Mary!" Martyn blundered out of the thicket. Their eyes met. "No sign," he said. Anna stumbled further downhill. The combe shallowed out ahead, blending back into the hillside. The stream wove down into thick, brittle, winter-killed undergrowth, almost as high as–

"There!" Mary stood in the bushes by the stream, the undergrowth almost to her shoulders. "There!"

She ran, Martyn outpacing her easily – over short bursts he'd always been the faster. Mary stood unmoving, staring across the hillside, even when Martyn crashed to his knees beside her, flinging his arms about her. Staring across the hillside. What at? What at? So Anna looked.

Ten yards away a hillock was limned against the pale winter sky, black in silhouette like the long narrow shape atop it. The wind keened; long black tatters flapped about the figure. A black cloak, in tatters. Her stomach clenched anew. No. It couldn't be. Anna stumbled to a halt. She couldn't look away. It wasn't all black, she saw; there was a pale blur of a face, which turned from Mary towards her.

From this range, in this light, she couldn't see it clearly, but something was wrong with the face, she was sure of that. The eyes were dark, unblinking. It stood watching, motionless. The wind moaned. The tattered cape crackled and flapped around a thin – *spindly* – body.

First the school; now here. No – first Roydtwistle, ten years ago, *then* the school, *then* here. Coming back, out of her nightmares, her madness – but for Mary, not for her.

"Martyn." Her voice was now a thick, dull croak. "*Martyn.*" He stayed hunched over Mary, oblivious. Sod him, then. She'd fight it herself, if he wouldn't. She almost hoped he didn't hear her. She'd had enough of being afraid.. "Martyn," she said again, and pointed.

Martyn looked. The Spindly Man didn't move. Oh god, he'd say nothing was there. She *was* mad, then. But wasn't that a relief? Wasn't that worth the price, if Mary was safe? Then his face tightened and he was on his feet, releasing Mary, brushing her hands away. "Look after her. Call the police."

"Martyn–"

"Daddy–" But Martyn was already moving upslope, gathering pace as he fought and mastered the gradient.

"You, you bastard!"

The Spindly Man turned to face him. Anna caught hold of Mary as she tried to go after her father.

"Daddy!" Mary struggled, kicked, but Anna didn't let go. She couldn't look away either. The Spindly Man didn't move, just waited for Martyn to close with it, and that was the worst thing of all. It didn't fear him. It would kill him – just reach out one long thin arm and wrench Martyn's head from his shoulders. And Mary would see it. Anna had to cover the child's eyes, stop her seeing–

"Daddy, don't!" But then the Spindly Man turned, darted away, so fast it was as if it'd only ever been a black cloak which now blew away, flapping in the wind. Martyn broke into a run after it.

"Fucking paedo *bastard*–"

Mary was crying. "Daddy."

Anna kept hold of her. Mary's face in her shoulder; Mary's tears hot on her neck. Martyn shouted again, muffled with distance.

Below, a footpath wound downhill to the Dunwich. The Spindly Man was a black, wriggling blob slithering down it, Martyn a narrow black mark weaving after him. They veered off the path and down one of half a dozen terraced streets; tin sheets glinted where the houses' doors and windows had been. The council had bought the streets by compulsory purchase for an abortive new development a few years back; they were still waiting on the wrecking ball. Anna fumbled her mobile from her shoulder-bag. What were the streets called? The police would want to know. The Polar, that was it. They were all named after explorers. Scott, Amundsen, Peary, Nansen, Franklin, and... who else? Yes, Shackleton.

"Daddy, don't... make him come back, Aunty Anna, make him come *back*."

Anna half-rose. Mary grabbed her sleeve. "Don't go." Her voice was cracking. "Please. Don't leave me alone."

"Hush now. I won't. I won't." Kissing the top of Mary's head, her forehead, her cheeks.

"Don't leave me alone, Aunty."

"I won't, sweetheart. You know I won't."

She held Mary close, and dialled.

CHAPTER NINE

MARTYN CHASED THE paedo down the hillside, smiling.

Why? Because he could deal with this. The endless, fruitless jobhunting, the depression, his marriage's slow collapse, Eva's death – they'd all been like sinking into liquid mud. You had to fight it but couldn't win – couldn't mark or break it, only wear yourself down and sink. But this fucker, here–

At the hill's foot, the Spindly Man hit the main road, heading into the Dunwich. Fuck. Stop thinking; get doing. Even on the Dunwich they'd care more about catching one of the Spindlies than clobbering Martyn for cash he'd not got.

Might even get his picture in the papers, if he caught the swine. Shouldn't think like that; it wasn't right, somehow. Christ sake, fucker'd been after Mary. Least he'd not laid hands on her. Not that he'd seen. Christ. Better not have. *Get the sod.* If he took a tumble Martyn wouldn't complain; coppers probably wouldn't either.

They might find the missing kids. They might even be

OK. Alive anyway. Never be OK again if some bastard kiddie-fiddler'd got hold of you. Better than death, though. If you were alive there was a way back.

Yeah, right. Like there was a way back from losing Eva. There wasn't. If he was honest he knew that. She'd been the core, the centre, what he'd loved most.

Don't think of that. Get this bastard. Coming near your kid like that.

But that was it, wasn't it? If he were honest. Nothing he could give Mary compared to the part of him Eva owned. He knew that and it shamed him. It wasn't supposed to be that way; your kids were meant to give you reason to go on even if your wife was gone. But it wasn't like that. Not for him.

He blinked, snapped out of it, focused on the chase again. That was the beauty of it, why he smiled: none of that mattered here. Life was simple again. Like being on the rugger pitch and your job's to stop the other wanker getting by you. Focus.

The Spindly veered off the main road and towards the Polar. Martyn followed, picking up pace. Easy to lose the bugger here.

The Polar was a grid of parallel streets; Peary, Scott and Shackleton ran north to south; Amundsen, Nansen and Franklin cut across them, east to west. Lots of corners to dodge round, and lots of cobbled ginnels running behind the rows. And all empty, on top of that; all condemned. Martyn kept on the road; it was cracked and potholed, but the pavement was a minefield of loose, cracked slabs.

Some of the tin shutters over the door and window-frames were gone, or hanging loose. Squatters, homeless, druggies. Or more of the Spindly Men; cunts could've been hiding out here all along, where no-one'd hear the screams. He could end up facing the bastard lot of them.

The Spindly glancing back at him from the corner of Franklin Street. A white dead face, eyes like holes. Well, what else would their eyes look like? The fuckers snatched kids. Summat wrong with that face though. Summat really fucking wrong.

The Spindly ran round the corner. Martyn reached it seconds later; the terraces loomed up each side. For a second he was afraid the Spindly would be gone; but no, there he was, skirting a burnt-out car and nearing the junction with Peary Street. He hovered at the corner, looking back at Martyn, then darted round it.

Martyn let out a roar and shot after him, but by the time he turned onto Peary Street the Spindly had widened the gap between them from ten to twenty yards. It was a long road, but Amundsen and Nansen Streets both cut across it; the Spindly Man could vanish down either.

Martyn's chest was starting to burn. Too many cigarettes, too many takeaways, not enough exercise. He was starting to flag. The terraces wheeled about him. Where the tin sheets had been pulled away the doors gaped: hungry mouths. The windows: eyes. Staring down – black, empty, dead. He thought he saw movement in an upstairs window. Looked away. Kids maybe. Homeless. Crackheads. Smackheads. Or Spindlies. Was that it? Was this one gonna turn around and a dozen more like him come racing out of the abandoned houses like so many cockroaches out from under the sink, the hunter suddenly the prey?

Watch him. Watch the git. Vision blurring. Focus.

Focus on him. Fucking focus. Not losing him. Not now.

Amundsen Street. The Spindly feinted right, then broke left. After him. Tripping on a cracked paving-slab; blundering forward, arms windmilling. *Don't fall.* He didn't. Bastard was practically flying over the road surface now; couldn't see the bugger's legs for the tattered cape. Like chasing a stick on wheels, that bloody Dracula cape flapping about it and that head on top. Bastard had been holding back before if anything, a fucking athlete – nearly at the next corner already.

Which street was this now? Couldn't tell; vision was blurred. The Spindly had stopped, looking back at him. Again. That face. What was it about that face? Couldn't make it out properly. Christ. Felt like a bastard heart attack. Fucker's going to get away. But something about that face, something not quite right.

The Spindly raised his hand for a second, like a wave, and then he was gone round the corner in a flicker of black. *Bastard!* Martyn staggered to the corner. The road ahead was empty.

Martyn stumbled sideways, caught hold of a lamppost, gulped breath. Chest burning; throbbing from his heels up into his belly. Heart thundering. It'd burst. What you get for being an idle sod. Bastard's got away.

Martyn pushed clear of the lamppost, stumbled into the middle of the street. Now he heard them: sirens, wailing. He swung this way and that. Think straight: shithead can't have run far.

Scalp and neck prickling. Some fucker was watching. But where? He scanned the terraces. Everywhere and nowhere.

The adrenaline rush was fading. Dread coiled tight in his belly. Fists clenching. Not afraid of you cunts.

Threaten my kid. I'll fucking have you. If he said it often enough, he might convince himself.

Another breath. His lungs still burned, but less now. The blood-thunder in his ears had faded. The sirens were wailing, getting closer.

Listen hard. Best chance of finding the bastard now: listening. He was in one of these houses. Listen hard and you might hear him moving about. Have to be clever now. Should've brought Anna along, then. No. Don't knock yourself. You might not be book smart but you're not fucking thick.

Which road was this? He looked up, saw the old street sign clinging to the wall. Shackleton Street. He walked down the middle of the road, listening. His foot caught something. He looked down. Something black. He reached down, picked it up. A black cloth cap. It was cold and greasy, and he didn't like holding it. He threw it aside and wiped his hands on his trousers.

He knew that cap, or one like it; wasn't so thick as not to recognise it. Spindly bastard'd been wearing it. And now he'd dropped it. Must've been more rattled than he'd let on. Martyn looked down at the road, the pavement.

Something else; it was pale, pinkish-coloured. The hell was it? No idea, but it was on the pavement outside a house where the front door was a gaping hole. Only the front door though; the big front window was still tinned up. Well, you'd want that, if there was stuff going on in there you didn't want folk seeing. He went closer to it, saw it, was still.

Half a face looked up at him. A forehead, an eyebrow, a near-black eye; a nose, most of a cheek. He nudged it with his toe and it moved with a tinny, scraping sound.

That was a relief of sorts – at least it wasn't real – but he still wasn't touching the bastard thing. He somehow knew it would have the same cold, greasy feel as the cap.

No wonder the fucker's face'd looked like there was something wrong with it. There bloody was. Must be deformed or summat.

Martyn reached into his pocket, found his key ring. Eva had given him a little key ring torch for his birthday last year. If it still worked–

He clicked the switch. A pale beam fingered at the dark. The sirens were louder still. Nearly here. Better get a shift on, you want to be a have-a-go hero.

Shining the torch ahead, he risked a step in through the door. The torchlight picked out peeling walls; bricks and lathwork showed through the gaps. There was a table with a bucket on it in the middle of the floor. He pointed the beam down at the floor. The boards were still there, at least; they hadn't been ripped up for firewood. That was about all you could say for them though; they were pitted and rotten. Would they bear his weight? One way to find out. Best foot forward, lad.

A faint, brittle sound. He flashed the torch at the kitchen door. Was that a flicker of motion? No. There was nothing there. Nothing.

He stepped forward, shone the torch around the room as the first police car screeched to a halt outside, and a horde of white, mangled faces swarmed out of the room's back wall. And all of them were screaming.

THE TESTAMENT OF PRIVATE LEONARD BLOOR CONCLUDED
and nothings changed has anything changed and
drinking drinking to blot it out and stump of

left thigh failed to heal properly and became
infected septicaemia set in resulting in and
lying in bed at home speckled with fagash and
vomit and crying crying crying for all the things
now gone and burning with fever heat and running
with sweat and floating and seeing visions the
old men will see visions and the young men will
dream dreams and saw my comrades my friends the
battlefields ruined plain spread out before me
and the eyeless bloodless limbless faceless dead
dying maimed crippled wounded disfigured scarred
in endless procession across it british french
german turkish italian austro hungarian russian
belgian serb who are they who are we what does
it matter all torn meat and churned mud linked
solely by the capacity to suffer kyrie eleison
and delirum coma and death from septicaemia and
into thy hands o lord but there are no hands were
no hands to receive me only darkness and the
howling void and no justice done no leg restored
no restitution recompense or peace

GUEULES CASSÉES

'C' BLOCK

Flakes of paint lie like brittle leaves on the cracked floor tiles. The exposed brickwork is fretted and crumbling. A peeling wooden door with a pane of safety glass stands ajar. Beyond it, decaying, eyeless faces stare emptily from the wall.

CHAPTER TEN

STAKOWSKI SAW TWO cars in the car park by Witchbrook when he pulled in: a white Nissan Micra and a police Land Rover, back doors open. A girl – nine or ten – sat on the running board, wailing in the arms of a thin blonde woman beside her. Two uniforms, both young, hovered nearby.

"Jesus Christ, they've just left her like that?"

"They're green, ma'am."

"Bloody will be when I'm done with them."

"Flu outbreak. We're short on experienced officers."

"Ask me if I give a toss." They got out. "They catch anyone?"

"Said they had a bloke in custody, but he says he's the kid's dad."

"Who's on scene?"

Stakowski central-locked the car. "Tranter and Wayland."

"Thank god. Was worried it might be Janson. Can you go supervise?"

"Aye. Just let's get a description of the dad first."

"OK."

The blonde woman wore minimal makeup and dressed like a maiden aunt; be pretty if she gave herself the chance, though. He knew her from somewhere, but couldn't place it yet. Mist drifted down the hillside. The woman's teeth chattered, but she still held the sobbing child close, stroked her hair.

"Get some blankets."

"Ma'am." The uniforms scurried off. Renwick stepped forward. "Miss…"

"Ms. Anna. Anna Mason. Mary's aunt." She half-rose; Renwick waved her back down. Where did Stakowski know her from? A uniform draped a blanket round the child; she flinched back from it, then settled.

"Detective Chief Inspector Renwick. Detective Sergeant Stakowski."

He smiled at her. She smiled back, shy but genuine, folding a blanket round herself. Hazel eyes that never seemed to settle. "We've met."

"You have?"

"The library, yesterday. You came in for a book. *Myths of Old Lancashire*."

"Oh, aye." Should've remembered. Getting old.

"It was the name I recognised," she said. "Stakowski."

He smiled. "No, not that common a name round here."

"Polish?"

"Me Dad was. Came over here after the war, married a local lass. Anyroad–" He looked down at the kid. Red hair, blue eyes. "So, you'll be Mary, then."

The girl huddled closer to Anna. "Where's Daddy?"

Stakowski's radio crackled; he stepped aside. "Stakowski."

"... arge...?" Tranter. "...opy?"

"Repeat. You're breaking up."

The static thinned. Other voices murmured, faintly, somewhere else. Then Tranter came through clearly. "Sarge?"

"Aye, lad. What's up?"

"You might want to pop over here, Sarge."

"Where's 'here'?"

"Shackleton Street."

"What's up?"

"There's some pretty weird stuff here. Oh–"

"Aye?"

"–and two dead bodies."

"Save the best till last. Be right over."

THE TESTAMENT OF SERGEANT EDWARD HOWIE an here i was in the crazy house the nuthatch the lunatic asylum call it what ye like they called it a military hospital but i called it madhouse madhouse madhouse populated with the shudderin an the twitchin an the jerkin an the rigid an the mute an the screamin relics of shellshock aye an i were one of them my father a butcher by trade id worked in his shop afore the war when i wasnt in ma room a busily readin marx engels kropotkin readin an learnin an dreamin of a new world youd have thought id know better than to heed the call and march to war but there was a girl emma who lived a few streets away id known her since she was a scabby kneed bairn an time was wed been sweethearts an never a question but we would marry but now she was older an her mother

had put airs an graces into her head told her i
was no good enough for her an besides her mother
was a patriotic fool lapped up all the jingoistic
pish in the newspapers an drummed it into her
daughters head till now she said she would na
consider a man who shirked his duty as she called
it so here was i twenty two years of age at the
wars outbreak old enough to know better but still
i signed up for the duration cursing myself all
the while

LEFT ONTO FRANKLIN Street, then on up to Shackleton.
Automatic pilot. He'd been called out to the bastard
Polar in his beat days often enough: the domestic
disturbance on Peary Street where the husband had
waved a shotgun at him; the ginnel behind Amundsen
Street where a boy had bled to death. Shackleton
Street had been the worst; seemed it still was. The mist
thickened as he drove. He turned the headlights on.

Blue lights flashed in the mist. He parked up behind
the police cars. A big man sat in one, chafing his wrists
and scowling. Tranter headed over. "Sarge."

"Colin."

Wayland followed, hands in his raincoat pockets,
chewing gum. "Sarge."

"Get your hands out your pockets, lad, you look like
a flasher. That the dad?"

Tranter nodded. "Checked his ID."

"Good work. Name?"

"Martyn Griffiths."

"Right. So where are the bodies?"

"Upstairs."

"And the 'weird stuff'?"

"There's a lot to choose from, but try this for starters." Wayland held up two evidence bags. "Says he found them in the street."

Stakowski turned the first one over. "A cloth cap? That's not weird."

"Matches what the Spindlies are supposed to wear, Sarge," said Tranter. "And have a look at the mask."

"Mask?" Stakowski saw. "Christ Almighty."

"Pretty much what we thought, Sarge."

"Yes, thank you, Wayland. Fair enough, *I* call that bloody weird too."

"Ever seen anything like it before, Sarge?"

"I'd remember if I had."

"What gets me is how life-like it is," said Tranter. "Someone spent a lot of time on it."

"And then just dumped it," said Wayland.

"Mm." Stakowski hefted it. "Pretty light, too. What is it, tin?"

"Tin or copper, I think."

"Alright. Get it down to Sergeant Brock at the station – signed for, tagged, the lot. And while you're at it, take Mr Griffiths down the station, get a statement off him. Everything. Every detail. Clear?"

"Sarge."

"Good. But first, get onto the boss and tell her Mr Griffiths is alive and well. His kiddie were sobbing her heart out."

Wayland nodded, didn't move.

"What is it lad?"

"Speak to you a sec, Sarge?"

"Alright." They moved aside. Tranter stood outside the gate, scratching his head. "What's on your mind, Paul?"

"Just–" Wayland bit his lip.

"Spit it out."

"DC Janson, Sarge."

"What? She sexually harassing you? Christ, I'll have nightmares."

"Er... no, Sarge. But she has been mouthing off something fierce."

"What about?"

"The way the investigation's being handled."

Wayland looked miserable. No-one liked being the school sneak. "Go on."

"Basically... we're wasting time treating the two cases as linked. The Khalid girl's an honour killing, Pakis being Pakis, nothing to do with the missing kid."

"I can imagine."

"And she keeps going on about the Spindly Men angle as well. Says that's wasting time too."

"Where's Sergeant McAdams been in all this?"

"Even Janson's not thick enough to gob off near him. But... we were in the canteen today and she was rattling on. Rest of us were trying not to take any notice of her – heard it a dozen times already. But, you know Inspector Sherwood?"

"Oh, shit."

"Yeah. He was on the next table, and you know what he's like."

"Oh yeah. Old Brown Nose himself. So by now he'll've gone straight to the Bedstead saying the investigation's a shambles and her own team think she's lost it."

"Thought you'd best know."

"Aye. Thanks lad. Owt else I should hear?"

Wayland bit his lip, glanced at Tranter, shook his head. "No, Sarge."

"Alright. Get weaving. Shift the evidence down the station, let the boss know 'bout Griffiths." Stakowski turned away. *Cover her back, Mike.* What, even though he'd most likely get pulled down with her? *Yes.* Didn't even need to think on it, really. "Tranter! Where's the rest of the weird stuff?"

"Inside, Sarge. We gave the place the once-over, made sure it was empty. Apart from that we've kept it clear for the SOCOs."

"You called in the circus, then?"

"Yes, sir."

"Good lad. Suppose we should wait for them to arrive, properly speaking."

"Suppose so, Sarge."

"Dr Wisher'll be *very* upset, otherwise."

"There is that."

Stakowski grinned. "Let's get in there, then."

"Sarge." Tranter passed Stakowski a pair of latex gloves and a torch; they went through. Stakowski shone the torch around; bloated white faces came out of the walls. "Bloody hell."

"Yeah."

They picked their way over the rotten floorboards. In the middle of the room, the table and the bucket on top. There was a stick laid across the top of the bucket, something dangling down from it. There was a car battery on the table too, wired to the bucket or its contents. "Shit."

"Don't think it's a bomb, Sarge."

"Oh, you don't, do you? That's nice to know."

"I've not touched it," said Tranter.

"Thank heavens for that. Might be wearing half the bloody street otherwise." Stakowski had seen a few bombs during his army years. And their effects.

"Think it's some sort of electro-plating gear."

"Plating?"

"Been a while since I did my Chemistry exams, but I think so."

"We'll let the circus get stuck into that." Stakowski went to the wall and studied one of the faces. "Plaster of Paris?"

"Looks like it."

"Plaster of Paris. Car batteries. Why's that sound familiar?" He studied the faces. One was missing most of its jaw, the mouth warped into a gaping wound. Another had a trench above the mouth where eyes and nose had been ripped away. "Someone needs to see the psychiatrist."

"They look like casts of some kind," said Tranter.

"Who of, though? Any bugger went round looking like that, we'd know about it." Stakowski stopped. The bucket. Plating. Something. He went to the bucket and looked inside, reached for the stick.

"Sarge–" Tranter began.

The bucket was half full of liquid. Stakowski lifted the object clear of it. A thin piece of copper, now almost completely coated with grey metal. It was a cast of eyes and a nose. Stakowski looked from it to the second mutilated face, then lowered it back into place. Leave the scene as fresh as he could. But what was the betting it'd fit like a glove?

"Where are the bodies?"

"Upstairs, sarge."

The stairs were rickety; the risers gave underfoot and the railing nearly pulled free of the wall when Stakowski reached for it. The air was thick and stale with dampness and rotten wood. But there were other smells, worse: excrement, urine and another one. Cold slowed down decay, but didn't stop it.

There were three rooms upstairs: main bedroom, bathroom – toilet still embedded in the floor, the bath long gone – and the spare room. The doors were all long gone, stripped out like anything else that might have been of value. The bedroom was dim; a tin sheet still covered the window. Tranter shone his torch.

Bare floorboards strewn with chunks of plaster. Rotten wallpaper hanging from walls and ceiling like coils of dead skin. A board creaked underfoot. In answer, the walls made a scratching, scuttling sound.

"Rats," Tranter said.

The bodies lay side by side in the far corner. They were casually dressed – jeans, sweaters. Good quality but dirty. Stakowski took a step forward.

"Careful, Sarge." Tranter pointed out a ragged hole in the boards. "Put my foot through there. Both female – late thirties, early forties. One had a wedding ring. Not dead long. Rats would've done more damage otherwise."

"Owt else?"

"There's more masks in the spare room like the one outside. Dozens. And the bathroom…"

"What about it?"

"Might be connected, might not."

"Show us."

A dozen candles had burned down on the floor where the bath had been, leaving thin black soot-trails on the wall tiles, where a photograph of a man was fixed. There were markings on and around it, in something dark and crusted.

"Is that blood?"

"Could be. Ever seen anything like this?"

"Not as I remember. And I would."

"I'm pretty sure that's an inverted pentacle there."

"A what?"

"Five point star, sarge. Used in witchcraft and stuff." Tranter shrugged. "Went out with one of those Goth girls for a bit."

"'Bout the rest?"

"Dunno, sarge. Same sort of thing, I'm guessing."

"Probably right, if that bugger's involved." Sirens nearby. "Come on. Sounds like the circus is coming to town."

"If who's involved?"

"Him in the picture."

A thin shape in the front doorway, hands on hips. "Sergeant Stakowski. We meet again."

"Dr Wisher."

"How nice of you both to trample over my crime scene. Hope you've had fun. Don't let me keep you from your real work. Assuming you have some."

Stakowski ushered Tranter outside. "Charming lady," he murmured. "Think you're in there, lad."

"So you know him, Sarge?"

"Mm?"

"The guy in the picture. You know him?"

"Oh aye. You don't?"

"Looks familiar from somewhere."

"Oh, you'll have seen that bugger around alright. That psychic johnny, off telly – bloody con-artist. Cowell, that's his name. Allen Cowell."

CHAPTER ELEVEN

THEY DIDN'T LEAVE until the afternoon; Vera dug her heels in over that.

"We have to go," he said.

"And we will."

"I'm not messing you around, sis. I saw them. It was real."

"I know. You've hardly said a word since. Just what needs saying. Only happens when you've had a real one. Normally can't shut you up." That was harsh. "Sorry."

"No. It's true."

"So we'll go. But *not* till I've mended fences with them in Liverpool. I'm still your manager, last I checked. Aren't I?"

"Aye."

Aye. The bastard North again. "Right. So. Pulling out like that could fuck your career. So, I've some feathers to smooth and a future appearance, by you, at no extra charge, to arrange. *I* care about that, even if *you* don't. So we'll go – today – but when I'm ready. Not before. Clear?"

They drove in silence, out of Manchester. City and suburbs thinned out quickly, and they were in another world: green, yellow and grey moors, crags and gullies, steel-coloured tarns, black spiky thickets of wind-warped trees. Places nobody went. A landscape made to hide the dead. Not far from here, on Saddleworth Moor, Brady and Hindley had buried their victims; some were never found. How many victims, out there, of crimes not even reported? They might pass Johnny, Mark and Sam, and never know. A wilderness of unmarked graves; a desolation of unpunished crimes. The few scattered towns were lumpen grey beleaguered outposts, on hills or in valleys in the rain that began to fall. So little distance travelled, and yet so much.

The light was failing, the dirty grey clouds thickening to a rotted velvet black above, but the streetlights hadn't come on. A road sign: *Kempforth 5*. God, almost there. No sign of it yet though. Nothing human in sight except three houses by the roadside, thin lampposts lined up into the distance, drystone walls criss-crossing the hills, and they all shivered in the rain like ghosts. They could wash away any moment and leave the moorland as it'd been centuries before. They'd believed in witches here; easy to understand why. By night here you'd believe in vampires, werewolves, the bloody lot. She hated the North, fucking hated it. And now here they were; the worst place of all. The black sun.

When the mist came down she pulled into a layby, almost crying with relief.

"We can't go on in this," she said.

"Put the fog lights on and slow down. Just have to be careful."

"Oh, for God's sake. Allen, we've got to turn back."

"Vera, we can't. We can't."

"But *look* at it, Allen, for pity's sake."

"I know. I know. But we've got to, sis."

She looked across at him. "Allen, please."

He looked out of the window. "Think *I* want to go back?" he said at last. "Do you?"

"No."

"No."

"Then *why*?"

"Cos I've *got* to. No choice. If *you* don't understand that, nobody will."

She didn't answer.

"There's a price on everything, sis. A price *for* everything. Law of life, that is. Sooner or later, we've all got to pay what we owe."

Vera realised she was crying. Her breath hitched when she tried to speak. "I can't. Allen, I can't. Please don't make me." She could feel it already. The pull of every brick and stone and turf of sod of the place trying to drag her back. *You belong here. Never left. We know you for what you truly are.* The years, the cosmetics, the elocution lessons, the bank accounts, the Bentley, the house on the Downs: all just shells. Shuck them away and there was just a skinny, scabby-kneed girl in grubby underwear, huddled on a stained mattress beneath an unshaded bulb and waiting for the door to open, the next punter to come through.

No. Not true. She was more than that. But the closer she got to Kempforth, the less she believed it. And yes, she'd got away, but it had dragged her back in the end.

She hated Allen then, hated him for bringing her back. She tried speaking but she couldn't, only sob. Headlights flared through the rain-speckled window as another vehicle skimmed past. A warm hand curled around her own. She looked up. Allen was crying too.

"I can drive the car back," he said, "Once it's over. Whatever it is. There's a railway station down there somewhere. You get the train back to Manchester."

"What about you, you daft ha'p'orth?"

"I'll settle up here. Pay someone to drive the car back."

And it wasn't that she wanted to say yes – anyone would've wanted to – it was that she almost did. She'd helped him keep afloat so long, so easy just to let go, to let him sink at last. She'd done her bit, hadn't she?

No, of course she hadn't. Her bit would never be done.

"Don't talk daft." Deep breath. "Can you get us the wet-wipes from the glove box?" *Talk daft. Get us.* The bastard North, creeping back into her voice again.

"Aye, lass." His, too. Kept growing back, like a cancer, no matter how much you cut away. She cleaned her face and reapplied her makeup.

Cars swished back and forth on the Dunwich Road.

"This is it," he said. "They promised me. If I do this, I'm free. All the debts'll be paid off."

She put her makeup back in her handbag and put it back in the footwell. "Alright, then." She turned the ignition key, pulled out. The streetlights had come on at last; dull blurred embers of orange and cherry red now lit their way.

THE TESTAMENT OF SERGEANT EDWARD HOWIE CONTINUED throughout but on reachin the front i proved myself to be no mean soldier gaining promotion

to lance corporal full corporal and finally to my
fathers pride an mothers concern i was made a
sergeant an even emmas mother could no say ought
agin me then i might even hope to gain an officers
commission given time should the war continue
long enough an i found a part of myself hopin
it would even though i knew it to be the ruling
class dividin the proletariat agin itself for at
the same time it brought my respect in emmas eyes
but then came

TUCKED INTO BED, all her usual wild energy gone, Mary
looked tiny and fragile as eggshell. Martyn tucked her
in, stepped back so Anna could kiss her goodnight.
Mary's eyes flickered open when she did.

"Look after Daddy," Mary whispered, and closed her
eyes again. A moment later she was breathing in and
out, deep, slow regular breaths. Fast asleep.

"Yes, ma'am," Anna murmured, and straightened up.
She didn't turn round.

"Brew?" asked Martyn.

"Please." Her voice was tight. He knew the signs. She
was going to kick off *big*-style. They went downstairs
and she managed not to speak until they reached the
kitchen, then it spilt out. "The *hell* did you think you
were doing back there?"

"What?"

"Back there. Running off like that."

"Protecting my daughter."

"Could have fooled me. Looked to me like you
couldn't wait to get away."

"Oi–"

Anna folded her arms. "Keep it down. She's asleep."

"I was going after that bastard!"

"And what about Mary? She was scared to death. She was terrified you weren't coming back. What if something had happened to you?"

The one real sodding thing he'd done since getting out of Roydtwistle, and she was pissing on it. "And what about the other kids they've taken?"

"It's *your* child I'm worried about. Somebody has to be around here."

"Don't talk to me like that."

"I'm trying to get some sense into your bloody head."

"You're so ruddy perfect, you look after her."

"Don't tempt me."

"Cos you're so bloody perfect."

"No. I'm not. But Mary comes first for me, and she should for you as well."

"Right." He looked down, didn't speak. Didn't trust himself to.

"Pretty good sprint that, though."

Kick the dog, then throw it a bone – but then he saw the faint smile on her lips and had to chuckle too. "Have me moments. How about that brew, then?"

"You make it. Do something useful round here for a change."

"Bog off."

They talked a little while; mostly about what Martyn had seen. The painted mask, the bucket on the table, the wall of white, disfigured faces.

Anna looked up, frowning.

"What's up?"

"Mm? Nothing."

"Just... looked like summat'd given you the collies."

Anna shook her head. "Dunno. What you just described–"

"'Bout it?"

"I'm sure I've seen something like that somewhere."

"What, round here?"

"Not sure…"

"Anna?"

"Sorry. Drifting off." She put her mug down, stood. "You know, I'd forgotten what a pain in the arse you can be."

"Soz."

But he smiled; so did she, and squeezed his arm. "Good to have you back," she said. "See you in a bit. Will you be OK on your own?"

"Think I can go to toilet without falling in. Where you off?"

"Upstairs. Something I want to check on."

THE STATION HOTEL, like the town, had seen better days; unlike Kempforth, it still possessed a faded grandeur. It was made of the same biscuit-coloured stone as most of the older buildings. Once-ornate satyr's heads, now badly eroded, leered above the lintels. In the lobby, oil portraits of the local gentry adorned the oak-panelled walls.

"Now what?" asked Vera.

"First of all, let's sort the room out."

"It's sorted, Allen. Booked it before we left. Their best room, apparently."

"Yes. Yes. Alright, we take our bags up. Dinner, maybe. Then the police."

"Police? You never said anything about the police."

"Why do you think we're here?"

139

"I don't know, Allen. How about you actually tell me?"

"Not here." Allen went to the desk and rang the bell. Vera saw a stack of business cards for a local minicab firm and picked one up; driving a Bentley round Kempforth didn't seem a great idea.

A fortyish woman shuffled through the door behind the desk. Bloodshot eyes; cheeks turning into dewlaps. Everything about her seemed to be sag. Vera had a brief sensation of looking in a mirror; this was her if she'd never left.

"Hiya."

"Hello," said Allen. "We have a booking? For a twin room?"

"What name?"

Allen glanced at Vera. "Latimer." Better than booking him in as Allen Cowell. Keep a low profile. But Allen Cowell was one thing, Alan Latimer another. Alan Latimer had never really left at all.

A lift with a grimy mirror took them to the third floor. The 'best room' had threadbare carpets and a wonky toilet seat. "Christ. Hate to see the worst one."

Allen was at the window, looking out. Vera shivered and hugged herself. You couldn't see much from here; the mist hid everything beyond the row of shops opposite. Victorian buildings, decrepit, old, boarded-up, blotched with decay and discoloration. Dying relics of an age of industry. The Christmas lights along the street gleamed through the mist; they looked lurid and cheap. But Allen wasn't looking at any of those.

After a moment, she went over, put a hand on his arm. His hand covered hers; they both looked out to where the Dunwich would be.

"So? You said you'd tell me."

Allen took a deep breath, nodded. "Bad things have happened here."

"I know *that*, Allen. They happened to us for a start." Oh, god. He was going to tell the police about *that*. Some idea of confession being good for the soul. No. No-one could know. Ever. "Allen, no. You can't tell them. Not about Walsh and–"

"It's not about him. This has all been in the last week."

She waited.

"People have disappeared. A young couple. A teenage girl. A child." Calm, quiet, flat. "They've been taken."

"What do you mean, taken?"

"Taken."

"Who by?"

He shook his head.

"Allen."

"I don't know yet."

"Allen, please–"

He turned to her. Tears shone. "They said they'd show me more when I got here. And then I have got to go to the police and convince them to let me help. I can do it. They have evidence; I can use psychometry to gather information from it. We might be able to find the missing people in time. But they told me, Vera–"

"What?"

"That it will be dangerous."

"Then–"

"No. Can't run away. Not this time. This is the price."

"Price for what?"

"Everything we have. Everything we've gained since leaving here."

"Whatever we've gained, we bastard paid for. About a million times."

"It doesn't work like that, sis. We left others behind."

"And I'm sorry. But I did what I had to. I watched Walsh die in agony and I would do it again. And with him gone, what mattered was getting us out. Getting *you* out."

"We should have gone to the police."

"How could we trust them? One of them was one of Walsh's sick mates."

"Only one."

"And we never knew who because of that bloody mask he always had on."

"Only Walsh knew. Think the cop would have stuck his neck out for the others?"

"But if they'd been picked up, they'd've talked about their friend on the police. He'd've been in danger. And then *we* would've been. For Christ's sake, Allen, we were *kids*."

"You were nineteen."

"So? You were still a kid, though. And you were what mattered. Not saving the whole world."

"We left them behind—"

"Yes. We did. I did. Not you, *me*. And I would do it again. We were nothing but *meat* to Walsh and his bastard mates. We had to get out. Fuck the consequences, and fuck everyone else, and fuck all this bloody *guilt*. Because the only reason we're feeling guilty about it now is because we can *afford* to. Back then we couldn't. I couldn't—"

She stopped. She could see her breath. Allen turned, swaying. His hands grabbed hers, hard. She cried out. His jaw clenched and his head went back, eyes rolling white.

The room's lights were dimming; so was the window's

pale square of twilight. In the corners blackness thickened, as if ink was welling up in them. It spread; the walls disappeared in it, and the door, engulfed in black. It flowed across the carpet towards them, across the ceiling. It welled up over the beds and swallowed them too.

The lights on the walls were the dimmest of embers. Now they winked out. The last pinpoints of fading streetlight in the window vanished. They stood alone on a shrinking patch of worn, pale carpet. She tried to pull away from Allen but she couldn't tear her hands free.

The beds were gone, the luggage, the bedside table; the room, the town outside, the *world* outside, all gone. Just her, Allen and a square yard of carpet dissolving steadily in an infinity of black.

The blackness lapped around their feet. She'd taken her shoes off. Her tights were no protection; the cold was searing – like standing in a bucket of ice, except the black wasn't wet. Only cold. Cold as the grave. And then the floor gave way and she was plunging – she and Allen, hands still clasped – down into the bottomless dark. She couldn't scream. The shock of the cold stopped her breath, nearly her heart too. And then she was blind. Thick black cloth wrapped around her eyes. She was numb – couldn't tell if she was falling, floating or standing, if she still held Allen's hands or he hers.

A flicker of light; bright, sudden, it hurt the eyes. She nearly cried out, stopped herself. That liquid black would pour down her throat, though, of course, she must be breathing it in already. The flicker was there and then gone, but something moved within it. She didn't know what and wasn't sure she wanted to.

Another flicker. Something black and tattered moved,

not quite fast enough to avoid being seen. It might have been human, once. She wanted to believe it was just the brevity of the glimpse that made it look so incomplete.

Half a dozen more such flashes followed in the next minute. In most cases whatever they lit pulled away before they could be properly seen, but the last shape was immobile; a dark-haired man in uniform, his back to them. He stood erect, head back, as if on parade. She didn't know why, but somehow he was worst of all. She was glad she couldn't see his face.

She couldn't hear herself breathing. She tried to whisper Allen's name, but there was no sound; she couldn't even feel the vibration in her throat.

Another, longer flicker, lighting the soldier again. He cocked his head, as if he'd heard something. Vera glimpsed part of his face. He wore a mask of some kind.

The light died. Alone in the dark again. She stared into it, waiting for the next flash. He knew she was there now. Was Allen still holding her hands? If she pulled free it might break the connection, so she wouldn't see this anymore. Or she might trap herself in the black forever; maybe only Allen could pull her back out. She didn't dare try.

The light came again, but it didn't vanish this time; it got brighter, stronger, flickered less and less. The soldier was still there and he was turning towards her. In a moment she'd see whatever served him for a face. She drew breath to scream, even though no-one would hear.

Another light flickered, two or three feet away. A child stood in it. He had his back to her too. Brown hair, jug ears. He threw up a hand and the soldier vanished. Vera caught the briefest impression of a dull red glare in the black. It felt like a scream of rage.

The child lowered his hand. The glow that lit him stopped flickering, became a bright, steady cone of light shining down from somewhere above.

To the child's left, another flickering cone lit a second boy, this time fair-haired. When the second cone had stabilised, a third one appeared to the first child's right. The child was black-haired. All three wore school uniforms – shoes, socks, shorts; green blazers, red caps.

She knew who they were, of course.

Now they began to turn, though their feet didn't move. She didn't want to look at them, but couldn't look away.

At last they faced her. They had no eyes. Under the blazers were white shirts, red ties. Their faces were smooth, unblemished. But they had no eyes.

From left to right, she knew their names: Mark, Sam, Johnny.

Hello, Vera.

Their lips moved together, but were soundless. She seemed to *see* the words instead, printed red on the black.

A thin tingle of feeling returned; she felt Allen's hands in hers, just as he shuddered and pulled free of her. She cried out, or tried to – still no sound – fearing she'd be trapped forever in the dark, but fell instead to her hands and knees on the blessed, threadbare carpet of the hotel room. And Allen; he crouched beside her, shaking, eyes shut.

They were back in the hotel room. Sort of. On their side of the room, the lights glowed in their sconces; outside the window, the streetlights and car headlights passing on the road lit up the mist and a pigeon on the windowsill spared her an incurious glance. But two feet from her, the carpet vanished into inky black. It was like the other side of the room had just been sliced away. And still, the silence.

One after the other, two small, polished shoes stepped onto the carpet before her as something came out of the dark.

She scrambled backwards with a cry that no-one heard. The brown-haired child didn't even look at her. His black eye-holes were trained on some spot on the wall behind her, over her head. Sam. That was his name.

The fair-haired child stepped out into the thin pale light a moment later. Mark. And then the black-haired boy, glasses with cracked lenses over his empty sockets. Johnny.

None of them looked at her, or Allen. All of them stared at the wall.

Again, in perfect unison, their lips moved.

You abandoned us.

And Vera had no answer. Not to that; not to them.

You left us to die.

Allen still crouched there, head bowed, tears dripping on the bare carpet.

Look at us.

Even though she wasn't looking at the dead boys she *felt* the command; its heat on her face, the meaning. She turned back in time to see the glowing, emberous words fade. The children's mouths moved again.

Look at us, Allen.

Allen must have obeyed, because then they spoke again.

There is always a price.

Oh god. Oh god. They should never have come here. Kempforth, dragging them back. The black sun. She should never have let him come back.

146

You never had a choice, the boys said. **You live. We died. We gave you wealth. Success. There was always a price to pay for it. Now it's due.**

Still the boys didn't look directly at either of them, just stared fixedly past them at the wall.

Allen, Johnny said. **Allen.**

Allen dragged his gaze to Johnny; his mouth formed the word *yes*.

There's somewhere you have to go.

Vera blinked; a couple of blurry images seemed to flicker in the air between them and the children for an instant; a flashing blue light, a helmeted policeman.

No, said Mark. **Not yet. There's somewhere you have to go first.**

The words faded away. Then Sam spoke.

You have to go back to the start, he said. **Shackleton Street. Both of you. Go there. Tonight. And you'll see.**

Shackleton Street. Oh god, no, not that place. But there was no point protesting. These were the judge and jury. There was no appeal.

But *you'll see*? What? What would he – *they* – see? Because it was *they* who saw now, not just Allen.

You'll see, the three dead boys said together, before the shadows welled up and swallowed them, their pale, solemn faces sinking away as if into deep, black water. Vera fumbled across the carpet for Allen's hand. The darkness retreated, draining away, back into the corners of the room and then disappearing, until only shadows remained, fading before the warm yellow lights on the walls.

Vera let out a white breath. Then another, but it was fainter. The third breath couldn't be seen at all. A moment later, she heard the swoosh of traffic on the road; a car horn beeped. Someone laughed in the corridor outside. She jumped at a muffled clatter from the window; the pigeon had flapped away.

Allen was crying; his hand slipped from hers. He lay on the carpet in a foetal position. She crawled to his side, put a hand on his shoulder. His hand crept up and covered hers. She felt the need in him, even before his free hand reached for her blouse.

"No," she whispered. Not again. Please not again. Not so soon; it'd only been last night.

"Please," he whispered. "Please."

"No. Allen, no–"

"Please. *Please*."

And she relented. She always did. "Alright," she said. He reached up to caress her face, leant up towards her, lips parted.

"Wait." She got up, went to the window. Outside, Kempforth was mired in mist and dull orange light, car lights flaring beneath it like fish below the ice. Behind her, the rustle of clothing as Allen undressed. What counted was what had to be done, not what she wanted. She pulled the curtains shut and turned to face him.

IN THE BATH, she hugged her knees to her chest and tried not to cry. "Can't do this anymore," she heard herself whisper. "Can't. Just can't keep doing this."

She washed herself out; did it again. They hadn't used a condom, there hadn't been time. Sometimes there wasn't. Hence the morning-after pills in her handbag. They weren't used often – with her usual choice of lovers there was no risk of pregnancy – but there were some things she would and could not face.

A soft rapping at the door. "Sis? You OK?"

"Yes." He must know it was a lie, of course. But he'd said that this would free him, if she could just help do it. If it freed him from needing her like this, she could manage.

"We're going to have to go."

"OK."

THEY ATE IN a Chinese restaurant on the High Street: prawns in oyster sauce, kung po chicken, egg fried rice. She picked over it but forced herself to eat. After what'd happened in the hotel room her body cried out for fuel, but the thought of Shackleton Street made her ill.

At the best of times – *ha!* – every brick, every square inch of yellowed wallpaper and scuffed lino was soaked in memories she'd have paid half their fortune to be rid of. And she'd relive them all when she saw the place. The dead boys sending Allen to face whatever vision awaited – she could've handled that, dealing with the aftermath was what she did. But they'd said **both of you**. It wasn't just Allen with dues to pay.

"I can't manage anymore."

Allen put his fork down too. "Neither can I." He signalled the waiter. He had a great knack for getting their attention; just lifted a finger and there they were. One of his few practical gifts. "Can we have the bill, please?"

Heading back onto Station Road, Allen stopped. Across the road, under the railway viaduct, there was a shop with a faded TO LET sign in the empty windows. The hoarding had fallen down; beneath it was the old sign, fading on rotten wood but still legible: FITTON'S.

The night sounds died away. A car swept by noiselessly, and a fat man in a butcher's straw hat and striped apron stood under the sign. His face was a white moon, his smirking mouth wide and lipless, eyes tiny, dark and pitiless. His mouth moved. **You, you little shit.**

Another car swept by. He was gone, and sound returned.

"Mr Fitton," Allen whispered.

Vera could hear the High Street traffic again; down the road, a drunk was shouting. Fitton: she remembered facing him in the living room at Shackleton Street, Walsh's corpse still cooling in the kitchen, and saying *I don't want anything more of yours than I can help. Just enough to get out of here and never have to look at your face or this shithole town again.*

A hand closed round hers; she nearly cried out.

"It's alright, sis," said Allen. "Just me."

He squeezed her hand. She squeezed back, then let go. Didn't want people getting the wrong – or worse, right – idea. They walked back to the hotel.

CHAPTER TWELVE

THE LAST PAGE of notes was printing off when someone knocked on the trapdoor. Anna went and opened it; Martyn blinked up at her. "Thought you might want a brew."

She had to smile. "Yeah. Come on up."

He climbed; the steps creaked. "What you about?"

"Printing some notes off."

"What about?"

She sipped her tea. Too much milk, as usual. "Ash Fell."

He sighed. "Worry about you, sometimes."

"What's that supposed to mean?"

"You know no bugger likes talking about that place. That's if they've even *heard* of it to begin with, cos no-one's *ever* liked talking about it."

"Yes, I do know. But it *is* local history, like it or not."

"That's the point. *Nobody* likes it. No-one's gonna want to read about it."

"Yes, alright, *thanks*, Martyn. It just so happens it

might be relevant to what's going on round here."

"Eh?"

"Those faces you told me about? On the wall, at Shackleton Street?"

"What about them?"

"I thought the description sounded familiar."

"What, from that place?"

"That's what I've been trying to find out. I've definitely seen a picture, and I'm sure it related to Ash Fell, but it's not in any of the material I've got here."

"T'internet?"

"Bloody thing keeps timing out on me. Doesn't matter anyway – there's nothing, and I *mean* nothing, about Ash Fell online. I speak from experience."

"So where's that leave you?"

"Work."

"Eh? What, that call you got from your mate t'other day?"

"Carole. Yeah. She found it."

"Found what?"

"What happened at Ash Fell was forgotten very quickly, mainly because everyone in Kempforth wanted to pretend it never happened–"

"Still do–"

"–but after what *did* happen, there had to be an inquiry. And they published a report. Got buried as quickly as possible, of course. *But* Kempforth Library had a copy, which ended up in the basement with everything else no-one wanted to read. Carole found it. It's in my desk drawer at work. Can't be taken off the premises, but I've read through a lot of it."

"And the picture's in that?"

"Think so."

"You think?"

"Need to get the report to be sure." She drained her coffee. "Sod it. I'll go now."

"Now?"

"I've got the keys. Go mad wondering, otherwise. What?"

He was half-smiling, shaking his head. "Can't remember last time I saw you like this."

"They came after Mary, Martyn."

He stopped smiling. "I know. I were there too."

"What if they come again?"

He didn't answer.

Downstairs, she pulled on coat and gloves, stuffed the notes in her bag.

"Christ on a bike, have you seen it out?" Martyn had the curtains open; outside the mist was thick and white.

"Can't drive in that. I'll walk it."

"Don't talk daft. Ring a cab."

"On a Saturday night? I'll be waiting forever. It's five streets, Martyn. And the police station's not much further."

"Well, I'm coming too, then."

"And what if Mary wakes up?"

"Anna–"

"She needs one of us here. And you're her dad."

He looked down.

"I'll be fine. Pepper spray's in my bag."

"Can't you just ring the coppers?"

"And say what? I need the report, Martyn. Otherwise I've got nothing."

"Then wait till tomorrow."

"If this has got something to do with Ash Fell, do you think anyone in Kempforth knows as much about it as me?"

"No."

"Then it could make a difference. Save someone's life, maybe. Can't risk waiting till tomorrow." He opened his mouth to speak. "Martyn, just stay here and look after Mary. I'll be fine."

THE TESTAMENT OF SERGEANT EDWARD HOWIE CONTINUED
the day a shell burst over our position an i
alone like ishmael lived to tell the tale though
aye an it was a close run thing to be sure for
i lay it four hours or more while fighting raged
trapped under a fallen earth bank that pinned my
lower body afore help came and all around me torn
an sundered into collops mince tripes an chops
riven and shattered into lights kidneys brains an
steaks were the men of my command an they lay all
about me in that yellow reeking mud an helpless
i could only watch as the rats crept into the
trench an began to chew at my mens remains whilst
others came to watch an stare beadily at me with
cold cruel black little eyes deadlier than any
germans for we knew the rats in the trenches even
though we gave them our grudging respect one
man i knew keeping one as a pet oh we knew them
to be pitiless and deadly and these watched me
steadily waiting to see when it might be safe to
devour my flesh also their grey and brown fur the
yellowish feculent mud of the trench an the red
an the white of blood an bone only the blue was
lackin to make a suitably patriotic spectacle
of the carnage an the water in the trench was
rising and i might drown but a patrol came by in
time an dug me out i was evacuated to a casualty

clearing station who found no major but i had
other injuries not apparent on the field

THE CAB DROPPED them on St Matthias' Road. Across the
road, the church's lights glowed through the fog. Vera
heard voices from inside: evensong.

Allen stood looking at the church. Vera touched his arm.
"Come on. We're after Shackleton Street, remember?"

"I know. Just... remembering."

"Surprised they kept the place open, after what
happened."

Someone came out of the front gate, stood gazing back
at them. He wore black. White at his throat. A priest?
But the service hadn't finished. But then she realised the
singing had stopped. So had the traffic sounds nearby.

The priest raised a hand and waved. And she
recognised him.

He lowered his hand and was gone. She blinked. The
evensong returned; the traffic sounds came back.

"Father Joseph," she said at last.

"Yes."

Her throat was constricted; she could barely speak.
"Is it ever going to stop?"

"What?"

"Me seeing what you see."

"I don't know."

The far end of St Matthias' Road led onto Scott Street.
Vera clutched Allen's hand. This close to the Dunwich,
it wasn't just the dead you had to fear.

"Here we are. Memory Lane, eh?"

"Don't."

"Sorry."

Some streetlights flickered; others had gone out completely, leaving pools of shadow. Uncovered windows and doorways gaped; the tin sheets over the rest seemed to twitch and shift. Scott Street felt empty and filled with watching eyes all at once.

Something scratched and scuttled above them. "What–?"

"Easy."

"What was that?"

It came again; sounds echoed in the damp air as if in a cave. She looked at the upstairs windows on either side, saw nothing. She pictured something moving on an empty upper floor, crawling maybe from house to house through the walls. Here, it could be the living or the dead.

Allen squeezed her hand. They walked. All around there were tiny noises in the mist: ticks, scratches, skitters, taps, the soft *hush* of fabric on stone. Rats, or the wind, she told herself; rats or the wind.

Amundsen Street. One end of the sign jutted into space; the brickwork at the corner had crumbled away. Fragments littered the pavement.

"Come on, lass." *Lass*. The bastard North in his voice again. He wasn't wearing gloves; his hand was slick in hers. The faint, tiny sounds followed them down Amundsen Street too. Something clattered on the potholed road behind them. She didn't look back, wouldn't. Just a tin can, blown by the wind. Except there wasn't any wind. She squeezed her eyelids shut. Her legs were weak. Shaking. God, why had they come?

"Here we are."

She opened her eyes, and saw the sign. Shackleton Street.

"Oh god."

"We've got to, sis."

He led; she followed. When had that last happened? Had it ever, before? She looked down. Brittle weeds sprouted from cracked tarmac; potholes exposed the cobbles beneath. The houses could be hiding anything. She breathed deep. Calm. Control. "Home sweet home," Allen said.

"Don't call it that."

They stopped beneath the streetlamp outside the front gate. Tin sheets covered the front room and upstairs windows. The front doorway was a black hole with incident tape across it.

Number 35.

Faint scratching sounds came from inside the house–

"Oh god–"

–and stopped.

"Listen," he said.

"Can't hear–"

"That's right."

There were traffic sounds and a girl's voice in the distance, shrieking insults at someone. "You can fuck off you fucking slag, go on piss off you cu–"

And then the sound died.

"Oh Christ no," Vera said, or tried to. But there was no sound, none at all, and then the lights on the other side of the street flickered and went out. The black fell like a curtain over the houses opposite. She turned to run, but Allen grabbed her arms. The lights beyond the bottom of the street went out too. Only the lights along their side of Shackleton Street remained. Outside their circle, the dark was absolute.

Allen pulled her close to the lamppost outside number

35. Soon it was the only light left. It shone on the cracked pavement and the tangle of weeds and brambles that had been their front garden, the short footpath from the gate, and the front of the house itself. But it didn't reach into the hole where the front door had been. She could almost believe there was a door there, only painted the most perfect black imaginable.

The incident tape across the doorway stretched taut, then snapped. Something moved inside the house; two long pale hands emerged and clutched the doorframe. And then the man dragged himself out into the light, and it began to flicker.

Scuffed brown and white two-tone shoes, tartan socks; light brown corduroy trousers. A check shirt; a brown cardigan with antler-horn buttons. Greying brown hair to his shoulders. A lined, perpetually-amused face; warm brown eyes.

Oh, yes, she knew him. Adrian Walsh; she'd never felt such hatred for anyone else, or such fear. Fitton had been dangerous; always full of violence and rage. Like sharing space with a hungry wolf; a moment's distraction and it'd strike. Father Sykes had wielded the threat of Hell over you, like a whip. But Walsh... Walsh had always been her personal monster. Even though she'd watched him die.

Vera clung to Allen and shrank back. He was doing the same, but there was nowhere to go. Children again, afraid of Daddy. Walsh's smile widened; crooked yellow teeth.

Walsh stepped onto the pavement. Vera backed away from the lamppost until Allen stopped her. She was close to the edge of the light. Walsh took a step forward and smiled his Special Smile. Oh, Vera knew that smile of old. From the outside, at a glance, it looked like a doting stepfather's. Indulgence; affection. Until you saw the eyes. The Special Smile was the promise you'd suffer, by his belt or his cock. Or both.

Walsh halted by the lamppost, slid his hands slowly into his pockets. His lips moved without sound. Words burned red in the black behind him. **Hello, Alan.** His eyes flicked towards her. The smile locked on his face; whatever pretence to warmth it had drained away. **And hello, Vera.**

None of it had happened. None of it. Nothing since the night in 1985 they'd caught the train out of Kempforth. A dream; nothing real. The Bentley, the house on the Downs – that wasn't their real life, *this* was their real life, waiting all these years to claim them back. Shackleton Street. The stained mattress. The bare bulb. And Daddy waiting with his belt and cock, his friends queuing up to take their turn.

Walsh's teeth parted; tiny filaments of saliva connected them. **That's right, Vera.**

She could've killed herself then – anything, if it put her beyond his reach. But his own death hadn't stopped him. Why should hers?

Now you understand, said Walsh. **Dead or alive, you belong to me.**

His foot lifted. Its thick, inevitable slowness was like movement underwater. Allen's fingers clutched her arm. But big sister couldn't help him now, or even herself. Walsh would touch them in a moment, unless they went into the dark. But Allen would have by now if he'd dared, and he knew this dark; she didn't.

The streetlight began to flicker. Vera wanted to scream. Perhaps she did. In that silence, she couldn't tell.

But the light wasn't fading, it was getting brighter. Walsh stared up at it, face screwing up in rage and – could it be? – fear. He opened his mouth to roar, but as the light brightened he walked backwards down the garden path to the doorway. It was like watching a film played in reverse. At the doorway, his arms flew out. The long hands clutched the frame's edges. His mouth yawned open, screaming. Rage or fear? Both? Impossible to say.

Walsh's face faded into the drowning black as he was pushed back inside. His hands remained, clutching the doorframe. The incident tape stirred, rose. It reattached itself to the frame, stretched taut, then slackened. Walsh's knuckles were white with strain. Then their grip broke and he was sucked away into the black beyond the doorway.

Allen turned, looked into the dark behind them. He took hold of her, moved her back from the edge of the light. As he did, the three dead boys, moving as one, stepped into the streetlight's glow. The black holes of their eyes stared past her.

Their lips moved. **Something new has happened here. The police found two bodies here. They found other things, too. Ask to see them.**

As before, Vera caught some blurred impression of Allen's thought. There was doubt there. Fear. He didn't know how he could convince them. They weren't one of his audiences; most like they belonged to the half of the country that thought him a fake and charlatan.

Her name is Renwick, they said. **Detective Chief Inspector Joan Renwick. Ask to see her. Give her these names: Roseanne Trevor, Tahira Khalid, Danielle Morton, Ben Rawlinson. Tell her this: the Spindly Men**

made Pete Hardacre tear his own eyes out before his heart burst. Ask to see the things the police found here. You will be able to see. And you will show them. Do this and you will be free.

As one, the children stepped back into the dark and were gone. A few seconds later, the streetlights came back on and Shackleton Street was restored. Vera shuddered. Dear Christ, to be glad to see this fucking place again. Allen swayed and sagged against her. She held him up. She'd need to find him food, first of all; chips, a kebab, chocolate from an all-night garage. Traffic sounds washed in.

"Free," said Allen. "You heard them, sis. Free. Free."

"Yeah. Yeah, I heard them."

"Have to. Have to do this. Have to."

"Yes. Yes, sweetheart, I know."

She'd call another minicab to take them there, get Allen restored enough to go to the police station. Convincing them would be hard enough, without him looking off his face on drugs. As always, presentation was important.

But they were going to the police, as fast as possible. Not for the missing; for themselves. This was the price, was it, for what they had? For getting out? Then they'd pay it and be gone, back down south, away from this. Pay the piper, pay the ferryman. Do it and they could go. And never come back. *Ever*. Fuck the North. However many punters there were up here, they'd never come back again.

ANNA SHOULD HAVE called a cab. In the mist every lamppost, waste-bin or junction box was a thick blurred shape you only saw when you were a few feet away.

They seemed to jump out of the white. She'd managed to convince herself half a dozen times already that she was about to be attacked. No matter. Not far now.

She should have called a cab, or let Martyn walk her there, get a neighbour to watch Mary. Pride, that had been; needing to be right, to be sure. Now look at her. But stay calm. Don't panic. It'll all be fine.

Behind her: click, click, click.

She stopped, turned. The footsteps stopped. Mist drifted past her, sodden orange with trapped streetlight. She could see nothing.

Move. Doesn't mean anything. Someone got where they were going, that's all. Move.

Walking again.

Behind her: click, click, click.

Stopping, turning. The footsteps stopped again. Staring into the mist but only seeing the same thing: drifting vapour, trapped streetlight.

Someone playing silly games. That was all. Just walk. Even her heels' rapid clicking on the pavement sounded panicky, and too loud.

But not loud enough to drown out the click, click, click behind her.

She didn't look back this time, not until she was across the road. She went faster; her breath was ragged but she was at the crossroads with Raglan Street. The library was to her left; to her right was the traffic on Dunwich Road. She stopped for a moment there, then realised she couldn't hear the footsteps anymore.

There. There now. She turned, looked back.

Click.

Click.

Click.

The pale cone of the streetlight three posts away from her flickered as something stepped into it.

It was tall and thin, in a long, tattered cloak. It wore a cap of some kind.

Tall and thin.

Spindly.

She couldn't see its face, but knew it was watching her.

Anna took two steps back.

It stayed still.

Then behind her: click, click, click. She spun. Across the road another identical figure stepped into the streetlight's glow.

And then, to her right: click, click, click. She knew what she'd see even before she turned around.

The third Spindly Man stepped into a cone of light further up Raglan Street, cutting her off from Dunwich Road.

Together, the three of them advanced.

CHAPTER THIRTEEN

Only one way to go; she ran left down Raglan Street, hands out ahead of her. The fronts of houses rushed past her in the mist. None of their lights seemed to be on. Even if they were it didn't prove the house was occupied; even if it *was,* they mightn't answer the door. Not in time. She'd seen how fast the Spindly at Witchbrook had moved. She was fit enough, but wouldn't outpace them for long.

She veered to avoid a lamppost, tripped on a paving slab, cannoned into a gatepost. She stumbled on, hip throbbing, glanced back into the mist, trying to hear over the thump of blood in her ears.

Footsteps echoed in the dark.

She spun and ran, arms still out. At any moment another thin, tattered shape might loom out of the mist to grab her. Whooping for breath now, she shouted for help, but if anyone heard, there was no sign. Her shoulder bag thumped against her side. Was that why they were coming after her? Ditch it and she might be safe.

And she might have, but then she saw the library's windows glint in the streetlight, across the road. She ran to it, arms still outthrust. *Would* it protect her? It didn't matter. Her lungs burned and she could hardly breathe, and their heels were clicking on the pavement behind her. She had to stop. Oh god. She fumbled in her bag for the keys.

"THE HELL HAVE you been?"

"Sorry, boss." Stakowski dumped three manila files on his desk. "Checking the archives."

"Archives?"

"Aye. Back when dinosaurs roamed the earth, we didn't have computers. So we had to write stuff down, and they had to use this stuff called paper."

"Mike... please. No jokes, not now."

"You OK, boss?"

"No. This case is turning into a real shitball. Always more pieces, and less and less idea how they're supposed to fit together."

"Boss..."

"Maybe Janson's right. Maybe I *am* just flailing around and making up connections where there aren't any. I dunno."

"You really think that, Joan?"

"I don't know what I think right now, Mike."

Renwick's phone rang.

"Let us have a deck at this. Let you know if I find owt." Stakowski picked up his phone and dialled. Renwick's phone kept ringing.

"Renwick."

"Chief Inspector." Banstead. No *Joan* this time.

"Sir. How are y–"

"Detective Chief Inspector, I've received... well, what I can only call a litany of complaints about the way the investigations are being handled."

"Sir, if you mean DC Janson–"

"Not just her. The complaints I've had indicate a disturbing lack of focus in both investigations."

Deep breath, Joan, he's tricky. But he's the one gave you the case, said they might be connected. Wayland said Janson was on her own, the others trying to ignore her. Stakowski would have told her about any issues with his half of the team, wouldn't he? "With respect, sir, the investigation–"

"Investigations, Joan, plural. I made that clear to you from the beginning."

"Sir, you indicated there might well be a connection and–"

"*Might*. It made sense to have a senior officer in overall charge in case there was. It's true, however, that I thought you'd be able to manage two parallel investigations." He sighed. Weary, martyred. Tom Baldwin in the dock; smug, pious, dishonest. "I was wrong."

"Sir, I've just investigated the relevant leads, pooled information–"

"And tried to hijack Detective Sergeant Ashraf's investigation, which is completely unrelated to your caseload. He's not a happy man either. And as well as that, you've even had Detective Sergeant Stakowski running to the library for books on local bogeymen. Who's your prime suspect? The Loch Ness Monster?"

"Sir, with respect–"

But all she could see was Stakowski, phone tucked

under his chin, scribbling on an A4 pad. You didn't go to him behind my back, Mike. Please, Mike. Not you.

"Well?" She couldn't speak; Banstead sighed. "See? Joan, your investigation is unfocused and hopelessly disorganised. You're flailing about to try and prove a connection that doesn't exist."

"Sir, that is not–" Voice rising; she could hear the strain in it.

"Please don't embarrass yourself or say something you'll later regret, Joan. I'm trying to prevent you causing irreparable damage to your career. Getting defensive and making excuses won't help."

ANNA GOT THE key in the lock, turned it. The door opened. Something moved in the mist. She turned and a thin, cloaked shape flew at her. She shoved the door closed behind her, locked it again. The Spindly Man stopped, black-hole eyes staring in his pale immobile face. He reached out; broom-twig fingers scraped the wire-meshed glass. She stepped back from the door. The Spindly Man pushed himself away, back into the mist.

Something beeping. The burglar alarm. If she didn't disarm it, it'd go off. Good. Let the police come. She wanted them. But she needed Renwick. Her mobile phone – no, couldn't find a network. The telephone at the counter – she punched 9 for an outside line, opened her purse and found the card Renwick had given her. Two numbers: the police station and Renwick's own.

The alarm began shrilling. She dialled the police station. Engaged. Try Renwick's mobile? But there was no network. Perhaps there was just a fault on her phone. She dialled. A recorded voice said: *It has not been possible to connect your call. Please try again later.*

The alarm shrilling. The police would come. Wouldn't they? Even on a Saturday night, fights probably raging in the pubs and the High Street? How high a priority would this be?

A flicker of motion. She looked up. Something thin and tattered flitted past a window, vanished into the mist. Other shapes moved there also.

The back of the building. They were heading there. There was a back entrance, a fire escape, windows they could break. There was a skylight above her; any number of ways in.

She had to stay calm. Mustn't panic. So much for playing detectives. Stay calm. Ring Martyn.

"IT'S AS MUCH my fault as yours," Banstead went on. "This was clearly the wrong job for you, after the Baldwin business. I think the best approach would be to hand both cases over to DI Sherwood."

Stakowski was watching her, frowning. He half-rose; his phone rang. He picked it up, still watching her.

"We always have a full caseload this time of year. There are plenty of other, less demanding investigations you can handle. If you write your report of all that's been done so far tonight, DI Sherwood can pick things up tomorrow with the minimum disruption."

"Boss?" Stakowski, phone cradled to his chest. "Call for you."

Renwick mouthed: "Who?"

"Dr Wisher."

"Joan?"

"Sir."

"About that report–"

"Sir–" Renwick stood. Everything was suddenly clear. "I'll have to call you back. Might have some new information here."

"DCI Renwick–"

"Call you right back, sir." She hung up. Her fingers shook. Stakowski stared at her.

"I'll be buggered," he said.

Please, Mike, not you. "Well, if I wasn't finished before…"

"Finished? What–?"

She held a hand up. "Just put Dr Wisher through."

"OK."

"Never thought I'd be glad to take a call from her."

"You know, Chief Inspector, my hearing really is rather good."

Shit. "Doctor Wisher–"

"But never mind that. Completed the post-mortem on the Dunwich body. Sergeant Ashraf *insisted* I called you. Said it's linked to another case."

"Is it Hardacre?"

"Unless anyone else has gouged their eyes out with kitchen knives this week."

"Hope not. Mind you, on the Dunwich you never know." Renwick chuckled, heard only silence. "Anyway–"

"I would have emailed you my findings but there seem to be problems with your internet server."

"Same story all over Kempforth. Nobody's been able to access the net all d–"

"Fascinating. Your mobile network seems to be down as well. No matter. Thought you'd like to know, toxicology report found mild traces of THC in the bloodstream, so he'd partaken of a reefer or two, but in my view that's unlikely to have caused a reaction that extreme."

"Any idea what did trigger the episode?"

"No."

"Can you tell me anything?"

"Just that it killed him."

"We already knew that."

"*No*, Chief Inspector. *Listen* to what I'm saying. He didn't commit suicide as a result of the episode; the psychotic episode *itself* killed him."

"How's that possible?"

"Cause of death was massive heart failure, brought on by the panic he experienced. He was unlikely to have survived in any case, of course. He wasn't particularly young and he'd subjected his body to years of drug abuse. Shock and blood loss would have probably killed him in the end, but neither got the chance to. Put simply, whatever he thought he saw, he was so terrified he not only ripped his own eyes out to avoid seeing it, but his heart burst."

"Are you telling me that Pete Hardacre died of *fright*?"

Wisher was silent for a moment, then said, quietly: "Yes. I suppose I am."

And then the lights went out. "Shit!"

"I beg your pardon?"

Renwick opened her mouth to apologise, but then the phone went dead too.

THERE WAS STATIC on the line as soon as the phone started ringing; when Martyn answered it became a mushy roar. "Hello?"

"Martyn? Martyn! Martyn, can you hear me?"

She thought he was shouting her name, but couldn't be sure, the static was too loud. And there were other voices mumbling in the background, like a dozen crossed lines at once. She thought she heard *Dace*, and *Ash Fell*, but that couldn't be right.

"Martyn–" The alarm stopped. A moment's relief, but the phone was silent too. "Martyn? Martyn?" She rattled the phone's cradle, but there was nothing. She replaced the handset, put her purse back in the bag.

The streetlights' orange glare was gone too. Mist swirled outside the windows; it looked dun-coloured in the dark. She clicked the light-switch; nothing. Power cut.

Tattered shapes came out of the mist; silhouettes with pale blurred faces. They came to the windows, pressed their faces and thin brittle hands to the glass. A picking, scratching sound from the far end of the library. Then metal rattling. They were trying to open the fire escape. She found a letter-opener with a six-inch blade in a desk drawer, gripped it two-handed, like a sword.

The fire door rattled in its frame. Footsteps thumped across the roof. Something picked at the skylight. There were faces at all the windows she could see. She gripped the letter-opener tighter. She wouldn't stand a chance. She bit back a scream as something smashed into the fire door. They'd be inside in minutes. Unlock the door and run? Stupid – they were waiting outside.

Another crash; the fire door gave way. Cold wind gusted into the library. A tall thin shape moved in the dimness at the far end of the library. Its footsteps were like the clop of hooves on the threadbare carpet. It stopped, stood watching her. Brittle fingers scratched at the window. She raised the letter-opener. The intruder came forward. In a moment it would be in the light.

The sound of glass cracking; she spun. One of the windows had almost shattered; a dozen long cracks splayed out from the middle, where one of them had punched it. He looked at the intruder in the library. The intruder stared back at him, then – went backwards, literally, as if mounted on casters. It glided back into the shadows. The window-breaker looked up at the skylight. The scratching stopped; the shadow vanished. He turned his head left, then right and, as he did, the faces at the windows vanished back into the mist. Finally he gazed directly at her, perhaps for as long as half a minute. That face. That immobile face. Of course. She realised now. It wasn't a face; it was a mask. She'd been right.

The window-breaker stepped back; the mist flurried and swallowed him. The cold wind blowing through the open fire door cut through her clothes to the skin. She should go and close it, but couldn't bring herself to go down there, not now.

She was shaking. She needed to move but was afraid to. Had to do something. Quickly. They might come back. But she felt frozen, a statue.

Move. *Move.*

And then she was moving, but not for the doors, not yet. She'd come here for something. To do a job, and prove she was sane as well, maybe. Already there was the nagging fear she'd imagined the attack. She hadn't. She knew that. Which made this madder. She should get out now. But she'd finish what she'd started.

The librarian's office. Her desk drawer. What if it was gone, or it'd never been? But no, here it was. The stained manila file; yellowed pages, faded photographs.

Her fingers shook as they found the photographs and turned them in the faint dim light. Staying here, the risk – it was insane, but she couldn't leave yet. She held up one of the pictures, then another. Yes. Here. The proof. Anna's not mad.

She stuffed the report into her bag, closed it tight, ran back into the library as light flared through the windows. Two lights; a pair. Headlights. A car door slammed. "Anna?"

"Martyn?"

She ran to the doors. Quickly. Move quickly. A tall shape loomed out of the mist as she got the doors open. A scream in her throat–

"Anna?"

Martyn was flushed; he looked focused, directed. Alive, like when he'd chased the Spindly Man.

"I'm fine. Come on."

The mist swirled white. No sign of movement, but there was no guessing what might be within. The headlights' glow made a luminescent channel through the mist, guiding her in, but that only made the murk on either side more impenetrable.

Minnie the Micra awaited, engine idling. She got the passenger door open. Any second and something would grab her from behind. But no-one touched her. She pulled the door shut, fumbled for her seatbelt. Martyn climbed in. Then Anna remembered–

"Mary. Where's Mary?"

"Got Mrs Marshall from next door over to keep an eye on her."

"You found the spare keys, then?"

"Aye. What happened?"

"I was followed."

"Who by?" *Had* something just moved there in the mist? "Was it–"

"Martyn, we can talk about this later. Can we just get to the police station?"

"You OK?"

"*Yes*. Just drive. Please."

CHAPTER FOURTEEN

"LEAST WE CAN have a brew. Thank god for the emergency generator." Stakowski peered out of the window. "Looks like the whole town's blacked out. You OK?"

"Yeah, but the phone's still dead. Mobile network's still down too."

"Power cut wouldn't do that."

"No. Damn. Can't call the Bedstead back now."

"Never all bad."

"Ha." Tinsel hanging from the ceiling. The Christmas tree in the corner. Dad and Morwenna would have one set up in the front room. Perfect couple. Except she was half his age. Daddy, how could you? The message he'd left; the quiet, resigned tone. She knew the face that went with that: lined, melancholy, gentle. Like Stakowski's. Love you, Daddy. Hate you, Daddy.

"Looks like it came at a good time."

"What?"

"The blackout. What did the Bedstead want?"

"What's the radio reception like?"

"Joan–"

"What's it like?"

"Sounds like it's going through a sack of tinsel. Well?"

"I'm to fill out a report for DI Sherwood so he can take over."

"What?"

"No focus. Flailing about. No evidence to link the cases. Ashraf's pissed off at me for nosing in on his investigation. The Spindly Men were the final straw."

"Christ."

She didn't answer.

"What's he said about me?"

"What?"

"He's said summat."

"No."

Stakowski pulled up a chair. "How long we known each other?"

"Four years?"

"Try five. Have I *ever* not backed you up?"

She looked down.

"Do I brown-nose for promotions?"

"No."

"Who warned you Banstead would try and fuck you over?"

"You."

"Who told you Janson'd been stirring the shit?"

"You."

"I know how that bastard works. Oldest trick in the book. Divide and conquer. Ashraf's not got a problem with you. Just not used to taking orders off a woman, that's all. But he's a professional, gets on with his job. So come on, what was said?"

"Nothing. Nothing specific or direct."

"What was it?"

"Does it matter?"

"Might. Was it to do wi' the Spindlies?"

"Yeah. You getting that library book out."

"Banstead's style. Throw something into the mix, make you think I'd gone behind your back. But–" He closed his eyes. "Tranter. Wayland didn't want to talk in front of him."

"What?"

"When he told me about Janson, at Shackleton Street, Wayland called me aside so Tranter wouldn't hear. Thought it was cos he doesn't like telling tales, even on Janson's sort. Wayland's loyal to folk he serves with. One reason I've a lot of time for him when he's not being a poseur. But then I asked if there were owt else."

"And?"

"He said no."

"But?"

"Hesitated."

"That doesn't prove–"

"Did you tell anyone about that library book?"

"No. You?"

"Haven't told a soul. But Tranter knew; he drove me to the library."

"Tranter? But why?"

"He's young. Ambitious. Doesn't want to spend his career in the sticks. Banstead's never gonna worry about Tranter wanting his job. He's after a posting to Manchester, or the Met. Little bastard."

"So he tells Banstead about the library book."

"And the Bedstead gets you wondering if you can trust me." She couldn't meet Stakowski's eyes. "So, what now?"

"Bastard can whistle out his arse for his report. We go through everything we've got. See if we can find something to go on."

"OK."

"So what did you find out about the Spindly Men?"

"A bit. There's what I told you, obviously. They came from Hell, according to the legend. And like I said, they had no faces. They wanted faces of their own more than owt else, so if you could give 'em one, they'd do whatever you told them."

"Give 'em one?"

"If you made them a mask to wear, for example."

"Interesting–"

"There's more. According to the tale, if they touched you, you saw Hell. And if that happened you'd either kill yourself or die of fright."

"Like Hardacre?"

"Aye." Light flashed through the window. "Ey up. Visitors."

Outside, a man helped a woman out of a minicab. "They look well-to-do."

"Have to be, pay a cabbie to go out in this."

Footsteps thumped along the corridor outside. "Boss?" Crosbie stuck his head round the door. "You're never gonna believe who's just turned up."

"Let me guess," said Stakowski. "Allen bloody Cowell."

"Jesus, sarge, you're the one who should be on the telly."

Stakowski stared at Crosbie; Crosbie looked at Renwick. "And he's asking to see you personally, ma'am."

* * *

Renwick breathed out. "Give me five minutes."

"Ma'am."

AN INTERVIEW ROOM. Three officers: Renwick, Stakowski and Crosbie. Two interviewees: Allen Cowell and Vera Latimer.

Cowell had come in looking pale, shaken. Not anymore. He took a deep breath, composed himself. He had an audience now.

Stakowski looked down at his A4 pad. He hadn't written on it; wasn't likely to. But it beat looking at Cowell.

"I cancelled tonight's show in Liverpool because I had a vision."

"A vision," said Renwick.

"A message, if you prefer. Do you know what a spirit guide is?"

"I watch television, Mr Cowell."

"Then you're familiar with my show."

"Not my cup of tea."

Crosbie chuckled. The sister glared at him. Hard bitch, that one. But you've read the case files, Mike. What they went through. Show some pity.

But he'd heard all the excuses in the world for being a bastard. Daddy never loved me; mummy locked me in the cellar. After a while you sickened of them. And besides, he couldn't get past Laney. Couldn't.

Well, try. Act like a bloody professional. He's part of this somehow. Try and see how. For her if not yourself, or for the kiddie.

"But," said Renwick, "I understand the concept."

"Mine told me I had to come back here. When I arrived, they sent me to Shackleton Street. Which was where I experienced–"

"This 'vision'," Stakowski said.

Cowell sighed. He sounded bored, but the corner of his mouth twitched. "There are always sceptics. Very close-minded way of looking at the world. You need to open your mind, Sergeant."

The sister smirked. Stakowski's fists clenched beneath the table.

"All very well, Mr Cowell," said Renwick. "But we do need evidence that can be used in a court of law."

"I appreciate that, Inspector."

"*Chief* Inspector."

"But what if I could point you in the right direction? Show you where to look? Because you aren't getting far at the moment, are you?"

"Oh, aren't I?"

"Four missing persons. Tahira Khalid. Danielle Morton. Ben Rawlinson. And... ah, yes, Roseanne Trevor."

Silence. Was she taking him seriously? Banstead would rip her apart if she did. Cowell was bad enough, but if he endangered her career–

"What if I told you something the general public hadn't been told?"

Renwick folded her arms.

"The Spindly Men made Pete Hardacre tear his own eyes out before his heart burst."

Renwick went still.

No, you bastard. You'll not fleece her like your kind did me. Sod the case files. Sod what happened to you. You won't.

He clapped, slowly. "Not bad. Quite impressive. Who'd you pay off?"

"Mike," said Renwick.

She had to see Cowell for the fake he was. "A copper?

Someone in Forensics? Some poor gullible sod who'll help you out if you give 'em a message from the dear departed? What's the plan? Give your sales a boost?"

"Mike, that's enough."

Christ. Losing control. He was supposed to be a professional. Vera looked ready to fly at him. Take the girl out of Shackleton Street, but you'd never take Shackleton Street out of the girl.

Cowell's face was twitching. Scared, close to panic. The sister leant forward, reached for him. Then his eyelids fluttered shut. His eyes rolled underneath. Cowell's head dipped forward. Great. Here came the amateur dramatics.

"Mr Cowell—"

Cold, suddenly. Central heating must be on the blink.

White breath poured from Cowell's mouth, and he spoke. "Elaine Rudleigh. She was a paramedic. You called her Laney."

The moment where it mightn't have been said; the moment where he realised it had been. The hollow feeling in his stomach. The roaring in his ears. Shock, disbelief. And then the rage.

"April 15th, 1998." Cowell opened his eyes, smiled. He looked tired, relieved, and triumphant. "The baby would've been a girl."

The next Stakowski knew, he was coming round the table, making for Cowell. Vera was on her feet. Renwick too – "Mike!" – but he wasn't stopping, even for her. His fist went back. Cowell looked up at him and said: "Paul Marshall. July the 12th, 1999."

The roaring in his ears became a wind. Any second it'd sweep him away. Nobody. Nobody alive knew that. He looked down at Cowell; Cowell looked up at him with a cold, flinty smile. *You wanted a fight? You got one.*

Renwick put a hand on his arm, waved back the sister with the other.

Stakowski pulled away. Christ. What kind of a copper are you? But of course he knew. *Laney. Marshall.* He wasn't fit to hold the warrant card, wear the uniform. He blundered to the door, wrenched it open, ran out.

RENWICK FOUND STAKOWSKI sat on the concrete steps outside the station's side entrance, shoulders slumped, head bowed forward, a cigarette smoked almost to the filter. For the first time, he really did look old.

She waited. Not long; it was cold. "Mike."

"How do, lass." She could barely hear him. He didn't look up.

"Do you want to tell me what just happened there?"

He dropped the cigarette stub, lit a fresh one. "You saw."

"Yeah. Believing it's another matter."

Silence. "Alright," he said finally. "I'll tell you."

She sat beside him.

"Laney were a paramedic here in Kempforth. Met her back in '94, when I were a probationer – got called out to a bad RTA. Not exactly the stuff of romance, picking up body parts and cutting survivors out of the wreckage. But, her and me hit it off. One thing led to another. Got married in '96. Same year I transferred to CID."

"You were married? You never said anything about–"

"Not summat I like dwelling on, lass." His voice was a whisper.

"What happened?"

"Early '98, she tells me she's up duff." A half-smile. "Bloody shat a brick at first. But after that – aye, I were happy with it. And then two weeks later, some bastard junkie stabs her six times. Eighteen bastard hours they tried to save her. They didn't manage."

"Mike–"

"She was always the one said folk like that were sick, needed help. I'd always just thought they were scumbags. Sell their own kids to a bloody paedo for the next fix. Laney taught me different. But then you see the damage fuckers like that do."

"When… when did this happen?"

"Oh, April 15th, just like he said. Wherever he gets his info from, he's good."

Renwick almost asked about the baby. Didn't.

"Went off the rails after that. Drink, mostly. Lower than I'd been in my whole bloody life. Even worse than when mam died." He chain-lit another cigarette. "I started going to Spiritualist meetings. I were raised Catholic, but I'd lapsed years ago. Just wanted… just wanted to speak to her."

"Yeah."

"Anyway. Couple of mediums got a lot of money out of me with 'private sessions' before I cottoned onto them. Parasites, bloody lot of them. Bleed folk white when they're grieving and vulnerable. There's not much lower than that. So I know Cowell's sort, and I bloody hate the bastards. He's so bastard fake you can clock it a mile off, but folk still think he's for real–"

"What about the other date?"

"You sure you want to know?"

"Mike."

"I'm trusting you, Joan."

"Tell me."

"Alright." He trod his cigarette out half-smoked. "Paul Marshall."

"Was he–?"

"Guess."

"The junkie."

"Gold star."

"And July 12th 1999?" Stakowski didn't answer. "If he was caught and charged at the time–"

"He was."

"He'd have been sentenced by then."

"They got it down to manslaughter. Can you believe that? Not responsible for his actions. Reduced sentence. Wasn't even double figures. Think that's what did it. Or maybe nowt would've been enough. I had... a friend. In the prison service."

"Mike–"

"You asked. I'm telling you. He's dead now, anyway. But he let me know that if I felt the sentence handed down to Paul Marshall was... unequal to the gravity of the crime... something could be done about it. An accident could be arranged. If I just said the word."

"And did you?"

"Laney meant everything to me. And then there was the kid." Stakowski half-withdrew another cigarette, put it back. "If I had it do all over again... I dunno. But you can't take it back, once it's done."

"So he had an accident?"

"On July 12th, 1999. Nasty one, too. Didn't die particularly fast, or so I understand. Great loss to humanity, I'm sure. Would've found a cure for cancer and everything." He glanced her way. "I know. Not the point."

"No." The wind blew.

Stakowski stared at the ground. "So what happens

now?" She could barely hear him.

"Well, you can start by making me a brew, you old goat." He looked up. "You don't get out of putting the kettle on that easily."

"Slavedriver."

"Yep." She took his hand. It was leathery, knuckly and cold.

"Aye. Come on. Get piles sitting here."

She held the door for him. "You gonna be OK?"

"I'll make it. Probably best not go back in there, though."

"Happen, sarge."

"Taking piss?"

"Aye."

Stakowski laughed.

"Mike?" Sergeant Graham called as they reached reception. "You alright, mate?" She looked from him to Renwick and back again.

"I'm fine, Joyce."

"You sure?"

"Aye, love, I'm alright."

Graham bit her lip. "Boss? Someone else asking for you."

"Oh?" She turned, saw a thin blonde woman. "Ms Mason." And some big lummox with her–

"Mr Griffiths," said Stakowski.

"Hi." She was pale, but determined too, in a way she hadn't been before. Angry, almost. "I've got some information you might find helpful."

"Mike, can you–?"

"Of course." He pulled himself up, breathed out. "You can rely on me."

"I know."

He smiled, turned. "This way, Ms Mason."

* * *

THE INTERVIEW ROOM had breezeblock walls and a wiry green carpet. They sat at a chipped, scored table; Stakowski passed out cups of tea. "Here we go."

"Thanks."

"No problem. Now then. Fire away."

"There's a lot of information." She took the file from her shoulderbag. "Not really sure where to start."

"Tell him about–"

"Let's give your sister room to breathe here, Mr Griffiths. How about we start at the beginning?"

She took two photographs from the file, pushed them across the desk. "Do these look at all familiar?"

He went utterly still. "Aye, lass. They do. So just what the hell are they?"

She wasn't nervous anymore; she was calm, even euphoric. She leant forward, fingers steepled, and began to speak.

CHAPTER FIFTEEN

"ANYTHING?" RENWICK ASKED.

Cowell put the Shackleton Street photo back down on the desk. "Standard publicity photo," he said. "Send out dozens of these every week."

"No way to trace an individual one?"

"Sorry. These symbols, though…"

"What about them?"

"They're occult in origin. That's a pentacle, there, five-pointed star. And this one…" he tapped a symbol composed of five zig-zag lines radiating from a central point, "is a old pagan religious symbol. It's called the Black Sun."

"Miss Latimer?"

"I'm fine."

"You sure? You looked–"

"Fine." Vera stared back at Renwick. At least she wasn't smirking anymore; she had been ever since Cowell had driven Stakowski out. Crosbie looked from one of them to the other.

"I think it's a kind of charm," Cowell said at last. "Meant to draw me there somehow."

"To Kempforth, or to that house?"

"The choice of location's hardly accidental."

"Sorry?"

"We grew up there," said Vera. "In that exact *house*. And no, Chief Inspector. Our childhood was not happy."

"They said…" Cowell began. "I was told to ask to see the things you found at Shackleton Street."

"What *things* are those, Mr Cowell?"

"I don't know. I was told only to ask to see them."

"By whom, Mr Cowell?"

"My spirit guides."

Crosbie sighed.

"Your spirit guides," said Renwick. "Of course. Forgot."

"I'm sure Sergeant Stakowski could testify to their accuracy."

Renwick really didn't want to think of Mike right now. "I suggest you leave Sergeant Stakowski out of this."

"He went to hit Allen," said Vera.

Who bloody deserved it, Renwick wanted to say, but couldn't. And if they wanted to complain there wasn't much she could do. *Oh Christ, Mike, I didn't want to know this.* Cowell smiled. "I'm quite prepared to forget what happened before, Chief Inspector."

"Glad to hear it. So that was your spirit guides, was it, told you that before?"

"About the Sergeant's wife? Yes."

"Tell me a bit more about your spirit guides then, Mr Cowell."

"They're called Johnny, Mark and Sam. Three boys I knew when I was little. They're dead now."

"What happened to them?"

"They–"

"No." Vera was shaking. "Enough. I won't... I won't be put through that again. I won't."

Cowell looked at her, then Renwick. "How relevant is this, Chief Inspector?"

"That's what I'm trying to determine, Mr Cowell. OK. We'll leave that part. For now."

Vera sank back into her chair, shaking.

"Do you know what 'psychometry' is, Chief Inspector?"

"Enlighten me."

"The ability to obtain information about an object by holding it. Who it belonged to, where it came from. It's quite impressionistic – isolated names, images, and so forth. Can be confusing sometimes. But if I can handle the objects you found at Shackleton Street, perhaps I can find out who's taken the child, and where."

The child. That was what it came down to. If it got out she was taking anything Cowell said seriously... Christ, Banstead'd have an orgasm. She'd be finished. But she was anyway, unless she found Roseanne. Maybe even then. But that didn't matter, if the child was found. She'd nothing else left.

"If – *if* – I allowed that, those items stay in their evidence bags."

"Of course. That should be fine."

"Should be?"

"It's hard to be exact. Varies from case to case."

"Uh-huh." She glanced at Crosbie. Would he phone Banstead the first chance he got?

Judgement call. Down to her.

"Constable?"

"Ma'am?"

"Get hold of Constable Brock. Tell him we'll need his help." She didn't take her eyes off Cowell. "And just so we're clear, Mr Cowell, lives are at risk here. So if this *does* turn out to be a publicity stunt, I will personally ensure you'll be holding your next séance at Strangeways Prison. Have I made myself clear?"

Vera looked furious. Cowell sighed. "I'm sorry you doubt me. But I suppose it's inevitable." He brushed imaginary dust from his sleeve; his fingers shook slightly. "Shall we go?"

THE TESTAMENT OF SERGEANT EDWARD HOWIE CONTINUED
aye that could no be seen by any surgeon patient
exhibited hysterical paralysis of the legs also
violent reaction to any sight of blood referred
to dr yealland at london hospital for course
of treatment with electricity dr yealland aye
i remember that bastard applyin electrodes in
dose after dose to ma legs talkin to me as if i
wasnt there as if i was not human he considered
me degenerate i must recover he said an return to
the front and serve my country that the times did
not allow for coddling of such as i the greater
good must be considered an he applied jolt after
jolt of electricity to ma legs to force response
an in a long long session an endless day he
forced me to walk again an i was weeping torn
between hatred of him an shame at my weakness
for what else could i call it my mind would not
allow my legs to move for i was terrified of death
an some word or another of it got back to emma
in glasgow for she wrote to me breakin off our

engagement since i was a madman or a coward or
both an she would have neither an so i returned
to the front without demur

THE EVIDENCE ROOM was at the back of the station,
long, narrow and breezeblock-walled. Ranks of tall
steel shelves on either side made it narrower still. In the
space between the entrance and the shelves, Renwick,
Crosbie, Cowell and Vera waited.

The evidence room was Brock's domain. His father
– also a copper – had got him a job, but nothing could
remedy Brock's lack of ambition. He'd spent his career
as a uniformed constable, the last ten years in the
evidence room, but he was happy enough with that; he
was far happier dealing with things rather than people.
He lived alone, had modest savings; in a couple of years
he'd retire. That was enough for him.

Wheels squeaked; Brock pushed a trolley slowly into
view. He was stick-thin – cadaverous was the word – but
slow and ponderous, like a much heavier man. Greasy,
tangled black hair with streaks of grey. On the trolley
was one of the plaster faces from Shackleton Street and
the painted mask. Brock halted, stepped back.

Stark striplighting flickered above them.

"Is that enough for you to get started?" Renwick
asked.

Cowell nodded, pale under the striplights. "Oh, yes.
More than enough."

"Well then. Whenever you're ready."

"Alright." Cowell brushed at his lapels. His fingers
shook; his face was grey.

He went round the side of the trolley and faced them.

A showman's gesture; probably didn't even realise he'd done it. He began breathing deeply, in and out. Brock leant back against the wall beside Renwick, arms folded; he reeked of stale sweat and cheap spray-on deodorant. Crosbie shifted impatiently; Vera hugged herself, bit her lip.

Cowell's fingers, shaking, settled on the plaster face. He closed his eyes. Brock sniggered. Cowell opened his eyes, blinked; Vera glared.

"Constable," said Renwick, sharper than she'd meant.

"Sorry, ma'am."

Cowell breathed deep. He looked afraid – of finding something, or maybe not finding it. His eyes closed again; his hands crept over the face. Its eyes were closed, the mouth agape, or what should have been a mouth. Below the upper lip there was just a gaping hole extending out into the cheek, down into the chin. Cowell sucked breath through his teeth. "Something institutional," he said. "I'm getting a hospital. No, not a hospital exactly. I…" His eyes flickered under the lids. His lips twitched, pulled back from the teeth. He sucked in another breath, this one vast; it seemed to pull the air and light from the evidence room. His head fell forward.

"This was… this was a real face." His speech had thickened and slowed. His head twitched left, then right, then left again as he spoke. "A plaster cast. He had to lie there. Wait for it to harden. He's still waiting. Pain. The pain. And the sorrow. Shame. Misery." He sucked in another breath; his head went back. The striplights flickered. He released the cast, fumbled for the mask.

Renwick breathed out; it hung white in the air. So cold, suddenly. She glanced at the others; Crosbie had pulled his lapels closer together, while Brock's arms were wrapped around himself. Vera's hands covered her mouth.

"We are the dead." Cowell's voice was thicker still. "We are the d–"

And then he was cut off. He didn't stop speaking. *We are the dead,* she saw him say, but she couldn't hear it; couldn't hear anything. Brock looked puzzled. Crosbie stuck his fingers in his ears, waggled them around. His mouth said *What?* but again she couldn't hear it. Vera had sunk back against the wall. Her mouth hung open; her eyes stared upwards.

At the far end of the room, a striplight flickered out; blackness poured into the space like a flood of ink. And then the next striplight died too. And then the rest, all but the one lighting the space around the entrance; the dark rushed forward. The last striplight flickered above them and blazed bright; the dark's forward surge halted.

Vera sank to her knees, face still in her hands. Brock kept mouthing the word *what?* He looked close to panic. Crosbie fumbled at his throat and mouth, repeating *what the fuck* over and over. He stared at Renwick. She tried to speak too; nothing happened.

The dark around them rippled and pulsed. It was alive. It would flood in and swallow them if it could. The remaining striplight was all that held it back. White mist streamed from her mouth with every breath.

She looked back towards Cowell. He was still clutching the mask, his head thrown back. His upper body kept jerking backwards. Over and over his lips formed the same words: *We are the dead. We are the dead.*

The striplight brightened; the glow spread. But the

evidence room was gone. The breezeblock wall was still at their back, and the door too – Brock was wrenching at the handle, trying to get it open – but the narrow room and metal shelves were gone. Behind Cowell was an endless floor of cracked asphalt, mud, stagnant water. And then the light widened a little further, and showed someone standing there in a tattered black cape, head bowed.

Crosbie took a half-step forward, fists clenched; Vera's hands had come away from her face and she was standing again, pressed back against the wall, eyes vast with fright. Brock was still trying to get the door open; Cowell just jerked back and forth, mouthing the same four words over and over.

The newcomer was tall and skeletally thin and wore a floppy black cap. Its head came up; a painted, immobile mask hid whatever face it had. If it had eyes, though, she couldn't see them; just the black holes punched in its mask. When it looked at her, the purest cold seemed to stream from them.

It was the same kind of mask Cowell was holding, but a different shape. The uncovered part of the face was blurred, dark and writhing. She couldn't focus on it properly, and didn't want to. Even trying to do so *hurt*. She was grateful for the mask; if the whole face was exposed, she didn't think she could bear the sight.

The light widened a little further; two more Spindly Men stood behind the first. One had a mask covering the top half of his face, with bright blue eyes painted on it; the other's covered the left side of his. The three stepped towards Cowell. The light flickered again; the shadows around them thinned slightly for a moment, enough for her to glimpse more immobile faces just beneath the surface of the dark.

Mafeking Street, Kempforth itself, seemed an eternity away, the last fading echo of an old life, something from childhood, vitally important once but now irrelevant, belonging to another time, another place. Only this abyssal blackness remained, and the things that swarmed in it; the deep-sea predator fish, circling and closing around a diving bell and waiting for its protective walls to give way.

Was there any way back to the evidence room, the station – concepts already grown so vague she fought to picture them? She didn't know. But if the light went out any chance would be gone. And now the first Spindly Man reached for Cowell.

She started forward, Vera too, but the other Spindly Men turned to them, the blue-eyed one staring at her, the other at Vera. So cold. Struggling to move. Like wading through treacle. The first Spindly's hand falling, relentlessly, towards Cowell's shoulder.

And then Brock flew past her, fell on his arse – the evidence room door was open, and the striplight flickered like a strobe, going wild. The scene was changing back and forth with each flash. One flash illuminated more ranks of Spindlies gathered on that endless field of mud and asphalt around them; the next lit the familiar shelves and walls of the evidence room.

A blur of motion – Stakowski. He vaulted over Brock, towards Cowell. Behind him Renwick saw the corridor, the striplights there flashing and flickering. Other people stood there – McAdams, Joyce Graham, Anna Mason and her brother coming out of the interview room.

Get the civilians out, Renwick shouted at McAdams, but of course there was no sound.

Stakowski – she spun back. He'd shoved Vera aside, lunged for Cowell. The blue-eyed Spindly reached for him. Renwick leapt forward, trying to shout his name.

Stakowski tried to wrench the mask from Cowell's hands, but it wouldn't budge. The first Spindly's hand was an inch from Cowell's shoulder. Stakowski balled a fist, drew it back. No, he wouldn't stand a chance against the Spindly Men–

But it was Cowell he was aiming for and he caught him smack on the chin, snapping his head back. Cowell's grip broke; the mask fell.

Vera screamed silently as Cowell pitched back into the dark–

The striplight overhead exploded in a shower of sparks, heralding an inrush of returning sound – a striplight in the corridor blew out as well. McAdams jumped aside as its plastic casing smashed to the tiled floor. A last flicker and the lights came back on.

"You fucking bastard–"

The Spindly Men were gone. The evidence room was the evidence room again: the steel shelves, the narrow aisle between them. Brock sat huddled against the wall, shaking. Crosbie stood by the door, blinking and dazed.

"Get off, woman–"

Crosbie ran forward to help Stakowski, who was trying to fend off Vera Latimer's blows. Renwick waded in, grabbed her wrists. "That's enough."

"He fucking hit Allen, the cunt–"

"You can take the girl out of Shackleton Street..." Crosbie muttered.

"And fuck you, Jock–"

"That is *enough*. Vera. *Vera*. Cool it. Now."

Vera blinked and stared at her. A thin whimper slid

out of her throat. Renwick released her wrists and she covered her mouth.

"I had to clock him. Only way to stop it. Brock, can you grab us a chair, please?" Stakowski helped Cowell to his feet. "Take it easy, Mr Cowell. *Brock*. A bloody chair."

Brock nodded, stumbled off to get one.

"Allen–" Vera went to her brother.

Renwick took a deep breath. Questions like *what was that* could come later. She turned to Crosbie. "Go help DS McAdams. Dave?"

"Yes, ma'am?"

"Make sure the station's secure, get the broken glass swept up. Joyce?"

"Boss?"

"Can you come take a look at Mr Cowell, please?" Christ, if Cowell was injured – Graham grabbed the first-aid kit and jogged down the corridor towards them. Behind her Anna Mason and her brother stood staring – Anna pale and shaken, Martyn bewildered with nothing to fight. "Alastair–"

"Ma'am?" called Crosbie.

"When you've a minute, can you arrange to get Mr Griffiths and Ms Mason home too?"

"Actually, ma'am–" Having installed Cowell in the requested chair, Stakowski stepped aside to let Graham through "–you might want a word with Ms Mason first. Think we might have a lead here."

Laughter. Cowell. "You see?" he said. "You see?"

"Allen, are you alright?" Vera gripped her brother's hand in both of hers. He patted hers. He was ashen, blood at the corner of his mouth.

"I'm fine. Better than fine. You all saw that. No-one

can deny it. What we saw. That was real. It was real." The laughter subsided slowly. "Chief Inspector?"

"Yes, Mr Cowell. You're sure you're OK?"

He'd stopped laughing, but he was still smiling. His eyes were bright. "I've never felt better in my life. I don't think any medium ever provided such clear proof of the supernatural as just now." A deep breath. "But I suggest we pool our resources. Share what information we have, and see where we go from there."

Renwick felt utterly calm and ready to jump with excitement, all at once. "Let Constable Graham finish checking you over," she said. "And then we'll see."

She headed out into the corridor. McAdams had found a dustpan and brush and was sweeping up the glass. "Take Mr Griffiths and Ms Mason to interview room one for the moment," Renwick told Crosbie. "Just let's keep them out of the way." She met Anna Mason's eyes. "If that's OK?"

"No problem." Anna shook her head. "I want to help. I'll wait."

Crosbie led her off; Martyn followed, dazed and dumb.

"Thanks, Mike," Renwick murmured.

"Any time."

"Good punch as well."

"Had to be done, boss. Only way."

"Not that you enjoyed it at all."

"No, ma'am. I didn't."

His hand shook; before she could stop herself, she gripped it for a second, then quickly let go. "Let's do this," she said. "Find out what the hell's going on."

CHAPTER SIXTEEN

ANNA SAT WITH Martyn in the interview room for nearly half an hour before they were taken up to the... squad room? Was that what the police called it, or was that only in America? It was on the first floor of the station and overlooked the misty street.

They pushed two desks together and sat around them. Eight in all: her and Martyn, Renwick and Stakowski, the big Detective Sergeant with the ginger hair and the Scottish one – Alastair, Renwick had called him. The man with the smart suit and expensive watch, pressing a cold flannel to his jaw. He looked familiar. An actor? The woman with him didn't look familiar. His wife, maybe? Pity, she was tall and elegant, equally well-dressed. Older than Anna by a good few years, but handsome. Groomed. Short hair, but not mannish. Just her type.

"Alright," said Renwick. "You all know who I am. I believe you all know Sergeant Stakowski as well. This is DS McAdams. DC Crosbie. This is Allen Cowell." A brief pause. "The medium."

Yes, of course. He had a TV series on one of the satellite channels. She'd seen it at Martyn and Eva's once.

"Miss Latimer, Mr Cowell's sister."

Sister, then. Vera's eyes met hers across the table. Light brown, almost yellow. Bright, clear, attractive. "Hi."

"Hello." Anna looked down. *Miss, though. Not married.*

"And this is Ms Mason, and her brother, Mr Griffiths." Renwick took a deep breath. "Alright. Let's begin. Mike, let's talk about the house on Shackleton Street."

Stakowski nodded. "We found various bits and pieces there, more about that in a mo. We also found the bodies of two women, which we've now identified as Elizabeth Fowler and–" he checked his notes "– Jayne Shore."

"Jayne?" Anna nearly jumped; Martyn hadn't spoken since they got here. "Jayne with a 'y'? Shore like in sea-shore?"

"Yes, that's right–"

"But she's dead. Liz Fowler too. I mean, already. They were–"

"Mr Griffiths–"

"They were in my wife's art class."

"Art class?"

"They were killed with her. Night the college burned down."

"Whoa. Hang on. Of course." Stakowski rubbed his eyes. "Sorry, lad. Forgot. Eva Griffiths, right?"

"Yeah."

"Anyroad, as you say, they were both listed presumed dead back in November after the fire."

"Presumed?" asked Martyn. "I thought–"

"It were a bad fire, Mr Griffiths. We never found all the bodies. Just... parts. Nowt we could ID–"

"Mike," said Renwick.

"Sorry." Stakowski rubbed his eyes. Martyn looked down. "Anyroad, they both died in the last couple of days. Not sure what of yet. Wearing the same clothes they'd been last seen in. Looks like they were kept as prisoners. Why, we have no idea. No ransom demands; neither was what you'd call wealthy in any case. But it's looking like the Spindly Men went to work round here a bit earlier than we thought. But the other stuff we found... no idea. Not till Miss Mason showed up. But anyway, Mr Cowell–"

"We'll get back to Ms Mason in a moment." Renwick turned to Cowell. "OK. Mr Cowell. What did you... see? In the evidence room. What can you tell us?"

Cowell inspected the damp cloth, folded it neatly and set it to one side. It was his moment; he was milking it. "It was different from the usual," he said. "Johnny, Mark and Sam weren't there."

"Who's that?" said Stakowski.

"My spirit guides. They weren't there."

"Johnny, Mark and... Sam, you said?"

"That's right." Vera put her hand on Cowell's. Pride in her voice. "Read any of his books. He talks about them there."

"I'll order one off Amazon once t'internet's up again."

"If we could carry on?" said Renwick. "Are they usually there when you perform..."

"Psychometry? Yes. They usually are. But this time... I'm not sure exactly what I encountered. Something... it was something very *powerful*, certainly. Like a wave, almost, rolling over me. All I got were... impressions."

"Impressions of what?"

"Rage. That was the first thing. This terrible sense of... rage. But suffering, too. Terrible suffering. I had images of... an institution of some kind. Corridors. Rooms. People wearing some sort of smock. The kind hospital patients wear."

Renwick nodded.

"I'd have said it was an asylum, but I had a sense of *physical* suffering too."

"Abuse of some kind?"

"Abuse..." He stopped. Vera took his hand and squeezed. "Perhaps. But there was more. Worse. Wounds. I don't know."

"Was there anything else?"

"Yes. Just one other thing. The military. Something... something to do with the military. A uniform. Uniforms. I'm sorry. As I said, it was very intense, but not at all controlled, just a jumble."

"You saying that all of this is random? No purpose to it?" Stakowski had been jotting notes on an A4 pad.

"Oh no. Not at all. There's a very definite purpose of some kind. But... it's like a huge train, hurtling past at top speed. The impressions I've had are like – glimpses through the windows." Cowell groped for the cup of tea in front of him, spooned in half a dozen sugars, stirred.

Renwick let out a long sigh. "And that brings us to you, Ms Mason."

Cowell looked sulky; pushed aside so soon. Vera looked at her sidelong, smiling slightly. Anna's cheeks grew warm; she opened her shoulderbag and took three pictures from the file. "Here's what I showed Sergeant Stakowski earlier." She handed the first photograph to Crosbie, who studied it and passed it on.

"When Martyn described what he'd seen," she

began, "I knew it was something I've seen before. And I realised it was connected with a book I've been planning. Local history. History was always my thing. Took my degree in it." McAdams stifled a yawn; her face burned. Enough. Block it out. "Anyway. My... er, area of interest ..." God, this wasn't going well. "Local history and the First World War in particular." Come on, Anna. Just tell them.

The picture showed rows of white mutilated faces like the ones from Shackleton Street. "This is the picture Martyn's description reminded me of. They're plaster casts of men suffering from facial wounds. Your face doesn't really have any vital organs, so it can take some pretty horrific damage and survive. Fighting in a trench left your head very vulnerable to bullets, shrapnel or grenade splinters, but steel helmets prevented a lot of fatal injuries. So there were literally thousands of men like this in World War One. The French called them *gueules cassées*, the men with broken faces."

"Jesus." Renwick passed the picture on.

"The surgeons did their best – a lot of what we know now about reconstructive surgery came out of World War One – but there were limits to what they could do and how many they could help."

She passed the second picture to Crosbie. It looked like part of a face had been cut off and laid out on a table. Just an eye, an eyebrow, a nose, part of the forehead. "What you're looking at here is part of a facial prosthesis, made in France in 1918 by Anna Coleman Ladd. Made from paper-thin galvanised copper, then hand-painted to look absolutely lifelike. It took a month to produce each one. A British sculptor called Francis Derwent Wood did similar work with tin masks." Anna felt Vera's eyes on her; she looked down. *God. Get a grip. You're not a teenager.* "They'd take a plaster cast, make clay or plasticine squeezes from it. Model the mask to match pre-injury photographs; hand-paint it to match the skin-tones. They looked real except at very close range. And of course, a mask can't move."

"Hand-painted? That's what you said, right? They were hand-painted."

"Martyn–"

"That's what you said, right?"

"Yes."

"They'd need painters to make the masks look right."

"Martyn..."

"So the women from Eva's class, that's why they were taken. Eva could..."

"We don't know that, lad," Stakowski said gently.

"Four missing persons," said Renwick. "Three deaths. More if there is indeed a connection with the fire at the college last month. And yes, some of the people presumed killed in the college fire may not have been. And then there's what happened in the evidence room."

"My department, I think."

"Mr Cowell–"

"It's supernatural. You've all seen that."

"If we hadn't, Mr Cowell, this discussion would *so* not be happening."

"I've never heard of a spiritual being causing *direct* physical harm. The few that have malicious intentions generally seek to mislead people in harmful ways, because, physically, they can't do anything. There's possession, however..."

"Possession."

"A spirit controlling a living person. Possessed people can display supernatural abilities. But this seems *entirely* supernatural."

"So what do we do?"

"I don't know, yet. But remember, I was told I *had* to come back here, which implies there's something I can do."

"Fine. So… World War One. What's the connection?"

"The Kempforth Pals," McAdams said, arms folded, looking down. Everyone looked at him; he'd been quiet throughout. "We learnt about it in school."

Anna nodded. "So-called 'Pals' battalions were recruited from towns, districts – the local men could all join up and serve together, instead of being split up between different units. It helped recruiting. But when they went into action, it meant the entire adult male population of a town could be mown down within seconds. The Kempforth Pals went into action on 1st July, 1916, at the Battle of the Somme. They were massacred. Only a handful survived."

"All that was left in Kempforth were kids and old men." McAdams looked up. "Same in towns like Accrington, Blackburn. It's where all the jokes about us being inbred come from. Not many eligible men left after the war. Lot of folk ended up closely related. 'Cept the Asians, obviously, they came along later."

"There's something else," said Anna. "It's just a spit away from here, but hardly anyone in Kempforth even knows about it anymore. Not something they ever liked talking about."

"Out of sight, out of mind," said Stakowski. "Heard of it when I were a kid, but… big scandal at the time, then folk forgot it. They wanted to."

Renwick coughed. "Could someone start making sense, please?"

Anna pushed more photographs across the table. "What do you see here?"

"Same as the others you showed me."

"No. Anna Coleman Ladd's studio was in Paris, Francis Derwent Wood's in London."

"So?"

"On the far side of a hill overlooking Kempforth, if you go into the woodland there, there's a large area that's fenced off. There are signs saying Keep Out, Danger. Officially it's unsafe due to subsidence, caused by a demolition carried out years before. In fact, beyond that fencing is a large complex of abandoned buildings containing, among other things, the studio where those masks were made."

"What?"

"The Kempforth Veterans' Hospital and Sanitarium, Chief Inspector. Otherwise known as Ash Fell."

CHAPTER SEVENTEEN

ANNA LOOKED DOWN; she could feel all their eyes on her. "Ash Fell was the brainchild of Sir Charles Dace," she said. "He was the head of the Dace family when the Great War broke out."

"The Dace family?" asked Renwick.

"They'd been the main landowners in Kempforth since the Norman Conquest," said Anna. "Moved into textiles during the Industrial Revolution. In 1914, they owned both the cotton mills and most of the land. Sir Charles encouraged all his employees to join the Pals, not that they needed much encouragement."

"Anything to get out of Kempforth," chuckled Crosbie.

"No," said Anna. "It wasn't that. They thought they were needed. It was... a sense of duty. Hard to understand now, we've got so much more used to distrusting authority, I suppose. Sir Charles enlisted, too, but with a different regiment; he served in Flanders and saw conditions at the Front for himself. And then he learned what'd happened to the Kempforth Pals."

She passed on a faded, sepia photograph of Sir Charles Dace: tall, lean, uniformed, swagger stick under one arm, chin up. Darkish hair; trimmed moustache, pale eyes.

"I've seen letters he wrote at the time. He believed in the Empire, but he was an enlightened imperialist. Believed there was a duty to the less fortunate – the 'lower classes' at home, the 'lower races' abroad. He felt responsible for the men of Kempforth. And most of them had now been wiped out. He couldn't do much about that – apart from contribute to the war memorial, which he did – but there were a lot of physically and mentally damaged survivors. So he did something for them instead."

"A hospital for war veterans," said Renwick

"Hospital and *sanitarium*. A hospital treats and cures people. A sanitarium cares for people who can't be cured. Kempforth Great House – the family seat – was on the hill overlooking the town. The opposite side, overlooking the moors, also belonged to the Daces too, including an uncultivated slope overgrown with rowan trees, otherwise known as mountain ash. Hence, Ash Fell."

"I've been on the moors," Renwick said. "I know the hillside you're talking about. Never seen any sign of a building there."

"It wasn't meant to be visible. Sir Charles wanted to give the patients a sanctuary from the outside world."

Renwick turned to Stakowski. "How come I never heard about Ash Fell, Mike? Especially last year when we were searching for a missing child."

"I were under the impression the place had been demolished, ma'am."

"Still an area where a body could have been dumped."

"Only with great difficulty, boss. But I scouted round the general area – with DC Wayland, in fact – and couldn't find owt. I was going to discuss getting authorisation to enter the grounds, but then... we found the Baldwin girl's body."

"Even so, I've been here nearly five years and never even heard of the place."

"*I* hadn't, till I were fourteen. And I grew up in Kempforth – me dad's farm were on t'other side of the hill from Ash Fell. As kids we were told not to go into those woods. Not that you could go far – it were fenced off, wi' danger signs all round it. Every bugger you asked had a different reason why. Hospital that burned down, madhouse where they all got left to starve, mad doctors doing human experiments... you heard 'em all. Never knew who to believe."

"Tell kids not to go somewhere, it's the first place they'll head for."

"Some did. I knew of two. It discouraged the rest of us."

"They died?"

"One did. The other got some sort of brain damage. He lived another fifteen years, I heard. If you could call it living."

"What actually happened?"

"Some kind of accident, in both cases. But no-one was ever quite sure what or how."

Renwick looked at Anna. "Sorry, Ms Mason. Go on."

"This is an aerial shot of Ash Fell. Unique as far as I know."

Another photograph. Thick woods. A long drive led up to a large oblong structure. Two corridors extended out from either side at the front before travelling down the slope, each terminating in a square, red-brick building. At the back of the central building, a shorter, stubbier corridor jutted out on each side and a longer one to the rear; another square building stood at the end of each. It always made Anna think of a scorpion crouching, claws raised to attack.

Below the complex, on the picture's bottom left, stood a cluster of smaller buildings by a stream; on the bottom right, a cruciform structure with stippled open space beside it. A round metal structure stood by the central building.

Cowell held up the picture. "This place–"

"Mr Cowell," said Renwick.

"But I know this place–"

"Allen," said Vera. "Let her carry on." She caught Anna's eye, smiled.

Anna smiled back, looked down, went on. "Ash Fell was built using a variant of the so-called radial plan. Different wings and wards radiate from a central admin block."

"So what's what?" Renwick asked.

"I'll start with the outlying buildings. On the left is the Home Farm. Asylums and big hospitals generally tried to be self-sufficient back then. It had livestock, plus a greenhouse, bakery, dairy. Wheat and cornfields. Even a water-mill to grind flour." She tapped the cruciform building. "Here's the chapel and cemetery."

"Cemetery?"

"If you died at Ash Fell, you were generally buried there."

Renwick tapped the central building. "Admin block?"

"Yes. The Warbeck building. The metal structure

beside it is the water tower." Anna produced another picture. "Here's a frontal view."

Warbeck was three storeys high, four if you counted the attic space. Red brick. Wide concrete steps led up to a portico. Big, black, heavy doors. A clock tower loomed above them.

"Warbeck was the centre of operations for Ash Fell. Operating theatres, kitchens, laundry, gymnasium, swimming pool, mortuary. The superintendent's quarters were incorporated into it too. Normally that would been a separate building, but Ash Fell wasn't normal."

"You're not bloody kidding," said Stakowski.

"What about these other five?" asked Renwick.

"The two lower wings are D and E Blocks. The three above are A, B and C. Each handled different categories of patient."

"Go on."

"A, B and C blocks all provided hospital care. C Block dealt with facial injuries."

"*Gueules cassées*," said Vera. Those yellow eyes met Anna's. Catlike. And what was she? A mouse? Was Vera assessing prey or a potential mate? "Right?"

"Right." Anna coughed. "Block B was for miscellaneous patients: cases of gas poisoning, a few amputees. Block A was psychiatric. As you can see, there was open space around each one for exercise and fresh air; between each block, and between D and E Blocks and the main path, they'd conserved patches of woodland. It meant each block was like a self-contained community."

"And D and E Block were for sanitarium care?" asked Renwick.

"Yes. Patients who were too badly damaged to ever function in the outside world again. Block D housed patients too badly disfigured for reconstructive surgery. Many of their loved ones couldn't bear to see them. E Block was psychiatric. There were catatonic cases. Others wandered around in a world of their own, reliving the past over and over – mostly harmless, except when they struck themselves around the head to try and drive the memories out. Sometimes smashing their heads against walls. They couldn't get past what'd happened to them. There were also some violent cases – they'd think they were back in combat, or overreact massively to every irritation. Your little boy won't eat his greens so instead of telling him off you smash his face into the table-top three times. And there were so many cases. There were over 20,000 men drawing pensions for shell-shock the year Ash Fell opened."

"Jesus," said Renwick.

Anna shrugged. "Stick people in filthy trenches, shells exploding constantly around them, waiting to go over the top and probably get killed, it'd drive anyone mad." She cleared her throat. "Ash Fell opened in 1923. It was – initially – a reasonably humane and well-run institution. Until Sir Charles Dace died, and his sons came into the picture: St. John and Gideon Dace."

Two photographs. Two men in evening dress. Chalk and cheese.

"St. John–" tall, dark-haired, regular features, a rugby-player's physique.

"Gideon–" pale, thin, narrow-faced, a lank blond fringe swept sideways across his forehead, hanging into his right eye. St. John stood up straight; Gideon slouched. St. John looked serious; Gideon's smirk never touched his eyes.

"St. John was the eldest and the favoured son. Promising athlete, reasonable academic qualifications, groomed to take over the business. Gideon, in contrast, was a sickly child, with a permanent limp from an accident when he was seven. Sir Charles never hid his disappointment in Gideon. He was very intelligent, though. First class degree from Cambridge, despite blowing most of his allowance on drink, gambling and prostitutes."

"What they'd call 'acting out' these days," said Renwick.

"Or being an arsehole," said Stakowski. "Take your pick."

"Gideon seems to have alternately craved his father's respect and hated his guts. Which might explain future events. When Sir Charles died in September 1929, Gideon was in Paris, celebrating his graduation; St. John had been managing the business day-to-day for several years. What they didn't know until the will was read out was that Sir Charles had spent virtually the entire Dace family fortune. First on building Ash Fell, then on establishing the Ash Fell Hospital Trust Fund to keep it running for years to come. He'd made over nearly everything that hadn't been spent on the hospital to the fund. As a result the business was almost bankrupt, plus the brothers had inherited Sir Charles' debts, which were substantial. St. John had some stocks and shares; he planned to liquidate them and plough them into the business, but–"

"The Wall Street Crash," said Stakowski.

Anna nodded. "St. John's assets were wiped out; Gideon didn't have any of his own. They had to sell the business to a competitor for a pittance to prevent it going bust. They also had to sell most of their land. Once Sir

Charles' debts were paid off, they still had Kempforth Great House, but that was pretty much it. And this was where Gideon came into his own. Whatever he lacked in physical strength, he made up for in cunning."

Renwick sipped her coffee.

"The fund was managed by a Board of Trustees, so the first step was getting onto it. The biggest opponent of *that* was the Chairman, Dr John Lethbridge. In late 1931, someone gave the police compromising photographs of Lethbridge with a young man. Anonymously, of course. Lethbridge was forced to resign and died in prison. In early 1932, St. John Dace was unanimously voted in as the new Chairman. Between 1932 and 1935, the remaining original Trustees resigned one by one."

"Blackmail?" asked Renwick.

"Impossible to prove, but most likely. New Trustees were appointed – friends of Gideon. Most of them had no medical background; none of them ever even saw the hospital. They just acted as a rubber stamp."

"They embezzled the Hospital?" Renwick asked.

"Slowly, over a number of years. They had to launder the money they were bleeding off. But the Great Depression was still going on, so under the guise of economic necessity, wages and equipment at Ash Fell were cut drastically from 1936 onwards. They stopped taking new hospital patients and trained, experienced staff were replaced with the cheapest possible labour."

"Gideon's work?"

"He was pulling all the strings, but someone else was always officially in charge. The tours were almost certainly his idea, but when they started St. John was conducting them."

"Tours?"

"Little brainwave Gideon had for some additional income. In the old days, people used to visit lunatic asylums for amusement. Come and look at the freakshow. Laugh at the funny mad people." She heard her voice grow raw. *Calm, Anna.* "Gideon revived the practice.

"The only patients at Ash Fell now were sanitarium cases. Gideon actively sought out new ones to fill A, B and C blocks. Ash Fell was designed to hold four hundred patients. By early 1937 the numbers were almost double that, all either seriously disturbed, appallingly disfigured or both.

"Gideon knew people who'd pay to look at the insane and the disfigured. Or worse. He found them; St. John guided them round the hospital. Groups of patients were penned up in communal areas, half-naked, left to soil themselves. Made a better spectacle. Gideon, as always, stayed well back from it."

"Plausible deniability," said Vera. Her fingers toyed with a cigarette pack. They were long. Clever-looking; nimble.

Anna nodded. "It made money, but it took its toll on St. John. He began drinking heavily, gained about five stone in weight. When the war broke out, he made a concerted effort to get into shape and enlisted. Anything to get away from Kempforth and Gideon, I think. He was posted to the Far East; tried again and again to get combat assignments. His superiors thought he had a death wish – go out in a blaze of glory, redeem the family honour. When that failed and he ended up in a succession of staff postings, he started drinking again. Caught malaria. He was demobilised in early '46 and went back to Kempforth. Nowhere else to go. While he was gone, Gideon had had himself voted onto the Board and things at Ash Fell got even worse."

"Worse? How?" asked Stakowski.

"Allegedly? Bringing in prostitutes to publicly copulate with the mutilated prisoners. Forcing the psychiatric patients to fight each other, sometimes to the death."

"They got away with that?"

"Who was going to report it? The staff weren't, and nor were Gideon's guests. The hospital doctors signed the death certificates and they were buried in the grounds."

"And what did St. John think of all this?" asked Renwick.

"God knows. He was pretty much a complete wreck by then. As far as anyone can tell, he spent the next year carrying on as before. No-one's sure if Gideon's wartime 'entertainments' carried on. But Gideon was losing interest anyway. Ypres and the Somme were old hat now; they had Auschwitz, the Burma Railway, Hiroshima, Nagasaki. Besides, the Trust Fund was nearly exhausted. All he wanted now was to get the actual land back. Some of the psychiatric patients were transferred elsewhere in late '46 and early '47. What he had planned for the surviving facial injury patients no-one's really sure. And then…

"May 1947. St. John led another guided tour round Ash Fell, finished up in E Block. No-one's quite sure exactly what happened. Somehow, the inmates got out of their cells. One woman managed to get out through a window. Got out of the grounds completely, in fact. She made it to a nearby farmhouse and raised the alarm.

"When the police and ambulance arrived, St. John and his guests were all dead. They'd been torn to pieces. St John Dace was probably dead before the patients got him. He'd shot himself with a pistol."

"Could he have let them out?" asked Vera. The tip of her pink tongue briefly touched her red top lip.

"That's one theory. Another is a member of staff whose conscience finally got the better of him, or a patient's relative taking revenge. Either way, it finally finished Ash Fell."

"And Gideon?" Cowell pressed the cold flannel to his jaw again.

"Oh, he escaped prison; legally he had next to no connection with the place, even though it was common knowledge he was behind it all. And of course he could afford some very good legal counsel. Some of the hospital staff were jailed, but most of the blame was put on St. John, who was conveniently dead."

"You're not saying the bastard got away with it?" said Stakowski.

"Oh no. He didn't. Gideon won the criminal case, but a dozen patients' families sued not only the Hospital Trust – which by now had no money – but Gideon personally. He was still on the Board; he had that one connection with Ash Fell, but it was enough. They won, and the trial judge awarded huge damages. Gideon tried to appeal it, but failed. Once the damages and legal fees were paid, he was ruined. All he had left was Kempforth Great House. And Ash Fell itself."

"Ash Fell?" asked Renwick.

"He'd been fighting a separate case to get the land restored to the Dace family when the Trust was dissolved – planned to sell it and the Great House, leave Kempforth, start over. But no-one wanted to buy it, especially not from him. In 1953, Kempforth Great House burned to the ground. And it wasn't insured."

"No way," said Vera. Her smile was cold, flinty. Anna couldn't look away from those yellow cat's eyes. "He ended up in the hospital?"

"That's right. The one thing he still owned. This huge *complex* of buildings, and he had them all to himself. From then until the day he died."

"Christ," said McAdams. "Drive you mad, that would."

"It did. Apparently he acted constantly as if he was being followed around – shouted at people who weren't there. Not that people saw much of him after 1953. No-one's sure how he survived as long as he did, but he managed somehow."

"How long did he live there?" asked Renwick.

"Around Christmas of 1985, one of the hill farmers – one of the few people who'd have anything to do with him – realised he hadn't seen Gideon for a while. So he went to the hospital. He found Gideon in the Warbeck building, lying at the foot of the stairs. He'd been dead for over a month. The post-mortem showed he'd broken his spine. He hadn't died quickly. He was seventy-seven years old."

"Nasty way to go," said Stakowski. "But if anyone deserved it..."

"After that, the council sold Ash Fell to a property developer who wanted to turn it into luxury apartments–"

"Christ on a bike."

"–but the company went bust in the 1987 crash."

"Serves the buggers right."

"Mike."

"Sorry ma'am."

"After that it became council property again. They

planned to demolish Ash Fell completely, but there were a string of accidents on site. Three workmen died, nearly a score were injured, equipment and materials either stopped working or went missing. Rumours started going around that the job was jinxed, Ash Fell was haunted. Nobody wanted to work on the site. The demolition costs were overrunning, and it wasn't as if the council had any particular plans for the land. It was just that most people in the area wanted to forget the place ever existed. In the end, they announced it'd been demolished and fenced the whole area off."

"Jesus Christ."

"I only found it was still there through a colleague at the council. I was trying to get hold of some pictures from the demolition for the book I was planning. That's when she told me that it was still standing but any access to the site was a complete no-no." Anna shook her head. "Chances of getting a book about the place published are pretty low. But I couldn't drop the project – it was fascinating, in a horrible way."

"Just outside the town," said Stakowski. "With plenty of room for people to stay, if you're not too choosy. Whether they want to or not. And practically nobody knows it's there."

CHAPTER EIGHTEEN

"MR COWELL, I am not taking civilians into a situation like this."

"Chief Inspector, you're going to need my help. You've seen for yourself you're not dealing with a run-of-the-mill kidnapper. Something supernatural – or paranormal, if you don't like that word – is involved. You may've only glimpsed it, but you can't deny what you saw. None of you can."

"We don't know who or what's up there, Mr Cowell."

Sweat gleamed on Cowell's forehead. "All the more reason to bring someone who does."

"And you do?"

His voice rose. "I'd say I'm the closest thing to an expert you have." Vera put a hand on his arm. Cowell shook her off. "This isn't a straightforward haunting. This is physically dangerous to the living, and you'll need more than a truncheon and a can of pepper spray to stop it."

"Mr Cowell–"

"Allen," said Vera. "Chief Inspector, you have to admit he has a point."

"Boss?" said Stakowski. Renwick turned; his gaze was steady. "Talk to you for a second?"

After a moment, she nodded. "Dave, Alastair, can you keep an eye on things here?"

"Nae hassle," said Crosbie.

"Don't worry," Vera said, "we won't break anything."

Martyn chuckled at that. But Vera was looking at Anna when she said it, smiling; after a second, Anna smiled back.

"OK, MIKE. WHAT you thinking?"

Stakowski breathed out, looked back up at her. "We should take Cowell along."

"Are you mad?"

"Look, I know he's at least eighty per cent horseshit, but–"

"Only eighty?"

A weak smile. "I'd've said a hundred before today. But you saw what happened in the evidence room."

"Thanks for reminding me."

"Hate to say it, but Cowell's right. He's the closest thing we've got to an expert."

"Come on. What about one of the local priests or vicars?"

"You'd have to convince them first, and word would get out. I assume you'd not planned on telling the Bedstead about this part of it?"

"Funnily enough, I think it's going to completely slip my mind."

"Good thinking."

"I have my moments. But if Banstead knew I was taking Cowell seriously…"

"Does he need to know yet?"

"No."

"If you get a result he'll not give a shit how you got it. Be too busy telling every bugger he believed in you all along."

"So you think I should bring Cowell?"

"And Ms Mason."

"Mike–"

"I'd be surprised if you'll find anyone who knows more about that place. You could try the council, but knowing them it'll probably take a fortnight before they even admit it's still standing."

"Fair point. But I don't like bringing civvies into this. There's any number of ways it could go tits-up."

"This isn't a normal case, ma'am."

"I had noticed. My priority's getting Roseanne Trevor out of there."

"If she's alive."

"If she's alive."

"And Tahira Khalid."

"Yes."

"And Danielle Morton, and–"

"Yeah, OK Mike, thanks."

"We might also consider bringing Cowell's sister along."

"Why not just print invitations?"

"She knows how to handle Cowell. God knows we don't need him getting any flakier than he already is."

"I must be going as mental as you. It's making sense." To hell with everything else; everything but getting the child out alive. "You're going to suggest we bring Griffiths as well."

"A: could come in handy if we find any of the women from the college. B: he'll want to come. And C: frankly, better he's up there with us than shooting his mouth off down here."

Renwick released a long breath. "Alright. We'll do it. But they keep to the rear, and out of our way."

"THE ORIGINAL PLANS for the building are lost – no-one's exactly sure when. But these are the individual floor plans." Anna handed more papers to Renwick. "One set for Warbeck, another for each individual block."

"Thanks. OK… DC Crosbie will run you back home. If you can make your way to the Station Hotel for 7.30 am tomorrow, that will be appreciated. And Mr Cowell, Miss Latimer, if you can be ready to go by then."

"I will be," said Cowell. "Believe me, I will. Don't worry, Chief Inspector. I won't let you down."

"OK. Everyone else? Good."

"Come on, Allen," Vera said.

"Alastair, if you can run them back? Thanks."

Alone with Stakowski, Renwick went to the kettle. "Tea, two sugars?"

"You're brewing up?" His smile was shaky. "I might faint. Aye, go on."

Renwick filled the kettle.

"So what's the plan, boss?"

"Leave as little to chance as we can. Go over the floor plans, work out our approach. And we draw firearms… whatever Cowell says, those things are solid enough to snatch people."

"With you on that. If you want me, I mean."

Renwick got the milk from the fridge. "What did you find out about Cowell?"

"All about contacts, police work. You know that. So I rang a mate of mine."

"You have *friends*?"

"Ha-ha. Ben Hardman – he's retired now, but he were a beat copper round Dunwich and the Polar back in the '80s."

"And?"

"Cowell's a stage name. He were born Alan Latimer."

"Latimer, like his sister."

"Aye. Anyroad. Father died when he were eight – late '70s, this'd be. Shortly after that a new feller came along, one Adrian Walsh. Which is where things get interesting."

"Go on."

"Their mother died not long after marrying Walsh. She were already on Valium – looks like she upped the dosage, or someone upped it for her. And one night she took too many."

"But nothing anyone could prove?"

"'Course not. Ben also gave me the number for a lass who were a social worker at the time. There were suspicions, apparently. Stuff that'd ring alarm bells in a flash these days. Both kids were quiet and withdrawn. Unexplained bruises. That kind of thing."

Renwick handed him his cup. "Left the teabag in. Never get it strong enough for you."

"I'm not happy till I can creosote the fence with it."

"So, there were suspicions."

"Nowt they ever proved. But… fast-forward to 1985 and a little thing called Operation Clean Sweep." Stakowski poked the teabag with a spoon. "Remember the other day, we were talking 'bout a suspected paedophile ring in Kempforth, back in the '80s? Not that they'd've called it that back then, but that were what it was."

"Yeah."

"I were still in the army when that were going on. But guess which case files I were reading before Cowell turned up?"

"You can read?"

"Bog off. Ma'am."

"STATION HOTEL," SAID Crosbie.

In the passenger seat, Anna glanced into the back of the car. Cowell gazed out of one window; Vera looked out of the other, eyes lost and distant. Martyn was squeezed between them, shoulders hunched in, scowling. Anna managed not to smile.

Vera got out without speaking, slammed the door. Crosbie caught Anna's eye, raised his eyebrows. She gave a little smile in return, then took a deep breath.

"Actually," she said, "can you let me out here?"

"Eh?" Martyn stared at her.

"I need some time to myself." She couldn't believe she was saying it. "I'll get a cab back, or book a room if it's late."

"But Mary–"

"Yes, Mary. One of us should be there when she wakes up. And it should be you."

"But–"

"Martyn, you're her father. And I'm never going to be her mum."

Crosbie climbed out, opened the passenger door. "Ma'am."

Was he flirting? "Thank you."

Vera opened the other rear door. Cowell sagged sideways. "Allen?"

"Tired. So tired." The energy of a few minutes before was gone; he looked old, raddled, an ageing drag-queen whose makeup had started to run. Vera released a long breath and helped him stand.

"Way past someone's bedtime," Crosbie murmured.

"Thanks for the lift," Anna said.

"See you the morrow, then."

"Yeah. See you, Martyn."

"Yeah."

The car pulled out; its foglights faded into the dirty mist.

Anna followed Vera and Allen into the hotel. The lobby was empty; a couple of battery-powered lanterns had been hung up for lighting. "Best ring the bell," Vera said.

"Yes." They studied each other, until Anna looked down. She shrugged. "Sometimes you just need a bit of time off from your family."

"Yeah. I know." The yellow eyes lingered on hers. "See you later."

Vera shepherded her brother to the stairs; Anna wondered if there'd been hints and hidden meanings there, too, of a kind she'd welcome more. Vera was definitely her type, and there was that sense of strength; coiled, catlike. Dangerous, but exciting too.

She shook her head. No time for daydreaming. Getting carried away there. Her grip on reality still wasn't perfect.

You might have a touch of it too. Might wasn't good enough, not anymore. She needed better answers than that.

She shook her head, chasing away an afterimage of yellow, catlike eyes. Even if Vera *was* gay, that didn't mean she was interested. She rang the bell on the reception desk and waited.

STAKOWSKI CRUSHED THE last flavour from the teabag, flicked it into the bin. "Like I said, nowt were ever proved, but rumour was Adrian Walsh wasn't just a kiddie-fiddler, but a pimp into the bargain."

"The paedophile ring."

"Oh aye. Equal opportunities – boys *and* girls. Late '70s, early '80s, about a dozen kids went missing round Kempforth way. Ben reckoned most of them were down to Walsh and co."

"Where did all this information come from?"

"A burglar, would you believe? Trying to trade information for softer treatment."

"And how did *he* know about them?"

"An old schoolmate, name of Tom Yolland. They were both 'bout eighteen, nineteen years old. Went drinking occasionally."

"How did Yolland come into it?"

"He were one of them. Sort of. One of the – alleged – members were a local butcher, ran a shop on Station Road. Name of George Fitton. Yolland worked in the shop. Lived above it, too, with Fitton. Anyroad, Yolland used to be one of the victims, and when he got too old for them, Fitton took a shine to him, for whatever reason, and kept him on. According to Ben's informant, Yolland got sledged one night and it all spilled out. He'd begun... participating in the ring's activities. Fairly full of self-loathing about it. He were a bit backward, apparently. Under Fitton's thumb, too, or so folk thought." Stakowski sighed. "There's some you hate, and some you pity."

"How many were involved?"

"Apart from Fitton and Walsh, Yolland mentioned three others. Father Joseph Sykes – parish priest at St Matthias' R.C. Church. Another one – you'll love this – according to Yolland, were a copper. Never substantiated, of course. No names. Yolland claimed he were obsessed wi' keeping his identity secret, so he always wore a mask when he were with a kid. Only Walsh knew who he was. Another reason they got away with it for so long. Never any lead on who this copper might be."

"If he ever existed."

"True."

"And the last one?"

"The last one wasn't what you'd call full-time; came from out of town every October. They called him the Shrike. No name, no description. Special kind of punter. Didn't just rape them."

"Killed them too?"

"Child predator. Worst kind of paedo there is, and they're all bloody bad enough."

Renwick shook her head. "And I thought Tom Baldwin was bad. But nothing ever came of this?"

"Nowt."

"Why not? Got as far as them mounting an operation."

"Well, first off, Walsh died – heart attack at Shackleton Street."

"Natural causes?"

"In a way."

"Spit it out, Mike."

"He wasn't alone."

"Who else was there?"

"Vera Latimer. Nineteen years old. She said she were upstairs in bed – women's troubles – and didn't hear owt. Even though he crashed around, pulled a drawer out. She came down an hour or so later to put kettle on and there he was."

"Think she knew something?"

"Ben said they found a fag butt in the kitchen ashtray, just one. Had her lipstick all over it. Could never prove it, but he reckoned she were there when it happened. And she just... watched."

"Jesus."

"Well, I'd not shed any tears for Adrian Walsh," said Stakowski. "Bear in mind he'd probably raped them both. And Christ knows how many others."

"You *are* Old Testament, aren't you, sarge?" Stakowski looked away. "Sorry."

"Probably looked like divine punishment, from where she were standing. Never seems to happen early enough, though, does it? And here's a thing. Vera Latimer took her little brother and scarpered out of town sharpish after that."

"How old was he, back then?"

"Fourteen, fifteen. My guess would be she tapped one of Walsh's cronies for money to skip town with. Fitton, most likely; he made a big withdrawal from his bank that day."

"Why would he pay out?"

"CID searched Walsh's house afterward – found cameras and unexposed film, but no sign of his porn stash. He'd have had one. You know these bastards as well as I do."

"You think she blackmailed him? A nineteen-year-old girl?"

"Stranger things have happened. If Fitton were in any of those pictures, she'd've had him over a barrel."

"Why didn't this masked copper step in?"

"Only Walsh knew who he was, remember? He were safest staying out of it."

"So what about Fitton and the priest? No-one try bringing them in?"

"Didn't get the chance. Remember Tom Yolland? George Fitton kept a twelve-bore in the house; same night Vera Latimer did a flit, Yolland got hold of it and gave the bastard – sorry, *alleged* bastard – both barrels. One in the bollocks, one in the face. Then he drove Fitton's van out to St. Matthias', waited for Father Sykes to show and redecorated the church with *him*."

"Jesus. And what happened to Yolland?"

"Drove out of town, to an abandoned farmhouse on Dunwich Lane. Place's still there now. Only a bit charred – he emptied two cans of petrol over hisself and struck a match."

"Fuck."

"And guess where the farmhouse is next to?"

"No way."

"Yup. Ash Fell. Tell you summat else too – those spirit guides of Cowell's?"

"Sam, Johnny and Mark?"

"Three lads, few years younger than Cowell, went missing round the same time Walsh died. Ben reckoned they were the ring's last victims. Samuel Morrison, John Kiley, Mark Danes."

"The Shrike?"

"It were October. About time for his annual visit. You

saw how Vera Latimer reacted when I asked about them. She acted like she had summat to be guilty about."

"Like what?"

"If they'd come to us, we might have been able to save those kids."

"Or they might have been dead already."

"True."

"And if one of the ring *was* a copper..."

"True."

"And that kind of thing, you feel guilty whether you should or not."

"And that's true too." Silence. "Anyroad, she buggered off to the big bad city – Manchester, then London. Made whatever living she could till Alan – Al*len* – started his medium act. She's a hard woman, Vera Latimer; like bloody nails. But you can understand why. And if there is one thing she cares about, it's her kid brother." Stakowski drained his tea. "So, what happens now?"

Renwick leant back in her chair. "You're an Authorised Firearms Officer, right?"

"Aye. You?"

"Yeah."

"You're sure you want me along?"

"Why wouldn't I, Mike?"

"You know why."

"I don't know any reason why I shouldn't be able to rely on you as I always have. Do you?"

A pause. "No ma'am."

Renwick smiled. "I'm glad."

"Me too, boss."

"OK. So, we get a team together, go up there soon as it's light."

"Sounds about right. Best take a look at this place's layout, then."

"Later."

"Why later?"

"First of all I'm going to brave the elements and see Banstead."

"The hell for? You can authorise use of firearms yourself."

"As far as he's concerned, I'm off the case and Sherwood's taking over. I don't need that gumming up the works. So I need to get at least one day's grace out of him." Renwick pulled her jacket on.

"You're going now?"

"Damn right. He's still full of the flu, remember? If I get him out of bed, I'll bet you any money he'll be sick, confused and not thinking straight. Which is exactly how I want the bald-headed bastard."

Stakowski chuckled. "Can I come too, then, ma'am?"

"I can handle Banstead on my own."

"Oh, I know. That's why I want to see it for myself."

"Alright then, you old buzzard."

"Good to have you back, boss."

ALLEN WAS SQUEALING in his sleep. The clenched, muffled sounds she knew so well. In the neighbouring bed, Vera curled up on her side, her back to him, tried not to hear.

He'd made noises like these back at Shackleton Street. Sometimes Walsh took them to the clients; other times the clients came to the house. They'd been the worst. Hers and Alan's rooms adjoined; so many times she'd heard noises like this through the bedroom wall.

The comforting had already started by then. As they'd

grown up she'd given Alan the only release she could. Until Walsh had died.

Oh, that'd been sweet, coming down to find him on the kitchen floor, croaking for help. And, yes, she'd pulled up a kitchen chair to watch the hate, terror and finally the nothingness in the bastard's eyes as he died, slowly, alone and in pain.

She'd been careful. She'd not trodden in the wetness on the kitchen floor where his bladder had emptied; even then she was planning what she'd say and do. No-one was going to know what had happened. She was taking Alan and getting them both clear, as fast as they could.

Yes, she'd looked for his hiding places until she'd found all of his filth, everything, and hidden it safe, where no-one else would find it. Fitton and Yolly had taken Alan away somewhere that day. She'd been afraid they wouldn't bring him back at all, but they did, and she'd stood up to Fitton with all the steel she had in her, all the while screaming inside. When they'd gone, she finally called the ambulance. She'd said afterwards she'd been upstairs, in bed – her period, she'd claimed – and had come down hours later to find him dead.

Two days later they'd packed their cases. Fitton had given them money; she'd told him where Walsh's filth was. She'd only heard years later about his death, and the priest's; about Yolly.

She'd got him away from there, made sure that no-one would ever know what they'd been put through – never prove it, anyway. First Manchester, then London, shaking the bastard North's dust off their feet.

Even though Alan had told her: told her how Fitton and Yolly had taken him with Mark, Sam and Johnny to an abandoned mill; how the Shrike had come and taken the other three, but rejected Alan as too old. Walsh had wanted rid of him, and then, presumably, it would have been her turn.

Fitton was taking the boys to the farmhouse on Dunwich Lane; the Shrike was waiting. Alan had begged her to call the police. But there was no trusting them; no knowing which one was Walsh's friend. And Walsh had loved to taunt her how Alan would be put in a home, become the prey of a dozen predators like Walsh or Fitton or Father Joseph, if the police ever knew. In retrospect, would that have happened, even then? Perhaps not, but she couldn't be sure. She was only just technically an adult herself, and she'd learned not to trust the authorities. Or anyone else.

So, no. No phone call to the police, even an anonymous one. Her priority was getting Alan clear. So, yes: she'd left three children to the Shrike.

Did it bother her? Some nights, if she let it. Guilt was a luxury. She had it now, she hadn't then. But it'd been different for Alan. They'd visited him soon after, shown him what the Shrike had done. He'd started to tell her. She'd begged him to stop.

Years later, she'd hired investigators to find them. Even Alan – *Allen,* by then – hadn't known. It was for her, not him. If they were alive, Alan couldn't have seen their ghosts. But there was nothing. Sam, Johnny, Mark had effectively ceased to exist one October day in 1985.

Muffled squeals from the next bed.

So tired of this now. She pulled the covers back, stood, stumbled across the room. Would tomorrow be the end of it? The debt's final payment? Oh, please. He'd retire; she'd make sure of it. And perhaps – oh, just perhaps –

he wouldn't need her comfort again. Perhaps she could finally have her own life.

She could ignore him. She could pretend she hadn't heard. Just this once.

No, she couldn't. She'd never left him at a time like this. It could kill him and then where would she be? Infected with his bloody Sight for the rest of her life? No bloody thank you. She knelt by his bed. She'd wake and cradle him, sing to him. Try to believe the price was worth paying for what they had. Praying she wouldn't have to pay it this time. Knowing she would.

"Allen. Allen."

Praying, most of all, that his embrace wouldn't pull her through the mirror again, into the world of his terrible Sight.

ANNA TURNED IN the narrow bed, pulled the covers tighter. Whenever she closed her eyes, it seemed a pipe gurgled, a floorboard creaked, footsteps sounded outside, or voices murmured through the walls.

She turned again, closed her eyes, tried counting. She'd read somewhere the human brain took seven minutes to shut down for sleep. Sixty seconds times seven. What were six sevens? Six sevens are forty-two. So all she had to do was count to four hundred and twenty. One... two...

Finally she switched on the bedside light and sat up. She got out of bed, went to the mirror. Crow's feet at the corners of her eyes, thin lines at the corners of her mouth. Age. Your one and only life, Anna. Slipping through your fingers like so much dust because you're afraid to act, to give up even a little control. Or you've forgotten how to.

And tomorrow, Ash Fell. She'd only glimpsed what had happened in the evidence room, but it had been enough. She might die.

And here she was wasting money on a hotel room and she didn't even know why. Or perhaps she did, thinking of a pair of catlike eyes. Christ. Of all the times to start acting on impulse. Tonight, tomorrow morning – it could be her last chance to see Mary, and she was throwing it away.

She whispered: "I don't know what's real and what's not anymore."

At least her reflection's lips moved. She'd half-expected it to listen in silence. Or answer her back.

What was worse: to see what wasn't there, or what was?

You might have a touch of it too. She needed to know more than that. Well, there'd be time to visit Stangrove Wood tomorrow, get what answers she could.

She peeled off the t-shirt, went into the bathroom, ran the shower.

ALLEN LAID HIS head on Vera's breasts; his lips moved against her skin. She stroked his mussed hair.

"I'm afraid," he whispered.

"What of?" As if she couldn't guess.

"Ash Fell."

She said nothing.

"I was here, to begin with. In bed, in this room. But then the dark came in, you know what that's like now."

Her fingers tightened in his hair. "Yes."

"It came, and this room went away. I was in... a

corridor. The paint was coming off the walls. There were pieces of it all over the floor. Mark and Sam and Johnny were there. And then they were gone, and I was alone. Something... I heard something coming down the corridor. It was coming for me. I had to fight it somehow. And I didn't know how. Still don't. I'm a fraud. I'm a fake."

"Then let's go. We'll tell them you're ill. Anything. Drive back–"

"We can't. I'll have no peace till this is done with, sis. That's been made very clear. I'm meant to be here, doing this. This might even be the reason I was given the Sight. Maybe afterwards, I won't have it anymore. We'll be free."

"Free?" A whisper; a prayer.

"But I don't know... I might not be able to do it, sis. I don't know if I can. And if I can't, I'll die. I know that. I'll die."

Either way, this would be at an end. An ugly, shaming thought, but true. She couldn't pay this price anymore.

At last he slept. He wouldn't wake again now, not until morning. I need a drink. I need something. Disentangling herself from him was a slow, careful job, but she managed. She was damp with their mingled sweat, and other fluids too. She felt filthy. Fouled. What decent woman would ever want her, if she knew? The shower, she decided, wouldn't wake him.

DRESSED, ANNA APPLIED makeup, brushed her hair. She'd let it dry naturally. She studied her reflection, nodded. "You'll do."

Go downstairs, have a drink. She doubted anything

would happen. Not in Kempforth. Should have moved back to Manchester a long time ago. Well, there was nothing to stop her going at weekends, if she made it through tomorrow. Get the train or the bus. Even stay overnight, maybe. A hotel, or somewhere else if she got lucky...

She picked up her handbag. Christ. At the end of the day, Anna, if you actually think having a drink in the hotel bar is adventurous, then god help you.

A last glance in the mirror, and she went out.

CHAPTER NINETEEN

LIKE STAKOWSKI, BANSTEAD lived in a converted farmhouse in the hills above the town. In the dark, in the fog, the drive had been a nightmare, but now they were here.

His living room was cold despite the log fire lighting it. The stone-flagged floor didn't help. Spartan, too; there were crosses and religious icons on the walls, not much else. No Christmas decorations, even. No photographs of Mrs Banstead either; she'd left years before.

Banstead huddled in his armchair in dressing-gown and pyjamas, hot water bottle hugged to his chest. He was in his fifties. A shaved head to hide baldness; pasty skin and pale, bulbous eyes. Cheeks becoming jowls, a pursed smug mouth. He looked diminished. Sat in the opposite armchair, Renwick thought of the Great Oz, finally unmasked as a shabby old man.

"Sorry to have to disturb you, sir," she lied. "But the phones were still down and as you can see, there've been developments."

"Yes." Banstead looked up at the ceiling. "Give me a moment."

"Sir." Renwick waited. Banstead coughed hard. She glanced at Stakowski, stood by the sofa, then back to Banstead. He looked up, gave a weak, insincere smile.

"My confidence in you clearly wasn't misplaced," he said at last.

Renwick kept a straight face somehow, waited.

"So. As well as the four previous mispers, we've now evidence that the kidnappers have claimed other victims."

"Yes, sir."

"And have been operating in Kempforth far longer than we thought."

"That's correct, sir."

"And indeed, these... Spindly Men are linked to the case. And Ash Fell." He shook his head. "That place."

"You'd heard of Ash Fell, sir?"

"Of course I'd heard of it, Chief Inspector—" a renewed bout of coughing "—but even I thought the place had been demolished. There'll be hell to pay with someone at the council over this." Banstead got up and shuffled to the drinks cabinet. "A drink, Joan?"

"Just a small one, sir."

"Sergeant?"

"Designated driver, I'm afraid, sir."

"Ah well." Banstead handed Renwick a glass. "Very fine single malt, this. Well... you were right, I was wrong. Let's say no more about it."

"Of course, sir. Ash Fell's a big place. We don't know how many people we'll be dealing with and we're short-staffed. So I'd be tempted to request outside support."

Banstead's face twitched. Direct hit on his raw nerve.

"But on the other hand, I'm loath to delay. We still don't know exactly what the Spindlies want the kidnap victims for. And there's the risk they might abandon Ash Fell if we don't move quickly."

Banstead licked his lips. "Yes, I see."

"So my plan's this. Get as many qualified AFOs together as we can, draw firearms and get out to Ash Fell first thing tomorrow. At the same time – if comms aren't restored – I'll send officers out by road, request some additional bodies from one of the neighbouring forces. With your permission, of course."

"It's your investigation, Chief Inspector. I trust your judgement."

Translation: it's still your neck if it goes wrong. But she could live with that if it stopped Roseanne Trevor becoming another Julie Baldwin. Renwick sipped her whisky; it tasted like burning earth. Definitely a male thing, she decided.

"Hadn't had a chance to speak to DI Sherwood about the investigation. Won't be necessary now. Joan?"

"Sir?"

"This could be a damn good result, careerwise."

"Sir."

"Hate to lose you, but I suspect it's only a matter of time. Promotional opportunities around here are thin on the ground."

We'll see about that. "Sir."

THE HOTEL BAR was lit by candles on the tables, until about ten o'clock, when the lights came back on. The half-dozen guests still there blinked and squinted; the bar staff went table to table snuffing the candles out, although they were left in place for now. Outside, the Christmas lights swung from the lampposts in low gusts of wind.

Anna had picked a quiet little table in the corner, good for people-watching. A couple had been cuddling in another corner, kissing occasionally. One had long hair, the other short. It was only now that she saw they were both women. The long-haired one was more self-conscious now. The more girlish of the two; the femme. The butch drew her close, kissed her mouth. Anna saw the fight in the femme's body, between wanting to yield and the fear of being seen. *Don't let me stop you, girls.* She tried not to look. But did.

A woman came in. Tall, elegant. *My type.* She went to the bar. Anna looked back at the couple. They'd drawn apart now. The butch was frowning, hands on hips. The femme's head was bowed. Arguing in low voices; she knew the sound. *Don't argue. Don't fight. Don't be afraid like I was.* Am. *Be happy. Show me the way.* The butch's eyes met hers. *Look somewhere else.* Anna glanced over at the bar.

The tall woman was looking at her. Yellow, catlike eyes.

Anna blinked. It was Vera Latimer. When had she seen Anna? And how much had she seen? Vera mimed taking a drink, raised her eyebrows. Anna nodded, mouthed *dry white wine.* Vera nodded back, turned to the barman.

She'd had a glass already, drunk it too fast; she wasn't used to drinking alone anymore. She'd have to make this one last longer. Too much, too quick. *She's just being friendly; she doesn't know anyone here. Doesn't mean she's a dyke. Don't make a fool of yourself.*

Anna blinked and looked down. When she looked up, Vera was coming over.

VERA DIDN'T GET out much on the gay scene. It was acceptable now, but hadn't been back then, not with Alan to take care of. Oh it had been legal, but she'd felt herself on thin ice as it were, a girl her age looking after Alan. If they'd known she was a lesbian, Social Services would have taken him off her in nothing flat. Put him in a home.

Alan then; Allen now. Allen; always Allen.

Or maybe not. Maybe she'd been paranoid about it. Old habits died hard. They still did: she rarely went out cruising for it. There was an escort agency she used; she couldn't get into a relationship. Daren't. Because of Allen. No-one else could know what went on between them. Keep everything separate. Strict little compartments. No-one getting too close.

Alan then; Allen now. Allen; always Allen.

Anyway, she had pretty good gaydar, knew another dyke when she saw one. Anna Mason hid it well, but Vera hadn't had to see her eyeing up the two girls in the corner to know, although it had provided the final confirmation. They couldn't go back to her room, of course, but they could to Anna's. Well... see how things went.

And if Allen woke alone in the dark tonight?

Then just this once, sod him.

"Hi."

"Hello."

"Couldn't sleep either?" Anna asked. A weak smile. She looked better now. A little makeup, not much, just enough to make the difference. Her hair was loose and had a shaggy look – she'd let it dry naturally.

"Pretty much," Vera said. Better than the truth.

They sat in silence for a while. The two girls in the corner went out, holding hands. The butch tilted her chin up, looking round as if asking *yes, and do you have a problem?*; the femme looked down, shy, uncomfortable. Anna watched them go.

"Something you didn't used to see round here," Vera said.

Anna giggled, nervous. "Still don't, much."

Vera smiled and studied her. Anna coloured, looked down.

"Have you always lived here?"

"Pretty much. Well, most of... actually, no."

"Make your mind up, woman."

A shy smile. "No. Just feels like forever sometimes. I grew up here." Didn't sound like it. The brother, though – *he'd* sounded Northern. Maybe this one had done better for herself. "Lived away when I was at University. And when I was married."

"You were married?"

"Hard to believe?"

"No. Not at all." Vera looked very directly at her. A few long seconds of silence where Anna seemed to be nothing but two rather pretty, very wide hazel eyes. *Rabbit in the headlights.* Vera broke eye contact to put her out of her misery, picked up her wine glass.

"I was at college with him."

"Studying what?"

"History."

"Should've guessed."

"Sorry?"

"Before. All the work you'd done on Ash Fell."

"Well, it's, you know, very interesting."

Vera smiled, ran a fingertip around the rim of her glass. "Sorry, I interrupted you."

"Mm? Oh, Peter. My husband. Ex. Nice guy, really. We just... weren't suited."

"So you came back here?"

"About... God, about eight years now. Wasn't supposed to last this long."

"What happened?" Let her talk; better discussing her past than Vera's. Everyone had skeletons in the closet, but hers was more of an ossuary.

"Well, after the divorce... Peter got a job overseas he'd been after for a while. Sold the house, split the money. All very amicable, really."

"Unusual, these days."

"Like I said, he was a good guy. We just weren't–"

"Right for each other." Vera kept up eye contact. "You said."

Anna cleared her throat. "Afterwards I... moved back here. Stayed with Dad for a bit, then I got a little flat."

She'd missed something out, there. What?

"It was just supposed to be for a few months, till I got back on my feet, decided what I'd do next. But – well – got stuck in a rut, I suppose. I'd hardly seen Martyn in years, he'd got married. And then there was Mary, my niece. She was about a year old when I turned up. She's lovely."

"None of your own, then?"

"No. You?"

"No."

"Anyway, I was planning to move. Back to Manchester. I'd studied there."

"Good gay scene there as well."

Another long silence, her eyes never leaving Anna's.

"Yes." More silence. "My dad died."

"Oh."

"Heart attack. And suddenly there were all these things to deal with. The will, the probate. It hit Martyn hard. Mary too. And there was Nan to look after."

"Your Nan?"

"Mm."

"Wow."

"Yes. She's still going. Hundred and two this year. But it was very hard on her, losing Dad. We were all very worried about her when that happened. There was lots to sort out, generally."

"So you stayed."

"Yes. And then… Martyn lost his job, and then Eva…"

"So you've never quite run out of reasons to stay then?" Vera sipped her wine, looking at Anna over the glass.

"I wouldn't put it like that."

"No?" And was Vera any better? Really? "You should move," she said. "When this is over. Get out of here, while you still can."

Too much said there, and she'd not even finished her first glass. They were on the cusp, here. It could go either way.

"Perhaps you're right."

The wide hazel eyes; the thin, parted mouth. She'd be fierce, passionate, if all those years of pent-up longing were released. But a one-night stand wouldn't be enough; she'd want more. And then it could get messy.

Of course, Vera would be down south again soon. There'd be hundreds of miles between them. She could just gratify herself and walk away. But being a hard bitch was one thing; a brand of cruelty so like Walsh's was another.

She sighed, looked down, rubbed her eyes. "Think I'll turn in."

"Yes," said Anna. Was that relief in her voice? "Me too."

Vera went out, headed for the lift. If Anna followed… but she didn't. Another opportunity passed over, because it never seemed to be the right time. Now and then she met someone like Anna; someone who'd be worth getting serious about under different circumstances. But there was Allen; always Allen. Perhaps soon she'd be able to consider herself before him. But not today.

"WHAT'S THE COMMS situation?"

"Phones are sort of working again, boss."

"Define 'sort of', Mike."

"They're fine long as you don't want to ring anyone outside Kempforth."

"What the hell's been wrong with them?"

"To be honest with you, ma'am, I don't think any bugger's quite sure."

"Internet?"

"Nothing. Server malfunction, looks like."

"Radios?"

"Interference is the worst I've ever heard. Some communication within the town, but even that's touch and go."

"So we're best sticking to our original plan of sending a couple of officers out in one of the Land Rovers to get a report to someone outside Kempforth."

"Yes, ma'am. Any thoughts on who?"

"Funnily enough, I do believe two of our detectives aren't AFO qualified."

"Aye. Tranter's not been in the job long enough. And Janson–"

"No-one in their right mind would trust her with a gun."

"You said it, boss, not me."

"OK. Get them on the road first thing."

"Is DS Ashraf a qualified AFO?"

"I believe so."

"Let's bring him in, then. It's his case too."

"As you wish."

"Fancy a brew, Sarge?"

"Sounds good."

"You know where the kettle is."

"Yes ma'am."

"Mike?"

"Ma'am?"

"Thanks."

WHEN VERA HAD gone, Anna put her wine down. Had there really been a moment when something almost happened? She didn't know; she might be getting better at telling what was real from what wasn't, but some things were harder to be sure of.

Well, Rome wasn't built in a day. And perhaps it was for the best nothing had happened. Not with so much going on. There was always Manchester; there was always moving away. But the mist was thick outside and there was no knowing what might lurk in it. And beyond the mist, in the hills, was Ash Fell. Maybe she should have made a pass; there mightn't be another chance. She raised the wineglass to her lips, drained it in a single gulp.

THE TESTAMENT OF SERGEANT EDWARD HOWIE CONCLUDED like a lamb to the slaughter my only regret being i was no longer fit to lead dared not have men depend on me for their lives but there was no escape only the firing squad or another trip to dr yealland with his cold eyes an electrodes so when the bullet found my throat it was a relief as i fell back into the trench mud an saw the great red parabola of my life leave me rise up into the air an fall back into my face like a bitter rain an it was for this i gave my life this shitten worthless land where they have learnt nothing forgotten everything an lie like fat bloated maggots being fed so-called news blatant lies a wean could see through findin distraction watchin their fellow men and women debasin themselves masturbatin over obscene pornography buyin worthless trash and trinkets to maintain industries that would otherwise collapse on an on like dogs like pigs devourin their own filth an i judge i judge an i hate an i despise an i call them unworthy unworthy unworthy of our sacrifice unworthy of life

WE ARE THE DEAD

'D' BLOCK

A room with a rusted bedframe and its barred window overlooking the lawn; for a moment a figure can – almost – be seen sat on the restored bed, its corrupted profile limned in silhouette, light shining through the gap where nose, cheeks, eyes, jawbone should be. Slowly it turns to face us. It is impossible to tell if it weeps, or has anything to weep with.

CHAPTER TWENTY

Sunday 22nd December.

ANNA WOKE IN darkness and lay for nearly half an hour staring at the ceiling, wanting sleep again and not getting it, stomach clenching at the thought of what she'd committed herself to. Her eyes stung and felt damp; each breath sounded like a sob.

Couldn't go. Had to go. They were counting on *her*? Relying on *her*? They must be madder than she'd ever thought she was. Couldn't go. Had to go. Oh god.

Her mobile's alarm shrilled. She turned on the light.

5.00 am.

She dressed, checked out, walked home. The mist had thinned; the streetlights turned it a sodden orange.

At 5.30 am. she let herself quietly into her house, went upstairs. In the main bedroom, Martyn snored. She eased the spare room door open. Mary lay curled up on her side, stuffed toy clutched to her chest. Anna tiptoed over.

Couldn't go. Had to go. Had to, for her.

Anna bent; her lips brushed the soft hair, the smooth forehead. Mary mumbled, shifted in her sleep. Anna went still, but the child didn't wake.

She wasn't mummy, or daddy, but that didn't matter. She shouldn't have stayed in the hotel last night, all that really mattered was here.

She tiptoed out again, closed the bedroom door. The pole and hook were propped on the landing, as always. She hooked open the trapdoor, pulled down the folding steps, climbed up into the loft.

She changed into walking boots, combat trousers, a thick sweater. She looked in the bedroom mirror; she looked pale and sick. A little makeup hid the worst of the damage.

She turned off the light, climbed down, pushed the steps back up, pulled the trapdoor into place, looked at the door of Mary's room. The urge to go in again; hold the child, breathe the sweet soft smell of her hair–

No. Let her sleep.

Downstairs was a thick waterproof jacket with a tuck-away hood, gloves stuffed in one pocket, a woollen cap in the other. There was a backpack, too. She packed quickly; her files on Ash Fell, a pair of wind-up torches, a half-dozen items from the medicine cabinet, two bars of chocolate-coated Kendal Mint Cake, a Thermos of sweetened coffee. It would be cold there.

She let herself out, easing the door shut behind her. It was 6.00 am.

THE TESTAMENT OF LANCE-CORPORAL MELVYN STOKES
for with pluck hes brimming full hes old john

bull and hes happy when you let him have his head
for its a feather in his cap when hes helped to
paint the map with another little patch of red
for its melvyn stokes i am and i am an englishman
and on this earth there walks no prouder race
for i fought for land and king nought in return
asking till a german shell blew off my fucking
face i fought not for a girl women are soft easy
and inconstant creatures fit only to be despised
for all that they breed the next generation of
englishmen sing hosanna god save the king no i
fought for my country for england for my race for
it is as simple as that

6.15 AM.

At Stangrove Wood, there was a light in Nan's window.
She always woke early; Anna had banked on it.

Nan picked up on the third ring, as if she'd been
waiting. A faint, indrawn breath, then: "Hello?"

"Nan, it's me."

"Anna? Thought so."

A buzz; the door opened.

6.18 AM. THE BRIEFING room at Mafeking Road. In front
of Renwick were Stakowski, McAdams, Wayland,
Crosbie, Ashraf, a Police Sergeant called Skelton and
twelve uniformed constables. This was it; all she had.
It'd suffice. It'd have to.

"Any questions?" Skelton – wiry and weathered, with
black, grey-flecked hair and beard – raised his hand.
"Frank."

"All due respect, ma'am, it's a pretty tall order for a team our size."

"I know. At present we can't get through to anywhere outside Kempforth on either landline or mobile. Same problem with radio, and the internet servers are all still down. I've sent two officers out by Land Rover to request some back-up."

"All due respect once again, boss, but mightn't it be better to wait for them?"

"We've a minimum of four mispers, possibly more." *Including Roseanne Trevor.* "We don't know what the kidnappers have in mind for them."

Skelton chewed his lip.

"I've no intention of needlessly risking any officer's safety. The kidnappers could be a comparatively small group we can handle with what we have. If not, we fall back, keep the area secure and wait for the back-up to arrive."

6.23 AM.

A thin dirt track, off a B-road off the Manchester-bound Dunwich Road South. A police Land Rover lay with its nose in a ditch. Colin Tranter sprawled in the long grass of the neighbouring field, still clutching the rock he'd smashed his skull with. He'd stopped screaming now.

Susan Janson lay across the steering wheel, face blackened. Older, less fit, her heart had burst before she could take Tranter's way out.

In the crackling static from the police radio were faint, murmuring voices. Some belonged to the living. Others didn't.

They weren't far from the main road, but their bodies would never be found and given decent burial. And their souls would never rest.

VERA LOOKED DOWN on Allen, lying tangled in the bedsheets. The thin, cruel early morning light showed the fine tracery in his cheeks that would become wrinkles, and the dark ugliness of the bruise flaring along his jaw. Stakowski, the bastard. His chest hair was almost all grey now. *Age*. He'd never looked so old, so depleted.

The bastard North had done this. Kempforth. The black sun. They should never have come back.

She snorted. As if there'd ever, really, been a choice.

As long as they got through this somehow. As long as *she* did. If nothing else, as long as she did.

Vera peeled off her nightdress and went into the bathroom; behind her, the alarm clock rang.

6.30 AM.

"How many of you are Specialist Firearms Officers?"

Four uniformed officers raised their hands.

"OK. Frank, I want six men on Dunwich Lane, along the old branch line, including two SFOs with precision rifles. If the kidnappers try escaping via the main access path, they'll have to come out near there. The other two SFOs come into Ash Fell with my team, along with yourself and four of your other armed officers."

Skelton nodded. "Very good, ma'am."

"We'll approach from the rear, through the woods. Search A, B and C Blocks first, then whatever's left of the Home Farm and Chapel. One we've eliminated them we can focus on the most likely locations – Blocks D and E, which have secure facilities for restraining violent patients, and the Warbeck building itself."

"Literally going round the houses," said McAdams. "Won't they spot us?"

"Ash Fell was built so the woodland hid each section from the other. With a little luck, we can use that to our advantage."

"It won't be a quick job," Ashraf said.

"No, but I can live with that. I don't want to delay anymore than we have to, but we won't help anyone by not doing it properly. We don't know their numbers or their capabilities." Or what they were. But now wasn't the time to think on that, if she wanted Roseanne to have a chance. That was Cowell's province. This was hers. "Also, there'll be four civilian advisers. Need to make sure they don't get damaged either. So, no heroics. Work in pairs, don't spread out too far. Questions?"

None.

"Alright. Report to the armoury."

WHEN ANNA FINISHED talking, she looked up; Nan looked back at her with calm, sad eyes. She nodded slowly, biting her lip, then picked up her teacup again.

"Suppose it shouldn't surprise me," she said at last.

"What shouldn't?"

"That place, darling. You really think I'd know nothing about it? We all knew. Even if we hadn't, your great-grandfather was there."

"Your dad?"

"Yes."

"He... he was a patient at Ash Fell?"

Nan shook her head, behind her spectacles her eyes glistened. "Anna, you've got to remember, dear, back in those days there wasn't any such thing as Social Security. You were on your own. And he'd lost an arm. Couldn't go back to his old work. Don't know myself a lot of what he did after the War. You didn't ask. Back then, the man provided for his family. That was it. You did what you had to do. He was a proud man. Strong, too. Even with only one arm, he was strong. Wouldn't have got the job otherwise."

"Job?"

"At Ash Fell, Anna. He wasn't a patient. He worked there."

"When did he..."

"In the thirties, love. Can't remember exactly when. Worked there through the war, and after. He didn't like to talk about it. It was awful for him. I mean, he'd fought at Passchendaele. Been through hell. He never talked about that, either, but... oh, it wasn't until all the other veterans started telling their stories that I realised how dreadful it must've been. I just saw what it had done to him and that was terrible enough. And those men, in that place... God, any one of them could have been him. But this was the Great Depression, you mustn't judge him too harshly, Anna."

Nan squeezed her eyes shut. Anna knelt by the armchair, took her hands. "I'm not judging him, Nan. I know how bad it was round here."

Nan pulled her hands free, half-raised them, let them fall back into her lap. "Oh, you don't know, Anna, you can't. It was terrible, terrible. And he'd come home and he'd drink, and I don't know what he was trying to forget, Passchendaele or that place." She took a deep breath. "But what choice did he have? In his state? Oh, that Gideon – Mister Gideon, he always called him."

"Gideon Dace?"

"Gideon Dace." Nan whispered it as if afraid to speak it aloud. "He was a terrible man, Anna. My da... only spoke about this once, you understand. Close to the end. He'd been drinking. He was ill. Very ill. Cancer of the throat, it was. Ah..." Nan shook her head. "It made him laugh to have someone like my father around. Most of his work was clerical, you see. But Gideon made him help with the tours as well."

"The tours?"

"Oh, you know, Anna. You know what those buggers did. He had to help. Open the doors for them, play the host. He was there the night it happened."

"What happened?"

"The night Mister St. John died. He wasn't supposed to be, but he was. He let them out, then locked the doors. No-one knew. Only me. He told me. And now you know too."

Nan sank back in the armchair. Anna took her hand again; Nan gripped it tight. The pictures on the mantelpiece: the tall man staring off into some terrible distance, the bowler-hatted man holding Nan's arm on her wedding day, trying to smile.

"Anna, love, I really don't think you should go."

"Go?"

"To Ash Fell. I don't think it's safe."

"Nan, I've got to. Eva could be there. There's a little girl missing. They need my help. I know more about Ash Fell than anyone."

"Don't bet on it, mate." Nan gave one of her fierce

little scowls. Anna laughed despite herself.

"I have to go," she said. "It's for Mary as much as anything else. Those things have come near her twice now. And... sometimes I'm not sure what's real and what's not, Nan. And that really scares me. But it's starting to look like some things I've seen were real, and–"

"Anna... we've never talked about this, I know. I don't think you wanted to, but I'm going to ask you now. When you were in the hospital, what did you see?"

Anna looked down. "Thought I saw Grandpa, once. And I thought I saw–"

"What?"

"The Spindly Men."

"It's the Sight, Anna. That's what it is. I think you got it from me, and I'm sorry for that."

"What are they?"

"*When the night wind blows on dale and fell, the Spindly Men come up from Hell*," said Nan. "That's what they used to say round here. I don't know much about them, love. Only that they were supposed to live on Ash Fell. And if they touched you, you died or went mad."

"I just wanted to see you first–"

"Because you know it could be dangerous."

Anna nodded. Nan stroked her hair.

"You're sure you have to go?"

"Yes."

"There's no other way?"

"No."

"Before you go, then, love, will you do something for me?"

"What?"

"Fetch my jewel box from the bedroom."

The box was a plain wooden thing, painted with a diamond-pattern of brown, beige and white; Nan had owned it as long as Anna remembered. There were only half a dozen pieces of jewellery inside; Nan took out a thin dull pewter cross, no more than three inches long, set into a pyramidal wooden base. A tiny metal Christ, detailed and agonised, was spread out on it. "Here. Take this."

Anna hesitated. "Please," said Nan, "for me." She folded Anna's fingers around it. "I'll say a prayer for you. I know you're not much of a one for God, but... maybe it'll help. Or maybe my father will listen."

"Your–"

He was here before, you know. I saw him. At the window.

"Has he been back?" she asked finally.

"Nearly every day. I didn't say anything. Knew you'd think I was going bananas. But it was him." She smiled. "It's alright. I'm not afraid. But I don't think I'll be here much longer. I think he's come for me. Expect it'll be quite soon now."

Anna just stared up at her. Nan was a constant; she'd always been there. Each Christmas, every birthday, she'd sigh and say this would probably be her last one. It was practically a tradition. But this was different: calm, accepting.

Nan winked at her, then reached out and, very gently, pinched Anna's cheek. "You go on now," she said. "Just take care, whatever you do."

Anna embraced the thin, hunched body. "Love you, Nan."

Nan's grip tightened. "Love you too, Anna." She let go. "Go on, now."

Anna nodded and stood up, blinking fast. Focused. There was work to do.

7.05 AM.

Silence in the kitchen. Martyn'd finished his cereal; Mary picked at hers, eyes down.

She'd woken a good hour before he'd got back last night. No aunty, no daddy; bastard power cut hadn't helped either. "Poor little mite were near hysterical," Mrs Marshall had said. "I know it's not been easy for you, but you've got to take better care of her." But she'd agreed to look after Mary today.

He should love her better than this, he knew. OK, the phones had been out last night, but he'd not even thought to try. But Eva might be alive; that pushed everything else out of his head. And if she was, if he could get her home, it'd all be right again. Just one more day, and he'd know.

And if Eva *was* dead after all? He wouldn't think of that. In fact, he *couldn't*; his imagination plain refused to go there. No surprise, that; not really.

"Love you, Daddy."

"Love you too, princess." And he did. He did. Just not enough; not the aching, unconditional way she loved him.

He wanted to tell her *Mummy's not dead,* but couldn't, not yet. *Mummy might not be dead*, maybe? But she wouldn't hear the *might*. Doubly cruel to raise her hopes, then dash them. Just a little longer, Mary lass. Then he'd know.

Mary pushed her bowl aside and looked up, eyes huge. Martyn went round the table, knelt, held her. She hugged him so hard he thought she'd crack a rib, her head against his chest. Her hair smelt clean and sweet. Martyn's back started aching, but he didn't budge. He'd stay like this as long as he had to. As long as Mary needed. He'd give all he could, all he had. He knew there should be more. Eva would've known, so would Anna. But he'd give all he had, even if it fell short.

Didn't matter. His head was clearer than in months. The depression, the flu-like debility, had drawn back, like he'd scared it off. He smiled at that; daft talk. But it felt like that. He had purpose again. If Eva was still alive, he'd walk through fire to get her back. And once that was done, everything else would fall into place. Everything would be alright. And there'd be enough love to go around for his wife and his child.

Mary's grip relaxed. She looked up at him, smiled; he ruffled her hair, smiled back.

"I've got to go out for a bit later."

"No!" Her grip tightened.

"Ow. Easy love. I've got to. But this'll be the last time. Promise."

"Promise?"

"Promise. Spend every bloody minute with you after this." If Eva was alive he'd have to spend time with her, of course. At home or the hospital. But Mary wouldn't mind that.

"Don't want you to go. Scared."

"It'll be alright. Promise. Anyway, thought we'd see if you could play round at Mrs Marshall's today?"

"'Kay."

"Thought you liked Mrs Marshall."

"Yeah. But…"

"Be back this afternoon, sweetheart. Back before you know it."

"Promise?"

"Promise."

7.10 AM.

Vera finished applying her makeup, clipped on two pearl earrings. A last touch of her hair. She nodded. Yes. She wore casual wear today – jeans, trainers, lumberjack shirt, zip-up fleece; all designer labels, of course. Simple but smart. Probably be ruined after today, of course. *The paint was flaking off the walls. Pieces of it lay all over the floor.* There'd be rats too; Shackleton Street all over again.

From the bathroom, the low insect buzz of Allen's shaver. He was humming: *Heelya ho, boys, let her go, boys...*

Vera washed the morning-after pill down with two quick swallows of lukewarm hotel coffee, put on her waterproof jacket. Their belongings were packed; they'd leave them at reception, come back for them after this.

The shaver's hum stopped; Allen came out of the bathroom, donned his shirt and white roll-neck and picked his long black coat up off the bed, eyes bright, hair brushed, skin cleansed and moisturised. The signs of creeping age were gone; he'd be ready to step out in front of the cameras, even if there weren't any.

"Ready?" she asked.

"Nearly." He took a powder puff, dabbed at his jaw to cover the bruise. "Where did you go last night?"

She looked at him. "The bar."

"On your own?"

"I had a drink with Anna Mason."

"Just a drink, was it?"

None of your bloody business. I've a right to a life of my own. "Yes."

"Really."

She breathed out through her nose. One way or another, for better or for worse, this was about to end. "Ready to go?"

A pause. "Yes."

THE PISTOL WENT in a hip holster. Then on went the bullet vest. Then the peaked cap with POLICE across it.

Stakowski looked across the room. McAdams caught his eye and winked. His own vest looked ready to pop free already, straining across his beer-gut. Wayland gave a last tug on his belt to ensure it was fastened properly, then put the cap on. No posing now. Crosbie pushed the magazine into his pistol and holstered it too.

The CID officers and Skelton all carried Glock pistols, the uniformed AFOs Heckler-Koch MP-5 carbines. The SFOs had G36 rifles, and there was a ram for door breaching.

Renwick tucked her hair under her cap. It looked too big; so did her bullet vest. She looked like a girl playing dress-up. She discarded the vest and picked a smaller one. Better.

Their eyes met. She took a deep breath, released it, and went out. Stakowski followed.

ANNA REACHED THE hotel at 7.15 am; she made straight for the breakfast room even though she'd rarely felt less like eating. Bacon, eggs, toast, sausage, black pudding: she could go all-out today.

She saw Vera and Allen at one table. Vera caught her eye; after a moment's silence, she indicated an empty chair beside them.

Anna sat down, smiled. "Hi." She wanted to tell Vera *you look lovely*. Didn't. Another might have been; another opportunity missed.

"Morning."

"Morning," said Allen, and looked away.

"Sleep OK?" Vera asked.

"Fine, thanks. You?"

"Yes." Vera's eyes didn't leave hers. Anna had to look away. Allen sighed loudly, rattled his spoon in his breakfast bowl.

Vera ignored him, glanced at her watch. "Ten minutes."

"Best work fast, then." Anna laid into her breakfast.

"Want a shovel with that?"

"Just stocking up on fuel."

"Well," Vera slipped her cigarettes and gold lighter from her handbag, "I'm stocking up on nicotine. See you in a minute."

Anna returned to her breakfast. "You sleep OK, Mr Cowell?"

"Like a baby." His smile was serene and utterly fake, eyes empty and screaming at the same time.

What would be up there, and what were they supposed to do when they found it? What good was a gun against the dead? Renwick and Stakowski must know that. And what did that leave them with? Cowell? She'd have called him a blatant fake before last night; she hadn't much more confidence in him now. Behind all the plans and preparations, this was madness. They must all know that. *And yet we're all going anyway, because we must.*

Had it been like this for her great-grandfather at Passchendaele, or the Kempforth Pals at the Somme? Waiting for the shelling to end, to go over the parapet and flounder through the mud into that vast, destroying machine? Like Moloch in the Bible, burning up a whole generation.

There'd been mutiny, like at Etaples, and rightly so. All those lives, sole, sacred, precious to their owners, cast away in their millions by incompetent brasshats and self-aggrandising politicians. The firing squad if you didn't go forward; the battle police waiting with cudgel and revolver if you fell back. There was courage in fighting that, too.

But they'd had a sense of duty, those men. There'd been courage, a readiness to sacrifice for the common good. Even the mutinies had come about when that had been abused. Was that gone too; did only a choice between greed and selfishness or bigoted fanaticism remain?

"It's half-past," said Cowell. He got up.

Vera was waiting in reception. Stakowski came in. He had his anorak zipped up, but it didn't quite hide the gun on his hip.

"Ms Mason."

"Good morning."

"Right. We all here? OK. Before we go, we're grateful to you all for your help, but this is a police operation. So we're in charge. You do exactly as we instruct you. Wherever we go, *we* go in first, you follow. And if you're told to get the hell out, you do exactly that. We clear?"

"Absolutely," said Anna.

"Mr Cowell? Miss Latimer?"

"Yes," said Vera. Cowell nodded.

"You OK, Mr Cowell?"

"I'll be fine, Sergeant."

"Alright, then. Appreciate this might not be easy for you, that's all."

Allen smiled tautly. "Thank you."

"The jaw alright? I'm sorry about that."

"It was necessary."

"I..." Stakowski coughed. "... I might have given you a harder time than I should, last night."

"I'm used to it," said Cowell. "But I appreciate..."

"Aye."

"Yes."

A pause. Stakowski coughed again. "Right then. This way."

Outside, he held open the Land Rover's door for her. "All aboard." Renwick sat in the passenger seat. Martyn was in the back. Vera and Allen got in another car.

"Is Mary OK?"

"Aye. She's next door."

"Mrs Marshall again?"

"Aye."

"The woman's a saint."

"Aye." Martyn grinned, then stopped as he saw Anna's face. "It'll be alright, sis. Once we find her Mam, it'll all be fine."

Oh Christ. "Martyn, we *might*. And even if we do–"

"She'll be fine."

"Martyn–"

"She'll be fine."

"Let's go," said Renwick.

Stakowski started the engine and pulled out. On top of one building, a line of pigeons, ranked along the edge of the roof like crenellations on a battlement. As the cars passed, they scattered in a metallic clatter of wings.

7.35 am.

THE TESTAMENT OF LANCE-CORPORAL MELVYN STOKES CONTINUED german brutes animals jealous of us our power england the empire was threatened what care i for the stinking french or weaselly belgians look at the mess they made of the congo not that i care overmuch for a few niggers if a whip is what it takes so let it be they are not as we are i am proud proud proud of my country i am proud proud proud of the sacrifice i made i will bear it without flinching even if my mothers shrieks still ring in my ears that one time she was allowed to see what the bastard hun had made of me my mothers shrieks my fathers groans the tears tears tears i could not see their faces only picture them for i had no eyes but the german shell had not harmed my ears oh no i could still hear

AT STANGROVE WOOD, Myfanwy pushed her walking frame to the window. Thin white mist drifted over the lawns; she couldn't see the hills. A shame; they reminded her of the Welsh landscape of her childhood.

The mist made things uncertain. The shadows beneath the willow tree halfway down the lawn, for instance;

she couldn't be sure if someone stood under it, staring up at her window.

"Just keep her safe," Myfanwy whispered. "You can do that, can't you? It's all I'll ask. I'll come with you without any trouble. I'm ready to go. But keep her safe."

Myfanwy waited, but there was no answer. Well; she'd done all she could. You did what you could and then you waited; you couldn't do much else. She turned away. She'd make a cup of tea, and then she'd wait. For the phone, the doorbell, or her father; whichever came first.

CHAPTER TWENTY-ONE

EARLY MORNING AND unable to sleep; Banstead shuffled into the kitchen in his dressing-gown, reached for the kettle.

Engines growled. He parted the Venetian blinds; outside, four police Land Rovers passed. Silhouetted figures sat inside; he glimpsed a rifle's barrel.

Banstead smiled. "Godspeed."

He released the blind, switched the kettle on.

ANNA PEERED THROUGH the window; the police were out of their cars and checking their weapons. Beyond, the woods were jagged and black; the trees were mostly evergreens, blocking the light out.

"Christ," muttered Martyn.

"You OK?"

"Fine. But... Jesus, this is real, isn't it?"

"Yeah." She nodded. With luck she'd be as certain of what was and what wasn't by the day's end. "Yeah, it is."

Stakowski opened the Land Rover's door, smiled. "OK, folks–"

Renwick stood waiting with Vera, Allen and an unsmiling uniformed sergeant.

"This is Sergeant Skelton."

Anna caught Vera's eye, smiled. Vera smiled back; it looked forced. *Concentrate, Anna.*

"OK." Skelton folded his arms. "My job's keeping you four in one piece. So, one: you all stay together so my men can protect you. There'll be three spread out in front, three at the back so you're covered from all angles. Effectively you'll be encircled. You stay within that circle at all times. Two: I tell you to do something, you do it. That's all. Ready when you are, ma'am."

Six officers – two uniforms with rifles, four with sub-machine guns – went into the woods; the others formed up around the civilians, and followed.

A barely visible path wound through the trees. Twigs and pine needles cracked underfoot. The pines' smell was fresh and sharp. Anna saw tiny flickers of motion in the corner of her eye – thin shapes ducking back behind the trees – but whenever she looked, there was nothing there.

Stop it.

"Hold up," someone whispered.

"What?" Skelton asked.

"Fence."

"Jesus," Stakowski murmured. A fine barbed-wire mesh stretched between twenty-five-foot concrete posts. "Meant business when they put this up."

"Get us in," said Renwick.

Crosbie and Wayland used cutters to snip a hole in the fence. Fresh movements off to each side, beyond the ring of armed officers; Anna forced herself not to look. *Nothing's there. You're imagining things. How are you going to cope once you're inside?*

They filed through the hole. The path through the trees was harder to find after that; no-one had come this way in years.

"We're here," someone said.

Ahead was an eighteen-foot-high red-brick wall topped with iron spikes, a small wrought-iron gate set into it, black and rust-pitted, with a weathered plaque saying ASH FELL VETERANS' HOSPITAL AND SANITARIUM. A rusted chain and padlock secured it. Beyond it an asphalt path led through ranks of thin bare trees.

Spindly trees could hide Spindly Men. So many things she might, at any moment, see, and no knowing which were real, which weren't.

Focus, Anna. You're finally here; finally about to see this place for yourself. You wanted that. Now you have it. So pull yourself together.

"Allen?"

Allen was staring into the woods. Vera put a hand on his arm. He blinked, patted her hand. "I'm alright." Anna wasn't sure which of them he was trying to convince. He took a deep breath, let it out again.

"Open it," said Renwick.

Wayland took the cutters to the chain, which snapped with a heavy *chunk*; Crosbie lifted chain and padlock free. The gate grated open; a low, moaning wind rose from nowhere and as abruptly fell, and the woods were still again.

*   *   *

THE PATH BULGED and cracked where roots grew under it; the sky was visible through the branches now, although they snagged at Anna's clothing. Allen snapped off a twig. "Rowans."

"AKA mountain ash," Stakowski said. "Hence Ash Fell." He winked at Anna. "Some of us paid attention. What about 'em?"

"They're also a traditional defence against witchcraft."

"Witchcraft?" Skelton's eyebrows rose nearly two inches. McAdams and Crosbie exchanged glances; Wayland blew out a long breath and turned away. Ashraf looked from one of them to the other, glanced up the path towards Skelton's men.

"Meaning?" asked Renwick.

"Maybe something. Maybe nothing." Allen pocketed the twig. His fingers shook. "But a little extra protection can't hurt."

There was a rowan branch inches from Anna's face; she snapped off a twig, slipped it into her pocket beside Nan's cross. The old faith on one side, the new on the other. Maybe one of them would help.

THE TESTAMENT OF LANCE-CORPORAL MELVYN STOKES CONTINUED oh mamma mamma no shut up mummys boy stop your skriking be a man stand up like an englishman face it uncomplaining triumph and disaster impostors both but brutes though they are who was behind the germans dreams of empire who inspired them to overreach themselves but the jews the jews the sheenies the yids the kikes pinchprick bastards christ killers dragging war and strife with them wherever they go lower jaw

shattered shell fragment utterly tore away upper
mandible nasal cavity flesh of cheeks cheekbones
eyes eye sockets partially destroyed but not
dead christ not dead still alive

THE WOODS GAVE way to open ground, and B Block
came into Renwick's view; a squat, flat, single-storey
building, but with a small tower at each corner.

"It's mostly on one level because of all the missing-
limb cases," Anna said, "but that didn't leave much of
a view. Hence the observation towers."

"Not much good if you couldn't walk," Renwick noted.

"There were lifts. But the idea was, if you could get
up there yourself–"

"You jolly well would."

"Pretty much."

Renwick half-smiled, then turned away. "Mike?
Frank?"

"Boss?" Stakowski approached, Skelton in tow.

"Just had a cheery little thought about what lovely
sniping positions those towers would make."

Stakowski nodded. "What d'you reckon, Frank? Keep
the marksmen back here for cover, send an advance
party to secure the entrance?"

"It'll do. Nice to know your army years weren't
completely wasted."

"The odd bit of information did stick in my head."

THE MAIN DOORS opened easily; inside, B Block was
mostly a succession of individual rooms, many still
housing stripped, rusty bedframes.

The lifts were beyond use – ancient iron cages hanging from rusted cables – so they climbed the observation towers' winding staircases to the top, but found only the pigeons' leavings: feathers, dried excrement, scattered bones.

But there were other rooms, too. In one, artificial limbs hung from hooks, waiting to be attached to stumps. After the last of the officers had filed out, leaving Renwick alone with them, they swayed slightly. No, that was the dim light playing tricks. There was no draught; the dust lay undisturbed. And that arm's fingers couldn't have moved; they were metal and terracotta, nothing more. They weren't curling slowly into fists behind her back when she turned away. Enough. She had work to do.

They found false legs, too, and perished rubber tubes and bags for the colostomised and emasculated. But no masks; not here. And no hostages, alive or dead. Only dust, long undisturbed.

Renwick met Stakowski's eyes; he bit his lip. The fear, now, that this was all they'd find. *No. Banish emotion. Do your job if you want that child to live.*

"Boss?" Ashraf. "Wayland's found something."

She found Wayland in one of the day rooms at the centre of the block, crouched over a familiar pattern etched on its dusty floor; five lightning zig-zag lines, connecting at a central point. The Black Sun, Cowell had called it. In its centre lay a small gold bracelet.

Renwick held a hand out. "Evidence bag." Stakowski passed her one. "Get a picture first."

"Ma'am." Crosbie snapped half a dozen pictures from different angles with a digital camera. When he was done, Wayland picked the bracelet up with a pencil and dropped it in the bag.

"Mr Cowell, can you tell us anything?"

"I think you know as well as I do what that symbol is, Chief Inspector. As for this..." Allen took the evidence bag, held the bracelet through the plastic. "It belonged to..." he closed his eyes. "Tahira Khalid."

"Considering there's a bit shaped into the name TAHIRA, I'd say we're having a good day all round for deductive reasoning," Stakowski said, and winked.

Renwick stood up. "Let's finish up here and move out. And stay alert."

Outside, it was lighter, the sun higher in the pale, clouded sky; it only made Renwick feel more exposed. At least it took her mind off what relic of Roseanne Trevor's they might find, in the centre of a symbol scrawled on a dusty floor. Or what purpose it served.

THE TESTAMENT OF LANCE-CORPORAL MELVYN STOKES CONTINUED unable to smell taste see even to eat pureed mush poured down my throat in a tube at least i didnt have to look on what they made of my face or the faces of the others here in this place this place this oubliette french word hate the french despise them but oubliette its a good word a place of forgetting an old cell hidden under castles in ancient times where you put folk you wanted forgotten about this place is one vast oubliette for people like me that nobody wants to be reminded of understandable as wars must still be fought and there are always faint hearts cowards communists anarchists and all their lily livered verminous kind seeking to sap our will to fight and what better fodder

for their **propaganda** than such as i who stand
mute witness to the sacrifice made and offered
willingly for the glory of the nation the empire
the race the land

CHAPTER TWENTY-TWO

A BLOCK STOOD two storeys high. A curved roof; high windows. From its side, the long connecting corridor snaked off through the woods towards Warbeck.

As before, once the advance party had reached the main entrance, the others crossed the overgrown lawns, ringed by Skelton's men.

Anna walked ahead of Vera, beside Martyn. She glanced behind her, smiled shyly. Vera smiled back, wished she'd tried harder last night, imagined kissing that thin mouth. Anna looked away.

Renwick tried the double doors; they were locked. "Alright. Ready?" Ashraf nodded. "Then let's go."

Ashraf and McAdams swung the ram between them; the doors flew wide with an echoing crash. Inside was only silence and dark. For a moment, Vera thought it would flow out to meet them.

COLD DAMP AIR that smelt of rotten wood, like her old

room at Shackleton Street. Moss and char, wet concrete dust, the ammoniac reek of animal piss. Vera imagined spores taking root in her lungs; she covered her nose and mouth with her chiffon scarf.

Flakes of old paint crunched underfoot. *I was in a corridor. The paint was coming off the walls. Pieces of it all over the floor.* Walls and ceiling were bared; wires hung down from above. In places the wooden tiling had come away from the concrete floor. The room doors gaped, ajar. Inside one was a naked bed frame.

Bare, wretched; like her room at Shackleton Street. Some of Walsh's clients had liked tying her up. But you didn't need that to feel helpless. No, *helpless* wasn't the word. *Powerless* was better. *Choiceless* was best of all: left only with the options of spreading your legs with or without a slapping to compel you.

Allen walked, hands in his pockets, occasionally running fingertips along the walls, looking solemn, sensitive and slightly puzzled. *Presentation, Allen, presentation.* It looked posed, faked. If only. None of this would be real; there'd be nowt to keep them here, nowt to have brought them to begin with.

Nothing, *not* nowt. Nowt *is Lancashire dialect. Nowt is the bastard North. Nowt is everything you wanted to get away from. Not* nowt. Nothing.

What if they were angry, the dead, about the lies he'd told, the times he'd faked it? She was as much in the firing line as him, then; she was the one who'd got him giving 'readings' to friends and neighbours, then doing 'psychic nights' in pubs. Who'd turned him, in the end, into a performer who didn't know if he was lying or telling the truth anymore.

Well fuck you if you're judging us. After what we'd

been through, we had no rights? The Sight was all we had – so yes, we used it. We gave something back. Charities – NSPCC, Barnardo's. Not enough? Well fuck you twice. We did what we had to. You fuckers didn't help, we got nothing we didn't fight for, so fuck you.

Had she expected an answer? None came. Only the black, hungry silence of the place. Hungry, yes. Expectant. It was *waiting*. Walking down the corridor, Vera looked straight ahead; if she looked into the rooms she might see people standing in the doorways. Except they wouldn't be people anymore. And she couldn't bear that.

THERE WAS A day room here, too, at the centre of the Block. It seemed inevitable they'd find something there. Tables and chairs were stacked neatly against the walls; in the empty room's centre the Black Sun was etched on the floor in something dark – Blood? Shit? – with a pewter ring in the shape of a skull at its centre.

"It's engraved," McAdams said.

"*To Ben from Dani 4 Ever,*" Allen said, staring at the far wall. McAdams looked at him, then Renwick. Allen turned. "Yes?"

"Well?" asked Renwick.

McAdams nodded, dropped the ring into an evidence bag. "Ben Rawlinson."

OUTSIDE, ANNA STOOD hugging herself; Martyn stared off into the woods.

Vera touched Allen's arm, drifted over to Anna's side. "You OK?"

Anna nodded. "Just… this place. Funny, spent so long trying to get to see it–"

"Yeah."

They looked at each other. Vera's hand stole out; her gloved fingers brushed Anna's. *Perhaps after this*, Vera wanted to say. But there wouldn't be time. Anna looked down. Vera took her hand away.

"Alright," Renwick said. "C Block."

THE TESTAMENT OF LANCE-CORPORAL MELVYN STOKES CONTINUED o the rage that churns within me when i think how our blood was wasted how we fought germany again and yet should not have for see what they had built and they were right about the jews i say it clearly right about the jews i would have fought alongside mosley and his blackshirts to save this country while there was still time but instead i rotted slowly here without a face no face faceless i was here being fed through a tube a tube a fucking cunting bastarding fucking bastard tube rule britannia britannia rules the waves britons never never never shall be slaves but so they have become the niggers the pakis the yids the chinkies and filthy disgusting queers sodomites and perverts sticking their dicks up one anothers arses where all the stinking shit comes from and sucking one anothers dicks loathsome creatures loathsome hitler was right about those too oh yes i heard all about him even in here

*   *   *

INSIDE, STAKOWSKI SAW, C Block was much the same as A Block. Paint flaked from bare walls, ceilings and the crumbling wooden doors of individual rooms that stood ajar to show emptiness within. Barred windows that opened no more than an inch so you couldn't jump out. You couldn't stop the truly determined, but you could litter their way with obstacles, buy them time to think better of it.

This time they went straight to the day room. Another Black Sun was etched on the dusty floor, a purse containing Danielle Morton's driver's licence in its centre.

After that they searched the rest of the block: operating theatres, steel tables, cracked glass cabinets. Bottles with faded labels, half-full of murky fluid.

Crosbie pushed open a door, shouted: "Sarge!"

Stakowski jogged over. Renwick was already there. Inside–

On the walls, hung with skeins of cobwebs: crumbling plaster-casts of broken faces. *Gueules cassées.* Below them, on a work-bench, were a dozen masks, the paint flaked off, the metal beneath gone to rust and verdigris.

On the floor: three women. Dead maybe a couple of days.

"Christ."

Martyn Griffiths stood in the doorway. Anna caught at his arm. "Martyn–"

"Get him out of here," Renwick said.

"Get back behind my men," snapped Skelton.

"I know her." Martyn pointed.

Renwick raised a hand. "What?"

He came in. "Friend of Eva's, from the class. Dunno her name. That one, though–" pointing again "–she's called Alison. Dunno the other one at all. Sorry."

Griffiths' face was pale. His sister hugged him about the shoulders, but he hardly seemed to notice. He'd gone like stone. Stakowski had to look away; he'd been there, with Laney, knew all too well what it was like.

Stakowski went to him. "Look, Mr Griffiths, maybe you coming with us weren't the best idea. What we might find here... you don't want to see it."

"Martyn," said Anna, "Sergeant Stakowski's right."

Martyn's lips parted wetly, gulped air. "I'm going on."

"We don't know what we'll find here, sir–"

"I'm going on," said Martyn.

Stakowski nodded. "Alright."

"Can I?" said a voice.

Renwick nodded.

Cowell skirted the bodies, went to the table. He reached for one of the masks, looked askance at Renwick.

"Go on," she said.

Cowell picked a mask up with his fingertips. It was brittle and fragile as an autumn leaf. He closed his eyes, sucked·in a breath.

"Anger," he said after a moment. "I'm getting... A terrible anger. But someone else... someone else needed the masks."

"Who?"

"But these were rotten. So they had to make more."

"Why?" said Renwick. "Are they disfigured too?"

Cowell didn't answer. He stared ahead, mouth open.

"Allen?" Vera reached out to touch his arm, but didn't.

Cowell released a long breath, sagged against her. For a moment, he looked wearier than anyone Stakowski had seen. "I don't know what they are." He blinked, straightened. "Not yet. We have to keep going. There's no other way."

The women were laid out side by side; they draped a tattered swatch of old curtain across their faces. They'd come back later, see the bodies dealt with properly. As it was, they had the living to worry about. Stakowski felt the Glock's weight at his hip. Let the bastards come into his sights; he'd pay them back, for this if nothing else.

THE TESTAMENT OF LANCE-CORPORAL MELVYN STOKES CONTINUED never blamed master st john no it was that gideon yideon more like a jew name some changeling some jewish cuckoo in the nest turned this place into his freakshow so i lived out the years here o the rage they put me in e block in the end transferred me over because even as i was i lived on and raged against him against them all the english lion roaring the spirit of the race the power of britain the simple british soldier i killed my germans without a thought pointed my rifle pulled the trigger and down they fell like coats falling off pegs another i slew with bayonet another still beat to death with my rifle battering his square head till the bone collapsed and felt nothing cared not a jot but now they walk beside me all my dead

D BLOCK'S BRICKS were damp with morning mist. For a moment Martyn thought the walls themselves were weeping, bleeding out the sorrow of the years. You could feel it somehow, here, the pain and the misery the place had known. Fuck. And he was supposed to be the unimaginative one. Dad had said so often enough.

Enough of that. The enemies here you could catch hold of. Dad's disapproval, the endless, hopeless hunt for work, the crushing weight of the depression – all of them had been like trying to fight half-set jelly. Nowt to grasp, nowt to fight or catch hold of. Not like this. Here, he'd grab the bastards and choke the life out of them if he could.

They'd checked the chapel and the Home Farm before coming here. The chapel had seemed alone and desolate in its field of tall, waving grass; Martyn hadn't seen the stubby brown headstones filling the field until they reached its door. He'd made out the inscriptions on two or three: name, dates of birth and death. Nothing else; no rank or decorations.

The chapel had been empty, pews and altar long since stripped out, a bent sapling writhing from a crack in the concrete floor, seeking the light from the glassless windows.

There was little left to search at the Home Farm: farmhouse, dairy, bakery and mill were all burned out, the roofs fallen in. The greenhouse was a naked, rotted framework, the silo a hollow, rusted shell. Only D and E Blocks remained; those, and Warbeck.

The doors to D Block opened; the air blowing out was cold and rank.

I'd have been in one of these if I'd been around back then. Signed up, taken the King's Shilling. Get shot to shit or blown to bits, gassed, drowned in a shell-hole, that or ended up somewhere like this. If I were lucky I'd get out one day, with a missing arm or a permanent twitch or a fucked-up face. If not I'd be here, or staring at the wall in E Block.

But this was the worst, for him. How much could you strip away from someone, before they fell apart? Not much, in his case – a fucking *job*. He'd been going even then, after months of fruitless searching. And then Eva–

No. He wouldn't think on that.

But if you took away their fucking *face*? No job, though you'd be fed at least; you'd not starve. But what wife would stick with you in that state? He would have lost everything he'd lost already, if that'd been him, but not even the faint glimmer of hope of getting it back – and without even a *face*, the one thing above all else that told you who you were.

They filed past a dust-covered desk, then down the corridors. The wooden doors hanging open; each little room beyond a well to collect the wept-out misery. If you still had eyes to weep with.

"You OK?" Anna whispered.

"I'm f–"

They were near the end of the corridor when the crash sounded. Anna cried out, clutched at his arm; Martyn pushed her behind him as he turned. Bloody near soiled himself as well, not that he'd ever admit to it. Stakowski's pistol was already in his hands, so fast Martyn couldn't believe it had ever been in the holster; Renwick and the other detectives drew theirs. Skelton's men were already aiming their rifles and sub-machine guns down the empty corridor.

Empty, yes, but clouds of dust swirled in it. And something else was different; the corridor was darker. It took Martyn a moment to realise what; the doors to the rooms had all slammed closed and shut out the light from the windows. All together.

"Jesus," said Wayland. Laughter rippled through the

group; a whistle in the dark. Wayland grinned, flushing.

"We're not alone," said Allen. God, he was an annoying bugger. Reckoned he was on TV all the time, even when there weren't a camera in sight–

A slow, soft creaking, and a door swung slowly open, then another. And then they were all opening, sending fresh swirls of dust across the littered floor.

The corridor brightened. Martyn wished it hadn't; the light coming in through the windows seemed too bright, like a floodlight outside the block, and it cast shadows across the corridor floor, stretching out of each doorway. They looked like people. Sort of. But very long and thin, too long and thin to be alive.

Pale fingers groped around the edges of the doors. There was no sound, no sound at all. Martyn couldn't even hear his own breathing now. But puffs and coils of dust rose up off the floor to roll into the corridor as the rooms' occupants came out into view. Not much better than silhouettes at first, but then his eyes began to adjust and he could see the ragged, dirty remnants of khaki uniforms and white patient's smocks they wore. Those, and the dully glinting masks that covered all their faces. And the worn and withered flesh they unmercifully failed to hide.

Stakowski stepped past him, shouting, but there was nothing, no sound, as he swept the pistol back and forth over the gaunt, silent ranks.

The masks wholly covered their faces. Or where their faces should have been. Because this had been the home of the worst ones – not men with broken faces but men with no faces at all, men who'd never again eat a meal not poured down their throats by a tube. Dust swirled from another door as an old-fashioned wheelchair rolled out into the corridor. Something was huddled in it. No legs hung down over the edge of the seat. In place of a left arm a sort of flattened paddle beat weakly at the air. A right hand lacking all but its thumb and forefinger clutched the doorframe and levered the chairbound thing out into the light.

Its head jerked round; it stared straight at him. The face the mask depicted was stolid, unexceptional. He might have been a decent-looking lad; no movie star, but he'd have had his share of girls back when Nan was a toddler. But not now, and never again. The pincer-like right hand rose towards the mask.

Simultaneously, in the same dead silence, the other masked figures raised their slow hands. The one closest to Martyn, in full uniform, had a mask that reached down from his scarred forehead to his chin. His face was thin and gentle-looking, or would have been had it been real.

The thing in the wheelchair began lifting its mask away; Martyn glimpsed a wet, lipless hole that might once have been a part of a mouth, gaping and wetly sucking at the dank, dusty air.

The uniformed man lifted his mask too. Martyn caught the dimmest impression of a black gaping hole beneath it, a nothingness that should've been a face, and he drew breath to cry out, even if it would never be heard.

The corridor dimmed again suddenly; the doors didn't close, but it was as if the floodlights beyond the window had gone out, plunging the corridor into darkness. Stakowski crouching, gun aimed. Torches flashed into the dark and seemed to fade out within inches, illuminating nothing, and then the sound returned.

"–your hands in the air, do not move, or I will have no alternative but to open fire–" Stakowski stopped as the dull natural light they'd had before returned, and the corridor was lit again. Dimly still, but not the near-dark of seconds earlier. The doors to the rooms stood open; the dust settled and stayed undisturbed. But beside one door near the corridor's end, empty, cobwebs trailing from its arms and handles, sat an old, moth-eaten wheelchair.

"Jesus," Crosbie said. The big Asian copper – Ashraf – held his pistol out ahead of him, muttering what sounded like a prayer.

"Did anyone else see that?" Anna's voice shook. Martyn put an arm round her. "Did you?" she asked.

"Aye, sis. Saw it."

"Did you?" She looked at Renwick.

"Let's all stay calm, Ms Mason. Everybody."

"Oh god." Anna was shaking. Martyn held her up. Vera put a hand out to her, then let it drop. "Oh god."

"OK," Skelton said. "Bishop, Desai, Larson, you stay here, cover us. Rest of you, with me. We're checking the cells."

ALL THE ROOMS were empty, of course. No sign of hidden trap-doors or ceiling hatches could be found. Stakowski holstered his pistol, wiped a thin sheen of sweat from his forehead. "Nothing, ma'am."

"I told you," said Allen. "We're not dealing with a flesh and blood enemy."

Skelton glanced at him, then back to Renwick. "What next, ma'am?"

"We carry on," Renwick said. "We search this

building, the same as the rest. Keep your eyes open, and remember why we're here. You're all serving police officers. I expect you to handle a damn sight more than a few party tricks."

"Party tricks?"

Renwick didn't look at Allen. "Party tricks, Mr Cowell."

"Chief Inspector, if I've ever encountered a genuine supernatural phenomenon–"

"Party tricks," Renwick stared him down. "Someone is here, and someone's playing silly buggers. Whatever that was, we have a job to do. So let's do it."

Cowell opened his mouth to speak; Vera caught his arm, murmured in his ear. She got it, even if he didn't. Renwick didn't believe the 'party tricks' crap any more than Martyn, but she was doing what she had to, to stop a panic in the ranks. That's what Cowell didn't get. There were people who needed their help.

She was right, they had a job to do. Martyn understood that; so did he. He was here to find Eva, and if the coppers all ran away they'd drag him off with them, and he wouldn't get to do it.

Thin fingers squeezed his arm. He turned. Anna. He managed a smile. She managed one back. She was white; the lines at her mouth and corners of her eyes showed stark against her skin.

"Come on," he said.

They searched the rest of D Block, and all they found was what they'd come to expect: the Black Sun painted on the day room floor, and in its centre–

"Aw Christ," Wayland said.

"Bastards," said Ashraf.

Stakowski turned to Renwick. "Ma'am–"

She raised a hand for quiet, not looking at him, not looking at anyone. Stakowski fell silent.

The pink romper suit lay at the centre of the Black Sun. Empty, of course. Renwick stood over it, looking down, not speaking, not moving, for nearly a minute. Then she crouched to inspect it more closely, reached a gloved hand out to touch it. Martyn found himself stepping backwards. This felt too close, too personal.

"She's looking for blood," Anna whispered.

Martyn looked back at Renwick. If she'd heard Anna she didn't react. At last, she stood up and let out a long breath.

"Roseanne Trevor?" asked Stakowski.

"No name tag. But she had a pink romper on when she went missing."

"Fuckers," Crosbie said. Even Skelton had his jaw clenched, so tight Martyn could see the muscles jumping in his cheek.

"Take it easy, folks," said McAdams. "Alastair. Deep breaths, mate. Mind on the job." But it still took him two attempts to get his pistol back in its holster.

Renwick stared down at the suit, not speaking; Stakowski coughed. He stepped in close, dropped his voice to a whisper. "Ma'am? What now?"

"What now?" Renwick looked up, took a deep breath. "Bag and tag the evidence, Sergeant. Then we finish up and move on. They're either in E Block or the Warbeck building. So we search those: every room, every corner, every inch." Her voice was quiet, clipped and level. "And we find these bastards."

CHAPTER TWENTY-THREE

E Block stood black against the bleached, washed-out sky. Its doors were battered and dented; old damage, from the night St. John Dace had died. Her great-grandfather's face, the eyes staring into that terrible distance. Fighting to smile on Nan's wedding day. *He let them out, then locked the doors.*

She'd tried a few drugs at university. Nothing serious, dabbling. A joke she'd heard: *there's a time and place for everything – it's called college.* She'd smoked weed – who hadn't? – sampled psilocybin, speed and, once, LSD. Lying on a couch in a friend's rented house, she'd seen a tree outside the window, backlit by pre-dawn light. Just for a second, the branches had shivered and *changed*, morphed into four cartoon warthogs peering in through the window. Only for a second, and then it was a tree again, but she'd lain there for almost an hour gazing at it, rapt, waiting for it to shift again. Since D Block, this felt more and more like a less benign version of that experience. At any moment the naked rowan trees threatened to shift into the mangled shapes from the D Block corridor.

We know it. We all know it. Whatever's waiting isn't human, or even alive. Bullets will be worse than useless. We can't harm them, but they can harm us. And yet we go. Like sheep to the slaughter, out of duty, obligation or simple herd instinct.

Like the Kempforth Pals, again, or Nan's father at Passchendaele. Anna's hand slipped into her jacket pocket, found Nan's cross. It gave her comfort, just for now, it couldn't hurt. And there was Mary. If any threat to Mary came from here and it took Anna's life to end it, so be it. The calm with which she accepted that surprised her. And she walked on.

Just for a second, the bedraggled lawns around the building were populated with thin, dark figures, some shuffling, some gazing, motionless, into some unfathomable distance. For an instant, heads turned towards her. But she blinked, and the grounds were empty.

Most of the ground floor was the canteen, vast and empty. Anna couldn't see any sign of life. A faint clatter from upstairs. Stakowski put a hand on his gun.

"Frank," Renwick whispered. "Let's check upstairs."

Skelton and Renwick led the way; the rest of the group followed, the civilians within the protective ring of Skelton's men.

Upstairs: two floors of dusty, peeling corridors, empty and lightless; doors that gaped open into bare, narrow rooms. Wayland and Crosbie went into one, moving out along opposing walls. Wayland covered the wall opposite him, plus the ceiling; Crosbie covered the other wall and the floor.

· The same exercise was played out in the other rooms, one by one. They were the same, at first glance, as in the other blocks. But then you started noticing things. The restraints hanging from the rusted bedframes. Dark stains on this wall; scratches scored by jagged fingernails on that one. On another wall, words cut out of newsprint: IN HERE THE BLACK SUN SHINES. Below it, a collage of yellowed drawings: jagged black-and-white pencil sketches of screaming faces, jumbled splashes of mud-brown, blood-red, flame-orange, poison-gas-green, battlefield-mist-yellow in wax crayon. Again the feeling something was about to shift: that the chaos of the drawings would shape itself into whatever the artist had been trying to depict. Or the grey air inside that wretched room would form itself into a human shape.

No. She wouldn't see.

But it was too late. As she passed another room, the shadows on the wall above the bed thickened and clotted, solidified and sagged forwards, pouring off the wall onto the bed and floor. The blackness drained out of them to leave the white of a stained, grubby hospital smock and skin denied the light for decades. The man sat on the bed, face prematurely aged, black hair streaked with grey, vast eyes fixed on some distant vanishing point a million miles beyond the wall. Only for a moment, the time it took Anna to take a single step, before he darkened again into shadow and his substance drifted away, dispersing in the light.

Not real. She shouldn't have come here. She hadn't taken drugs in over a decade, but was this some sort of flashback? Or worse: was her sanity going, after all? They could always lock her up in one of these rooms.

She almost laughed. Mustn't. For a moment she was back in Roydtwistle. She'd had a small room there, with a window, a door, off a corridor like this. Oh god, she should not have come; the place was coming alive around her. Her mind was all she had, and it would be so easy to lose it here.

"Jesus," said Stakowski. A heavy iron door stood ajar; inside the walls were padded, like mattresses had been stuck to them, the door too except for a little gap for a spyhole. "An honest-to-god padded cell."

"Restraint room for violent cases," she said. "There were four on each level here."

"Four?"

"Some of the patients were seriously disturbed."

Like you, Anna? And she felt the shift coming. So easily done, the flick of a finger on Ash Fell's part. *You're so easy, Anna. I can flip you in a heartbeat, at a whim. You belong to me.* The dirt and shadows on the walls shifted from black to red; blood, and a clump of matted hair. Even with the padding, someone had injured himself. There was shit smeared on the floor too and something squatting in the corner in a torn straitjacket, gaunt face bleeding where its own nails had raked it, its lips curled back from brown and yellow teeth, eyes wide and bulbously staring. It was trembling. Fright? No, not fright; fury. The first figure had seen only the past; this one saw the present, but only through the prism of its rage. Suddenly it went still. Blinked once. Its head swivelled, a gun coming to bear, until those pale eyes found her.

Silence fell. Stillness; a wait that seemed endless. And then it straightened its shit-streaked legs, pushing itself up the wall to stand, eyes never leaving hers. It shuffled across the cell to the doorway – would no-one stop it, no-one help? Its clenched teeth looked like yellowed bone in a bloodless, unhealed wound; it stared at her with killing hatred, trembling as if bitterly cold. Everything else seemed to fall away; there was only this thing and its eyes.

And then it looked down, at the straitjacket sleeves across its chest, and its arms slowly slid apart, unfurling from its chest, bloodied hands emerging from the unfastened sleeves, the nails sharp. It looked up at her again. The hatred in its glare was undiminished, but the white-lipped snarl gave way to a distorted smile before it lunged for her with a soundless screech–

She yelped, recoiled, and its substance flew apart, scattering in the dim light that fell through the barred window high above, and the red stains on the padded walls were just the black of old dirt.

"Ms Mason?" Stakowski, frowning.

"Anna? You OK?" Vera was at her side, a hand on her arm. It felt like a tiny shock, her touch. Forget about that. Now wasn't the time. Martyn coming over as well; she waved him back. All eyes on her. Her face burned.

"Sorry," she mumbled. Act normal. Don't let them know you're crazy. Maintain control at all costs. "Thought I saw something." *Smile*. "This place. Sorry."

"I can relate to that," said Vera.

"Me too," said Stakowski. "You need to get out?"

"No. No. We won't be here much longer, will we?"

"Just to search the rest of it. But there's still the Warbeck."

"I can handle that. It's just this place." Her face still burned. This place disturbed them all, but she was the one who'd admitted it.

Mary. Focus. Keep going. Do what has to be done. Whatever it takes.

"OK, if you're sure."

She nodded.

"Let's crack on," Renwick said.

Vera squeezed Anna's hand. Anna squeezed back. A thin smile touched Vera's mouth.

"Come on, Vera," Allen said. "We've work to do."

Vera rolled her eyes, let Anna go. They moved away. *Probably best. Need to focus.*

"Sure you're alright, lass?" Stakowski had come to her side.

"Fine."

"Alright."

Martyn fell into step beside her, not speaking. Cowell had looked almost jealous. Did he know about her and Vera? Stupid. *What* her and Vera? Nothing had happened. *Almost* didn't count. Did it? But what was it to him anyway? Maybe he was used to having all big sis' attention.

Or perhaps he just wanted to get this done. Maybe what she'd just seen was a glimpse of the world he saw.

"No sign of anyone, ma'am," Skelton said.

Renwick nodded. "OK. Let's check out the canteen."

Following the others down the staircase, Anna glanced out of the barred window over the lawn. The grass was a tangle of green, with blotches of dead-brown scattered across it, all the way out to the woods. Dead-brown; khaki, almost.

The blotches shifted and stood up. Some leant on crutches or lolled in wheelchairs. Others had stumps for limbs – some with prostheses strapped to them, some not. Others lacked jaws, noses, ears, eyes. She saw a face where the skin had been drawn over the empty eye sockets and stitched shut. Others had no faces at all, just gaping bloodless half-healed holes. They closed in on E Block – some walked, some limped, and the wheelchairs rolled across the lawn with no-one pushing – as the bare trees at the woods' edge accomplished the shift they'd been threatening and more figures began crowding the lawn – the crippled and disfigured, the vacantly staring, the murderously raging – until they were crammed shoulder to shoulder, staring up at her. At *her*.

"Sis?"

Her eyes stung, blurring – she blinked.

"Sis, you OK?"

The lawns were empty. Tears, warm on her cheeks. She found a tissue, dabbed them.

"Anna?" Martyn said.

She managed a smile, even patted his big, decent, concerned face. "I'm OK. Let's just get out of here."

THE TESTAMENT OF LANCE-CORPORAL MELVYN STOKES CONCLUDED but i was one of those who came for st john dace o i was still a fighter a thing of terror i homed in on their screams like a bat hunting echoes and i killed killed until master st john shot me it must have been him who else would have had a gun it was nothing personal against master st john he was a good man once but gone soft weak probably yideon doping his drink with opium god knows what capable of anything the eternal jew and he fired into the hole that had been my face finished the job the german shell began all those years ago and nothing changes

this place still our prison and outside is the
last of england a swamp of niggers darkies jews
filthy disgusting queers the race doomed now lost
too late to be saved weakened and miscegenated
interbred with lesser races god king and country
mocked derided sneered at all that remains is a
fat bloated decadent remnant now deserving only
a quick death to end its misery its mockery of
life

ONE OF THE canteen windows was smashed, the bars
wrenched out; wind and rain blew in, mould and fungus
sprouted and instead of dust was a patina of mud, wet
dirt that had dried, softened and dried again, layer on
layer, one atop the other. In the centre of the canteen,
they found what they'd been looking for: the chairs and
tables had been pushed aside, and in that empty space
someone had drawn the Black Sun.

"Summat's different here," Stakowski said. "Nowt in
the middle."

Renwick let out a long breath. "So they're not done
yet. They want someone else. Maybe the others are still
OK."

"Boss—"

"I said *maybe*, Mike."

"Aye."

Cowell crouched by the symbol. "Of course. Five
blocks around a central building. Like a five-point star;
a pentacle. Or like the Black Sun itself."

Stakowski frowned. "Some kind of a ritual?"

"Oh yes." Cowell stood up, brushing his trousers and
coat. "I'd've thought you'd guessed that by now. It's a

ritual, alright. The question is whose."

"Sh," said Skelton, looking up. From above came footsteps, descending the stairs.

Stakowski, eyes still fixed on the ceiling, put his hand on his pistol.

"All civilians," said Skelton, "bunch up. Lads – form up."

The armed officers moved to encircle Anna and the others.

"Shit," said Renwick.

Anna turned. Suddenly there were people at the far end of the canteen. They hadn't been there before. Even in the dim light they were impossible to miss. Some wore stained white smocks; others, army uniform. Some sported missing limbs and faces; some grinned empty grins or stared into other worlds, barely aware. Some stood with bodies bent awry or continually jerking in response to bombardments long ended for everyone but them. And some snarled with perpetual rage, crouching as if to attack.

And in front of them, like a line of police at a demonstration, were the Spindly Men, with their masked faces and black, tattered capes.

Footsteps rang out from the far end of the hall. Anna turned; a similar crowd was forming there.

The devil, and the deep.

After all these years, her nightmares from the psychiatric ward had come, at last, to find her.

CHAPTER TWENTY-FOUR

"OH GOD," WHISPERED Vera.

For an instant the years between her and Shackleton Street vanished and she was huddled weeping on the bed, waiting for the next punter to come up the stairs. A victim again; prey. But then the moment passed; she'd never given anything up without a fight in her whole adult life, and she wasn't fucking starting now. Allen was white-faced, gawping. Vera grabbed his arm, looked for an exit.

Renwick drew her Glock. *Stay calm. Do your job.* Levelled it, two-handed, as the Spindlies closed in. *Pick a target.* The one in the middle, that one. She steadied the gun on him, right between the black-hole eyes in the mask. Stakowski moved to her side, raising his own weapon. The Spindlies came to a halt and stood regarding her and the other cops.

"Form a line!" Skelton snapped. His men fanned out and knelt between the Spindlies and the civilians, shouldering their rifles and carbines. Wayland and

Crosbie stepped behind them and aimed their pistols over them; Renwick, Stakowski and Ashraf fell back to join them.

"Mike?"

"Ma'am?"

She didn't look directly at him, didn't dare take her eyes off the Spindlies and the lost souls behind them. "Get the civvies out."

"What about you?"

"I'm not planning on croaking here either. Just get them out. That's an order, Mike."

Behind Skelton's line, Stakowski saw Allen and Vera sidling towards the smashed window. Yes, they could make it that way, if they were fast and if the mob at the other end of the hall didn't spot them. But the Spindlies seemed to be focused on the coppers. He saw Martyn square his shoulders, clench his fists. Anna pulled his arm, looking from him to the Spindlies to the window. She was white and breathing fast, almost hyperventilating, eyes so wide the whites encircled the irises completely. Stakowski sidled towards them. Slow, careful; don't attract attention.

Vera dragged Allen to the window, knocked the remaining pieces of glass out of the empty frame. "Climb over. Now."

He blinked, then nodded and started clambering out.

"Martyn." It was like trying to shift a statue. Anna knew he wanted to fight them, get Eva back. But they were already dead, the Spindlies and the horde behind them. "Martyn, come *on*."

"With me." Stakowski whispered. He had his gun out, pointed at the floor. "That means you, Mr Griffiths. *Move*."

One of the smock-clad patients turned his grinning head, looked past them at the window. Cowell was outside already, his sister crouched on the sill, half-in and half-out of the killing room. The dead started moving, and Stakowski raised the pistol. Renwick had given him a job; he'd bloody do it. "Behind me," he hissed, "and keep fucking moving. Don't make a sound."

The line of police started backing up. Vera climbed the rest of the way out. Her brother was already legging it across the lawns; she pelted after him. Two down, two to go.

"*Griffiths,*" said Stakowski.

Martyn stood rooted. Anna pulled at his arm. "Martyn."

"Armed police officers," Renwick shouted. "You're all under arrest on suspicion of kidnapping and murder."

Heads turned to study her. Shit. Now what? The other officers were waiting for orders. "Put your hands on your heads, lie down on the floor, you won't be harmed." Oh Christ Christ Christ. Dad. Daddy. Christmas with him and Morwenna, was that so bad? She should've rung him last night, before the phones went down.

The Spindlies began moving forward. "Stay where you are." She shouted it; her finger tightened on the trigger. Careful. You can't unfire a gun. "Hold still or we will open fire."

They had no guns that she could see, but they hadn't needed them to kill Pete Hardacre. Just a few yards between them now.

"This is your last warning," she shouted.

The Spindly in her sights paused for a moment, cocked his head. Impossible to tell with that mask on, but she thought he looked amused. And then he took another step forward.

"Fire!"

Renwick squeezed the trigger as she gave the command, and a neat little hole appeared in the Spindly Man's forehead; cracks raced out across the mask, but he didn't fall. Barely even hesitated, in fact. Just took another step towards her.

There was no fear, or even surprise. It seemed inevitable, somehow. She only blinked when every gun in the canteen went off in a fusillade, deafening. The rifles and carbines fired short, chattering bursts; the muzzle flashes lit the canteen's dim interior like a strobe. The Spindlies twitched and lurched back; the patients didn't even seem to register that. 'Her' Spindly reached towards her; she fired three rounds in his chest and he tottered backwards, then straightened and came forward again.

"Fall back. Move move move–"

But the screams had already begun. Two of Skelton's men fell writhing; Skelton stood his ground, firing at first one, then the other of two advancing Spindlies. One lunged, touched his face. The scream that came out of Skelton was higher, shriller, wilder with fright than Renwick would have believed possible. He dropped the gun and clawed at his face before falling, the shriek choking suddenly off. He lay still.

"Fucking move!" Stakowski screamed, and Martyn finally shifted. He ran, Stakowski with a hand at his back, and then there was a cry–

Stakowski spun – Anna had tripped, gone sprawling. Crosbie and Wayland had already turned, reaching down to grab her and heave her bodily at him. Stakowski caught her, reeling back under the weight, as the Spindlies lunged at Wayland and Crosbie. One touched its fingers to Crosbie's temple; he screamed and fell.

"Bastard–" Wayland avoided the first lunge at him, spinning and firing, half a dozen rounds slammed into the Spindly Man, but it hardly even slowed; just gathered itself over him and dived, hands reaching for his face. Wayland was screaming too now; Crosbie was on his knees, hands to his face, blood running through his fingers.

Movement to Renwick's side: McAdams, backing calmly up, firing again and again, every one a hit but changing nothing, until her Spindly – she could tell by the bullet-hole in its forehead – reached out, fingertips sinking into McAdams' chest. McAdams screamed; his arms flew out, his gunhand swung towards her and the Glock fired wild, again and again.

Stakowski saw it, of course. How could he *not* be watching out for her, whatever the circumstances? As soon as Martyn bailed out of the window after Anna Stakowski turned. He saw other officers falling, guns useless, the Spindly Men dropping them with the merest touch of a long, clawlike hand, but it was Renwick he sought and found, just as McAdams' gun fired wild, and when the first bullet hit her, Stakowski thought of body armour, that it'd keep her safe, but then she took two more hits and there was blood, and that silly peaked cap that'd made her look like a girl playing dress-up flew off and she was falling, and that was it, the end of Mike Stakowski as a copper. Oath, rank and duty fell away. Only one thing mattered and it was bleeding out on the canteen floor. Ashraf ran in front of her firing; a Spindly hand raked across his face and he was shrieking, thrusting his pistol into his mouth and firing–

Stakowski shouted at Griffiths and his sister to fucking well *run*, and then that was it, job done, duty discharged, and he ran across the canteen floor, firing the Glock empty at the bastards as he went until he fell to one knee beside her, reloading the useless bastard gun at them and firing again, again, again, bullet cases raining on the floor, useless but it was all he had to keep the bastards off her even for a minute, and he fired one-handed while the other hand reached out, grasped her shoulder and tightened on it, just so that she'd know.

ALLEN WASN'T AFRAID as he ran. He knew where he was going – across the lawn and then through the woods. The path was nearby. The ground was uneven, but he didn't stumble, as if his feet were guided. And of course, they were.

This was about *him*. It was his job, fixing this. Always had been. The police, the rest – they'd been required, to get him here, right place, right time – but they'd played their part. It was him now; him alone. He'd been born for this; this was what they'd given him the Sight for.

"Allen!" Vera, behind him. Go away, big sis. She wasn't needed either now. Not for this. She was free. She thought they were heading back down the hill, away from here; well, let her. He knew better.

He wasn't surprised when he looked up the path towards Warbeck and saw three small boys in short trousers, their backs to him. He blinked sweat from his eyes and they were gone, but, as if he hadn't already known, his path was clear.

This could be the last time. Pay off his debts and retire. A normal life, whatever that was. If he could do that, he'd face whatever it was in Warbeck and be glad.

Something – he glanced at his left wrist; his watch

was gone. He laughed. It didn't matter. The watch was nothing. Replaceable.

Chosen. I was chosen. I always knew that. He was walking now, fast. *The dead chose me to talk with them: that's special, but not unique. This is. I'm here to finish this. To give them rest. Of course that's it. What else could it have ever been?*

"Allen!"

He kept going; it'd take too long to explain to her. It had to just be done. He followed the pathway between rows of silent rowan trees. And then he was through, and the Warbeck building was in full view at last.

Ranks of windows, some broken, some blinded with chipboard or tin sheeting, some glinting like dead, unblinking eyes, beneath twin gables that rose like horns above the façade. Tin sheeting, like the windows of the houses on Shackleton Street–

He stopped, looked down. The gravel rippled and swam like the bed of a fast clear stream. Deep breath; the rippling stopped.

"Allen!" Vera, her vaunted elocution fraying, the Kempforth burr she hated coming through. He walked. Gravel gritted underfoot; weeds, sprouting from the cracked surface, snatched at his ankles.

Stone steps, flanked by stone lions on plinths. Above the lions twin pillars supported a stone marquee, the words WARBECK HOUSE engraved on it.

And beneath the marquee, recessed into an archway, a set of wooden double doors. In front of them stood Johnny, Mark and Sam, their backs to him again.

"Allen!" Vera, close now. Wind, howling

The wind, and Vera's voice, died. Thick silence spread out and the double doors swung open to reveal a black, aching void that flowed out, down the steps and up over the façade of Warbeck House. And then the dark engulfed Allen too, and there was only blackness until a pool of light formed, illuminating the three boys as they swivelled to face him; faces wizened and eyeless, fretted lips drawn back from yellowed teeth.

Go in, Alan. You have to go in. Find what waits for you and do what has to be done.

But do *what*?

You'll know, Alan. There's someone waiting for you. A guide. He'll show you what to do. Listen to him. Listen to him and do as he says.

Alright. He nodded.

Be brave, Alan. Be strong. This is for us, to end things at last.

He nodded. In perfect unison, they nodded back.

Goodbye, Alan.

The light around the boys died. The dark rushed back in, only to disperse, and sound returned. The Warbeck building loomed before him.

And the doors were open.

"Allen, for Christ's sake!"

He didn't look at Vera as she ran up. He waved her away; she was an irrelevance now. He didn't need a business manager, or a minder. This was more important than she'd ever understand.

"Alan... Allen – don't go in there."

He went up the stairs to face his destiny. She ran up the steps, caught him, tried to pull him back. But big sister wasn't so big any more and he threw her easily aside. She fell down the steps and landed with a near-comical squawk, legs aspraddle, skirt hiked up, looking up in anger, shock, humiliation and dismay.

"I'm sorry," he said. "I have to." For her as much as him. He turned and made for that black, gaping wound of a doorway. The Sight shackled them together; while it tortured him, he couldn't leave. But if it didn't, anymore – if it served its purpose and was gone – then she'd be free too. They both would.

And he owed her that if he owed her anything; the one thing his money could never buy.

VERA FUMBLED IN her pocket for a tissue, dabbed blood from her nostril. Her backside hurt where she'd landed on it, but she'd live.

"Bastard," she said. But there was guilty relief there too. The Black Sun had finally claimed its own; it had never really been in Shackleton Street; it had been waiting for him, here, all these years.

"ANNA, WAIT UP!"

She looked; Martyn blundered after her. Her life in a bloody nutshell – she had the strength and speed to outrun all the crap, but something always held her back.

The worst had happened. The ghosts were here. They could kill, and they had. So, perhaps she wasn't mad, after all. Perhaps she had the Sight, she saw things others didn't. Either way, she had to keep moving.

There was only silence from E Block now. No shooting. No screams. Stakowski had been right behind her but he'd turned back, gone back in. She'd liked Stakowski. The only sound now was the wind's keen.

But she couldn't help him or the others now. Mary was what mattered; that meant getting out of here. As

Martyn neared her, she started running again, outpacing him easily.

The Warbeck building came into view to the right; her feet crunched on gravel. And then she saw Vera outside it and she veered, running up the path. Behind her, Martyn shouted her name.

Vera leant against a pillar, biting her lip.

"Vera? You OK?"

"Just bruised. Fell down the steps. Or rather, Allen pushed me."

"He did bloody what?" Martyn, arriving, chivalrously outraged.

"He saw his bloody spirit guides again. They said he had to go in there, so he did. Tried to stop him, but he shoved me down. Little sod."

Martyn was already going up the steps.

"Martyn, what're you–"

"Her brother's in there," he said. "And Eva too. Must be. Only place we've not checked. "

"Martyn–"

But he'd stepped inside. Anna turned to Vera, but her head was bowed, a tear running from under her closed eyelids down one powdered cheek. She suddenly looked old; Anna reached out to her. Vera looked up, dabbed her eyes with a tissue, straightened her shoulders, tightened her jaw and followed.

And that left Anna. What now? She could go. Someone had to look after Mary if Martyn didn't return. But she knew that wasn't really why; a shameful part of her would pay any price for freedom. And what if Eva was alive, waiting to be found? Mary would have her parents back, and Anna might be free to go. Manchester wasn't far. She could still have a future, if she wanted one.

Anna took out one of the torches she'd packed and walked up the steps. She hesitated briefly before the thick, churning dark, its cold, dank breath on her face, then took a deep breath and stepped into its heart.

CHAPTER TWENTY-FIVE

DEEPER AND CRUELLER than the normal winter chill, the cold fell around her like a shroud. And it was dark; she could see nothing, no-one.

"Hello?" Her voice echoed. She wished she hadn't spoken.

"Anna?" Vera's voice, right next to her. She turned, shining the torch; Vera flinched back. Beside her, Martyn scowled.

"Helps if you've one of these," she said. "Lucky I've got a spare—"

"Ta." Martyn plucked the second torch from her hand. "Let's find him 'fore he does hisself a mischief."

"Which way?" asked Vera.

Anna pointed. "Only one way, really. Main corridor, down there."

"Well, let's crack on, then," said Martyn. "Catch him up before we lose him."

A match struck, orange flame playing across Vera's face; a faint tang of sulphur, then burning tobacco.

"God," she said, and came over to Anna, took her arm and breathed deep. Scared; Anna could feel it. She opened her mouth to speak.

"Come on, you two."

Vera breathed out, nodded; they went after Martyn. She kept hold of Anna's arm. Anna didn't try to shake her off.

ALAN DIDN'T HAVE a torch, but he didn't need one here. Three pools of light were arranged along the corridor; one of the dead boys stood in each, to help him find his way. Johnny was closest. As Alan drew level with him the light went out; the blackness washed back into place behind him.

Alan, yes, not Allen anymore. Latimer, not Cowell. With any luck, Allen Cowell was gone forever. He'd never been real; just a mask, an act. Alan Latimer from Shackleton Street had been the one to see the dead. Such a relief, at last, to let the lies slip away. So, he was plain Alan Latimer again. Who needed help – therapists, counselling. That was fine; he could afford it. But first, this.

Another light bloomed further up the corridor. Johnny stepped into it, stood waiting. Alan looked back; grey shapes moved beneath the darkness like fish under lightless water. He glimpsed military uniforms, white hospital smocks, faces–

Alan.

He turned back to face the three dead boys.

Don't look behind you. Look forward. Not the past. The future.

Yes, of course. They were right. He walked towards

the next pool of light; it blinked out and reappeared further down. Allen – *Alan* – followed, and didn't look back.

PAINT FLAKED FROM the corridor walls; nests of ancient wiring hung from ceilings like tangled cobwebs. Doors stood open, revealing long-empty offices. In some, files still stood open on desks. A sink, a toilet, both blotched with rust. Sometimes dust swirled about them; years' worth, decades.

It felt like they'd been following the same unending corridor for hours. For all she knew, they had. They could've circled the place twice already.

"Anna?" Vera's fingers were tight on her arm. "What time do you make it?"

"Time? It's…" Anna looked at her watch. "Stopped. Midnight, it says. That can't be. Can it?"

"Don't know. Don't think so. Mine was playing up before. Now it's stopped too, both hands at twelve. Same as yours. And my mobile's dead. Only charged it up last night." Her voice shook.

Anna checked her phone. "Mine's dead too."

"Just have to keep going then," said Martyn, up ahead.

"I just want to get out of here," Vera whispered. "While we can."

"What about Allen?"

"Sod him–" Vera put a hand to her mouth. She made a trapped, tiny noise.

"It's OK. I didn't want to come either."

Vera looked up the corridor to Martyn, then back to Anna.

"I'm not leaving him." The grip on her arm slackened; Vera's eyes darted to the torch. Anna stepped back. "No, Vera."

Vera's lips trembled. She blinked back tears. "I'm sorry. I'm just…"

"I understand." She glanced at Martyn. "Let me talk to him. Martyn?" He ignored her, kept going. "*Martyn.*"

"What?" The torchlight flashed into her face. She squinted. God, big brothers never changed.

"Martyn, come on. We can't stay here."

"What?" He flicked the torch-beam at Vera. "Her brother's in here too–"

"And what good are we going to be? You've seen the size of this place. And what if we run into something?" Vera caught Anna's arm again, drew close to her.

"I'll sort the buggers." Martyn stood, feet apart, like the rugby forward he'd once been.

"They're dead," said Vera, in a taut, trembling voice. An unlit cigarette shook between her fingers. "Don't you get it, for Christ's sake? They're fucking *dead*. Normal rules don't apply here."

"If they're ghosts, they can't hurt us, then," said Martyn, "can they?"

"Oh for God's sake, Martyn." Anna managed not to stamp her foot. "What do you think happened to the others? Old age?"

A muscle jumped in his cheek. "Alright, then. You two get going. But I'm stopping here."

And it would've been so easy, but she could hear Dad's voice even here. *The family, lass. Always the family.*

"Martyn, no," she said. "We've *all* got to get out of here."

He shook his head. "I'm not going without her."

At least he wasn't still pretending it was about Allen. "Martyn–"

"What?"

"Martyn, you know she has to be–"

"Don't say it, sis."

"Martyn, you've got to accept–"

"I said *shut up, Anna*–"

Vera snatched the torch from her hand.

"Vera–"

"You heard him. Let him stay. He's a grown man–" Vera broke off. She was shining the light back down the corridor, the way they'd come.

"What?" Vera whispered. No more than ten yards behind them, a brick wall barred their path.

"That can't be right," said Anna. From behind her came Martyn's heavy, scuffing footsteps. She took Vera's arm, gently took the torch back, went to the wall, held out a hand.

"Don't touch it," said Vera.

But Anna did. Her fingers encountered cold, damp brickwork, nothing more. Solid.

"Fuck," said Martyn.

"We have to get out of here." Vera's voice shook.

"The window." Martyn yanked at one of the window bars. It made a gritting, scraping sound and a little powdered rust fell, but it didn't budge. Martyn let out a muffled roar and yanked harder.

"Anna?" Vera's voice was thin, tiny. She was looking out of the window, across the lawns, which weren't empty anymore. There were maybe twenty or thirty of them, advancing over the grass, swaying slightly. Some wore uniforms, others hospital smocks; some had the dulled, slack faces of people staring into a different world, while others wore the now-familiar masks. And others still displayed faces lacking jaws, noses, eyes, faces with gaping bloodless holes and trenches sunk into them, faces where the skin seemed to have crumpled inwards as if shrink-wrapped, moulding itself to the absent bone; brandishing their mutilations at the world. They halted, staring at the building.

There weren't so many of them at a glance, and they were spread out thinly. It was almost possible to believe you might avoid them if you ran fast enough. Except that Anna doubted they were as slow as they looked. Even if they were, by the time Martyn could force a way out through the window they'd have ample warning and would have closed in around it before the first of them could even try and wriggle free. And even then, beyond them were the woods, where the tall thin shapes of the bare trees seemed constantly poised to shift into something else.

"Martyn, no," she said. He was still gripping the window-bar, poised to wrench at it again. "It doesn't want us to leave."

"What do we do, then?" Vera's voice was almost level now.

"Like you said," Anna told her, "the normal rules don't apply here."

"So what do we *do*?"

"We keep moving until we find a way out," Anna said. How calm she sounded; more surprising, how calm she *felt*. "Normal rules don't apply. Some kind of rules must. So we work out what they are and we might just get out. Come on."

"OK." Vera nodded.

"You gonna be alright?"

"I think so."

"Martyn?" He was staring out of the window, pallid light playing across his face. "Martyn, come on. We need to get going. *Martyn*."

He blinked, looked across at her, finally nodded. "Alright," he said at last, then released the window bars and followed.

THE DARK WAS alive with whispers. That was unusual. Normally Alan only found silence among the dead. That blanket, velvet hush. Well, it didn't matter. He saw Johnny, Mark and Sam up ahead, in their pools of light, guiding him on. Alan kept his eyes on them, not looking at the shadows or what moved there.

THE CORRIDOR TURNED right, leading deeper into Warbeck House. No windows here to shed light; only the endless corridor and the dead ends of empty offices. The only light came from the torches. And Martyn's was fading.

"Shit." He rattled it, thumped it with the heel of his hand. Anna looked back at him. "It's going out." He felt stupid even as he said it.

"It's clockwork. Just wind it up."

He fumbled with the handle and looked down. His face burned. Stupid. He'd just wanted to find Eva, get her out, but this place didn't play fair. Childish and petulant, yes, he knew that. But he was tired now. Empty. Anna had talked about learning the rules, but that wasn't going to count. The house was playing with them; they'd no chance of getting out. It was choosing when and how to finish them. But that didn't matter, nothing did, if he couldn't find–

"Martyn. Baby. My big bear. Martyn. Baby. My big bear."

Martyn stopped.

"Martyn. Baby. My big bear. Martyn. Baby. My big bear."

"Martyn?" Anna said.

"Sh." He held a hand up. "Sh. Listen."

"Martyn. Baby. My big bear. Martyn. Baby. My big bear."

"There," he whispered.

"Martyn. Baby. My big bear." It came from the right. He turned into a long, deep corridor. He didn't think it'd been there before. "Martyn. Baby. My big bear." He could hear the words echo.

"Martyn?"

Martyn shone the torch ahead. The beam didn't seem to reach very far. He remembered the winding mechanism and cranked it.

"Martyn," Anna said.

"You can hear it too. Don't pretend as you can't."

"Martyn?" He wouldn't look at her, *would not see* the pity in her eyes. "Martyn, it's not her–"

"Bollocks."

"Martyn. Baby. My big bear. Martyn. Baby. My big bear."

"It's her. I know my own wife's fucking voice, for Christ's sake."

Anna tried to grab his arm but he shook her off, and then he was walking, then running, and it was easy because the corridor was straight. He heard Anna behind him, shouting his name, but she got fainter and further away as he ran, and then the corridor bent round and he couldn't hear her anymore.

Martyn disappeared round a bend in the corridor. Anna followed, and found herself facing a blank wall.

Vera sucked breath in through her teeth and gripped her arm tighter. Anna reached out and touched the wall, pushed at it, hoping something would yield. Nothing did.

"Martyn!"

Vera gripped her arm. "Sh." Anna shook her off.

"Martyn!"

"Anna, for Christ's sake."

Anna put her ear to the wall. For a moment she thought she heard a fading echo of a woman's voice.

"What now?" whispered Vera. "Where are we?"

"I don't know." She took Vera's hands. "But we stick together, OK?" Vera was nodding. "I mean it, Vera. Whatever you see or hear, we don't split up." She gave the blank wall a last glance. "This place is playing games with us. If we get separated, we might not be able to find each other again." She wouldn't think of Martyn. Mustn't. He could take care of himself. Her best chance of helping him was saving herself. "OK?" she said.

Vera nodded, breathing deep. After a moment, Anna stroked her cheek; Vera closed her eyes and leant into the caress. Despite everything, it would have been so easy to take things further. In that giddy moment, Anna was sure she could take things as far as she chose. But now wasn't the time. She took her hand away, tracing a line down Vera's cheek with the tip of her thumb. Vera breathed out, opened her eyes. "What now?" she asked.

"Back the way we came. Come on."

Was she relieved Martyn was gone? Not that she'd ever admit it, but perhaps she had a better chance of getting out now. Nan still needed looking after. And, most of all, there was Mary.

They hadn't retraced their steps very far before coming to a bend she knew hadn't been there before. Beyond it, the corridor forked.

"Left or right?" asked Vera.

If the house was playing games with them, what difference did it make? But they had to try; if they just stayed here they'd never get out.

"Let's go right," she said at last.

"OK."

SAM VANISHED AS Alan neared him. That was nothing new by now, but he didn't reappear. Alan stopped, waited. Up ahead, Johnny and Mark gazed at him. The whispers had faded; there was only silence now.

Come on, Alan.

As Alan reached Johnny, he vanished too. Like Sam, he didn't reappear.

Alan looked at Mark. There might have been sorrow in that round, pale face. Alan didn't move. When he reached Mark, he'd go too. And Alan would be alone, in the dark. And he'd never feared anything more.

Mark shook his head. **You won't be alone, Alan. And I won't go straight away.**

But he would.

Yes. Everything has to end one day. But don't be sad. It means you'll soon be free. We all will. You won't have the Sight anymore, after this. You'll have a normal life. But you have to do what comes next on your own. And I won't leave you without saying goodbye.

Was it just Alan's imagination, or had Mark

emphasised **I** and **you**? No more than Alan deserved if he had.

He reached Mark's side; his hand hovered briefly over the head of blond hair below him. Mark looked up with those black holes, eyes once clear, blue and innocent. **It's alright.**

Alan had never touched one of his dead before. Mark's hair was fine and soft, the scalp beneath warm. Nothing to suggest he wasn't alive.

"I'm sorry," Alan said, and realised he could hear the words – faint, muffled, but they were there.

The skin between the worlds is very thin here. That's why you can hear yourself. You'll be able to hear him too. It'll be like talking to a living man.

"Who? Hear who?"

Alan?

"Yes."

I'm sorry too, said Mark.

And Alan was alone.

ANNA STOPPED. "WAIT. Listen."

"What?"

"Listen."

The shuffle of feet, the faint mumble of voices, growing louder in the stillness. There was an alcove in the tunnel. Anna shut the torch off and ducked into it, pulling Vera after her.

A torch-beam flickered down the corridor, inches from them. Vera huddled behind Anna. The footsteps shuffled closer; a man, jowled, sagging and oyster-eyed, black hair threaded with grey. He wore his officer's uniform; must have been wearing it the night he died, part of the act. He looked tired beyond words and full of grief. As he passed she saw the exit wound in the back of his head.

Others shuffled after him; dressed in 1940s fashions. One man, bloodied face beaten almost shapeless, eyes gouged out, was guided by a woman in a yellow dress marred by a dozen red stab-wounds; white as chalk, her sunken eyes gazed off into the distance, void of hope. There were a dozen more.

They shuffled past, oblivious, until the last of them, an ashen-faced, severe-looking woman in trousers, hair gathered in a tight bun, stopped and slowly turned. There was a ragged wound in her face where half her lower jaw had been torn away; a jagged piece of bone stuck out. She stared at Anna. The others stopped and turned as well, then began to advance, faces dull and empty. Emaciated, grey-white hands reached out. Behind her, Vera was keening.

Light flashed into Anna's face; she flinched, heard Vera gasp. Then it moved away. When she dared look again, it was playing over the faces of the dead. One by one they lowered their eyes, and as the uniformed man flashed the beam back and forth over them, they shuffled back towards him. He shone his torch into Anna's face again, then aimed it back along the corridor and began walking again. Heads bowed, the others shuffled after him. The procession rounded a corner and was gone, the light dying away and the soft shuffle of footsteps swallowed up.

"That was him, wasn't it?" Vera whispered. "St. John?"

"Yes, it was. And by the look of it, his last tour party too."

"But didn't they die in E Block?"

*Your great-grandfather was there the night it
happened. The night Mister St. John died. He wasn't
supposed to be, but he was.* "Yes."

"So why are they here?"

"Maybe the ghosts in E Block don't want them. Come
on. Let's go."

Up ahead, a dim, hazy light. Alan went towards it. Go
towards the light sounded like the kind of thing he told
his audiences. Up ahead, the corridor opened out into
a room. It was bare, wide and long; archways held the
ceiling up. To his left, a row of windows; the pale light
came through them and lay in weak, watery pools on
floorboards crusted with feathers and birdshit. Here
and there were pigeon bones.

Alan looked out through a window. Below were the
lawns and the woods; beyond them the moors and hills
rose clear. He hadn't been aware of climbing upwards,
but he must have done. He was in the attic space of the
Warbeck building.

He heard rustles and whispers. Pale shapes moved in
the shadows. They never came too close to the light,
but he glimpsed faces like faded photographs; in one,
a gaping trench between forehead and nose obliterated
the eyes. Another was a shiny globe of burn scars; eyes
stared out, bared teeth and gums snarled, through
ragged holes where fused lips and eyelids had been cut
away.

A wheelchair creaked; a truncated, malformed figure
shifted in it. Alan moved into the light. The shadows
teemed with motion; they circled him, crowded close as
they dared. Like fish in a tank.

A match scraped and hissed; the dead sank away into the shadows. Alan glimpsed the match's flare before it died, and a face. "Who's there?"

The faint tinkle of the match dropping to the floor. A figure stepped through a pool of light further down, then back out into the shadows.

"Who is it?" Alan breathed deep, strove to sound calm. "Who's there?"

Footsteps clicked. A man in evening dress stepped into the pool of light opposite Alan. Not a police officer, or Martyn Griffiths; this must be the one he'd been told he'd meet. The man took a cigarette from his mouth and blew out smoke, obscuring his face, but he was familiar, somehow.

The man stepped out of the light. His shoes clicked on the floor; slow, deliberate, a clock counting off a condemned man's last seconds. In the black, the cigarette glowed.

The man stepped into the light with Alan. He was pale, with a narrow face, sharp nose and fair hair swept into a side-parting; a long fringe flopped across his forehead, nearly covering one eye. His wet, loose lips looked perpetually on the brink of a smirk; his eyes were near-black and emotionless. His left hand slid into his trouser pocket, brushing his suit jacket back from his side; his right hand brought the cigarette to his lips again. The coal glowed blood-orange; the tobacco crackled. He blew smoke off to one side, and smiled.

"Hello, Alan," said Gideon Dace.

CHAPTER TWENTY-SIX

"ANNA."

"What's up?"

"Can't keep going. Got to stop."

Anna bit her lip.

"*Please.*"

"OK."

Vera slid down the wall. "Where are we?"

"I don't know, to be honest."

"You don't know? You're the one with the plans."

"The corridors stopped matching the layout a long time ago. We should've at least found a window by now, or an office. Something."

"Map's not much cop, then, is it?"

"It's this place. Playing with us."

"Christ."

After a moment Anna put an arm round her. She rummaged in her backpack, dug out a Mint Cake bar. "Here."

Vera shook her head.

"Take it. Keep your strength up."

Vera's eyes were red. "What good's that?"

"I'm not giving up. You need to keep up your energy. So bloody get this down you. Half now, half later."

"Yes, Mum."

Anna unwrapped the other bar for herself. "There's some coffee here as well, if you want."

"Ha. Might as well eat a hearty supper."

Anna opened the flask, half-filled the cup. "Here."

"Thanks. So what now?"

"Keep going. Find a way out."

"How? Even if we do those things will be waiting for us."

"I'm not giving up. Got Mary to get back to."

After a moment, Vera smiled. "Tougher than you look, aren't you?"

"Dunno about that. Not in a place like this."

"You're not just talking about the spooky shit either, are you?"

"What?"

"I saw you, back in E Block." Vera looked away. "Sorry. That was…"

"Yeah." Anna studied Vera's profile. "True, though."

Vera glanced back at her.

"After I got divorced. My husband…"

"You don't have to talk about it."

"We'll go in a bit. I want some of that coffee first. Peter was a good man. Wish I could say he was a bastard, sometimes, but… he wasn't. We'd met at college, gone out a few times, seemed well-suited."

"But you weren't."

"Didn't realise till later. The physical side was – well, OK, I suppose. Considering. Neither of us had much prior experience. And–"

"You were still in the closet?"

"Hadn't even admitted it to myself back then."

"Not an easy place to grow up gay, Kempforth."

"No. You done with that coffee yet?"

"Sorry." Vera drank off the coffee, returned the cup to Anna. "So?"

"So, I cheated on him. No-one steady. Just... I'd go out when he was away on business, find someone. Told myself at first it was a phase. I was getting it out of my system to save my marriage. But–"

"It wasn't."

"No."

"What happened?"

"I got careless. He caught me. I think I wanted him to. He was pretty decent about it, to start with. He'd had a job offer abroad. Good timing, really. We'd sell the house, split the money, that'd be it."

"But?"

"The job fell through. Company went bust. And all of a sudden it didn't seem like such a good deal to him. We ended up fighting over the house. He won."

"And you?"

"I had a breakdown. Stress. Guilt."

"Guilt?"

"He wasn't a bad man. I'd hurt him. When things got ugly, I didn't feel I had much of a leg to stand on. Morally, I mean."

"Jesus. Being a bit too nice for your own good there."

"Maybe. Anyway. I was sectioned for three months." She looked up. Vera didn't look afraid, or judgmental. "And when I got out..."

"You came back here."

"Nowhere else to go. It was only meant to be for a

few months. But there was stuff with my Dad. He'd found out. About the women. It wasn't easy for him."

"Sod him. It's your life."

"He was my Dad. I loved him. I'd always been his favourite. I had to fix things with him first. And then Mary was born and... I just adored her on sight. And there was Nan to look after... selling her house, getting her into Stangrove."

"Sounds like you were making excuses."

"I was going to move back to Manchester, get things started again. And then Dad died. Heart attack. No warning. And there was a funeral to arrange. It was particularly difficult for Nan, she'd just lost her son. Wasn't easy for Martyn either."

"And the next thing you know, you've been here how long? Ten years?"

"It wasn't that simple," said Anna. "I was going to move a couple of years back. Dad left me the house. I was going to sell it, split the proceeds with Martyn and clear out. But then he lost his job, and the housing market went down the pan at the same time."

"I'd've sold the place for what I could get, bunged him a share and got out of this shithole fast as I could."

"Maybe."

Anna looked down. Warm fingers found hers and squeezed.

"Sorry," said Vera. "Just being a bitch there." The corner of her mouth twitched; her thumb stroked the back of Anna's hand. *To hell with it all*. Anna leant forward; Vera parted her lips.

Light flashed; they sprang apart, shielding their eyes. Someone was at the end of the corridor, shining a torch on them. It raised a hand, beckoning. Then it turned and began to walk away, flickers of receding light playing on the wall.

Anna re-packed the Thermos and stood. "Come on."

"But what if…"

"Would you rather wait here and die?" She managed a smile. "We can pick up where we left off later."

Vera smiled back, and stood.

The figure waited silently for them to catch up, then walked on. Anna glimpsed the khaki of a uniform, but didn't shine her torch. Maybe it was best not to know. Nothing to do now but follow, and hope.

"YOU KNOW WHO I am?"

"Gideon Dace."

"*Sir* Gideon. I inherited the title from St. John when he died."

Alan wouldn't gratify him with a title. "Your father built Ash Fell. You…"

"Yes?"

"Embezzled the hospital funds, tortured the inmates, and finally died here, alone and despised. Have I left anything out?"

"A great deal. But I'll overlook your manners. There's a lot you've left out, but that's hardly your fault. Or the Mason woman. She knows more than anyone alive, but this place has secrets it keeps from the living."

"Even I know that."

Gideon glanced around. "It's never quiet," he said. "In here you can never be alone." He turned back to Alan and smiled. "But I digress. This way. We've a lot to discuss."

Gideon stepped out of the light. Alan hesitated; all

around him were whispers, like feathers brushing glass.

Gideon laughed. "Not afraid, Alan, surely?"

Alan followed, keeping his eyes on Gideon; better to see him than the other shapes around him.

"I was no angel, I'll admit. But I have suffered a somewhat bad press."

"You think so?"

"Of course." At the end of the attic, Gideon descended a flight of steps, opened a door at the bottom. "I wasn't the son my father wanted – too much the Hedonist, not enough the Stoic – but I applied myself diligently enough to my studies. Certainly enough to try to put right my father's wrongs."

He ushered Alan onto a landing. There was no visible light source, but nonetheless Alan saw quite clearly. "Wonderful Sir Charles Dace! Noble Sir Charles Dace! Noble? Ash Fell is one great monument to my father's vanity. However high-minded his aims, he not only beggared his own children, but almost destroyed a business that had run for almost two hundred years – and which, in case you've conveniently forgotten, was the town's chief employer. Bankrupting the family business was bad – even humiliating – for us, but a potential catastrophe for the men who worked in those mills. I found a buyer for them at a fraction of their true value. If I hadn't, thousands would have lost their livelihoods." Gideon breathed out, forced a smile, drew on his cigarette. "Note that it was *I* who found a buyer and saved the mills from collapse. Oh, I've no doubt St. John was a *better* man than I – more honourable, chaste, temperate and so forth – but he was nowhere near as worldly. He didn't understand betrayal."

"And you did?"

"I've experienced treachery as well as dealing it out, Alan, I can assure you. St. John was father's favourite, remember. And he looked up to father... you know, I honestly think that to him, father was almost a god. He was devastated by what father had done. Paralysed, in shock. He could do nothing. But *I* could."

"Is there a point to all this?"

"Only that I wasn't acting from purely selfish motives. My family was a consideration, trying to preserve and restore it. And there was – *is* – a thing called *noblesse oblige*. A contract between the leaders and the led. Most people just want sufficient food and water; shelter, a wage. They don't *want* to wrestle with issues of state. My... *class*, for want of a better term, takes care of those things. We provide leadership and stability; in return we need the common herd to work the factories, harvest the crops, buy the goods–"

"Fight in the wars?"

"Yes. I'm afraid, Alan, that wars are sometimes necessary. When they are, we do what we have to, to convince the herd. That's the system, and it works. Even after Passchendaele and the Somme, even after the parade of ruined and mutilated souls that passed through here and places like it, we could still send the young men marching if needs be. Not because we want to, not because we're cruel; because we must. It's how the system survives and maintains itself. And before you decry it, consider the other systems out there. Compared to, say, the Kaiser's Germany, the English ruling class of 1914 were positively benign."

"Matter of perspective."

Gideon snorted. "Well, I'm sure the Irish peasantry and African natives might take issue. But there was give as well as take. Surely even you can't deny our colonies benefited from our presence also. In any case, we're straying from the point. We each have responsibilities to the other. And 'from him to whom much is given, much will be asked'. If I recall the Gospels correctly." Gideon led Alan off the landing and into a corridor. "My father, however worthy of respect you find him, failed in his responsibilities. Someone had to retrieve his error. St. John was incapable, so the task fell to me. My methods might not have been the prettiest, but you can't always choose the time or place of your battles, or the weapons at your disposal. I didn't create the situation, remember."

"I understand," Alan said at last.

"Do you?" Gideon smiled. "I hope you weren't hoping to lay the ghosts of Ash Fell with a single expression of sympathy. We're rather past that now."

"I thought as much."

"And it's not me who needs laying to rest; I'm not the villain of this piece."

"Then who is?"

"In my time, Alan, not yours."

"But that doesn't explain everything."

"Oh?"

"The treatment of the patients, for example."

"Unfortunate, but I was left with little choice. Had to raise money somehow. Again, St. John's responsibilities devolved on me. He couldn't do what had to be done, but I could. I plead guilty to an excess of zeal." He looked around. "And anything I may have done, I paid the price for. Remember how long I've been here, living and dead."

"Why vanity?"

"Mm?"

"You said this place was a monument to your father's vanity. But he built this place to help others. Even if it caused your family hardship... what?"

"I'm sorry. I'm sorry." Gideon dabbed his eyes with a yellow handkerchief; his titters died away. "But to hear you paint him as some dewy-eyed humanitarian... My father had far bigger considerations than that, Alan. Do you really think he'd throw away everything the family had built up over a few loonies and missing noses?"

"Well, I thought that's what he did."

"No. Ash Fell wasn't built out of humanitarian motives, I can assure you."

"Then why *was* it built?"

"You'll see."

ANNA LOST COUNT of the twists and turns their route had taken, but finally their guide led them out into a large, pentagonal hall, with a spiral staircase in its centre. The uniformed man turned and went up the staircase; it creaked and rattled as he climbed.

At the top of the staircase was a landing. The uniformed man walked down it. Torchlight gleamed on grimy, frosted glass in the doors along his way. Anna and Vera followed in his wake. Anna had turned her torch off for now, but kept ready to switch it back on, just in case.

The uniformed man stopped, shone his torch across the plaque on a door and stepped into the room. Anna stopped outside the doorway. Bright, pale sunlight streamed in through the wide window opposite. In front of it was a desk, a tattered swivel chair behind it. There were bookshelves and a pair of armchairs, split and shedding stuffing. The door-plaque read DIRECTOR'S OFFICE.

The uniformed man turned to face her: tall, thin, with reddish-brown hair, a neatly trimmed moustache and pale eyes.

Sir Charles Dace raised his hand and beckoned. Anna shuffled in; after a moment, Vera followed. Dace looked from one to the other of them. For all Anna could read of his expression, he might as well have worn a prosthetic mask. Was there sadness in his gaze, regret? Pity or contempt? She couldn't tell.

Dace took a deep breath and pointed across the room. Anna looked, saw a print of an undistinguished country landscape. Dace gestured to the floor; after a moment Anna crossed to the picture, took it down. Dace waved her aside; he stared, unblinking, at where it'd hung. His pointing hand opened, until the exposed palm faced the wall. Then he curled his fingers into a fist.

The floor shuddered. The desk rattled. Old, loose papers drifted to the ground; a book toppled from the shelves in a flurry of dust. Powdered concrete spidered down from the ceiling as the wall began to crack.

GIDEON – OPENING YET another door, leading onto yet another flight of steps – stopped, cocked his head. "Now, whatever can that be?"

"What?"

"Can't you hear it? Or feel it?"

Alan touched the wall; a faint trembling seeped through it. From somewhere in the distance came a groaning, rumbling sound. "What is it?"

Gideon chuckled. "Father, I believe. Talk of the devil.

Still trying to interfere, even though it's far too late. We're beyond his reach here."

"Interfere with what?"

"You'll see, soon enough. It's all to do with why you're here. He can't get to us, so he's trying something else. It won't work, of course. He'll just antagonise the others, and they won't like that at all. Silly pater. Still, he's a big boy."

Gideon's smile made Alan want to run, but he didn't. This was where he had to be. "Daddy never loved me," said Alan. "Is that really the best you can do?"

"I wasn't aware," said Gideon, "that I needed to justify myself to you. Do you really think that I've been waiting all these years for you to absolve me? Do you really think that *your* approval is what will make the difference between damnation and salvation? If so, you're sadly mistaken."

Allen swallowed hard. "Shouldn't we be getting on?"

Gideon's smile vanished; his eyes were black empty voids like the barrels of guns, tunnels to nowhere. "I lead, not you. You, Master Latimer, follow."

"Alright."

"It's this way."

THE CRACK WIDENED, spilling dust and gaping black. Dace pulled his now-clenched fist in towards his face. The room juddered; dust-streams hissed down from above.

"Oh Christ, what now?"

Anna held Vera's hand between hers. "Easy." Still, she was oddly calm. This was easier for her than Vera, perhaps; Anna was used to going with the flow, bending with the wind, while Vera, she was sure, was used to being in control. But the cold fact was that right now there was little she could do.

A final climactic shudder; something fell out of the crack to thud on the worn carpet, and the room became still. A few last motes of dust drifted down.

Dace's hand dropped to his side, then gestured weakly at the object on the floor.

Sounds outside; footsteps in the corridor. Dace put a finger to his pursed lips and walked past them, out into the corridor. The door clicked shut behind him.

"Wh–" began Vera.

"Sh."

From outside came the sound of a struggle – the dull thump of blows connecting, the thud of feet on the landing, a crash as bodies cannoned into the locked door. But no cries; not a word, not even a gasp or breath.

Finally, the struggle subsided; the plodding footsteps began to recede. With them came the sound of a heavy object being dragged away. And then at last there was silence again.

After a few minutes, Anna crossed the room. The object that had fallen from the wall was wrapped in oiled cloth. At the desk, Vera at her shoulder, she unwrapped it to reveal a battered tin box. It must have been sealed in the wall for decades, but the lid came off easily enough.

"What is it?" asked Vera.

"Some kind of journal." A small, brown, leather-bound book, yellowed pages covered with thin, precise handwriting. Underneath was a wad of paper – several large sheets, folded several times. She spread them carefully out across the desk. "Bloody hell."

"What?"

"I think these are the original plans for Ash Fell."

"The ones that were lost?"

"I think so. Careful, they're old. Each different building, floor by floor, and... that's interesting."

"Come on, Anna, stop playing games."

"Sorry. But have a look at this."

She tapped the centre of the plans for the Warbeck building. "Right here. See? In the middle."

She felt Vera leaning closer. "Is that–"

"Yes. Some sort of secret chamber. In the shape of a pentagon. It's not on the plans that were available to the public. Seems to be directly under the centre of the Warbeck building. Buried deep, too. Under the sub-basement, as far as I can make out."

"But what for?" Vera's hands rested on her shoulders; Anna slipped free of them. *Not now, not just yet – later, if we live.*

"Let's see if the journal sheds any light."

GIDEON LIT A cigarette. "My father was certainly a man of parts. Soldier. Businessman. Dabbled in politics at one point. He was also a student of the occult."

"The occult?"

"Oh yes. Surprised you, didn't it? I'm not sure where it came from; even dead, we don't talk much. He kept it quiet, of course. Regular churchgoer. I never suspected, in his lifetime or even mine."

Gideon trod his cigarette out. "I don't know how seriously he took it, till after the War. He believed in the Empire, you see. Thought it was a genuine force for good, and that it was now doomed to collapse. The war had weakened it economically, killed thousands of its young men. Britain had become almost unrecognisable to him. But worse, people didn't have faith in it anymore – not their leaders, or the monarchy, or the Empire. There'd been a great deal of social change – votes for women, the rise of Socialism. Everything was changing, in flux. My father was convinced this would lead to the collapse of the Empire, and to permissiveness, decadence, moral laxity. The last three being my favourite things, of course. Well, he was right. But you can't turn the clock back. Can you?"

Alan wasn't sure if the question was rhetorical.

"But what to do? There were political movements, of course, but my father believed the damage was irreversible in normal terms. However, he had other options."

"The occult?"

"Oh yes. There are spells for almost everything. Make someone fall in love with you. Heal a broken heart. Even raise the dead. But they're meant to be used on individuals. Father wanted to affect an entire nation. An *Empire*. However, he was an industrialist; adapting a process for mass production was his business."

"How did he do that?"

"The first problem was power. Does the phrase 'there's a price for everything' ring a bell?"

"Yes."

"Thought it might. Ritual magic requires energy, like any other process. A motor needs fuel; a watch requires winding. Some spells draw their power from the focus and concentration required by the ritual itself. But others require sacrifice. It all depends what you want. In this case, nothing less than a blood sacrifice would do, and the scale of the task meant a sacrifice on an almost unimaginable scale. And then he realised, it had already been made. Oh come on, it's obvious."

"The War?"

"Just so. My father realised that the First World War constituted the greatest blood sacrifice in history. Millions had died, to say nothing of those condemned to a lifetime of suffering by disfigurement or madness." Gideon offered Alan a cigarette.

"No, thank you. But it'd already happened. How could he use it to... reverse itself?"

"He wasn't trying to bring them back to life. That wouldn't have worked. But he *could* use that energy to reverse some of the war's ill effects. There was still time to harness the energy that had been released. And *that's* why he built Ash Fell." Gideon tapped the wall. "He paid agents to... harvest the battlefields of Passchendaele, the Somme, Loos, Mons, the Marne, Verdun."

"What do you mean, harvest?"

"They collected items he could use. Simple as that. Earth from the battlefield. Spent bullets, broken bayonets, guns, even human remains. All of which found their way into the walls of Ash Fell."

Something finally clicked for Alan. "Of course. It was right in front of me."

"Oh?"

"Five blocks around a central building. Like a five-point star. A pentacle."

"Close," said Gideon. "But not quite. You can't see it, because it's hidden. But don't worry. I'll show you."

"Think it's safe to smoke?"

"No idea."

"Do you mind?"

"Go on, then."

Vera settled back in the least ratty armchair and lit a Sobranie. Calmer now. Christ, she'd dealt with Walsh and that bastard priest, faced Fitton down. "Was he mad?"

"I'd have said yes before today." Anna adjusted her reading glasses and turned another page. "You'd have to be to believe in this."

"He reckoned he could change the whole world to fit what he wanted. Sounds pretty mental to me."

"There was a lot of it about, in those days." Anna turned another page, studied it. "Good grief."

"What?"

"According to this, there's a small fortune in silver in the walls of this place."

"Silver?"

"It's how Dace designed it. Every patient's cell, every treatment room, was designed to capture human suffering."

"He did what?"

"What it says here. He didn't just build relics of the victims and the battlefields into the walls. He went one better than that."

"The patients?"

"Not just the remains of the dead and the weapons that'd killed them. The actual, still-living victims of the war. Especially in D and E Blocks, where they were never going to get out. Each one was like blood sacrifice in slow motion."

"So where does the silver come into it?"

"Magic properties. That's what he's put here. There's a thin silver plate under the floor of each cell. Looks like Gideon never even twigged. That's why Dace hid the original plans. Too much of a temptation, anyone knowing about it."

"So the silver plate, what, catches the patient's suffering?"

"Yeah."

"And then what?"

"There are silver wires leading from the plates, down through the walls and connecting to these." Anna tapped one of five thick black lines radiating from each vertex of the pentagon. Each was jagged, like a lightning rune.

"What are they supposed to be?"

"I think that's – wait, yes – some sort of silver rail. Below sub-basement level. See, they all converge on–"

"The hidden chamber."

"That's right. And... *Jesus*."

"What?"

"Look. *Look* at it. Can't you see it?"

"They all zig-zag. So, what, did he get the angle wrong?"

"Vera, they're lightning runes. Five lightning runes, intersecting at a single central point. Sound familiar?"

"No. Yes. Wait..." Allen. Something about Allen. "That symbol they showed us. On that picture of him they found at Shackleton Street."

"The Black Sun. That's what he called it. A pagan religious symbol. That's what this is, Vera. Ash Fell was built as a gigantic Black Sun."

THIS CORRIDOR WAS cold and damp; the air clung wetly and stank of mould.

"We're now below Warbeck's sub-basement," Gideon said. He pointed at the floor. "The silver rail's under the floor. Can you believe that? A small fortune. Actually, not so small. I was sitting on a fortune, and I never knew. Not until it was too late, of course."

"After you were dead?"

"Oh no, before. You don't think I remained here out of choice?" Gideon looked around. "The former occupants of this place made certain that I couldn't leave. I'd lose all sense of direction, become violently ill, if I went too far away; I'd always end up back here. So, yes, a solid silver rail, directly underfoot. Channelling all that misery down here, towards the centre."

"And is that where we're going?"

"Of course. Where else?"

And what then? Could anything Gideon Dace wanted be a goal Alan should help achieve? Or was Gideon serving out some sort of penance? He hardly seemed repentant.

Unless, of course, the energy Ash Fell had stored had to be dissipated before it caused further harm. Like defusing a bomb, or shutting down a runaway reactor. That must be it. He couldn't understand what else it might be.

"What my father failed to consider," Gideon said, "is that there's a lot of anger out there in the netherworld. You're a long time dead, and believe me, the tales you tell your audiences don't even come close to the truth. No Heaven or Hell, no Elysian Fields, no eternal rest or reincarnation. Just a cold, dark place of ashes and dust and stagnant water."

Gideon trod out his cigarette. "All that's truly valuable is in the world of the living. If you're lucky, you get to walk among them, see this flawed, befouled but beautiful world yourself, but even then you're like the poor child outside the sweet shop, nose pressed up against the glass. You can see, hear, smell even, but never touch, taste, *feel*. And the living don't realise. The lines of communication are so chancy. Besides, people hear what they want to hear. No-one wants to be told what's *really* waiting. The dead wouldn't have even the brief contact with the living they have. You're not unique, Alan. There are others like you, so sure they know everything when they know *nothing*. Nothing at all."

"The dead can't touch or feel? Then what happened back in E Block? I saw—"

"Ah, well." Gideon lit yet another cigarette. "Over the years, there've been many trespassers here at Ash Fell. They all died, because they all made the same mistake. They assumed the rowan woods are meant to keep them out. But you and I, I think, know better. We know that rowan wood is a charm against witchcraft. The woods weren't planted to keep something out, but to keep something in."

"Keep what in?"

"The creatures you call the Spindly Men. Do you know, Alan, what the name 'Kempforth' means?"

"No."

"*Kemp* is a Saxon word, meaning *warrior*. A *forth*, or *ford*, is a *bridge* or *crossing*. Thus, Kempforth is *the warrior's crossing*. In old legends, it was a place where slain fighters passed through to the afterlife. Another reason Daddy dearest built the hospital here. It's one of a handful of places on earth where the lands of the living and the dead overlap."

"And the Spindly Men?"

"'When the night wind blows on dale and fell, the Spindly Men come up from Hell.'"

"You said there was no Hell."

"The Spindly Men live in a sort of limbo, between life and death, belonging wholly in neither world. That limbo is a dreadful place, worse than the land of the dead. It's as close to the religious concept of Hell as you're likely to get. The Spindly Men have no faces; none at all. And without faces, they can only grope blindly, hunting by touch. The rowan trees confuse them and ensure they can never find their way out. Unless someone gives them a face."

"The masks."

"Yes. The dead, you see, can't do much for themselves. But Ash Fell belongs to them if it belongs to anybody, and there were still old masks here. They'd suffice, until the women from the college could make new ones. You see, if you give a Spindly Man a face, you free them to walk in the world of men, and they're bound to you. They'll do your bidding. So, if you need someone to start a fire, or bring someone to you..." Gideon released a long breath of smoke. "And if necessary – well, you saw how the police died, in E Block. And you heard about the man who died on the Dunwich Estate?"

"Pete Hardacre?"

"Yes. And how he died?"

"Yes." Alan swallowed thickly. "He tore his own eyes out."

"And did you wonder why?" Before Alan could answer, he carried on. "'The Spindly Men come up from Hell,' remember? They live in a place we can't even contemplate. That's the other part of the legend, you see. If a Spindly Man touches you, you'll see Hell. And the sight'll strike you dead in an instant, or drive you mad."

"But why?"

Gideon smiled. "There's power here. A limited reserve, slowly accumulated, but power's a bit like money. The more you have, the easier it is to get more. Opening a door is always simply a matter of applying the correct amount of force in the correct manner."

"I don't understand."

They'd reached a heavy wooden door. "You will, Alan. It's all about to become perfectly crystal clear."

"WELL?"

Anna took her glasses off, rubbed her eyes. "It's madness."

"I could have told you *that*. Go on."

"What he seems to be saying is that the power generated at Ash Fell could then be used to invoke, and then control, the souls of all the war dead."

"All of them?"

"The greatest blood sacrifice in human history, remember? All of this is about raising and controlling spirits of one kind or another."

"Was it supposed to take this long?"

"Don't think so…" Anna looked up from the journal to the hole in the wall. "Hang on."

"What?"

"This passage is dated 20th August 1929."

"And?"

"This looks like Sir Charles Dace's handwriting. But 20th August was the night he died. So how did it get sealed up in the wall?"

"Don't ask me. So what does it say?"

"'I've been a fool. I barely escaped the Nexus Chamber with my life…'"

"Nexus Chamber?"

"The hidden chamber under the building, I think. 'I had sufficient protection to escape the Chamber, but not the building. Their rage is at the whole world, but for now it's focused on me. At present, they control the whole building. I have managed to erect some defences here in my office; if they hold till morning, I may escape alive, but I doubt they will. The telephone does not work and none hear my cries. Even if they did, they could do nothing.'"

Vera stubbed out her cigarette.

"'How could I have been so blind? I no longer control the forces I've invoked. The dead whose souls I tried to call on are filled with anger – against the world they were torn out of, the Empire that sacrificed them and, of course, me, for attempting to press them into service after they had already made the supreme sacrifice,'" Anna read. "'They aren't just seeking vengeance. They want me dead to ensure my silence. Only I know the machine's purpose–'"

"The machine?"

"The hospital, I think. 'They seek to control the machine, for their own ends. They, not I, will sing the Black Song...'"

"The what?"

"The Black Song. According to his notes, it's the final stage of the process – whoever sings it gets control of all the energy that's been built up. 'I will not survive the night; thus it must fall to others to avert the cataclysm. I will use a spell of concealment to hide this journal in a place of safety, until the time is right.'"

THE FIRST THING Alan heard, as he went through the door, was the crying. It wafted out to meet him on a cold damp wind, the kind of weeping Alan knew too well. The low, relentless sobbing of a child beyond hope.

He stood in cold, dank darkness. Whatever night vision he'd had before was now gone. Behind him, the door clicked shut.

"My father isn't your enemy, Alan," Gideon said. "Or St. John – he's here, somewhere, wandering endlessly with a procession of dead tourists. It isn't even me. The enemy you're facing are your heroes."

The weeping grew louder. It came from all around now.

"The glorious dead," said Gideon. "The fallen. So many names for them. For some, it's the broken promises: a land fit for heroes, a war to end wars. For others, it's decadence and immorality – interracial marriage, homosexuality. Others see hard-won rights and freedoms stripped away; saw a better world built in the years following their death, and now see it dismantled with no-one lifting a finger to stop it. Whatever your political or religious bias, there's ample food for your discontent. You've heard the saying: for our tomorrows, they gave their today. Well... some of them don't consider it a fair trade, and they want to cancel the deal."

"So how do I stop them?"

Gideon laughed. "You don't."

"What?"

"They control this machine my father built, and allowed it to keep running in order to build up greater and greater power. As I found out when I became its sole resident. They didn't waste a moment paying me back. And when I died..." His smile faded. "I've been here nearly sixty years, alive and dead. The ones since

I died have been the worst. They're very inventive, and they can torture me for eternity, if they want – or release me, if I do as I'm told. Which I have. You're not here to stop anything, Alan. On the contrary. You're part of this. You always have been."

The room seemed to spin. "But my spirit guides." Alan's voice sounded strangled and feeble. "They told me you'd show me what I had to do."

"Ah yes. Them."

A pool of light appeared nearby; three small figures stepped into it.

"I'm sorry, Alan," said Mark.

"'THEIR SACRIFICE WAS in vain,'" read Anna. "'The world they saved is unworthy of it. So they are crossing. The Great War's dead are coming back, to dispossess the living.'" She stopped. "Oh."

"What?"

"'Five are needed. Five who possess the Sight. Four may be brought by any means, but the last must come to the Nexus Chamber of their own free will. At their sacrifice the Black Song will be sung, and the gates will be opened.'"

"Allen," Vera whispered.

CHAPTER TWENTY-SEVEN

MARTYN HAD BEEN walking for a long time now. Wasn't sure how long. Wanted to rest. *Needed* to. But couldn't. Whenever he thought of stopping and resting – just for a moment – Eva's voice seemed to grow a little fainter, and he'd press on lest it vanish altogether.

"Martyn. Baby. My big bear. Martyn. Baby. My big bear."

He put a hand against the brickwork, closed his eyes. No. Don't weaken. Close to her now. Close. He pushed himself clear. He ached but he'd keep going. Dedication. Devotion. He wouldn't stop.

"Martyn. Baby. My big bear. Martyn. Baby. My big bear."

Guilt? Yes. He'd abandoned Anna and Vera back there. A gentleman didn't do that. *Fuck off, Dad.* They wanted to go, he wanted to carry on. Let them go their way; he had to go his. Best this way. He wasn't leaving without Eva. Get lost anyway, if he tried to go back.

"Martyn. Baby. My big bear."

She was calling him, knew he was here. Just round this next corner. No? The next one, then. He kept promising himself he'd stop and rest, but kept on going.

The endless corridor forked into three; he couldn't tell which Eva's voice came from. Didn't help he was so bloody tired, or that he was one long ache from the knees down.

He shouted: "Eva. *Eva!*"

But all that came back: "Martyn. Baby. My big bear."

He fell to his knees. He was crying. Like a big kid. Fucking mardarse. Mum, Dad, take me home; don't like this game anymore. But he was far from home now, that state of innocence was long gone.

And then: "Martyn. Baby. My big bear." It came from his right, clearer than ever. "Martyn. Baby. My big bear."

Martyn stood. Stumbled to the right-hand corridor. Cold air blew in his face.

"Martyn. Baby. My big bear."

Stand, you bastard. Walk. Find her.

"Martyn." He stood up straight.

"Baby." A first, lurching step.

"My big bear." Down the corridor, closing in.

"I DON'T UNDERSTAND," Alan said. "You said it was the last time, before."

"It should have been." Like Gideon, Mark spoke normally now; Warbeck belonged far more to the dead than the living. "But we had to see you again."

"Why?"

"Do you know how it felt," Sam said, "when you left us to die?"

"Sam, I–"

"It hurt," said Mark. "It felt like betrayal."

"We do understand," Johnny piped up. "Your sister only wanted to save you. You just wanted the pain to stop. We understand that *now*. But at the time…"

"It's our turn to betray you now," said Sam. "But we wanted to face you."

"Get on with it."

"Shut up, Gideon," Mark said. "We're sorry, Alan, for what it's worth. But we've suffered enough. Do you know what death is? What it really is? It's not like the fairy stories you tell people. There's no miraculous transcendence to a higher state. We died brutalised children, and that's how we remain. Prey."

Alan looked at Gideon. "What about him? Gideon Dace died in his seventies."

Gideon tittered. "Tell him. You're going to love this, Alan."

Mark closed his eyes, or at least the lids briefly covered the empty holes that had been his eyes. Alan had never seen that before. "Promises are kept here. In the Nexus Chamber. There's a lot of power in Ash Fell. You don't need me to tell you that. Power to change things. In Gideon's case, to restore his old appearance. A partial inducement." He spat the words out.

"They needed my help, you see, Alan," Gideon said. "Even in death, there's no justice. You can always make a plea bargain."

"For the dead to come back," said Mark, "they needed five people. You know the first four: Tahira Khalid, Roseanne Trevor, Danielle Morton, Ben Rawlinson."

"Why them?"

"They all had the Sight. Maybe only a touch, but that's enough. It's a rare gift. There are only two others in Kempforth, and they were both forbidden. One of the dead, one of their leaders – they're his family. And he said, don't touch." Mark shook his head. "But that didn't really matter."

"The Spindly Men could only take four by force," Johnny said. "The fifth and last had to come of his own free will."

"You had a vestigial trace of the Sight," said Sam. "When we died, the others here came to us. They offered us something we wanted if we acted as your guides, developed your gift…"

"And won your trust," said Gideon. "Oh yes, Alan. The plan went back as far as your childhood. Your whole life has been a preparation for this. Once you were here, I could guide you. It'd stop you guessing the truth till it was too late. I agreed, in return for… parole. I've done my time. So I'm restored, and free to go."

"Better than you deserve," said Mark, "but we'll let that pass."

"Well, if we're going to debate morality, Mark, it was you who mentioned betrayal. What's in this place can't reach far beyond Kempforth. But your trusted spirit guides could." .

Alan couldn't speak. He looked at the boys, their empty eyes.

"We wanted to have the courage to tell you to your face," said Sam. "And to show you something."

"What?"

"The price *we* demanded."

The light behind the boys widened, to expose three men kneeling naked in the centre of the room. Their hands were lashed behind their backs, ankles tied together, ball gags in their mouths. On the left, a big, fat man with piggy eyes; on the right, a lean one with a craggy face and iron-grey hair. "Mr Fitton," Alan whispered. "Father Sykes."

"Yes," Johnny said.

And in the middle–

"Walsh."

"Yes. The policeman's still alive. But we'll take him soon. Tonight."

"What about the Shrike?"

"He's beyond reach," said Mark. "He isn't truly human. He's nothing to do with this. Just something… that passed through." He looked back down at Walsh, Sykes, Fitton. "This was our price. The power to take revenge. For you as well as us, Alan."

Gideon slow-handclapped. "Deeply moving. Can we get on with this?"

Mark sighed. "Alright."

What happened next took a moment and an eternity. The skin of the boys' faces dried and stretched, grew woody and hard. The black slits of their eyes filled up with a livid red glow; their mouths stretched impossibly wide, their teeth growing triangular and serrated like a shark's. Their hair fell out. They turned and advanced on Walsh, Fitton and Sykes. Walsh was whimpering; Fitton snarled curses through his gag, and Father Sykes seemed to be praying to a god who, if he'd ever existed, had abandoned the priest long ago.

The three dead boys raised their hands, which had now become long, reptilian claws. The light changed as they leapt, became a jagged flicker like a strobe. Walsh and his friends started screaming; it almost drowned out the gobbling snarls of what the boys had become. But not quite. Their shapes blurred, until there was no telling who was screaming in torment or snarling in bloody triumph. A jumble of faces; the flicker grew blinding, the light cut out and they were gone, leaving only a few last, fading screams.

The light returned, a steady pool; Gideon stepped back into it. "Now," he said, "let's begin."

The light spread to fill the chamber.

The chamber was pentagonal in shape. The door they'd entered through was halfway along the base; the pentagon's apex was straight ahead. Symbols covered the walls. Some – pentagrams, black suns – he recognised; others were beyond what little occult knowledge he'd ever had. At each corner was a stone plinth. The one ahead of him, at the apex, was empty. The others… weren't.

On one side was a man in his twenties. His lower half was embedded in the plinth. The stone had grown into and through him; a spar of rock pushed out through the flesh of his cheek. He stared off to the side; his lips moved weakly, without sound. To the other side was a thin, dark-haired girl about the same age. The plinth's mass had grown upwards over her belly and her right forearm; the other arm hung limp and twitching. Two stone fangs tore through the skin below her collarbones. Her head fell backwards and forwards; tears splashed on the tattered t-shirt whose remnants barely covered her meagre breasts.

"Go forward," said Gideon, breath warm and rank on the back of Alan's neck. Alan skirted the chamber's exact centre, where lines of pale-coloured tiles ran from each corner to converge on a silver plate chased with symbols he couldn't name, the focus of all Ash Fell's suffering. A low, resonating chant began, coming from all around him.

Ahead and to the left was an Asian girl in her teens; she might have been pretty once. The part that appalled Alan was that she was still alive. The stone wasn't swallowing her up like the others; at first glance she just seemed to be sitting on the plinth, but it was as if a spiky tree of stone had grown up through her body and sprouted in all directions. Long thin spines of rock emerged from her thighs and arms, her belly, breasts and back, her neck, her cheeks. The top of the tree came out of her mouth, forcing her head backwards; she stared up at the ceiling, tears dripping from the corners of her eyes.

But the worst – the worst was the last one. The child. How old? Two; Renwick had said something about it. It had been personal for her, anyone could see. Renwick was dead; better, perhaps, that she hadn't lived to see this.

At least the physical damage was hidden. All he could see of the child was a head and weakly flailing arm; the rest was buried in the stone. But the dull, resigned anguish on the child's face was bad enough.

And up ahead, the last plinth awaited him. The shadows beyond it teemed with motion. The Spindly Men moved forward to meet him; behind them other figures, malformed or rocking, twisted with lunacy, shuffled in their wake.

He turned, and any thought of escape died as Gideon stepped backwards, smiling, and more Spindly Men sealed off Alan's retreat.

There was no point fighting, and Alan didn't even try; he'd come here of his own free will, but he had none now. The boys' betrayal had drained everything from him. And perhaps this was what he'd always really deserved. Clawlike hands guided him to the plinth. A last, bitter thought: he was ending as he'd begun, the unwilling means of another's release.

CHAPTER TWENTY-EIGHT

THE CORRIDOR WAS narrow; if Martyn stretched out both arms he could touch the sides. His feet were killing; it helped him carry on.

But there was light up ahead, and Eva's voice was clearer than ever. With the last of his strength, Martyn stumbled on.

"ANNA, ARE YOU sure about this?"

"We've got to try it."

"No, what we should be trying to do is get out of here, tell someone."

Anna stuffed the Ash Fell plans back in her bag with Sir Charles' diary and zipped it shut. "Number one, good luck convincing them. Number two, what makes you think we'll be allowed to leave?"

"Allowed?"

"Sir Charles led us here. I'm guessing he wanted us to try and stop what's happened."

"Sod him. Let him stop it. It was his bloody idea."

"Not this. Ash Fell's not doing what he built it to anymore. He wanted to regenerate Britain, not turn it into the land of the dead."

"This place won't let us out." Vera opened her mouth, closed it, sagged. Anna put both hands on her shoulders.

"If we can find the hidden chamber – that's the focal point. Best chance of throwing a spanner in the works."

"Find it how?"

"Well, we're now at the exact centre of the Warbeck building."

"So?"

"So the hidden chamber–" She wouldn't say *the Nexus Chamber* "–should be directly underneath."

"Should."

"Should."

"This place shifts about to suit itself."

"Don't see what alternatives we've got. Plus..."

"What?"

"According to the plans, there's a secret passageway to the chamber from the director's office."

"Where?"

Anna crossed to a bookcase, pulled; she jumped back as it toppled, crashed to the floor, dust billowing up.

"Jesus!" Vera ran to the office door, peered through the glass, checking if anyone – *anything* – had heard.

Anna coughed, waved the dust away

"Can't see anything," Vera said. The walls were oak-panelled; there was no visible join.

"Keep watch." Anna pushed the rest of the bookcase clear. When that was done, she felt around the oak panelling. There had to be a catch or join.

"Anna, someone's coming. Anna!"

"Bar the door. Something. Wait–"

She found something; a join, and then a catch. She pushed it. A click, and a section of panelling swung out. The escaping air was cold and dank.

THE END OF the corridor; Martyn could see it. There was a door, ajar.

"Martyn. Baby. My big bear."

He staggered the last few steps to the end, fell against the doorway, stared through it into the room beyond.

There were rows of tables. Buckets and car batteries stood on them, and painted masks. Plaster casts on the wall. Shackleton Street must have been an outpost, a base of operations in the town; they'd fallen back here when it was discovered.

"Martyn. Baby. My big bear."

"Eva?"

"Martyn. Baby. My big bear."

The room was huge; he never seemed to get any farther along it, but maybe that was just exhaustion. He kept going, of course; wasn't giving up this close to her.

The first woman was curled up on her side by one of the tables. He knew from the blonde hair that she wasn't Eva, but he checked anyway, felt her throat for a pulse. Nothing, of course. He didn't recognise her, but he'd only known a few of Eva's mates from the class. Besides, Christ knew what a month here left you looking like. He closed her eyes. She was somebody's sister, daughter, mother, wife. As he went on, he saw others, laid out on the floor.

"Martyn. Baby. My big bear."

He went from body to body, checking each one.

Young, old, fat, thin, blonde, brunette, redhead, grey-haired. None of them were Eva, but still she called.

"Martyn. Baby. My big bear."

So. Real then. Alive. "Eva," he mumbled. And stood up, and walked on.

SOMETHING SLAMMED AGAINST the office door.

"Shit." Vera backed away.

"Vera, through here."

"Hang on." Vera applied a last trace of mascara.

"You're touching up your makeup at a time like this?"

Vera patted her hair. "If I'm going to die, I at least want to look good."

"Take my word for it. You do."

A moment's silence; they studied each other. Vera smiled. "Let's go, then."

"OK."

Anna flashed her torch through the open door, down a flight of damp stone steps littered with brick and plaster. It was dark except where light glinted through holes in the wall. A steel rail was set into the wall. Anna went through; Vera followed and, as another blow hit the office door, dragged the hidden door shut behind them.

"MARTYN. BABY. MY big bear."

The far end of the room. There was a door with a cracked frosted glass pane; through it he could see a spiral staircase. But there was a woman huddled against the wall. She was alive, and she was talking. But even without that, and even though her head hung forward, he knew who it was. He knew by the way her bell of auburn hair fell over her face, by the intricately worked silver ring on the little toe of her bare left foot.

"Eva," he whispered. "Eva." He said it as a Christian might say *alleluia*.

"Martyn. Baby. My big bear."

He knelt beside her. "I'm here, love," he said. "You're safe now." That wasn't true, but he'd bloody make it so. "I'm gonna get you out of here."

"Martyn. Baby. My big bear."

"Yeah, love, it's me. Eva, it's me. Eva? Eva?"

"Martyn. Baby. My big bear."

"Eva–"

When he tried to hold her she was like rock; rigid, wouldn't budge. And when he managed to force her chin up, her eyes were staring sightlessly into forever, not knowing he was there or caring. She was talking to some other version of him, far beyond his reach.

HALFWAY DOWN THE steps she heard the screams. It took Anna a few seconds to make out the words, or rather word; a woman's name, screamed over and over.

"Martyn–" The screaming came from nearby, almost next to her. And then she saw the hole in the wall inches from her. She looked through it and–

–and there was Martyn, kneeling, embracing a woman with reddish hair. Anna saw the woman's face; Eva.

"Martyn!"

He looked up, blinked. She shouted him again, stuck her hand through the hole in the wall, and he saw her. "She's gone," he said; Anna saw Eva's blank stare and the slackly, silently moving lips and understood.

The shadows behind him moved; tattered black cloaks swept the floor, elongated claws unfurled and the Spindly Men's pitiless masks stared down. "Martyn–" She pointed.

Martyn saw them, but didn't seem to care. He made a token effort to rise; he might have tried to run if he could have brought Eva with him, but she was immobile. He looked at her, then Anna, and sank back down. "Go."

"Martyn–"

"Just bloody go," he shouted, pulling Eva to him, burying his face in her shoulder. And then Vera was yanking her arm, shouting at Anna to move, and then she was running too.

HE MUST'VE KNOWN it all along, deep down; she couldn't have survived. He'd never had a chance of finding the red-haired, blue-eyed girl who'd come down the church aisle in a cream dress and veil. She was gone; she'd been gone since the fire on Armistice Day, and ever since then he'd been on borrowed time. It was almost a relief, now he knew. He could stop now. He could just give up.

Martyn buried his face in her hair, breathed the sweet, lingering scent of her. Anna would look after Mary; this was where his life had always been. He had time to whisper Eva's name once more before cold dead fingers touched his forehead; it was the closest he could come to a prayer.

CHAPTER TWENTY-NINE

"COME ON." ANNA scrambled down the steps. "There's no time–"

"Anna, wait up–"

"No time." *Martyn*. She wouldn't think of him. She might feel something if she did, and that would be death here. She felt numb; that was best. *Martyn*. She had to get out, find Mary... Christ, she'd have to *tell* Mary. And what might he have told Mary about Eva? *Martyn*.

No, she mustn't think of him. Had to focus on this place. The gates were opening, or about to. She had to try and stop it, if she could. And then? God knew.

"Come on!" Vera, at her heels. Did Vera think Anna was getting them out? Sorry, Vera, no. Had to keep going, do whatever could be done to stop this if there was a way. But Vera was following her, down the stairs. It was getting colder now; darker too. No more light coming in through the gaps in the walls. Below ground level. Basement, sub-basement, and the Nexus Chamber. The cold black dark and only the torch to probe it; it seemed every step would bring something monstrous lunging up to meet them. But it didn't.

She held onto the rail as she went; suddenly it vibrated, thrummed like a live cable. She snatched her hand away, almost overbalanced. A low humming sound; threads of dust spidered down from above.

"What...?" said Vera. The steps shook; she swayed and nearly fell.

"Grab the rail," Anna shouted, seizing hold. She glanced back to see the older woman clutching it two-handed. The humming became a full-throated roar; the building juddered. More dust rained down, tiny pebbles, fragments of concrete.

"Christ! The whole lot's coming down!" Vera yelled.

Anna looked up at the concrete ceiling; if it fell, they wouldn't have a prayer. The roar got louder still. She'd been to a heavy metal concert once at college, with Peter; when she'd stood too near to one of the speakers it had felt like this, a deafening blast of sound that shook your internal organs. Except this was much more powerful. Christ, if the building didn't collapse this might kill her. She thought she heard someone screaming somewhere, but couldn't be sure.

And then the building simply juddered to a stop, so abruptly she lost her balance, nearly pitching down the steps. The dust hissed down a few seconds longer, then stopped. A thin whine sounded in Anna's ears.

"Anna? The fuck was that?"

She brushed dust from her hair. "I think it's started. Come on. Got to try."

The staircase opened out into a corridor. To their left, it ended in a brick wall. Anna blinked; for a moment she thought she saw a corridor extending into the distance, a figure in evening dress, but then it was gone. To the right, the corridor led to another wall, but this one had a door in it.

"The Nexus Chamber, I'm guessing," Vera muttered.

As they neared the door, a weak, relentless moaning came through the pitted wood. Her legs didn't feel steady. She didn't want to see whatever was behind it, but she knew she'd have to. Avenge Martyn. Stop whatever was happening. Most of all, protect Mary. Forget everything else, that last was her bottom line. She turned the handle.

The pentagonal room beyond was almost empty of the living. Someone knelt by the plinth at the opposite end, swaying back and forth, hands over his face. Anna could see the bowed head, the dark hair with its traces of silver.

"Allen." Vera stumbled to him. As she did, Anna saw the other plinths, and the bodies fused into them. The boy in one corner. The girl in the other. And, flanking Allen, a teenaged girl and – *Jesus* – a toddler, little more than a baby.

They were all dead; their stillness, the lack of breath hanging like smoke in the cold air, the unblinking eyes all told her that. She didn't need to seek a pulse, although she did. They were still warm, cheeks damp with tears. Each one someone's child. And some of them would have had brothers and sisters. Like she'd had Martyn. White pain flared in her at the thought, but it was distant; there were other things she had to focus on now.

She didn't know how, but she managed to close all their eyes, the child's last of all. Renwick had been so determined to save her.

"Allen. Allen, let me see."

Anna went over to her. "What's wrong?"

"His face. Something."

Maybe something had gone wrong; maybe he'd been hurt somehow defeating Ash Fell's purpose at the last.

"Allen, let me see."

Allen's hands came away from his face; Vera cried out.

The face beneath wasn't Allen's; it was thinner, with a neat moustache, and immobile. Close to, you could see it wasn't flesh and blood. Another prosthetic mask. There was blood on his hands, dripping out from under the mask.

Allen reached for the mask; Vera caught his wrists. "Allen, no – oh god – Allen, don't, we'll get you to a hospital."

Allen tore his hands free, got hold of the mask and wrenched at it. A muffled scream escaped the immobile mouth. Fresh blood splashed his already soiled shirt. Vera cried out, reaching for him, but he flailed at her with one hand – and at Anna when she tried to help – while the other kept pushing at the mask. He bellowed as the lower part of it pulled away from his face and levered slowly upward.

"Allen!"

The mask came away, fell from Allen's fingers to the floor. What lay beneath was raw and slick with blood. He reached for his face again, wiping the blood away from what she now saw was another mask, slightly smaller than the first.

Allen hooked two fingers into the eyeholes, his thumb into the mouth, pulled; with a wet ripping noise the mask tore free, clattering on the floor beside the first.

Beneath this mask was another, and another beneath that. Each was smaller than the last, and deeper set. Each was sunk deeper into the front of Allen's head. The latest mask was set at the back of an ever-deepening cavern of raw, red flesh. No bone, no brain, though both should have been reached by now; just mask after mask in an empty, hollow head that, even though it shouldn't have been capable, screamed and screamed.

Vera was screaming too, pushing herself away from the sight on her bottom; Anna couldn't move.

They'd come too late. This had been years, decades, in the brewing. She'd been an idiot to think she could stop it now. She pulled Vera to her feet. Allen, still moaning, still tearing off mask after mask after mask, crawled across the floor, towards the silver plate in the centre of the room.

There. The centre. The heart of the machine. If she could stop him reaching that, there might be a chance. If she killed him. He was as good as dead already; it'd be a mercy. She had to find a weapo–

But a pale light, coming from no visible source, already suffused the centre of the room, and vague, inchoate shapes moved into it out of the dark. The Spindly Men, in their tattered black cloaks, and behind them, the vanguard of this army of the lost and damned. And as they closed in on Anna and Vera, they began to sing.

CHAPTER THIRTY

"MIKE?" THE DECEMBER wind's low keening, through E Block's broken windows. "Mike, are we dead?"

Stakowski opened his eyes at last. His arm ached from holding the gun. His knees ached too. How long had he been crouched like that?

"*Mike*! Over here, you bloody mushroom."

Joan–

Stakowski looked round, not daring to believe. She was trying to get up. "Easy, lass."

"Don't 'easy, lass' me. What the hell happened?"

"Every bugger else died, basically." Stakowski propped her against the wall, rubbed his arm and winced.

"What about the civvies? Anna, Martyn, Cowell–?" She was pale, eyes sunken, blood crusted down the side of her face; a bullet had clipped her just above the ear.

"Last I saw, they were pegging it for the main path. They've any sense, they'll keep going."

"You didn't go with them?"

"I got them out, like you said. I weren't leaving you here on your tod."

"You should've."

"Well, I couldn't." Stakowski reloaded his Glock, got up.

"What you doing?"

"Checking for survivors."

Empty cartridges clinked underfoot; the air stank of gunsmoke, blood, death.

Stray specks of dust danced in the light. Stakowski reached McAdams first, did his best to close his eyes. Poor bastard's face would give the Devil nightmares; he'd died screaming and it showed.

It was the same story with them all. Most, like McAdams, just seemed to have collapsed, hearts giving out. Crosbie had gouged his eyes out before dying; Wayland had beaten his head in against the floor. A couple of others had shot themselves, like Ashraf.

"They're all dead."

"All of them?"

"Yeah." Stakowski caught her as she almost fell. "Jesus, boss, take it easy."

"Fuck that."

"Shurrup." She'd been hit three times; one round had struck the body armour over her chest, another had plucked the meat of her left shoulder; the third and last was the head wound. Stakowski cleaned and bandaged both. "You'll probably have a fine set of bruises on your chest and all," he said.

"Doubt anyone'll be looking at my boobs for the foreseeable. Where's my Glock?"

"Here. So what's the plan now?"

"Find the others and pull out. Just for now. We've

still got the Warbeck building to search. Chances are the mispers are in there."

"Boss, we need to get you to a hospital."

"I'm not giving up till I'm sure."

"Joan, there are two of us left. What good are we gonna do?"

"Hang on. What's that? There. Look."

Something lay glinting in the centre of the Black Sun on the floor. "Gold watch."

"Not just any gold watch. Look at it. It's a Rolex. They are *not* cheap."

"Jesus. It's Cowell's."

"What?"

"The watch. It's Cowell's. I'd know that lump of bling anywhere."

Renwick swayed, then steadied herself. "Cowell's watch. Tahira's pendant, Rawlinson's skull ring, Morton's necklace." A pause. "Roseanne's romper suit. But this one was empty before. Oh Christ. We're bloody idiots, Mike. He was being called back, alright. Whatever's here wanted Cowell. And we hand-delivered him."

ALLEN CRAWLED ACROSS the floor, towards the cold, unnatural light at its centre. If Anna could pull him back from the centre, could she stop it? Yes, for as long it took the Spindly Men to reach her. She'd seen what their touch brought. Not that staying where they were would save her, or Vera; the Spindly Men were closing in.

They hadn't meant to kill her before; they'd just herded her like a sheep and given her that extra scare to

convince her she was right, to ensure she gave Renwick
Ash Fell's history. Just as Allen had never been in danger
when they'd appeared behind him in the evidence room;
it'd all been a show to convince the police he was for
real, to make sure that they brought the fifth and final
sacrifice here, so he could come to the Nexus Chamber
of his own free will.

Another bloodied mask fell from the hole in Allen's
head and clattered on the floor. The dead parted to let
him crawl through, then closed ranks as he passed, their
song, their chant, never faltering.

The Spindly Men turned towards her and Vera, and
stepped forward.

Hands reached for them. She shrank back, Vera with
her, but there was nowhere to go. So this was how it
ended – so much left undone or deferred, for such petty
and stupid reasons. She shut her eyes, then opened
them. She'd flinched from things too long. She'd die
with her eyes open if nothing else.

And Mary? Martyn was gone. Eva was gone. Anna
was all she had left. She couldn't die. Mustn't. There
had to be something–

Her pockets. She fumbled for the rowan twig, Nan's
cross. Desperation now, but she had to try. She found
the twig first. She thrust it at them like a gun, sweeping
it this way, then that. For the briefest instant, she
thought they hesitated, but then they came forwards
again and cold, elongated fingers plucked the twig from
hers, snapped it in half, flicked it aside.

The cross. Nan had thought it would help. Nan had
the Sight. Would it help you, if you didn't believe? She
held it up; the hands kept reaching.

And then they stopped. The chamber fell silent,

broken only by Alan's moans as he crawled. Then the hands were lowered; the Spindly Men and the vague, shuffling shapes behind them moved aside. A Spindly Man advanced – tall, masked, dressed in tattered black – but this one was different. His hands, she realised, were those of a human.

He reached out. His fingers brushed the cross. The Spindly Man caressed it, almost tenderly. Then he reached up and took off his mask.

The face beneath it was unmarked. Perfectly recognisable. Anna knew it well. She'd seen it a hundred times in Nan's wedding photo, bowler-hatted, weary and unsmiling, puffy with drink.

Of course. This place had fed on him too. He hadn't escaped. But he'd been the man who locked the E Block doors, delivered up St. John Dace and the others for vengeance. Who better to lead the army of the dead?

For a moment, it was just the two of them. The Spindly Men, the other dead, Alan, even Vera; all of them disappeared and there was just the past, looking into the eyes of the present it sought to sweep away.

Her great-grandfather's hand rose; a finger pointed. Her own family. Was her life so devoid of redeeming qualities, or was he powerless to show mercy? She shrank away, but others closed behind her.

A single fingertip touched her, just above the left breast. A moment of searing cold; she cried out, almost fell. But she was still alive, and her great-grandfather stepped away from her. The ranks of the Spindly Men and the dead parted too, leaving a clear path back to the chamber door. As the chanting began again, a young man in evening dress stepped forward to open it, met her eyes and smiled: Gideon Dace.

Allen had almost reached the centre. Vera moved towards him, but Anna's great-grandfather barred her way, pointing at the door.

"Come on," said Anna. "Before they change their minds."

"Alan–"

"There's nothing you can do."

Vera let herself be led. A faint noise came from her throat as they passed the hunched, crawling shape, but she carried on.

Gideon's smile didn't waver as they went through the door and his empty eyes never left hers. Anna looked back at the threshold; so did Vera, and cried out as the pale light from the floor flickered into the red, gaping hole that'd been her brother's face, illuminating the inside of a head that had been hollowed to an empty shell. He shouldn't have been alive, let alone able to scream, but he did, as if he'd somehow seen his reflection. There was pain there, and fear; misery too, grief. And then the chanting rose to a crescendo and the glow from the plate brightened, became a column of cold glittering light that flared brilliantly and consumed him in the instant before Gideon, smirking, closed the door on them.

Light glowed through the edges of the doorframe; a low roar built as the floor shuddered underfoot. Tattered, skeletal shapes darted past them; Vera screamed. The Spindly Men. But they weren't interested in Anna or Vera now. They'd done their job. The gates were opening. It was in the hands of others now.

Anna dragged Vera towards the stone steps, back into the director's office. More streams of dust hissed down past them as they ran out onto the landing and down the lurching spiral staircase. She was still clutching Nan's crucifix; she thrust it into her pocket, before using both hands to grasp the rails. The spot above her left breast burned, as if a piece of ice was pressed to it.

"Where now?" Vera shouted in her ear.

If they were allowed to leave, if the building had played the last of its tricks on them – if it had, the reception area would be straight ahead. "This way. Come on."

THERE WAS A low, rumbling roar as Renwick and Stakowski reached the main path and a wind blew up from nowhere. Renwick staggered, clutching Stakowski's arm; he steadied her.

"The hell's happening now?"

"Christ knows."

The front doors flew wide; two figures almost tumbled down the steps. Renwick drew her pistol, ran forward.

"Joan! For Christ's sake!" Stakowski followed. It looked like his policing days weren't done just yet, after all.

"Ms Mason?" Renwick asked.

Anna swayed, shaking, one hand pressed clawlike to her chest; Vera sank to her knees and wept.

"Where's your brother? Where's Cowell?"

Anna shook her head, mute.

"They wanted Cowell," said Stakowski. "The place did. He was the last part of whatever was going on."

"Well, it's got him," sobbed Vera, "it's bloody got him now."

THEY FLED down the path, through the trees, until it

opened out onto a flat concrete platform.

"The hell's this?" Renwick said, leaning on Stakowski.

"Old railway platform," gasped Anna. "Remember, there was an old branch line running along Dunwich Lane? Where do you think it led?"

"Jesus."

They clambered down from the platform and stumbled through the woods. "Police officer!" Stakowski kept shouting as they went. "Police officer! Hold your fire!"

The Land Rovers were waiting for them, along with half a dozen officers pointing rifles.

"DS Stakowski. This is DCI Renwick. Hold your fire, you bloody idiots. Right. Now move. We're getting the bloody hell out of here, back to Kempforth. You, give us the keys to that vehicle."

The engine ground into life. Vera huddled in the front seat; Renwick slumped in the back with Anna.

"Christ on a bike."

Renwick stared out of the side window; Stakowski looked. Clouds of yellowish-brown mist were pouring thickly down the wooded hillside. "What the bloody hell's that?"

"Something we need to get away from, Mike," said Renwick. "Drive."

Stakowski could see shapes moving in the mist. All kinds of shapes. All were, or had been, human; some seemed incomplete. At least one seemed to be in a wheelchair that moved down the hillside. "Yes, ma'am."

"And Anna, talk to me. Tell me what's coming."

"What's coming?" Anna's laugh was faint and shaky, close to madness. "Hell."

BLACK SUN RISING

'E' BLOCK

Beside the hydrotherapy bath are the rusted controls controlling the volume and temperature of water; beside the heavy bathtub, crumpled, stained and rotted, lies one of the heavy canvas sheets that once covered it except for a hole to admit the patient's head. The tub is now almost overflowing. The water is murky; in it wave green fronds of water-weed that have found a home there. The relentless drip of water echoes through the corridors, the patients' rooms where fingernail marks still score the peeling paintwork, and through a heavy steel door yawning wide to show padded walls catching the thin thread of light from a tiny window high above.

CHAPTER THIRTY-ONE

AFTERWARDS, THERE WAS silence in the car, except for Vera's sobbing. Anna fumbled Sir Charles' diary back into her backpack; her face burned. Even with Vera to back her up, who'd believe her? Even Renwick and Stakowski had only glimpsed a fragment of what Ash Fell had to offer; Anna doubted she'd ever adequately describe what she'd seen.

Didn't matter. As long as they didn't lock her up. *She* knew it was true – as long as she could get home, find Mary, get her clear–

"So what the hell do we do about it?" Renwick asked.

Anna blinked. "What?"

"Even I can tell when the shit's about to hit the fan. So?"

"I don't know. There might be something in the journal. The only other thing I can suggest is – perhaps – if Ash Fell can be destroyed."

"Destroyed?"

The icy sensation above her breast sharpened, like a

jab; Anna winced. "Blown up. I don't know if it would work, but Ash Fell's the focus."

"Need the army for that," said Stakowski. "Or the RAF."

"Ordering air-strikes is a bit outside my remit," said Renwick. "I'll have my work cut out convincing Banstead."

"I think you'll manage, boss."

Stakowski nodded at the rearview mirror. Yellowish vapour boiled out of the woods onto Dunwich Lane; shapes moved within it, advancing. It was spreading across the hillside above, rising towards the top.

Renwick covered her mouth and nose. "Christ, that *smell*."

"Like a swimming pool," said Stakowski, "but worse."

"It's chlorine gas," Anna said. The cold spot was still there. The skin felt numb. She thought of frostbite, the flesh turning black, gangrenous. That might be happening now; maybe her great-grandfather's touch had just condemned her to a different kind of death. She wanted to look; didn't dare.

"What?"

"It got used a lot on the Western Front."

"Fucking hell. Mike, is the radio working?"

"Think so."

"Get onto the station. Tell them to evacuate the town, now."

"That mist's going to be all over the town in an hour, if that," said Stakowski. "Christ, we'll never get 'em all clear in time."

"I'm fucked if I'm standing by and watching the whole bloody town wiped out. Fucking get on it, Sergeant."

"Yes, ma'am."

Vera stared out of the window, silent. Anna cleaned her face with a wet-wipe. "I need to get to Mary. Martyn–" The pain flickered, distantly, like a fire at the edge of her vision; she refused to look at it directly, focused on Mary instead "–left her with a neighbour."

"Drop you at the station? Your car's still there."

"Yes. Yes, that's fine."

"We'll take Dunwich Road South, head for Manchester."

"Can I come with you?" Vera asked. She'd stopped crying; her face was composed.

After a moment, Anna laid a hand over hers. "OK."

THE TESTAMENT OF PRIVATE OWEN SHORE and the rain beats down foul stagnant trench water laps around my groin i grip my rifle tighter with sodden gloves shivering with cold staring across the pulverised landscape of mud ponded with great drowning shellholes full of fouler water still and i stand here i stand alone with the comrades bodies scattered round and the germans starting to advance this was not the cause for which i joined my country called i answered it welshman though i was i was a briton too part of a mightier whole i came to be a man to face that challenge i envy you my lad said father youll make me proud i know only wish i was of military age for i too would go prove my manhood but what manhood is there waiting in a sodden hole in the ground to be killed and the rain beats down

*   *   *

ANNA LEAPT OUT of the Land Rover before it had even stopped at Mafeking Street and ran across the car park to the Micra. She scrambled in, slammed the door behind her, got the key in the ignition and turned it. The motor caught and growled.

Martyn folding Eva to him, burying his face in her. What about Mary, you selfish bastard? What about your bloody child?

Something banged on the passenger window; Vera. Anna unlocked the door, fastened her seatbelt as Vera got in. "Belt up," she shouted, and hit the accelerator.

Out through the gates; she'd stop for no-one now. *The family, lass. Always the family.* Had to get Mary. Nan, too. But Mary most of all. Sirens wailed. The cold spot burned at her breast, a dagger of ice pushed slowly in. She pushed the accelerator down. It was time to see how fast the Micra could go.

"YES, SIR. I'LL take full responsibility. Please... please just pass the order along. Thank you."

Renwick put the phone down. Even through the double glazing, she could hear the amplified voices blaring from the police cars as they spread out across town. *There has been a chemical spill. The town is being evacuated. Please leave for your own safety. You will be able to return when the situation is under control. If you do not have a car, the bus companies are providing transport; report to the following pick-up points.*

The yellow clouds swirled around the top of the hill. She'd tried ringing Banstead to warn him, but his phone was dead. The mist was coming down the Dunwich

Road, too. Soon it'd swallow up the Polar. Goodbye, Shackleton Street. And then it would hit the Dunwich itself.

"It's a bloody emergency," Stakowski was shouting at the next desk. "Get those bastard buses out to those pickup points. Any queries, refer them to my superior, but just get bloody moving *now*."

Nothing to take from her desk. The photo of her parents wasn't there anymore. It was back at her flat. No time to go back there. She gripped the windowsill for a second. A wave of giddiness. She shut her eyes, opened them again.

"Done," said Stakowski. "Buses are on the move."

"Good. Thanks."

"You OK?"

"No. This is a fucking shambles, Mike. Just made it up as I went along."

"What else could you've done, lass?"

"We need to evacuate the whole fucking town. We're not even gonna shift a fraction of them. People are gonna die."

"That'll happen whoever's in charge. There's not enough time."

"I've fucked this up, haven't I?"

"Number one: I've just heard you convince four superior officers we need to evacuate. Number two: it were your idea to get onto the bus companies. Each of those'll save Christ knows how many lives. Number three–"

"What?"

"Stop feeling sorry for yourself and get your arse in gear. I'd offer to make a last brew, but I don't think we've got time."

Renwick smiled back; in that moment she loved him deeply. Maybe she always had. "Probably not."

"Best go."

"Aye." Christ; he'd made a northerner of her at last. They ran for the stairs.

ANNA PULLED UP, gave Vera the house keys. "Get food, anything we can carry. There's carrier bags in the cupboard under the sink. Use them."

"Anything else?"

"The photos on the front room mantelpiece. If you've time. And, there are presents under the tree."

Always the family.

"And some books and toys from the little spare room upstairs, Mary's room."

"Gotcha."

Vera ran to the front door. Anna eyed her reflection in the rearview mirror. Wild hair, bloodshot eyes. Dirt and dust on her clothes.

That cold spot was still burning. Quickly. Now. She unbuttoned her blouse, pulled it back from the skin above her breast. There: where her great-grandfather's fingertip had touched her, the skin was hard and white, like a chicken-pox scar. Still numb, and ice cold when she touched it.

She rebuttoned her blouse with shaking fingers, tidied herself as best she could and then went up Mrs Marshall's drive.

A few streets away a police siren sounded; an amplified voice blared out: *There has been a chemical spill. The town is being evacuated. Please leave for your own safety. You will be able to return when the situation is under control.*

She rang the bell. Mrs Marshall opened the door. "Anna? Oh my god, what happened?"

Anna shook her head. Mrs Marshall bit her lip. The sirens. The blaring voice. "Anna, what's going on?"

"They're evacuating the town," Anna said. "Everyone's got to get out. Some kind of chemical leak."

Vera came running out of Anna's house holding two or three bulging carrier bags. "Ready," she called.

"Is Mary OK?" asked Anna.

Mrs Marshall's eyes flicked from Vera to her. "She was until about an hour ago. Then she started wailing for her Dad. Sobbing her heart out, she was. The bloody hell does he think he's playing at? She thinks the sun shines out of him."

Anna could only shake her head. She didn't think she could speak of it yet, not without falling apart. Mrs Marshall put a hand to her mouth.

"Don't tell Mary–" Anna said at last.

"Aunty Anna?" Mary ran down the hallway. "Where's Daddy?"

"We'll see him in a bit." Anna didn't dare look at Mrs Marshall's face.

"Where is he?"

"We've got to go now." Everyone would be trying to leave Kempforth at once. If they were caught in a traffic jam they wouldn't stand a chance.

"Where's Daddy?"

"Mary, I'll explain, I promise. But you've got to trust me for now, OK?"

"No!" Mary's fists were clenched. "I want Daddy. I–" Her bottom lip shook; her eyes filled up.

"Mrs M, do you need a lift?"

"No, no. I've got my own car, I'll be fine. You just go. Be safe. Take care."

Anna bundled Mary into the car. "Put your seatbelt on, princess."

"What about Daddy?"

"We'll see him in a bit." The lie made her sick.

"Who's that?"

The engine turned over. "This is Vera. Vera, meet Mary."

"Hi."

Mary just blinked. Anna looked away.

"Where now?" said Vera.

"Nan," said Anna.

CHAPTER THIRTY-TWO

MYFANWY LOOKS OUT over the misty lawn. Is that someone under the willow tree? Her eyes are too weak to tell. But she has another Sight. It's been years since she last used it; she thought it was gone – just one more thing age had taken from her – but now it's back again. And it takes only the tiniest effort to open that other, unseen eye, and search for Anna.

She closes her eyes, and sees.

THE TESTAMENT OF PRIVATE OWEN SHORE CONTINUED and the rain beats down foul stagnant trench water laps around my groin i grip my rifle tighter with sodden gloves shivering with cold staring across the pulverised landscape of mud ponded with great drowning shellholes full of fouler water still and i stand here i stand alone with the comrades bodies scattered round and the germans starting to advance complete

```
catatonic withdrawal no response to external
stimuli occasional increases in respiration
perspiration heartrate indicate distress
attributable to recollection of war experience
but withdrawal so complete external signs
virtually undetectable
```

FROM HIS KITCHEN window on the twelfth floor of Macy Court, the old man who called the police to Danielle Morton's flat looks down on a sea of churning, yellowish-brown smog, hiding everything below the fourth floor.

Someone's screaming. In the corridor, alarms shrill. Outside, amplified voices blare; sirens wail.

Too late for the Dunwich. Always first to get the bad, last to get the good.

Ah, well.

The kettle boils. He pours. One last cup of tea.

The screaming's from next door. Melanie; that's her name. Three kids; as many different dads. The screaming stops; a thud as a body falls.

The old man fishes the teabag out. He's always liked his tea weak. Good job, too: might have time to drink it. He sits at the kitchen table, sips.

Melanie's kids are screaming now; thin, piping cries, swiftly cut off. He sucks air through his teeth. Perhaps a mercy. Poor little sods.

He doesn't hear the door go, but someone steps into the kitchen. A brown serge uniform, and the face... no. It has no face. Just this gaping, bloodless hole. The old man takes a deep breath, drains his cup, and stands up straight. Cold white hands grip his head and–

*   *   *

MYFANWY BLINKS AND bites her lip. That's the trouble with the Sight; you don't always see what you want to, and you don't always want to see what you do. The willow's branches blow in the wind. Not long now, but she isn't ready to go yet. There's something she needs to know first.

So she closes her eyes, and sees.

BANSTEAD KNEELS NAKED in his room, thrashing himself across the back with a knotted rope. There are still those who'd persecute him, if they knew, for the past. They don't understand, of course. He's made penance: suffered guilt, prayed, mortified himself. The good in his life outweighs the bad. He's paid for his sins.

No, you haven't.

Banstead leaps up. Why's it so dark? The light's fading. He can't see his bedroom anymore. He reaches for his clothes, but they're gone. And instead of carpet he's standing on a cold earth floor.

The blackness is total. A pool of light appears; three small boys stand in it.

Hello, Mr Policeman.

The boys move forward, revealing three men: Adrian Walsh, George Fitton, Father Sykes – kneeling, bound, naked, gagged.

Remember this?

Something falls at his feet. He picks it up: the leather mask he always wore.

He's flung to the ground beside the others, then forced to kneel. Cords bite into his wrists and ankles. Something's forced into his mouth.

The boys have changed; their hands are claws, their faces like withered jack-o-lanterns.

It's our turn now.

Banstead screams through the gag, but there's no sound.

MYFANWY RECOILS, SHAKES her head, grips the walking frame to steady herself. She wishes she hadn't seen that, but at least she won't have to live with it for long. She closes her eyes again.

And sees.

"THIS WAY, GIRLS. This way, please."

Constable Brock's voice sounds thin and weak and reedy to his own ears as he jogs after the two girls – the last of the stragglers he was detailed to round up – out of the Station Hotel, towards the two buses outside it. They're holding hands, he notices. Sweet. Everything's so loud. He wants the comforting quiet of his evidence room again, but it's not to be had.

"Stay in line!" The bellow from the bus in front hardly sounds like Sergeant Graham at all, but it's her alright. "No pushing. Get back in your place, please sir."

"This one," Brock tells the girls, pointing, but they're already scrambling on board the rear bus. The doors hiss shut behind them. A roar and the bus pulls out, headlights blazing, vanishing into the mist. The other follows.

There's a stink like a swimming pool; it's burning his nose and throat. The mist is thickening round the hotel steps; dark shapes come out of it.

"Brock!" Sergeant Graham's by her car. "Get your fucking arse in gear unless you want to bloody die."

He runs over, scrambles in. The engine roars; the car pulls out. Brock's hands are shaking and he feels he's about to piss himself.

"Good work, Brock," Sergeant Graham's saying. "Knew you had it in you."

He can't tell her that he doesn't; he's got nothing left after this. He just fumbles his seat-belt into place, shuts his eyes and doesn't look back.

MYFANWY TAKES HER glasses off, plucks a tissue from her sleeve, carefully dabs her eyes. But she still hasn't found what she's looking for, so she closes them again.

And sees.

MR LEE, PROPRIETOR of the Good Luck restaurant, has not been idle; his wife, sons, daughter and three grandchildren are crammed aboard his van, and they're already turning onto Dunwich Road South.

His hands are steady on the wheel. He remembers China dimly; the Civil War, the Cultural Revolution, and the many killed by both. His father got them out. His mother fell sick and died along the way, but he and his father reached Britain.

Another war, another country, another world, and now he's become a refugee again. He isn't afraid; he's calm as he drives. He's proud of the business he has built up, but if it now has to be abandoned, the money from the wall safe is under the front seat. Once they're clear of immediate danger, he can empty his bank account, too. If you're still alive, you can always start again.

MYFANWY SMILES; SHE doesn't know Mr Lee, and Chinese food's too spicy for her – give her a stew or hotpot, or one of the old Welsh dishes she grew up with, *cawl* or *bara brith* – but she knows a kindred spirit when she sees one. The quiet, steady courage that doesn't win medals and often goes unnoticed; she's had to find it many times. Anna has it too. Poor Martyn never did, and now he's dead. She knows that. But it's Anna she has to know about.

The willow branches part; someone steps out, looks up at her.

So, here at last. But not yet. She has to know, first, that Anna's safe.

And she closes her eyes. And for the last time, sees.

WHO'S THIS IN the car with her? Some woman? Well, Myfanwy's always had a feeling about Anna. She doesn't judge. Little Mary's safe in the back; that's what matters. Never any doubt Anna would take care of the little one. And there's something else only Myfanwy sees; a point of cold, white light, glowing like a tiny star above her breast. She knows who put it there. A mark of protection. It'll keep Anna safe; she'll live, if she wants to.

On the street outside, the dead are everywhere. One steps back from his victim and motions them on their way; another kneels, head bowed, over a body, as if mourning. This is an invasion like no other; there'll be invaders seeking to spare their descendants from what's coming. Some will succeed, and others won't.

She's coming here. No Anna, don't. The mark will keep you safe from the dead, but this mist will kill you if you're caught in it. Don't burden yourself with an old woman who's lived out her span, who always knew today was her day to leave.

MYFANWY OPENS HER eyes, looks down at the empty lawn. There's a cold shadow on her back; she knows who it is.

"Hello, Da."

He doesn't answer. He takes off his mask and cap. He looks so tired still, so prematurely old.

"She'll be safe, won't she?"

He nods.

"You've come for me, then?"

He nods again.

"Will it hurt?"

He shakes his head.

"Quick? No pain?"

A nod.

Myfanwy takes a deep breath. "Alright, then. Just give me a moment."

She lowers herself into her favourite chair, makes herself comfortable as her father comes over, a cushion in his hands. A different death for her, then; quieter, more peaceful. Is there anything important she might have left undone? She can think of nothing. Better luck than most, then. She nods, settles back.

And closes her eyes.

* * *

"Aunty Anna, you're going too fast."

"It's OK, princess. We've got to go fast today." Anna swerved up the drive to Stangrove Wood. "I'll leave the engine running," she whispered to Vera. "If something happens–"

"I'll look after her."

"Don't let her see anything." Anna climbed out of the car.

"Aunty Anna!"

She'd almost reached the entrance doors when they swung wide; her great-grandfather stepped out, Nan cradled in his arms.

"No. *No!*" She almost flew at him, hopeless though it'd be, until she saw the sorrow on his face. Nan's, on the other hand, was quiet, composed, with the faintest trace of a smile. She looked like she was sleeping.

Mary, screaming.

Her great-grandfather stepped around her, walked down the drive into the thickening mist.

She climbed back into the car. Vera opened her mouth. Anna held her hand up; she didn't trust herself to speak. Mary, sobbing. *You said you wouldn't let her see.* She turned the ignition key.

On the road she passed him, still carrying Nan. He turned down a side street, towards Trafalgar Road.

THE MAIN ROADS were already clogged; Anna wove her way through the back streets to the outskirts of town. Beyond that, the Micra bounced and rattled over narrow lanes and dirt tracks, loud thumps coming from its already martyred suspension, finally joining the column of vehicles on Dunwich Road South near the front.

"Where now?" said Vera.

"Join up with Dunwich Road South, head for Manchester. What do you reckon, princess? Trip to Manchester? Go for a Chinese, maybe?"

"What about Daddy?" Mary's voice rose. "You said we'd see him."

"Anna," Vera said, and pointed; behind them the mist was coming, like a relentless river.

Anna pulled out into the right-hand lane, floored the accelerator; other cars were already flashing by. Horns blared. Cars swerved into her path up ahead; Mary screamed.

The road sloped upwards, over a rise, and they cleared it. Only half a dozen more cars did. Brakes screeched; steel and glass shattered and tore. There were screams. But no mist came over the rise – at least, not yet.

A couple of buses. A van with *Good Luck Restaurant* emblazoned on the side. Two or three police Land Rovers. Twenty or thirty cars. Anna kept looking back as they drove on, but no-one else came over the hill. She put her hand in her pocket again, gripping the cross. More about Nan than any faith; holding it gave her some sort of strength. She didn't know what kind it was, but she'd take whatever from wherever she had to now. For Mary's sake, and her own.

CHAPTER THIRTY-THREE

ANNA CHECKED THE rearview mirror continually, but there was no further sign of the mist. For now, at least, the immediate danger seemed to have passed.

As they drove, though, ugly knocking sounds came from under Minnie's hood, and a rattling from somewhere in the chassis. Anna fumbled a cassette into the deck. Sibelius. Mary liked that. *Fantasia*. She'd seen the film. Soothe Mary, calm her down. And herself.

The knocking didn't stop; it got louder. That last tearing rush to get out of town and the cross-country dash over rough roads had been too much for the old girl. *Museum piece*, Martyn had used to say.

Vera stared dully out of the window, chewing the skin around a thumbnail; Mary rocked, pale and silent, in the back, a stuffed toy clutched to her chest.

It was too easy to imagine Minnie broken down at the roadside, and her pounding on passing cars' windows, begging them to at least take Mary. Until the killing mists, and what moved in them, drifted down the road.

Vera snorted a laugh.

"What?"

"Just thought. Our Bentley was back at the hotel. We could've travelled in style." Vera's voice almost cracked. "Fine. I'm fine."

"I'm so sorry, Vera."

She shook her head. "At least he's out of it now. It's over for him. He's not in any more pain."

Anna didn't answer. Nothing she'd learned of the life to come had given any comfort so far.

Crossing a stretch of moorland, the column slowed; the police cars were pulling over. The other vehicles halted. Renwick got out of a Land Rover, pale and haggard, Stakowski beside her, close enough to catch her if she fell. Anna pulled Minnie in nearby, steam drifting out from under the hood.

"Anna. You made it."

"Just about, but my car's had it."

"Doesn't look too healthy. What do you reckon, Mike?"

"Aye. Think we've room for a little 'un."

"OK. We'll take you."

"Thanks."

"Got through to Manchester on the radio. It's bad."

"How bad?"

"They've got satellite pictures. Kempforth's gone. Probably guessed that."

"Yeah." Didn't make it easier, though. Witchbrook, the Creamery, Trafalgar Road – gone. Whatever she had thought of the place, it had been home.

"The mist has expanded east and westward, mainly. Swamped Burnley, Accrington, Oswaldtwistle, god knows how many little villages in between. They're estimating thirty, forty thousand dead. At least ten thousand refugees."

"Oh Christ."

"Seems to have stopped for now, anyway. Wind's not even shifting it." Renwick's voice shook; she dragged her sleeve across her eyes. "They're setting up refugee camps in safe zones, prepping to evacuate as far as Manchester if it comes to that. Meantime they're calling the army in, to try and contain it somehow."

"How? They're already dead."

"We've got to try."

More lives thrown away. The Somme; Passchendaele; nothing changed, nothing learnt. The same wastage. Maybe the ghosts were right to be so enraged.

"You never know," said Renwick, "maybe this is it. Maybe it'll stop here."

"No," said Anna. "I don't think it will."

"Well, we'll just have to do our best. They're going to target Ash Fell with an air-strike, like you suggested. Maybe that'll work. Anyway, I've been given directions to the nearest refugee camp. First priority's to get everyone to safety. Mike?"

"Ma'am?"

"Make sure everyone else knows where we're heading. Also, make sure the other vehicles are all roadworthy. If any of them aren't going to make it, let's find out now and get the passengers on board one that will." She touched her blood-matted hair. "I'm not losing anyone else."

ANNA WATCHED THE Micra recede into the distance, then turned back to Mary. She had an arm round her but the child sat iron-stiff, stroking her stuffed toy's head.

"Mary, I've got to tell you something."

"Don't bother." Her voice was tiny, thin and brittle, like an old woman's. "I'm not stupid."

"What?"

"It's Daddy, isn't it? He's dead. Like Mummy and Nan."

"Yes." Anna squeezed Mary round the shoulders, but the child didn't respond. "Mary, I'm sorry."

"You lied."

"I had to."

"You lied to me." Anna had been braced for howling and sobbing, but this was worse: flat, cold, a boil festering into an abscess instead of venting its poison. "I hate you," Mary said, a crack in her voice. "I hate grown-ups. You tell us to tell the truth and then you lie and you go away. You all go away and leave me and you die and it *hurts*–"

"Mary. I won't leave you. I promise."

"Daddy promised too. He lied. I hate him. I hate you all."

"Mary–"

"Go away!" It was a scream. "Just… just bloody go away. You all do. You go away and you die. You never stay. You promise you will and then you don't. Just go away!"

"Hey." Vera touched Mary's hair. "Hey." Mary looked up at her. "It's not your aunty's fault. Or your daddy's."

"Who are you?"

"I'm Vera. I lost my daddy, and my mummy, when I was about your age."

"You used to be my age?"

Anna nearly laughed. "Yes, I did, you cheeky little madam," Vera said. "It hurts. I know it hurts. I had to take care of my brother when it happened. It wasn't easy. He was... so hurt by it all. But I had to be strong. I was the eldest. I would have done anything to stop him hurting. But I couldn't. And that was the worst of all. I know exactly what it's like, sweetheart."

Mary sniffed a couple of times.

"It's OK," said Vera. "Come here."

Carefully, hesitantly, she put her arms round Mary. The child stayed like rock for a second, and then she was screaming, punching and pounding Vera with her small fists. Anna reached for her; Vera waved her back, held on. The child fell against her, sobbing, howling against the suit jacket, curling up around the pain. Vera's eyes met Anna's. Neither of them could say anything.

"Anna?" said Renwick. "Have you still got your notes?"

"Yes. Sir Charles' diary, too."

"Good. Have a look while we're en route. See if there's anything that can help us."

Anna nodded.

"Anna?"

"Yes?"

"I need to ask you..."

"Yes?"

"The missing child. Roseanne Trevor. She's definitely dead?"

"Boss—"

"Shut up, Mike. Anna? Is she?"

"Yes."

"Did she suffer?"

Anna didn't answer.

"Joan, don't go bloody torturing yourself."

"Mike, I told you to shut up and just fucking drive. Anna–"

·"I'm... I'm sorry. Yes."

The air went out of Renwick; she sagged over the dashboard.

"Boss?" Stakowski reached a hand out.

"Keep your eyes on the road!" Everyone jumped. Stakowski withdrew his hand; the Land Rover's engine purred. "Sorry. I'm sorry. Just... everybody, thanks, but... leave me alone for a bit."

Renwick sat back in her seat and looked out of the window. Stakowski drove, looking straight ahead. Anna fumbled the book open; beside her and a million miles away, Vera sang, voice wavering with her own grief:

"Heelya ho, boys, let her go, boys, swing her head round and hold together..."

A shrieking whoosh from overhead; she looked up. Half a dozen jet fighters, streaking towards Kempforth.

A little later there were muffled explosions, bright orange flashes in the distance. Then nothing. The mark on her breast stung. She looked back to the journal, tried to focus. Couldn't. What good was it? Oh, she had the Sight alright, but what good had it done? Seeing something didn't mean you could stop it; it just left you feeling more helpless.

"Heelya ho, boys, let her go, boys, sailing homeward to Mingulay..."

THE TESTAMENT OF PRIVATE OWEN SHORE CONTINUED
seeing always the dead the loneliness the bodies
everywhere cringing in the trenches under the

constant hammering of exploding shells constant
dread of the gas that might roll in at any moment
of the snipers of the german flammenwerfer but
worst of all is the waiting the helpless waiting
and the rain beats down foul stagnant trench
water laps around my groin i grip my rifle tighter
with sodden gloves shivering with cold staring
across the pulverised landscape of mud ponded
with great drowning shellholes full of fouler
water still and i stand here i stand alone with
the comrades bodies scattered round and the
germans starting to advance i did not run desert
or shirk my duty i forced myself to fight the
war come what may forever and ever war without
end amen even dead it does not end for oh yes i
am dead dead but dreaming dreaming eternally of
the war trapped almost always in the monotonous
horrors of the moments i lived and can never now
escape and the rain beats down foul stagnant
trench water laps around my groin i grip my rifle
tighter with sodden gloves shivering with cold

JUST BEFORE DARK they reached the camp on the moors.
Floodlights lit tents and prefab huts, ringed with a
barbed-wire fence. Soldiers patrolled a perimeter
dotted with sandbagged machine-gun emplacements;
helicopters clattered overhead. Their column was
directed to a separate, neighbouring enclosure, joining
a motley collection of parked-up civilian transports.

A tall black army sergeant ran up. "Inspector Renwick?"

Renwick climbed out slowly, as if bearing the world's
weight. "*Chief* Inspector."

"Sorry, ma'am. Sergeant Itejere. Welcome to Camp Dunwich."

"Thanks."

"Our OC would like to see you when you've a minute."

"Be right there." She swayed. Stakowski caught her elbow. She shrugged him off. "I'm fine."

"Boss, you need to see the MO."

"Later, Mike. There's more important stuff. Sergeant, how did the airstrike go?"

He shook his head. "Missiles veered off-course. None of them even hit the target. And then we lost contact with the planes."

"Christ. Anna, did you find anything? Anything at all?"

Anna shook her head; truth be told she'd just stared miserably at the same page throughout the whole journey.

Renwick squeezed her shoulder. "You've done everything you can. Go and rest up."

"D'you want this?" Anna held out the journal.

"You hang onto it for now." Renwick looked grey and haggard, one eye still bloodshot. If anything, it looked worse than before. "Sergeant, can you–?"

"Yes, ma'am. This way, everybody." Itejere smiled at Mary as she passed, ruffled her hair. Mary just blinked up at him with old eyes, as if viewing someone she knew was fated soon to die.

THEY WERE WEDGED into a tent with twenty or thirty other refugees; you got a blanket, a pillow and just enough space to sit up or to curl up in. It was warm, at least, but Anna could barely breathe for the reek of sweat, flatulence, feet and worse. From outside a muffled voice boomed through some kind of speaker. And any moment the alarm might sound, signalling some new threat.

"This is horrible," Mary said, huddled between Anna and Vera. "I want to go home."

"We can't, chuck," Vera said.

"Why not?"

"Because it's gone, love."

"Vera–"

"Can't cosset her all the time, Anna. You've got to be straight with her."

Mary sniffled; Vera stroked her hair, sang to her softly. *"Heelya ho, boys, let her go, boys…"*

Anna turned away. So this was her fate; after a brief period of kidding herself she mattered, she was sidelined again. Couldn't help Renwick, couldn't even help Mary. Insight without influence. Knowledge without power.

Stop feeling sorry for yourself. Mustn't cry in front of Mary. Oh Christ. Have to get out. Stay and you'll blubber like a kid.

"Can you look after Mary for a few minutes?" Vera nodded. Anna picked her way through the limbs and bodies tangled on the tent floor and out into the night.

Going away again. All of you, you always go away.

CHAPTER THIRTY-FOUR

THEY'D SET UP a TV screen on a stand in the open space near the tents. A crowd had gathered; Anna saw jeans, t-shirts, tracksuit bottoms, saris, shalwar kameez.

The Prime Minister was speaking: "… any measures to defend our people against this cowardly, unwarranted terrorist attack…"

"Terrorists," someone mumbled.

"Fucking Pakis," said someone else.

Anna saw several Asians start to move away. Heads turned. Someone grabbed one of the Asian men by the arm. Shouting, a scuffle; then the fists started flying. Screams. The soldiers moved in; Anna walked quickly off. Her hand slipped into her pocket and gripped Nan's cross.

She found a row of latrines between the tents. Inside they'd been partitioned into sections – not individual, but at least you had some privacy. Despite the cold weather she gagged on the stench. She rummaged in her backpack, found a jar of menthol rub. She rubbed some under her nose; the smell diminished.

The grief was a dull, throbbing ache, sealed behind a wall. But then she remembered Martyn hiding his face in Eva's shoulder, Nan's arms tightening around her at that last goodbye, and the wall cracked. She doubled over, felt her face contort. The sobs felt like she was trying to vomit up her grief. After a few minutes it seemed to be over. She wiped her eyes, breathed deep, tried to compose herself, but then the weeping hit again.

Grief was like a virus. She'd been like this after Dad had died; that or sunken, listless, unable to function.

Stop feeling sorry for yourself and do something then, Nan would have said. For a second, Anna thought she'd *heard* Nan say it. She blinked, sat up straight. Something was digging into her clenched hand. She looked; it was the cross. No. Nan was right. Focus. So she'd lost people? Who hadn't?

She dug out Sir Charles' journal again. If there was any solution it would be here, and she'd been too stupidly numb to look for it. He hadn't just cowered there waiting to die. He'd hidden the book in the wall, guided her and Vera to it. *...it must fall to others to avert the cataclysm. I will use a spell of concealment to hide this journal in a place of safety, until the time is right.* There was something here; something that'd help.

After Sir Charles' last diary entry, the book was half-full of blank pages. She combed through the filled pages, searching. But what for? She had no background in the occult; even if she found it, she wouldn't recognise it.

Sir Charles' neat copperplate gave way to blurred, unmarked yellowish-white, and then, three or four pages of black scribble flickered past. Anna leafed back through the journal until she found them again.

The White Song, it said at the top.

The Black Song had opened the gates.

She read.

If all else fails, one hope remains. The White Song requires little effort compared to the Black. The Black Song violates Nature's laws; it is like pushing a boulder up a near-vertical slope. The White Song is more of a gentle push; it tips the balance and sends the boulder rolling back down the mountainside.

"But how?"

I reproduce the text of the White Song phonetically overleaf. Two conditions must be met for it to be effective.

Firstly – it can only be sung by one who witnessed the gates opening.

Secondly – a blood sacrifice was required to open the gates; another is needed to close them. Fortunately the sacrifice is much smaller in magnitude.

The White Song must be prefaced by the sacrifice of the singer's child. Male, female, eldest or youngest, are immaterial. The child may even be adopted; ties of affection, not blood, are what count.

Unless both these conditions are met, the gates remain open.

She and Vera were the only witnesses; neither had any children.

Ties of affection, not blood–

Mary.

Anna slammed the book closed. She wanted to rip out the pages, stuff it into the latrine, burn it.

But it could be the only chance–

No. Never.

But what pressure might they bring to bear? Even torture, if there was no other way to stop the dead?

She wanted to laugh. Again, she could see what others

couldn't, but it brought her no joy. *Alas, how terrible is wisdom when it brings no profit to the wise.*

The harrowed, wretched faces in the tent. The reek of the latrines. The stench of chlorine. The low sobbing. The misery. Kempforth gone, the mist advancing, perhaps until it blanketed the earth from pole to pole, shore to shore. If that was the choice, could she, in all conscience, refuse to give what was required?

If it was Mary? Yes.

She stuffed the book into her backpack. There might be a way round it. Small print. Something. If Vera asked, she'd say she was reading the journal still, looking for help, but for now at least, she'd say she'd found none. She desired Vera, had even come to rely on her to an extent, but she wasn't sure she'd trust anyone with this–

Outside, a klaxon blared; shouts, running feet. Someone screaming. Then more screams, breaking glass–

Mary.

She jumped up, ran outside, almost colliding with a soldier sprinting past. He wheeled on her, swung his rifle up, lowered it.

"Get to your transport," he shouted. "We're evacuating. The mist's coming in."

THE TESTAMENT OF PRIVATE OWEN SHORE CONTINUED staring across the pulverised landscape of mud ponded with great drowning shellholes full of fouler water still and i stand here i stand alone with the comrades bodies scattered round and the germans starting to advance unaware of where i was taken the indignities heaped upon me till at last i died and the rain beats down foul stagnant

trench water laps around my groin i grip my rifle
tighter with sodden gloves shivering with cold
staring across the pulverised landscape of mud
ponded with great drowning shellholes full of
fouler water still and i stand here i stand alone
with the comrades bodies scattered round and the
germans starting to advance and the corridors
decay and the other dead search for me till one
at last enters my unending dreams and says

"OK, MOVE ALONG. *No shoving.* Keep in line. Keep
moving. We'll get you all out."

Was the soldier trying to convince the herd of refugees
shuffling towards the camp gates, or himself? Anna
clung on to Mary, Vera to her. The klaxons blared.
Engines revved nearby.

Movement was maddeningly slow. There were so
many of them, packed nearly shoulder to shoulder. She
couldn't see over their heads into the cold distance;
couldn't see the mist. It was maybe best not to know
how close or far it was. There was no sign of Renwick
or Stakowski, but then they were police officers. They'd
have orders to follow, work to do. It was all on her now.

"Mary? Sweetheart?" The child stared, eyes vast in
her numbed, white face. "Mary?" Anna's voice shook;
Mary shut her eyes.

"Easy." Vera squeezed her shoulder. "She's just shaken
up. She's lost a lot."

"She's lost everything."

"We all have."

"What's going to happen to her?" Anna touched
Mary's hair.

"She'll survive. Just got to get her out of here. We can sort the rest out later."

"Yes. Knuckle down. Get through this. Like they did in the trenches. God." She almost laughed.

Vera gripped her arm tight enough to hurt. "Anna."

"Ow. OK. OK. I'm alright."

The mark above her breast stung coldly.

"We'll make it," said Vera. "The three of us–"

Screams; shots rang out. The crowd heaved and spilled backwards. Anna stumbled; Vera held her up. For a second, the crowd parted; the way to the main gates was clear. She could have run if she'd wanted, but she didn't. Just beyond the wire was a wall of yellowish-brown mist. It poured through the open gates, and shapes – some with leering faces, some with shattered ones – leapt out of it to embrace those at the head of the column.

More screams. Somebody cannoned into Anna. Bodies piled against her, forcing her back. Vera, though... Vera was clear, struggling towards her. Anna only just managed to thrust Mary at her – "*Take her!*" – before she was driven backwards.

"*Aunty Anna! Aunty Anna!*"

She had to get back to Mary. She mustn't fall. If she fell, she'd be finished. The crowd was bearing her away from Mary. Anna tried to slip sideways, out of it. but there were more screams, and the crowd surged. Oh Christ it was a stampede, a panic.

Anna bulled her way to the side, trying to break out of the column. She stumbled, started falling; she grabbed at a man to save herself. He punched at her face. The blow glanced off her cheekbone; her glasses slipped awry. If they were lost, she'd be blind and good as dead. The stampede surged and buffeted them; she clung to her aggressor. His eyes were wild; he was bearded and shaggy-haired – an academic, a musician, a biker? The flood was slacking and she tried to pull away, but he came at her and threw another punch, missing. He swung again. When she tried to avoid this one her foot slid and she fell. He kicked out at her; it glanced off her hip with a shock of pain that almost made her vomit. He raised his foot to stamp on her; she caught it and twisted, pushed back. He shouted in pain and fell on his back. If she let him get up he'd kill her.

All at once she was terrified and full of rage, and at the same time utterly calm; things moved too fast for her to feel anything and at the same time everything was in slow motion, except her. She got up. She needed a weapon. A tent had collapsed nearby. The pole stuck out of the canvas. She grabbed it, pulled it free. The man got up and lunged at her. She hit him in the face. He staggered back, clutching his eyes; Anna ran in and hit him in the throat. His scream choked; he fell. She hit him again. And again and again; the thrill of the impact sang up her arms. No bastard would come between her and Mary.

"Anna!" Someone caught her arm. She spun. Vera. "Come on."

The man was still. Blood and hair covered the tent pole. She didn't look at it after that. The man's face was a red blob. He looked dead. Well *fuck* him. She didn't care. Her own thoughts' coldness scared her. There was a thin whining noise in her ears; her head felt light. The bastard had got what he asked for. She'd done what she had to. End of story. That was what you did to protect—

"Mary? Where's Mary?"

"She's safe, I told her to stay put. *Shit*!" Vera was

pointing at a collapsed tent. There was no-one there. "Oh, shit!"

"You *left* her?" Anna heard her voice become a scream. "You fucking left her, you–"

"I had to help *you*."

"We've got to find her."

"Fucking how, in this?" Vera didn't push the point; she could see Anna wasn't going to give way. And she wasn't running off on her own. *She needs me more than I need her.* Again that coldness of thought, as liberating as it was frightening. "Where? Where would she go?"

"I don't know. I don't–" Yes she did. "She'd hide. Inside the tents." She ran forward. "Mary. *Mary!*"

The mist was rolling in, and the dead with it. Up near the gate, soldiers in insectile respirators were standing their ground, firing at the dead without effect. Already they were falling back. The dead rushed after them, but Anna ran on.

"There–" Vera pointed. A tiny, red-haired figure scrambled out of the half-fallen tent.

"Aunty Anna! Aunty Anna!"

"Mary–" Anna ran forward. *She's screaming for* me. *Not Vera, not Daddy,* me. *I'll keep you safe, princess, I'll–*

"Aunty Anna–" And then the mist took her and Mary screamed, voice choking off; Anna ran forward, screaming too, Vera's voice shouting vainly for her to stop.

"BLOODY *DRIVE*, MIKE."

Stakowski floored the accelerator; the Land Rover roared along the camp's perimeter. Out in the mist they could hear screams and the jagged rattle of rifle fire.

"Get us round the back," Renwick said from the passenger seat.

"Alright. Put your seatbelt on." Renwick fumbled with it, fingers thick. "Christ, why didn't you see the MO when we had the chance?"

"Too much to do. 'Sides, there were plenty of others in a worse state."

"Yeah? Seen yourself in a mirror lately? You look like death on a stick–"

"Just do as you're fucking told Mike, get us round the back–"

"We're here. They're bloody streaming out. Sod-all chance of finding anyone."

"We're trying, Mike." Renwick sat up straight, teeth clenched, sweat on her brow. "We're bloody trying to find them." To find that kid, find Mary, save this one at least.

"Never said we wouldn't, boss. Now put your bloody seatbelt on."

SOLDIERS RAN PAST her; one shouted, snatched at her arm. She pulled free and ran on. In the mists, shadows fought. Running men and men who stood to fight both fell at their enemy's touch.

The edge of the mist. The swimming-pool reek of chlorine. It'd kill her if she went in. But it was killing Mary now. Wait. On the ground. Two soldiers, both dead. *The paths of glory*. They wore respirators; she pulled one off. The rest, too – the soldier was in a full suit. If the chlorine got into a cut; chlorine mixed with water became hydrochloric acid, even she knew that. She stripped the soldier, mumbling an apology as she went. Suit, gloves – *quickly, quickly* – and then she ran.

There. The tent. And Mary thrashed beside it, tearing and clutching at her face, kicking feebly. Little lungs, so easily damaged. How long? A minute? Less? More? How long did it take?

The dead rose up and wafted towards her and then away, swaying clear. The mark on her breast burned. Searing cold. Bless Nan's father for giving her the chance to save Mary. Damn her for endangering the child to begin with.

Two of the dead approached Mary; a huddled shape in a rattling wheelchair and a tall figure with a black void where its face should have been. Anna ran shrieking at them, brandishing the tent pole; they sank away into the mist. She fell to her knees beside Mary. There was froth on her lips and her eyes were bulging. Anna threw aside the tent pole and gathered her up.

"Anna–" She rose, half-turning; a shape thundered out of the mist towards her. The face was deformed, insectile. She groped for the tent pole–

"Anna!" Not an insect's face, a gas-mask. The voice, she knew it. "Anna, it's me. Vera."

Anna stood; Vera gripped her elbow and they ran, the mist foul and deep around them.

REFUGEES SPEWED OUT of the rear gates; fleeing vehicles' red taillights wove away into the night. There was a thud, screams. Stakowski saw bodies on the ground, cars bouncing over them, and turned away.

The Land Rover was halted by the gates. So far none of the refugees had noticed it, but if they did? Would they swarm over it, try to break in? He grasped his pistol, then let go of it. He had to get Renwick out of here, get her looked at. If the mist ever stopped, they might have a chance.

"Can you see anything?"

"Plenty, but not what you're talking about." A last few figures ran out through the gate; the mist was uncomfortably near. Nothing living would come out of that.

He still kept shying away from it, who they fought. On his father's side, Poland had been a different front, a different war. But his mam had talked about the men on her side of the family who'd joined the Kempforth Pals and never come back. Might be them, coming for him in that mist. Might be them behind what had been done to Roseanne Trevor and the rest, behind all the death that had followed.

The mist was almost on top of them now. He was about to tell Renwick it was hopeless, they should go, but then two figures ran out of the mist, gas-masked, one with a child in her arms. He knew the child's face, and when one of the women pulled her mask off, he knew hers too.

STAKOWSKI FLOORED THE accelerator, spun the steering wheel. Anna glimpsed shapes on the ground in the car's path, caught in its headlights; she shut her eyes. The Land Rover's wheels thumped and bounced over uneven things. *You could stop this. You could stop it.* Behind them, the mist swallowed up the perimeter fence.

She pulled off the gas mask, gulped the clean air. "Thanks," she gasped.

"Mention it." Renwick said thickly. Stakowski glanced sideways at her. "Keep your eyes on where you're going, Mike."

"Aunty. Aunty Anna–" Oh god, that voice. Mary's voice. A grating, whispering croak. "Make it stop."

"Don't try to talk." She gripped Mary's hand. Her arms and legs shook. Muscles ached in her back; her hip throbbed from the kick she'd taken. Vera squeezed her free hand.

"Thank you too," Anna got out.

Vera smiled faintly, brushed Anna's hair with her fingers. "It's OK."

Tall high rows of lights glimmered; the motorway. Red taillights wove ahead of them, down towards it.

"Where to now, ma'am?" Stakowski asked.

"Just get us away from this, Mike. Hell for leather. Get on the radio while you're at it, see if you can... if you can..."

"Boss?"

"... can..."

"Joan! Christ–" Renwick flopped sideways; the car swerved. Anna grabbed her shoulder to stop her falling; Vera cradled Mary, let her prop Renwick upright. "What's wrong with her?" Christ, his voice had nearly cracked.

"Looks like a stroke or something."

"A stroke? Christ on a bike. That headshot she took. I thought she'd been looking bad. Told her to see the quack for Christ's sake. Should've known..." Stakowski fought to steady the wheel. "We need help. OK. One of you watch behind us. Other one look after her."

"We've a little one to look after, too," shouted Vera.

"Well, bloody multi-task then. You're supposed to be good at it."

They passed a car that had flipped over; blurred,

wide-mouthed shapes flew towards them. Hands smacked at their windows; Mary let out a strangled cry. Anna glimpsed wide eyes and mouths, caught screamed threats and pleas. Stakowski shifted gears, trod harder on the accelerator; the cries faded, were gone.

"Oh god," said Anna. "We just left them–"

"Would you rather it was us?" asked Vera. "Or her?" She nodded at Mary.

"No."

"Well, then."

But it wasn't just *well, then*. It couldn't be, because she could have stopped it. Was that on Anna's head too? Was every death that happened because she wouldn't sacrifice Mary? Fuck anyone who said so. She wouldn't kill her child for anyone.

Another car lay at the foot of the motorway embankment, but there was no-one in sight; it looked like the occupants had been lucky. Stakowski fought to keep the Land Rover under control. A huge chunk of the barrier was gone; the soldiers must have ripped it up as they went. Stakowski steered through the gap onto the motorway, drove hard and fast, overtaking again and again as the speedometer climbed towards 100. The other vehicles fell behind. Some of the tension ebbed out of him.

The motorway looked deserted; he could see nothing up ahead. The sodium lights above glinted off concrete, broken glass, the ruffled fur and feathers of roadkill. "How we doing?"

"Can't see any mist," said Vera. "Think we've left it behind, for now."

"Good... oh Christ."

The motorway lights flickered, flashed twice, and went

out; the dark piled above and around them, rushing in.

"Mike!" Anna shouted; for a second she sounded like Renwick. He cut the speed as fast as he dared, turned the headlights on full beam.

Behind them, more headlights blinked into life, following.

Anna held Renwick's hand, stroked Mary's hair. "Where now?"

"The hell should I know?"

"Try the radio," said Vera.

He did, but heard only a mush of static, and dull, leaden voices full of dead, empty misery.

None of them spoke after that; the voices of the dead filled the car. Behind them, the other headlights shone in the black; the few who'd escaped. Stakowski shut the radio off, and they drove on in silence through the endless night.

CHAPTER THIRTY-FIVE

Monday 23rd December.

STAKOWSKI WOKE, BLINKING crusted eyes. He was lying on a hard surface; his head ached. His mouth tasted foul; he was bloody cold.

He sat up, hugging the coarse blanket around him. The room was bare. Blanket-wrapped bodies covered the floor. In the corner, a couple of blankets had been hung up in front of a row of buckets. Despite the cold, they reeked. The only sounds were snores and heavy, sleep-laden breathing.

In the distance, gunshots and an explosion's muffled thud.

Stakowski uncurled and rose stiffly to his feet, stretching aching muscles and wincing at the crack and creak of joints and bones. A few sleepers twitched and stirred as he picked his way over to the window, but no-one woke.

The window was cracked; a thin blade of wind

keened through it. His reflection's eyes were tired and bloodshot; there was greyish-white stubble on his face. He looked old; felt it too. And he stank; hadn't changed his clothes in two days. He felt greasy, dirty. He'd have killed for a hot bath and a leisurely soak.

His grey hair was matted, odd tufts sticking out. *Shouldn't let you out on our own at your age*, Renwick would've said. His teeth were furred, and started to chatter; he clenched them.

Cold morning; a thin snow falling. Jesus: two days to Christmas.

Half a dozen squaddies jogged down the street outside. Someone shouted orders. Stakowski heard engines revving.

The dead's dull, leaden voices had faded as they'd driven, Renwick lolling in the passenger seat, the kiddie coughing and retching in the back. Around three in the morning they'd found a living voice and been guided to an industrial estate on the outskirts of Leeds, pressed into service as an emergency refugee centre and ad hoc hospital. One blanket each, a space on the floor and a bucket to shit in.

Refugee. Stakowski tasted the word; it was bitter. His father had been one. That was why he'd come here, because Britons didn't become refugees. It hadn't all been plain sailing. If Ulster hadn't been a civil war Stakowski didn't know what was – but compared to most other countries, it had been safe. Maybe they'd been lucky to last this long.

Outside was an army Land Rover, a machine gun mounted on the back, engine running. Across the road was the 'hospital'; a defunct haulage firm's offices. Renwick was there now, and the little girl.

Best not think of Renwick now. Drive himself mad. He was having trouble thinking about yesterday, full stop. But he'd done his job, got the sick to the hospital, seen Anna and Vera securely billeted, before collapsing. He'd managed that, but he didn't know how much he had left for anything else. Stakowski breathed out; condensation bloomed across the glass.

He picked his way towards the door; Anna blinked, groped for her glasses. "Mike?"

He put a finger to his lips.

Anna nodded. Beside her, Vera started to stir.

"Wake her up," said Stakowski, "and let's go."

IN THE HOSPITAL block, they found an army medic, a haggard-looking corporal with a missing front tooth and a thick moustache.

"Griffiths, Mary..." He went down his list. "Yeah. She's here."

"How is she?" asked Anna.

"Not brilliant, to be honest. Gonna be touch and go, but we've done everything we can. You her aunty?"

"Yeah."

"She's been asking for you."

Anna half-smiled, then covered her mouth, face crumpling. Vera put an arm round her. The corporal glanced at Stakowski, opened his mouth, closed it. From outside came shouted orders, the sound of movement. Shuffling footsteps, groans, coughs; they were getting the civilians up and about.

"What time you moving out?" Stakowski asked.

"The next hour."

"Bad?" asked Stakowski.

"What do you think?" The corporal lit a cigarette, glanced round. "Only just got the word – our comms have been banjaxed. The mist's streaming south, practically in a straight line. Looks like it's being *directed*, somehow."

"Directed where?"

"On the current trajectory? London. We got a satellite picture half an hour ago. It's hit Manchester already, early this morning. The whole city's gone."

"Oh god." Anna whispered.

"It's travelling at nearly 60mph. At the current rate, it'll hit London this afternoon, early evening." He shrugged. "Makes military sense, I suppose. Take out the capital, plus it'll split the country in half. We're moving south. Try and intercept."

"And what then?"

"Hold it off as long as we can. The grey funnel line are commandeering anything that floats and shifting people offshore. Islands off the coast, neighbouring countries. Norway, Sweden, Finland are pitching in – Denmark, Holland, Belgium, Germany, even the Frogs."

"Grey funnel line?" Vera looked dazed.

"Navy," said Stakowski.

The corporal raised an eyebrow. "Where did you serve?"

"Omagh."

The corporal nodded. "Lived in Northern Ireland for a bit. My dad was stationed there. Anyway, the plan's to get you civvies to an evacuation point on the coast, probably Scarborough or Filey. There'll be a skeleton force acting as escorts. Me, I'm heading south. We can't take any patients with us, so they'll be moved out with the rest of you. Some of them aren't going to make it,

state they're in, but there's not much else we can do."
He saw Anna's face. "Keep your kid warm, fresh air if
you can get it. Other than that, pray. Hard."

Anna covered her mouth.

Stakowski coughed. "There's another patient came in
with us."

"I'll have a shufti. What name was it?"

"Renwick. Joan Renwick."

The corporal ran his finger down the list, then
stopped. Stakowski bit his lip, clenched and unclenched
impotent fists.

"Shit." The corporal looked up. "I'm sorry."

"When?"

"Oh-seven-thirty-five. Never regained consciousness.
Best guess is a brain aneurysm. Nothing we could do."

Stakowski nodded. His body was a huge, leaden suit
of armour that he was trapped inside; a tiny, wearied
speck expending its finite energy in flexing its limbs.
"I'll take you to the little one," the corporal told Anna
and Vera. "Will you be OK?"

It took Stakowski a moment to realise the corporal
meant him. He turned away. The window facing him
was vast and swam with winter light. He stepped
towards it, swayed, leant against the wall. A hand on
his shoulder; Anna. He shrugged her off. He couldn't
bear anyone's comfort, not now.

"Come on," the corporal said again.

That was it, then; all over. Their footsteps clicked,
faded, became silence. Stakowski went to the window.
Below was the haulage yard. In it, stacked in piles, were
dozens of bodies. Outside the surrounding wall, thick
black smoke billowed up. He was glad the window was
tightly sealed; he knew what it'd smell like.

*   *   *

ENGINES GRUMBLED; REFUGEES stumbled out into the street. A truck rolled past. Stakowski glimped white, drained faces staring out from the back.

He saw his reflection in a cracked window; he looked even older than before. Gaunt. He touched the whitish stubble on his cheeks. Did his hand shake? Didn't matter now. Nothing mattered.

The tiny spark within him was still working his limbs, but it was growing ever more feeble. Anna, Vera and Mary would get a ride to the coast, a chance of survival. He didn't give much for the kid's chances, but he'd keep his fingers crossed for her.

And him; what of him?

He still had his Glock; a minute alone was all he'd need. Then he saw the corporal outside the hospital building, puffing on his cigarette. No, there was another way. He took a deep breath, made his choice and walked towards the hospital.

THE TESTAMENT OF PRIVATE OWEN SHORE CONCLUDED and the rain beats down foul stagnant trench water laps around my groin i grip my rifle tighter with sodden gloves shivering with cold staring across the pulverised landscape of mud ponded with great drowning shellholes full of fouler water still and i stand here i stand alone with the comrades bodies scattered round and the germans starting to advance and someone finds me says theres a way out an exit from this nightmare if you dare take it if you will fight one last time a new front a new enemy we can break out and all shall be well

all shall be well all manner of things shall
be well and the rain beats down foul stagnant
trench water laps around my groin i grip my rifle
tighter with sodden gloves shivering with cold
staring across the pulverised landscape of mud
ponded with great drowning shellholes full of
fouler water still and i stand here i stand alone
with the comrades bodies scattered round and the
germans starting to advance and i turn to him and
what can i say but yes

"MIKE?"

Stakowski blinked and turned. "Been looking for me, lass?"

Anna nodded. "You in the army now?"

He glanced down at his hastily slung-together uniform, the rifle in his hands. "They took me back, you might say. Not much else I'm good for, with her gone."

The hazel eyes glistened. "I'm so sorry."

He waved it aside. "Nowt to be sorry for, lass. Did all you could. Be a damn sight worse else. Lot of folk who'd not've made it, if it weren't for you."

"But there's so many who didn't."

"Well, that's not your fault, is it?"

She looked down. "No," she said at last. "No."

"Aunty," whispered Mary, holding out a pale hand. Anna took it.

"Anna," said Vera, "we've got to–"

"Yes." She kissed his cheek. "Goodbye, Mike."

Stakowski blinked. For a moment, he saw Renwick there. "Take care, lass."

Anna looked away. "Good luck," said Vera.

"You too."

"Anna–"

A voice shouted orders; Stakowski put his helmet on. "Gotta go," he said.

He ran to the waiting truck, climbed aboard. Someone passed him the camouflage paint. When he'd applied it he lit a cigarette. They'd issued him with a respirator; that would help, for a time.

The truck pulled out.

Better this way. Nowt else left. He patted the rifle. What he'd seen of the afterlife wasn't promising, but with a bit of luck he'd see Renwick again. Might get complicated if Laney turned up too, though.

Stakowski smiled. It faded fast. He finished his cigarette, flicked it out over the tailgate; it bobbed in the slipstream and fell away.

CHAPTER THIRTY-SIX

THE MILES UNFOLDED; the mist, at least for now, receded. Anna sat in the back of a truck full of casualties, Mary huddled against her in a blanket, pale face sheened with sweat, coughing. Mary had refused to let Anna's hand go, croaking *Aunty* over and over again, and the soldiers had let her ride with the child.

The truck bounced and jolted over the frozen roads. Too fast for weather like this, but there was no choice. Flurries of snow whipped past; the winter landscape went by. Empty houses, Christmas decorations still hung in their windows. Cars abandoned by the roadside, doors ajar. A discarded suitcase in the middle of a road. A small, huddled body on the pavement. Above, ravens wheeled, tiny black arrowheads, against the bleached and empty sky.

Mary coughed; there was blood. Anna wiped her lips. The White Song. *No.* She might die anyway and any chance to stop this would be lost. Mary gripped Anna's hand so tightly it hurt. But this pain was sweet. Anna squeezed gently back. *No-one will harm you.*

They reached Scarborough in the early afternoon. There were tailbacks on the roads outside the town. They were waved in once the previous batch of refugees had been ferried away. The streets were empty; the town's population had already been evacuated. Houses stood open to provide billets for the refugees.

Mary was gently taken from her arms, carried to a seafront café serving as a makeshift clinic.

"Anna, love?" She turned; Vera. "Come here."

Vera guided her to a small terraced house they'd been allocated. The electricity was still on; voices seemed to be coming from inside, but it was only the television in the front room that someone had on. Every TV channel showed only a series of test cards, jumping and flickering with interference: EMERGENCY BROADCAST – AWAIT FURTHER INSTRUCTIONS. Shattered, mangled faces superimposed over the picture, their leaden mumbling voices in the static from the speakers. In one corner stood a Christmas tree, lights aglow, almost bowed down with the weight of tinsel and baubles adorning it. The presents were still stacked underneath. Had Vera had time to grab Mary's presents? What did that matter now? They were worthless now, meaningless. To Mary, to anybody. To her. *All I want for Christmas is Mary's life.*

Anna collapsed beside Vera on the sofa. Vera reached out; Anna clung to her. She wasn't sure any longer who was giving comfort and who was receiving it. She shook. It was all waiting now, for a boat out. Waiting and hoping the boat reached Scarborough before the dead.

Vera's lips brushed hers. A small, agile tongue, warm and moist, darted into her mouth. Anna responded.

Fingers slid under her sweater, stroked her breasts through her shirt and bra. Her nipples hardened; warmth gathered in her belly. She reached down and caught Vera's wrists.

"I need to see Mary–"

"Anna…"

"I want it too, but–"

"OK." Vera withdrew from her, faced away.

How long are you going to put it off for, Anna? How many more chances do you think you'll get?

"Vera?"

"What?"

"Come here."

They kissed again. Vera's hands back under her sweater, Anna's fingers unbuttoning Vera's blouse–

Someone banged on the door.

"Shit."

"I'll go." Anna disengaged herself, stumbled to the door. "Who's there?"

"Army."

She opened the door. "Sergeant… Itejere?"

"Yes, that's right." The big man studied her. Further down, other soldiers stood at other doorways. "You were with DCI Renwick, weren't you? 'Fraid I never got your names."

"Anna Mason. Vera Latimer."

"Nice to meet you both. Just letting you know, ma'am – transport should be arriving in the next couple of hours. Get you offshore ASAP."

Two hours. Would that be soon enough? "Thank you. Is there any news?"

Itejere hesitated. "Nothing good. London's gone."

"Oh god."

"They flew the government and the Chiefs of the Defence Staff out to a secure location, or tried to, but that's gone too. Deputy Chiefs got flown out to Belize for safety, but we can't reach them. Or they can't reach us. Either way, we're on our own. And, apparently, the mists are expanding outwards in all directions now."

How did you get your head around something on that scale? London was *gone*. She shook her head. All she could think of was Stakowski, bits of ill-fitting army kit pulled on over his civilian garb, rifle in his hands, tufts of disarrayed hair poking out.

How far out would it go? When would it stop? Where? Britain? Europe? The world? And she could have stopped it, could have saved Stakowski, London, how many millions from this–

"So basically, get your stuff together and be ready to go at a second's notice."

"What about my niece, she's sick. Caught a dose of the gas…"

"Best see the medics about that. But get some rest first. You look all in. They'll be doing everything they can."

"Thanks." She could tell him now, about the White Song. If they didn't believe her, her conscience was clear; she'd tried, she'd failed. But what if they did? And so she said nothing, and Itejere moved on.

"You heard the man." Vera hugged her from behind. "Beddy-byes for you?"

Oh, just for a moment – just for a moment – could she think of herself? "But not straight to sleep?"

"Not if you don't want to."

Anna smiled. "Upstairs, then."

Up the stairs. The bedroom. Photos on the dressing table. A smiling couple. Children. Where were they now? *Mary*.

Vera pushed her down onto the bed, slipped off her shoes. Oh, to forget everything for a moment – Mary, the race against the mist. Just for a moment.

"There," Vera said, leant down and kissed Anna on the lips.

AFTERWARDS SHE CRIED again; Vera held her until it stopped. Then:

"Mary."

Anna half-stood, swayed; Vera caught her arm. "No, you don't. You need to rest, girl. You're all in."

"Mary."

"I'll go see her. You get some sleep. Come find us when you're awake."

"But – the ships…"

"I'll come get you. Rest."

Anna tried to argue – she had to see Mary – but she was too exhausted. She couldn't fight anymore; she closed her eyes.

THE SIREN WOKE her; a low dull wail, rising and falling. Air raid. No, that was World War Two; it was World War One coming back to bite them. Or were they all coming back now, all the dead?

She woke. A strange bed in a stranger's house. The first thing she remembered: Kempforth was gone.

The next: Mary.

The siren, wailing.

Outside, she heard screams, the clatter of feet, soldiers shouting orders.

Mary.

She sat up, shivering. Cold. Her glasses were on the bedside table. On a chair by the bed, her jacket and backpack. Her other clothes were scattered on the floor; she pulled them on.

The hospital–

Blundering down the stairs. Vera, you lied. You said you'd come–

Enough of that. She ran through the streets of Scarborough, dodging the crowds, the soldiers. Someone shouted after her but she went on and nobody chased her. Homing in on the café, praying she remembered the way correctly.

There it was. She ran towards it. People were already spilling out. And there was one she knew

"Vera!"

"Anna." Vera was crying; her head was bowed, as if in prayer.

"Where is Mary?"

"Anna–"

"Where is she?" She screamed it.

"Anna, I'm sorry."

Anna blinked. "What? What for?" But the dread was gathering, hard and stony in her gut.

"I'm so, so sorry."

"What?"

"They tried everything."

"Wh…" But she could only mean one thing. "No."

"I tried closing her eyes," said Vera, "but they wouldn't stay shut."

The keening noise she heard, could that really be her? Were those her hands, flailing at Vera's face? "You were supposed to look after her. You were supposed to look after her. You were supposed to watch her and keep her safe you bitch you fucking bitch you killed her you killed her!"

Vera warding her off. Hands grabbing her, lifting her away. Blood on Vera's face, streaming from a cut cheek. Had she done that? But she had to keep screaming, raging; the minute she stopped it would be real, it'd crash in on her that Mary was dead and—

Too late. Against death or its knowledge, the fiercest rage was a straw defence. She howled, collapsed in the arms holding her. No fight left in her. She was a wound that could only bleed.

Howling, weeping, she sank down. Vera stood over her, speaking to someone. "It's alright, you can leave her alone, we'll be OK." Vera tried to hold her; Anna fought, then let her. Vera was talking, but she couldn't make out the words.

The siren. Screaming, shouts. Gunfire. An officer's voice, shouting above the rest. Running footsteps. Hands pulling at her, trying to make her rise. An acrid, swimming-pool smell in the air.

People running past. Vera shouting, screaming at her now, trying to pull her to her feet. Anna looked up, past Vera, and saw the mist, dirty and yellowish-green, swirling on the hills above the town. Oliver's Mount and the Castle were already fading to shadows in it, disappearing altogether as the mist rolled forward.

With London gone, the war was effectively won. All that remained was the mopping-up, and they could do that at leisure now. The war for Britain, anyway. *The Great War's dead are coming back, to dispossess the living,* Sir Charles had written, but how much did they actually want? Just Britain, or would the mist roll out further to cover all Europe? Or the world?

"Anna, come on!" She snapped back suddenly into the here and now – the screaming was sharp and jagged all about her, the gunfire's chatter and the bullets' wasp-buzz alive, close and dangerous. Vera pulled at her arm. "Come on, get up!"

She shook her head.

"Anna, for fuck sake, I'm not arguing with you. Come *on*! We've got to go!"

"Leave me–"

"Anna–"

Anna threw Vera off. "Leave me!" Vera stumbled back, blinking. Anna went towards the café. "Just leave me," she said. "I'm not going anywhere."

Vera backed away, hesitated. A stream of bodies rushed past, and she'd gone – run away perhaps, the old self-preserving instincts resurrecting themselves, or swept along by the fleeing crowd.

She went in through the café door, calling Mary's name. No answer, of course; what had she expected? Fake snow sprayed on the windows. A plastic Santa on the wall. The place was empty, but for a dozen or so shapes stretched out, silent, on the tables or benches serving as beds. That one was too big. That was too fat. And that one… was Mary.

She took the last few steps towards Mary's b– No, she wouldn't think it, even to herself; that way it might not come true. But she pulled back the sheet and Mary's eyes were open and sightless, staring upwards, a dull glaze already on them. She felt for a pulse. *Please, please, please*. This couldn't be real. "Mary. Mary." Her voice was rising. Holding the thin shoulders, shaking her. *Wake up. Wake*. "Mary–"

Mist outside the café window. The smell of chlorine.

Didn't matter. Nothing did now.

She gathered Mary up. Still warm. Like an ember. You could nurse an ember back into a fire. Couldn't she do the same with Mary? Couldn't she?

The mist thickened. Things moved in it, came close to the glass. A face whose mouth was a gaping, toothless hole stared in at her.

"Bastards!" The face recoiled into the mist. She loved the rage for the second it lived in her; anything other than this dull, smothering pain. But then it died. Didn't matter, though. Nothing did.

But her traitor hands fumbled in her bag; inside was the survival suit she'd stripped from the dead soldier. Her traitor lungs held her breath until she'd pulled it on. The mist poured into the café, but it didn't kill her. And so she sat, Mary cradled in her arms, stroking the child's hair.

CHAPTER THIRTY-SEVEN

SHADOWS MOVED ABOUT her. She didn't look up; they didn't come near.

The shadows left her, and she was alone.

Time was trickling away, like a fistful of sand. The dead wouldn't harm her, but they wouldn't stop either, and when they reached the harbour there'd be no more boats, no exit; she'd be trapped forever in the mist, on a cold island peopled by the dead. Death would be better than that. She could take off the mask and inhale, but death by chlorine was neither quick nor peaceful. Perhaps she could find a gun.

But even that wouldn't be the end. No heaven, only a bleak and lonely desolation. Was that where Mary was now? And Martyn, Eva, Renwick, Stakowski, Allen, Nan, Dad? The promise of oblivion would be a blessing.

The mark on her breast burned cold. She looked down at Mary; the blue eyes stared up at her; the mouth hung slackly open, rimmed with bloody drying froth. This wasn't the bright and laughing child she'd loved.

For better or worse, for whatever foreign field departed, that child was gone.

There was one last thing she could do; Vera had tried, but failed. She closed Mary's eyelids with her thumbs. This time they stayed shut.

She laid Mary down on the table, wiped her mouth clean and closed it, tucked the blankets tight around her. She looked peaceful, quiet; she looked at rest. Anna drew the blanket up over Mary's face.

And then she thought: *The White Song.*

She could never have made that sacrifice herself. Abraham and Isaac? If a voice from the skies bade her sacrifice Mary, she'd have told it to fuck off. But Sir Charles Dace hadn't made a sacrifice; he'd made use of one.

Yes, and look how that had ended.

But it had worked.

The idea felt foul.

Outside, bodies lay in the street. Men and women. She couldn't see any children, but they'd be there, of course.

And there was the rage again; it flared weakly through the fog of her grief like a distant lighthouse. But stronger now, brighter. *Alright, then, you bastards.*

She would not, could not call it a blessing in disguise. Her reason for living was gone. But she'd have no more deaths on her conscience. She'd say, at least she'd tried.

She fumbled in her bag. Quickly, now. Even her great-grandfather's mark mightn't save her if they realised what she was doing.

She opened Sir Charles' book, found the right page. 'I reproduce the text of the White Song phonetically overleaf.' The words were barely pronounceable, but she forced her mouth to shape them. Her other hand gripped Mary's thin wrist through the blankets. *Sweetheart, I'm so sorry. Forgive me. Please.*

How would it work, if it worked at all? Would it stop here or roll back? If so, how far? Would it be as if none of this had happened? Martyn, Eva, Renwick, Stakowski, Nan – would they be alive again? Or would nothing happen at all?

At last she came to the end of it. She stopped. Silence. Slowly she looked up. In the mist outside, shapes pressed their faces to the windows, but they didn't move. Nor did the shape under the blanket. There was only stillness and silence, stretching on and on. Then one by one the figures stepped away from the window and shuffled off through the mist.

So; she'd done what she could, whether or not it had achieved anything. Now the big question; when you'd lost the one thing you'd die for, walk through fire for – without it, could you walk at all? Could you even stand?

For the briefest second she saw Nan, tutting and rolling her eyes at such self-indulgence. A world war, a husband dead, and *she'd* had to keep going; this was no different. Was it really Nan, or just the memory of her? It didn't matter; what mattered was that somehow she was able to stand, then walk, and then run. She put her hand in her pocket, grasped Nan's crucifix. It wasn't about faith, or the god she still denied. It was about Nan. Anna had believed in her.

THE SIREN STILL wailed. Shots rang out in the distance as she ran. Had this part of the town changed greatly, since the Great War? Here was a row of terraces that looked as if they pre-dated the conflict, although the Spar store at the end didn't. A lone figure stood outside it, head cocked. At first she thought it was studying its reflection in the window, but as she came closer – unafraid, as none of this felt real – it reached out, fingers brushing the glass. Its hand grasped empty air and twisted to the right, as if trying to turn a handle.

Anna ran on, feet sliding on the cold, wet pavements. A cat lay twitching in the gutter; a dog lay dead in the middle of the road. Movement inside one of the terraces – a figure that had cast its mask aside to show the wreckage of its face stood inside. It rocked back and forth as if laughing, wagging a finger at an empty chair. Then it reached out, encircled an imaginary waist, drew an imaginary partner close to kiss them with what remained of its mouth.

And then she understood, and then she was running again, laughing and crying, crying and laughing, towards the dying winter light that burned through the mist. She stumbled, nearly fell. A body, at her feet. A woman in police uniform, her skull crushed. Her face; Anna knew the face. It was the desk sergeant from the station in Kempforth. Sergeant Graham.

She looked back. The mist swirled and shifted; the thin black dead moved like predatory fish under its surface, waiting for it to rise. Anna ran on.

The mist thinned, dispersed; another street, no different from the one she'd left–

A shout, something flew past her eye with an angry wasp's buzz. A moment later, she heard the crack of the shot.

"Don't move!"

Soldiers, rifles aimed at her; she fell to her knees, arms

raised. One of them grabbed her arm, dragged her away from the encroaching mist, wrenched the gasmask off. "The hell are you? Where did you get that suit? It's military issue—"

She couldn't speak. What could she say?

"Leave her, Dan," another soldier called. "You can see she's a bloody wreck. Love? Harbour's this way. Come on. Everyone's getting out."

THE HARBOUR.

A gaggle of boats and ships; black smoke fouled the air. Some boats headed out to sea, others hove in towards the quayside, where the waiting crowds piled on. Dunkirk, but in reverse.

Soldiers patrolled the outskirts, but inside the cordon it was chaos. Anna was jostled, pushed, shoved. There were shouts, screams.

"Anna!"

Someone grabbed her arm: Vera, face white and streaked with tears. She pulled Anna close; after a moment, Anna hugged her back. Nothing else to cling to, either of them.

Screams: Anna looked round. The mist was billowing down the streets that opened out above the harbour. In minutes it'd be upon them.

A rifle fired, up into the air. "Alright!" a soldier bellowed. "Move it! *Move!*"

THE TRAWLER PULLED clear of the quay, wallowing low in the water from the weight of its passengers. Another boat hove in to collect the last dozen soldiers on the quayside, their rifles aimed into the encroaching mist; no more heroic sacrifices today.

The mist swirled in over fallen suitcases scattered on the quay; excess baggage there hadn't been space for. Anna's day-pack, at least, had made it. A discarded police tunic lay on the ground.

Anna looked across the crowded decks; a familiar face caught her eye. Thin, gaunt. Another of the coppers from Kempforth. Brock, that was it. No tie, no tunic. He was shivering in his shirtsleeves. His eyes met hers. Did he recognise her? Was there a plea in his eyes?

She looked away. So his nerve had broken. So, he'd only wanted to live. There'd been enough soldiers like that on the Western Front. She could tell someone. But what'd be the point? Let him live. And if he felt guilt, that was the price he paid for survival; there was always a price. You did what you had to, and lived with it.

Someone was sobbing hysterically as they pulled out to sea. Someone else sang; a thin, wavering lost voice, seeking meaning and consolation in vain: "*God rest ye merry, gentlemen, let nothing you dismay…*"

Vera sagged against Anna; Anna stroked her hair. *The last of England*, she thought; *the last of England*.

"*For Jesus Christ our Saviour was born on Christmas Day…*"

She had to be strong. And she would be. She only wavered when she remembered: everything Sir Charles had done had involved harnessing the souls of the dead. Why should the White Song be any different?

What might she have done with Mary's soul?

"*To save us all from Satan's power when we were gone astray…*"

No. She wouldn't think that. She wouldn't. She

wouldn't think of Mary, full stop; she mustn't if she was to survive.

"*Oh, tidings of comfort and joy, comfort and joy; oh, tidings of comfort and joy...*"

And so she stood by the rail, and watched the last of England vanish into the gathering dusk beyond.

Would I never of have all he says and say well [...]

[...] be a lesser man the any [...] and say well [...]

[...] any the [...] or [...]

[...] the [...] thing [...] the [...] good and be desire

[...] fear that he be number one [...] at a time [...]

CODA: THE LAND OF MIST

And still he felt no pain. Only a terrible sadness that a ritual could use so much power and achieve so little.

–Joel Lane, 'Playing Dead'

WARBECK

Old paper files and log books wait on desks for hands to brush the dust off and write in them again. A wheelchair rusts forgotten in the corner of the canteen; in the kitchen the great ovens crouch like cyclopean dogs of stainless steel, still and silent now, but waiting for the fires to start again. Like idols of Moloch; so easy to imagine ranks of human figures carried in unending succession into the fires' heart.

The Spindly Men have gone; a few still prowl the woods around Ash Fell out of habit and familiarity, but most, their duty done, have left for other pastures; this now is the land of the dead, and they can walk in it freely.

Here at last is Ash Fell's heart, slowing, stopping, a dead, empty shell at last. Or is it? On cold days yellow veils of mist hang in the corridors; at night they turn the colour of milk, white amidst the black. In them and in the offices, kitchens, store-rooms, staff-rooms, dormitories, day rooms, library, the voices and footsteps still echo and whisper. Those sounds, and those who made them, died long ago. But some things leave a mark that can never wholly pass away.

CHAPTER THIRTY-EIGHT

From *Ghosts Of War: Ash Fell and the Legacy of World War One* by Anna Mason:

The Industrial Revolution began in the late 18th century. Over two hundred years later, we're just waking up to the pollution and climate change it's caused. The era of modern industrialised warfare began in September 1914; a century later, its consequences manifested themselves catastrophically at Ash Fell Hospital, in Kempforth, Lancashire.

Since World War One, countless other conflicts have sowed the same grim harvest; the Spanish Civil War, World War Two, Korea, Vietnam, Cambodia, the myriad undeclared killing grounds of the Cold War and the 'War on Terror'. Will these toxic legacies come back to haunt us too? It's a question only time will answer.

* * *

"THE RUSSIAN GOVERNMENT has refused to rule out the use of its experimental thaumaturgic weapons system if the crisis in…"

"Thaumaturgic?" Vera asked. How different she'd become: cropped hair; a vest top, pumped-up biceps, a tattoo on her arm. More mannish, but more at peace. But less Anna's type.

"Fancy word for magic," Anna said.

"Why not just say that, then?"

"'Magic' would sound silly."

"And 'thaumaturgic' doesn't?"

"More scientific."

"Hm. Anna?"

"Yeah?"

"Katja's here."

"Oh. OK then."

"My stuff's all packed, so…"

"OK."

"I'm no good with this crap," said Vera. "Goodbyes and stuff. And, no point moping about the past, right?" Anna didn't answer. "Well. Never gonna agree on that are we? Oh well. Onwards and upwards."

"I'll see you off."

"You don't have to… you OK?"

Anna rubbed her belly. "Little one's kicking, that's all."

"I'll see you around then, yeah?"

"Yeah, right." Silence. "Take care, Vera."

"Yeah."

"I mean it."

"You too."

Outside, Anna watched her carry boxes out to Katja's pickup.

Katja nodded to her. She was younger than Anna; late twenties. A slight accent – Polish, Czech? "Hi."

"Hi." Silence. "Take care of her, yeah?"

"I will. I knew her, before."

"I know. It's alright. You were with the escort agency she used to use."

"Back in–"

"Back in England."

"Yes."

"Yes. It was before she and I met. Surprised really. She doesn't like being reminded of the past."

Katja shrugged. "We'll see how long this lasts. Will you be alright?"

"Fine," Anna said. "Just make her happy. She deserves that."

"Katja? I'm ready."

"Alright. Best go. Nice to meet you, Anna."

"You too."

Vera looked back once, then away. *Find peace*, Anna thought. *One day, stop running*. When the pickup was out of sight, Anna shut the door and went upstairs. The house seemed larger now, and emptier. She tried not to look at the gaps on shelves and wardrobes; too many of them seemed poised to shift into something else. The Sight had been quiescent since she'd left Britain, but now and again there were moments like this, a threat or promise to return. The room blurred with the first tears; shivered when the first sob wracked her. Was that someone standing in the corner of her room? No. Just the tears.

When she'd finished crying she washed her face, lay down and closed her eyes. Blackness. A pool of light. Nan stood in it, mouthing urgently, reaching out.

Beyond her, another circle of light in which Mary knelt in a white dress, her back to Anna. Anna reached for her shoulder, but the moment seemed to slow. There was an irrational fear of what Mary's face would look like when she turned round. But still, she reached out.

She woke, sat up in bed, went downstairs. Life went on; work had to be done. She made herself a sandwich- she was always hungry now – and ate it staring at the computer, trying to decide what came next; when the doorbell rang, it was almost a relief.

"Miss Mason?" The man was in his fifties, bald on top, long grey hair gathered in a last defiant ponytail; the woman was a pretty, pre-Raphaelite redhead half his age.

"Ms."

"Sorry. I'm Arnold Renwick. Joan Renwick's dad."

THE TESTAMENT OF GIDEON DACE so here we are we three sole or should i say soul ha ha tenants now of ash fell the unholy trinity father the son and the wholly goat ha ha well the dead kept their promise i will say that much the years of torment inflicted on me are at an end but still they got the last laugh ha ha i am confined to the grounds unable to venture outside

THE TESTAMENT OF SIR CHARLES DACE oh shut up gideon you vile little bastard bastard oh how i wish you were little has been so hard or unwelcome in my life or death as acknowledging you are indeed my child you perverted this place from its original intent exploiting those who sacrificed for us

THE TESTAMENT OF GIDEON DACE CONTINUED as did you pater dearest in building ash fell or had you forgotten if indeed you ever considered it at all

THE TESTAMENT OF SIR CHARLES DACE CONTINUED mine was for a valid purpose a good cause not for my own aggrandisement gratification or profit something you never would or could understand

THE BACK GARDEN was warm with the summer sun; the air was sweet with pine resin. A wooden picnic table; they sipped Orangina, ate baguettes with Brie and grapes.

"I was a university lecturer," Renwick's father said. "Social Sciences. Lorraine – her mother – was a social worker, often dealing with a lot of abuse cases. As far as Joan was concerned, we were the classic woolly-minded liberals. I remember her shouting at me once that I never *judged* anyone. Always saw both sides, never took a stand or *did* anything. She saw the damage we had to patch up, her mother especially. When she joined the police, she said she wanted to stop the kind of people we spent our lives clearing up after. At first I treated it as a sort of youthful rebellion." He half-smiled. "Which just made her angrier, of course."

Morwenna stroked his arm, gazing up at him adoringly. She seemed genuinely in love with her much older husband, which was rather sweet, but Anna could understand how Renwick could have found her maddening.

"She was something of a wild child when she was younger. But she was doing well in the Manchester police. And then Lorraine died. Joan was angry, more than anything else. Didn't understand why I wasn't, or didn't seem to be. I wanted to help her, but... Lorraine's death only pushed us further apart. And then she moved to Kempforth. And then–" He smiled at his wife, squeezed her hand "–I met Morwenna, and that just made it worse. To be honest, I'd almost resigned myself to losing Joan. But I kept trying. I kept telling myself she was an adult with her own life, but... she was still my little girl."

"I'm not sure what you want me to say," said Anna. "She was a very brave woman. Determined. She saved my life. And Mary's, for a while at least. If it wasn't for her, no-one would've got out of Kempforth. If she could have rescued the missing child, she would have. That's all I can tell you. I'm sorry I didn't get to know her better."

Arnold nodded, eyes bright. "That sounds like my girl," he said at last.

The three of them were silent for a while.

"And what about you?" he asked.

"What about me?"

"You seem happy," Morwenna said.

"In some ways."

"You lost a lot, too."

Anna shifted in her chair. "I think everybody did. But something good came out of it." She stroked her belly again. Her breasts were tender, sore. Except for one spot. The piercing cold of the white mark had faded within a few weeks of leaving Britain, but the skin remained hard, numb and dead.

"When are you due?" Morwenna asked.

"Another five months." She leant back in the chair. "It was Vera's idea. We had a male friend who was willing to provide the necessary." She smiled. "Plus a turkey baster."

"Oh." Morwenna looked a little queasy. Anna managed not to laugh, feeling a little cruel.

"But you're not together anymore?" asked Arnold.

"No. I wanted the child too, but – I think for Vera, it was a way of trying to... almost... *make* me choose the present over the past." That was Vera's reason; she wouldn't talk about hers.

"To replace your niece?"

"Not to replace Mary, no. You couldn't, but – help fill the gap, maybe. You see, the big difference between us was that if I could have Mary back, I'd have things back the way they were in a second." That was the question; how much did you have to accept, and live with, and how much could truly be undone? "I wouldn't have to think about it. But Vera wouldn't want her old life back on any terms. A big part of her's glad that Alan's dead. If it was a choice between the life she has now, and having Alan back, he'd stay dead. Does that make sense?"

"I think so."

"That's really why we split up. I made her feel guilty." She shrugged. "Well. I'm used to being on my own. A lot of people aren't, but I am. I'll cope."

Arnold held her gaze. "Yes. I think you will." He looked out to sea. "To think it's all gone. Theirs now, not ours. What will they do with it?"

The mist had continued to expand for several hours after Anna sang the White Song – perhaps because of that, perhaps not. By the time it stopped, virtually the entirely UK mainland was engulfed, along with the Isle of Man and even parts of Northern Ireland. Some of the outlying islands – the Orkneys, the Hebrides, the Shetlands – had been spared. Some remained inhabited even now, unlike the mainland.

A few odd patches of the Cornish, Scottish and Suffolk coasts remained clear of mist. Now and again some brave or (more often) avaricious soul would land on one of them, armed with gas mask and camera. They always brought back the same thing; grainy footage of shadowy figures moving in empty streets and ruined houses, with a soundtrack of hissing static. Overlaying both, dancing in and out of the interference, were images of ghostly, gossamer faces and a faint chorus of overlapping voices, each reeling off an endless unbroken monologue of suffering and loss.

"I caught a glimpse," said Anna. "They just wanted to go home. But their homes, their families, weren't there anymore. They were acting out scenes from the lives they remembered, as if they were still there. But they're not. Some things, once they're lost, you can't get back. That's the worst thing. The utter pointlessness of it all."

THE TESTAMENT OF GIDEON DACE CONTINUED a damned cheat i call it leaving me penned up in here served my penance did my time kept my word to them

THE TESTAMENT OF SIR CHARLES DACE CONTINUED you deserved every indignity and torment they heaped upon you and more but dear god what they have put me through in this place tried to remonstrate with them to explain it was for england but they would not listen

THE TESTAMENT OF ST JOHN DACE shut up both of you shut up you both deserve it we all do all three

of us the punishment is just we all used them as
fodder grist harvest

THE TESTAMENT OF SIR CHARLES DACE CONTINUED
enough st john this maudlin self laceration
serves no one

THE TESTAMENT OF ST JOHN DACE CONCLUDED no father
be silent and you gideon also this is my testament
i will say this only and nothing ever more to
both of you their lives were yours to do with
as you wished in life and death you to rebuild
your dreams of empire gideon to rebuild his bank
account the same principle on a less exalted
scale and i in my weakness and my cowardice
acquiesced i am as guilty as you both and so i
say our punishment is just and will complain no
longer only endure farewell

ARNOLD PECKED ANNA'S cheek, squeezed her hand. She
squeezed back, exchanged brief and insincere air-
kisses with Morwenna, and walked them back to their
Citroen.

"It must be strange. You're effectively the leading
authority on Ash Fell. The files you brought out of
Britain with you, I don't suppose you ever envisaged…"

"No."

"A shame that book of Sir Charles' was never found."

"Might be for the best. Look what's been done with
the information that *did* come out."

"True. A new arms race. Cheaper than nuclear bombs,
anyway."

"Or perhaps more costly. We don't know. If you start tampering with what's *real*... where does that end? One mistake..."

"That's the question, isn't it? It's not where you start. It's where you stop."

"Frightening."

"But attractive, too. Wouldn't you say?"

He knows. "Perhaps."

"I suppose, in the final analysis, it would come down to the conscience and judgement of the person with that knowledge." He smiled. "I'd like to think that if it still exists, it's in good hands."

The moment hung between them in the dying sunshine. "Well, time to go, I think. *Au revoir*, Anna."

"Goodbye, Arnold."

When their car was gone she went back inside and began to pack. Only what she needed; she was travelling light. From the mantelpiece, the pictures of Nan, Dad, Mum, Martyn, and – always, always – Mary. And a small metal crucifix, set in a pyramidal wooden base. You couldn't cling to the past, but you couldn't just discard it, either. What were you, after all, if not the sum of your scars?

But some scars could, and should be erased; men had gone into Ash Fell, and places like it, faceless and been given something like a life. Sometimes a scar could diminish you, make you less than what you were.

THE TESTAMENT OF SIR CHARLES DACE CONCLUDED st john st john drat the boy where is he ah well all shall be well all shall be well all manner of things shall be well my notes still remain they

```
can be brought back restored there is still time
all may yet be set to rights once more
```

```
THE TESTAMENT OF GIDEON DACE CONCLUDED oh do put
a sock in it pater dearest no one is listening i
can assure you pater pater where are you father
where are you daddy dearest oh i see gone off
in a huff have we pater tally ho gone away fuck
you then daddy dearest this place of darkness it
now appears is mine and mine alone well then i
shall make it my own believe you me ah well tis
very well.
```

THE TRAIN ROLLED south, into the deepening night. Anna had bought a ticket for Marseilles; she'd get off before there, of course. Disappear. A minor miracle no-one had come looking for her yet.

Alone in the compartment, she opened her backpack.

The journal still smelt faintly of chlorine, but the words of the White Song were clearly legible.

Even Vera hadn't known she had it; even Anna didn't know what effect the incantation had had. It hadn't rolled back the dead, but then she could never have sacrificed Mary. Dace's diary had spoken of them claiming the world back; perhaps she'd stopped it at the British coast.

The singing of the White Song must be prefaced by the sacrifice of the speaker's child... without that sacrifice, the gates remain open.

She stroked her belly. If done properly, with the correct sacrifice, how much would it restore? What? More importantly, who?

For the briefest moment, a patch of light and shadow in the empty seat opposite shifted; became, just for an instant, a small thin girl, about eleven years old, with red hair, blue eyes, and an impish smile that melted Anna's heart. And then was gone again.

When the thing that gave you the reason for living was gone, did you live without it, find something else to live for, or did you try to bring it back?

The train rattled on through the night.

Who was she to make this choice? But then again, who was she not to?

Anna returned the book to her bag, looked out of the window into the gathering night, and wondered what future, if any, she would give her unborn child.

In war, there are no unwounded soldiers.

–José Narosky.

ACKNOWLEDGEMENTS

Jenni Hill, who said 'we should publish this.'

Jon Oliver – of course – who agreed and commissioned this novel, as well as waiting patiently *waaaay* past the deadline and helping refine it into its final shape.

Mike Rathbone and Gillian Rathbone, for psychiatric information.

The other Simon, for advice on matters military and medical, and for eleventh-hour proof-reading.

The year leading up to the writing of *The Faceless* was at times a difficult one; I can only offer my heartfelt gratitude to the many friends whose kindness, affection and support helped me through it. Bernard and Clare Nugent (and Mac), Vicky Morris, Roberta Lannes-Sealey, I'm looking at you in particular, along with:

Andrea Power, for ideas, helpful information and support.

Gary McMahon, for architectural advice and feedback on the early chapters.

Joel Lane for casting an eagle eye over most of Part One.

Mark West and Anna Taborska for two rather cool book trailers.

Pat Kelleher, for additional World War One-related info.

Adam Higson of Greater Manchester Police, for information on police kit.

My grandmother, Lilian Iris Gillespie, for sharing her memories of my great-grandfather Richard James Lynam, who fought at the Battle of Passchendaele.

Clare Bland, Jenny Bent and Sara 'The Milf' Jones.

Dark Sanctuary, Lisa Gerrard, Azam Ali and Ladytron for the writing soundtrack.

Other sources of information included *War Is War* by 'Ex-Private X' (A.M. Burrage) and *War Against War!* by Ernst Friedrich, the poetry of Wilfred Owen, Siegfried Sassoon, Charles Hamilton Sorley and many others, *Repression of War Experience* by W.H.R. Rivers and *Hysterical Disorders Of Warfare* by Lewis

Yealland (in which the doctor's methods are the most unsettling aspect of the book.) All this provided a wealth of material, only a fraction of which made it into the present novel. Anything I've got right is due to the help of those people and sources listed; any mistakes, intentional or otherwise, are my own.

There are many people who have helped, in one way or the other. If you're one of them and your name's not on this list, it's down to my lousy memory, not any lack of gratitude or appreciation on my part.

ABOUT THE AUTHOR

Simon Bestwick was born in 1974. His short fiction has popped up all over the place, in the UK and the States, and is collected in *A Hazy Shade of Winter*. His first novel, *Tomes of The Dead: Tide of Souls*, received wide critical praise and, more recently, he has been nominated for the Bram Stoker award.

Find out more about Simon at
Simon-Bestwick.blogspot.com

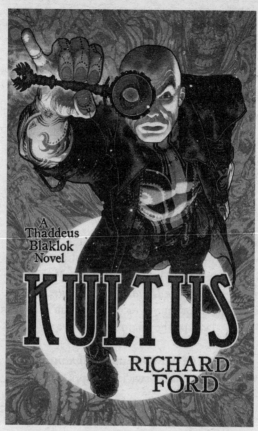

A
Thaddeus
Blaklok
Novel

KULTUS

RICHARD FORD

'Menacing
and uncanny'
The Guardian
on Mortality

'Immaculately
sinister'
TLS on Mortality

Regicide
Nicholas Royle

UK ISBN: 978 1 907992 01 8 • US ISBN: 978 1 907992 00 1 • £7.99/$7.99

Carl stumbles across part of a map to an unknown town. He becomes convinced
it represents the city of his dreams, where ice skaters turn quintuple loops and
trumpeters hit impossibly high notes... where Annie Risk will agree to see him again.
But if he ever finds himself in the streets on his map, will they turn out to be the land
of his dreams or the world of his worst nightmares?

WWW.SOLARISBOOKS.COM

Follow us on Twitter! www.twitter.com/solarisbooks

UK ISBN: 978 1 907519 95 6 • US ISBN: 978 1 907519 94 9 • £7.99/$7.99

Imagine a place where all your nightmares become real. Think of dark urban streets where crime, debt and violence are not the only things you fear. Picture a housing project that is a gateway to somewhere else, a realm where ghosts and monsters stir hungrily in the shadows. Welcome to the Concrete Grove. It knows where you live...

 WWW.SOLARISBOOKS.COM

Follow us on Twitter! www.twitter.com/solarisbooks